Goodreads Reviews for the Dr Power Books

The Darkening Sky (4.44 Stars)

'Absolutely enjoyed this first novel.'

'I have read many a crime book, but this book was different. I never for one moment guessed how the story would unfold.'

'Loved the way the two main characters (Superintendent Lynch and Dr Power) interacted with one another.'

'Illustrations were brilliantly drawn and brought the characters to life.'

'Thoroughly enjoyed this debut novel from Hugh Greene.'

'Brilliant. Very much enjoyed – a new detective series based in England.'

'It is a good crime and psychological thriller and will keep any reader interested to the end.'

'I love British Mystery stories, and The Darkening Sky is no exception. Well written, with great development of characters; I felt that I knew Power & Lynch personally. I look forward to further volumes in this highly entertaining and somewhat edgy series. Hugh Greene is a writer to start paying attention to in my opinion. Highly recommended.'

The Fire of Love (4.62 Stars)

'Good plot and enjoyable read - away to locate more books in the series.'

'This is a gripping story, I was hooked from the first page and found it difficult to put down. The description of the house and its history and the man who built it was very true to the time and the author really brings it to life.'

'I love the illustration by Paul Imrie on the cover, it is very striking and beautifully drawn as are the black and white illustrations inside.'

'A well written book with a well-thought out storyline, I enjoyed it very much and definitely want to read the next one.'

'There are lots of twists and turns and complex characters to keep the ending hidden from you and difficult to guess.'

'After the first chapter I could not put it down.'

'The Illustrations were brilliant evocations of the Power/Lynch world.'

'I love the little links between the books in the illustrations. Dr Power as drawn is quite dishy. I think I am falling in love with Dr Power!'

'A good read that I would recommend to anyone who enjoys crime novels and psychological thrillers. The writing is constantly good and interesting.'

The Good Shepherd (4.38 Stars)

'I was attracted by the cover of this book, which I thought it very striking and enigmatic.'

'There was drama and suspense and a nice twist at the end. It was quite compulsive, I felt I had to read more to see what happened next.'

'It is a very enjoyable and intriguing read. Well-written, it evokes the spirit of the times, the mid-nineties.'

'I enjoyed this book. The characters were interesting and I felt the book was well researched.'

'The story builds well with excellent attention to detail paid to the places that the main characters visit.'

'The pace of plot was gripping, and makes me want to know what is next. The illustrations were fantastic, and really added to the story.'

'An excellent read, loved it.'

'I was hooked from the first paragraph.'

Also by Hugh Greene

The Darkening Sky

The Good Shepherd

Schrödinger's God

Omnibus of Three Novels in a Single Volume
The Dr Power Mysteries

Short Story Collection
Dr Power's Casebook

The Fire of Love

A Dr Power Murder Mystery

Hugh Greene

Illustrated by Paul Imrie

Copyright © Hugh Greene 2014

Hugh Greene asserts the moral right to be identified as the author of this work in accordance with the Copyright, Designs and Patents Act 1988

All material in this book, in terms of text and illustration, is copyrighted according to UK and International Law. All rights are reserved. No part of this publication may be reproduced, stored in a retrieval system or transmitted in any form or by any means, electronic, mechanical, photocopying, recording or otherwise without prior permission of the copyright owner.

A catalogue reference for this book is available from the British Library

ISBN 10: 1502458195
ISBN 13: 978-1502458193

First Edition Published Worldwide in October 2014
Revised Edition March 2015

Typeset in Cambria
Proofreading and typographic design by Julie Eddles

All characters appearing in this book are fictitious. Any resemblance to real persons, living or dead, is purely coincidental.

www.hughgreene.com
twitter: @hughgreenauthor

Chapter One

But not before my heart had kindled
With the fire of love
And deep within me had burst
Into songs of love.

Incendium Amori,
Richard Rolle, 14th Century.

Proud Heaton Hall sat foursquare in the most secluded and beautiful Cheshire countryside. Its Victorian architect, Alfred Waterhouse, had chosen his site with care. Heaton Hall been built in 1870 from the proceeds of the first owner's success in the cotton industry. The house stood on sunny uplands overlooking a village, which the owner had built at the same time. His village, Heaton village, housed only his workers from the mill in the valley and the lands thereabout. He regulated all of their lives with a ruthless beneficence. On Sundays he allowed them a day of rest, but only if it was largely spent in the church the old man had built them. The village had changed little although the cotton mill and its mill hands had long since gone. The wealthy old mill owner, resplendent in top hat, black frock coat and white beard had spent the years of his retirement strolling through the leafy lanes of the lands he owned. Although he was honoured by Royalty and courted by politicians he was not a pompous soul and would, on his country walks, pass the time of day with any. However, once he had returned home and was ensconced within the thick stone walls of his Hall, the rich man guarded his privacy with zeal. Through his political connections he ensured that no modern-day railway or highway encroached upon his land.

The old man had planted a green wood to cloak his hall from

prying eyes. In the decades after his death, the wood had grown thick and virtually impenetrable. To glimpse the Hall's ashlar columns and classical pediments it was necessary to pass the locked gates and the servants at the Lodge.

All future owners of the Hall who followed on from the old man had been just as jealous of their privacy. The modern-day occupant was no exception. He had good reason for his obsession with security, for like his grandfather, the old man, Sir Ian McWilliam was an important man, a Minister of the Crown.

Sir Ian McWilliam had come into his inheritance on the death of his childless aunt, Lady Marian, four years before. He was just coming to terms with the heavy burden that a vast Victorian estate could be. It was taking much of the income from his considerable investment portfolio to keep the estate manager off his back and keep the house, the village and the farms about in reasonable repair. His wife had taken something of a dislike to the cold Northern rooms and intended to spend as much time as she possibly could in their London flat and with her friends until Sir Ian had refurbished the place.

Accordingly, Sir Ian McWilliam would take the Euston Pullman north at the weekend accompanied by a stack of ministerial red boxes in the temporary care of some minor civil servants, and take up residence in his family home. There he would take what pleasure he could muster from being Lord of the Manor. On Friday night he would wind down with a bottle of port and silent company of the despatch boxes. On Saturday he would be visited by the estate manager, and at the same time as hearing the village gossip would listen to a summary of the estate accounts. Sometimes his wife and one or both of his children would arrive on Saturday afternoon. He would tour the estate in the estate's Land Rover Discovery, visit a country restaurant in the evening and return back to the Hall for telephone briefings from Whitehall and Central Office, and see any visitors who awaited him in his study. But Sunday would see him decamping and moving south. Through the week the people of the village who worked on the land immediately around the Hall would look up at its elegant facade. Seeing the dark windows of the Hall they would wonder how long their jobs on the land would last.

One Friday in early spring, in the second year of the Parliament, Sir Ian arrived at the Hall by chauffeured limousine. His new Private Parliamentary Secretary joined him for a late supper and they talked until eight-thirty. They broke off their discussions to allow Sir Ian to take two phone calls, one from his wife in London and the other from his constituency agent. Sir Ian made one further call himself to his son. They had a short conversation characterised by raised voices, which the civil servant diplomatically pretended not to hear. After these telephone calls the Minister and his civil servant ate a frugal meal of cold meat, pickles and a stick of French bread that Sir Ian himself had warmed through in an Aga oven in the echoing, deserted kitchens.

At ten o'clock Sir Ian dismissed his civil servant. The security guard, walking a German Shepherd through the woodland paths, saw the silhouette of Sir Ian against the hall light as his Parliamentary Private Secretary was driven away in the Ministry Rover Sterling. The police at the Lodge noted the Rover as it sped through the gates and off down the hill towards the village and the motorway beyond. After that, according to his later statement, the police sergeant made radio contact with the two private security guards who were contracted to patrol the grounds throughout the time that Sir Ian was in residence. The civil servant looked up once as his car sped through the country lanes. The car headlights picked out a slim, young woman walking out of the village towards the car. Her eyes seemed wide and staring and she bent down to peer into the car at him. They were past her in seconds and the civil servant paid her no further heed and instead turned his attention back to the radio.

Sir Ian locked away his despatch boxes and went round to check all the doors downstairs. He switched off the lights except one in the dining saloon where he had been all night. He hated to think that whilst he was in bed the downstairs rooms were all in total darkness.

A personal thing. He made his way upstairs to the newly decorated apartments he would share with his wife. Tonight though he would be sleeping without her. Sir Ian undressed quickly and feeling the plush blue carpet between his toes climbed into the rose-coloured bed. For a little while he listened to the noises of the dry, old house. He suddenly found himself thinking about a certain lady again and shook his head as if to shake the very idea of her out of his mind. He nestled his head down on the firm, broad pillows and let the realm of dreams overwhelm him.

If the security guard had been passing the Hall at two a.m., he might have seen the light on in the downstairs room, just as Sir Ian had left it. At three a.m. he might have noticed that not only was there a light in the dining room, but that there was also a light in the library. But the guard did not pass by on the hour, as he was supposed to do, and as the inquiry found afterwards. And because of the lapse there was no-one to raise the alarm.

The light in the library was of an altogether different kind to the light in the dining room. This was no steady electric light, but a dancing, flickering glow. From a single matchburst the flame had grown greedily into a raging inferno that licked at and tasted first the old wooden furniture and then the red binding and yellowed paper of Sir Ian's leather-bound books. The gloomy stone-flagged corridors were brightly lit by shooting tongues of flame that caressed the dry wooden panelling before devouring it. Red stair-carpet burst into blossoming flowers of flame. The old timbers of the floors and ceilings shivered and cracked in the furnace heat. The fire burned as if empowered with a frenzied excitement at its own unbridled life. The sound of fracturing glass mixed with the raging crackle of the flames that swept through the hallways and up the heat vortex of the stairwell.

From the sleep-stilled village below the Hall nothing could be seen of the downstairs windows as, one-by-one, they filled with orange flame. The dense wood screened the Hall from all those who might have summoned help. Inside the Hall, smoke curled and curdled its way through the first-floor corridors pushed by the acrid hot air as it ascended the stairs. Fingers of smoke touched Sir Ian's snoring lips, rushed on his sucking breath to clog and smother his lungs. He coughed automatically at the hot and foul-tasting smoke, but he never woke up. By four a.m. the old Hall was a massive timber-dry beacon that lit up the darkness, reached out arms of flame to the surrounding trees, roasted the buds of spring and coloured the dawn sky an angry orange-red.

Chapter Two

When the fire of love has really taken hold of the soul
It clears out all vice, it puts away the trivial unnecessary,
It creates beauty in every virtue.
Incendium Amori,
Richard Rolle, 14th Century.

Dr Carl Power parked his Rover 101 with care; easing its glossy carapace into a parking space in the shadow of the wall. The hot sun was beginning to rise in the sky and the wall's shade would prevent the car from becoming too hot for when he returned. Power's thoughtful brown eyes stared out of the car window at the high, implacable concrete wall. He had motored through beautiful countryside to get here: passing through silent Cheshire villages; past post offices and country inns with names like The Sun and The Plough.

A single sign on a narrow country lane had pointed him south towards an ill-conceived council estate that spread its greyness malignly over the green land. In the midst of the seventies prefabricated housing, was a high wall that suddenly rose up, interrupting the houses' sprawl like a cliff wall standing firm against a grey and heaving ocean.

The wall in question surrounded the remand centre that Dr Power, consultant psychiatrist, had journeyed to visit. The wall forbade those outside a glimpse of its regime and forbade those inside the fantasy of freedom. It held the person Power had come to see tightly within its grip and was an abrupt separation from everyday life. For the traveller, going inside the wall was like being in a galleon sailing over the edge of the world.

Power reached for his battered leather briefcase and got out of the car. He locked it with pride and made his way through the grim car park to the high wooden gate of the prison. He knocked on the six-foot door inset into the right hand gate. A camera watched him with its single eye. Power had gone through this ritual many times. The solicitors who requested his services for their clients knew him to be an expert witness. Those criminals and innocents caught up in the legal system who might benefit from a psychiatric report were often sent to Power, whose academic reputation lent him extra standing in the court. Although he had visited many prisons; Power was unfailingly numbed by the process of locks and keys and gatemen. He managed to pass the occupationally suspicious gate guard and signed his name in the HMSO issue ledger. Two thick-set, white-shirted, black-tied guards joined him. With a bare minimum of conversation they steered him over the gravelled paths to the medical centre where he would interview his client. Power was settled in an over-warm office and offered tea. He declined. The prison officer who ran the medical centre and hospital wing nodded. "Right you are, Doctor." His tone was decidedly military.

The guard stood in the doorway while Power seated himself at the desk. This was where the regular prison doctor sat. Power took off his soft corduroy jacket and hung it over the back of the chair. He took the case details and legal depositions out of his briefcase. As he was taking a wedge of empty A4 paper out of the folder his eye was caught by the bookshelves by the side of the desk. The prison doctor's books. He noted the up-to-date editions of emergency medicine and surgery and then felt a wave of smug happiness overtake him as he saw a copy of his own book standing with the others; *The Unconscious Mind* by Dr Carl Power. He pulled the book from the shelf. There were actually signs that it had been read. Power thought of the prison doctor reading it, and his estimation of prison medicine rose. Yes, the spine was cracked; the pages dog-eared. It had definitely been well-read. His friends and colleagues would never have called Power a vain individual, but what vanity he did possess was massaged by the notion that the book was frequently referred to.

The medical orderly broke into Power's fantasy about his books.

"Ahem . . . would you like to see her now, Doctor?"

"Oh yes, of course. I'm sorry; I was miles away. I was thinking about this book." He closed its covers and replaced it on the shelf.

"That the book on the unconscious?"

"Yes, You know it?"

"Well, you'll read anything on the night shift, won't you?" Power's ego was neatly punctured and deflated. He smiled at himself as the prison medical officer continued unaware that the book's author sat in front of him.

"Don't believe a word of it either . . . tries to say something about the unconscious causes of crime. I know about crime. Worked here for twenty years. Some of 'em . . . most of 'em . . . in here; they're just bad. Nothing to do with the unconscious or their mothers or anything like that. Just bad. Bad through and through."

"Oh . . ." said Power, wondering whether to launch a counter argument.

"I finished the book though. Always finish a book once I've started. No matter how bad. Actually it's quite a good read that one . . . good stories . . . but that's what they are . . . fiction. Shall I get her, sir? You don't want to hear me blabbing on."

Power was still digesting the earnest but indirect criticism he had received about his life work. 'Everyone has their opinion,' he thought; trying to comfort himself, but half wondering if the orderly's opinions were nearer the truth than the columns-worth of praise that more academic reviewers had lauded him with.

"Shall I get her, Dr Power? You've only got till eleven forty-five, you know. I'll have to get her back to her cell spot-on, you know. Can't over-run. Disrupts the workings of the prison."

Power decided he could take the criticism. He forgot the book and concentrated on the girl. He needed time with this client; particularly in view of her notoriety. After the interview today he would have just two weeks to write a report for the defence. His written report and his verbal evidence in court would be subject to the most rigorous scrutiny by the media and the legal profession. His opinion would be compared with an earlier report prepared by the country's foremost expert in forensic psychiatry, Professor Anastasi. Since Anastasi's evidence was being put forward by the prosecution and Power's was to be for the defence Power knew that his report would have to be as perfect as he could make it.

The Crown Prosecution Service barristers and their hired medical experts would tear it to bits if it was any less. And here was Power worrying about one guard's ill-formed opinions of his book. He didn't have time to indulge his pride. And if the guard didn't understand the significance of the unconscious, Power certainly wasn't going to educate him now. He and his client didn't have time.

"Bring her along, please," said Power. "Quick as you can."

The hospital officer left to summon the remand prisoner and her escort. Power was just the latest in a long line of visitors, variously legally or medically qualified, to seek an audience with Zoë Allen.

Whilst he waited Power glanced through the three inch thick pile of letters and depositions that the defence solicitors had sent him. The first piece of paper on the heavy pile was their letter to Power. It read:

> We represent our client Miss Zoë Allen and aware of your expertise in matters of the mind, we would like to commission a report from you on the mental state of our client now, and at the time of her alleged offence.
>
> You may recognise her name from the recent press and television coverage, if not then we feel sure you will recall the recent death of Sir Ian McWilliam. Our client has been charged with the arson of Heaton Hall and with Sir Ian's murder.
>
> The prosecution allege that the fire which killed the Cabinet Minister was started deliberately by Miss Allen. They point to a large body of letters written to Sir Ian by our client, produced after his death, by his family. Our client freely admits to having written at least some, if not all, of these letters. They can best be described as love letters. The early letters are strong and passionate; the latter ones are bitter and threatening. It is these threats which have added fuel to the prosecution case.

The prosecution case has been helped by the expert opinion of no less a psychiatric expert than the eminent Professor Anastasi, whom we feel you will be well acquainted with. He is of the mind that Zoë Allen was infatuated with Sir Ian to the point of a dangerous obsession, and that, because Sir Ian McWilliam did not reciprocate her love, she torched his house in a jealous rage. He concludes that she is a dangerous individual, and because she shows no remorse for the death of Sir Ian, is probably a psychopath, who if found guilty should not have her mandatory life sentence reduced in any way. He leaves room also for the court to order her to a Special Hospital, say, the Ashworth Hospital, for an indefinite stay.

We seek your opinion as to her mental state with a view to perhaps following the path of diminished responsibility, which would allow for a lessening of the charge from murder to manslaughter.

We must apologise for the relatively short notice. The trial date has been brought forward, which gives you only two weeks to prepare your report. In view of your expertise in these matters, we are prepared to offer you, in the first instance, a fee of £600 for the report and trust that this is satisfactory to you.

Yours sincerely,
Gravett & Partners

The sum of £600 was welcome. For a court report it was a substantial sum, but the prospect of having to take on Professor Anastasi in the witness box, made the inducement seem that much less; Anastasi was a small, dark-eyed man, whose compelling and persuasive character had often made mincemeat out of less able psychiatrists' opinions. The psychiatric profession listened to Anastasi's pronouncements with awe, and it was only a wise man or a fool who begged to differ with him. Should Power disagree over this case, he would have to think very carefully before choosing to broadcast the disagreement in a report that would have to be argued against Anastasi's in court.

But Anastasi was human wasn't he? He could be mistaken? After all, thought Power, could a psychopath really fall in love so intensely? Power turned the photocopied pages over to reach one of Zoë's handwritten letters.

She had written it about twelve months before Sir Ian's death.

Although he had never met her, Power imagined Zoë to be a tall, thin, willowy girl, who was perpetually dreamy and withdrawn from the world. Maybe she'd written this on a kitchen table over coffee, or late at night, tucked up in bed and balancing a book on her knees as a writing surface. But these were just Power's daydreams. He would meet her soon enough and test out his fantasies about the girl. For now he must confine himself to fact. He read quickly, but carefully:

> *Monday*
> *Dear Ian,*
> *Saw you leaving on Sunday, probably driving down on your way south. I worry in case you work too hard, racing between your home and Westminster. You passed me in your car, (driving too fast). I saw you looking out of the window at me. You wanted to stop, I know, but you couldn't ask your chauffer to stop. I understand that. You have a public image to keep. I know how you feel for me though – unable to express what you really want – made to do what they want you to all the time. I saw the anguish on your face through the window. I know you were dying to stop and take me inside, but you weren't allowed, were you? And I walked back alone, through the cold wet grass to my cottage.*
>
> *I lie awake at night thinking of you, waiting until you can see me again. I lie naked on the bed with the curtains open, so that the moonlight falls on my body. When I look down my skin looks like silver.*
>
> > *I'm waiting for you,*
> > *Love Zoë*
> > *xxxxxxx*

And from the next month:

> *Thursday*
> *Dear Ian,*
> *Looking forward to seeing you again this weekend. Hope you'll be here. Hope you've left your wife behind this time. Saw her on Sunday when she passed here. I don't want to criticise your taste in women, (that would reflect on me, wouldn't it?), but she's not right*

for you, is she? I hate her. I'm sorry, but I do. When I think of her in your bed, all legal and proper ... I just want to die.

I sent you the photograph of me I know you wanted.

Why haven't you phoned this week.

    Love Zoë,
    xxxxxx

And from the week before Sir Ian's death:

Ian,

I rang you and I rang you on your direct line. First there was no answer, then I spoke to some man. He wouldn't let me talk to you. He said that you didn't want to talk to me. He said he was going to tell the police. That you never wanted to hear from me again. That I was pestering you! I know he was lying. He was trying to keep us apart ... so I am writing to let you know just how I feel. So you know I care.

I care so much abut you. My love is everything. Everything I see and everything I touch is my love for you. If my love were to be shattered I am sure the whole world would simply dissolve – all the streets and cars would simply fade way. I would fight for my love. I would die for my love. I would kill for my love. I would kill.

    Phone me, love, Zoë.

The letters all seemed to have been written very quickly. They were demonstrative in their passion. Reading them in the cold light of day Power tried to understand the intense feelings that lay behind each and every word. How old was this love-sick girl? He looked through the notes for her exact date-of-birth and calculated her age. She had been about eighteen when she wrote the first letter. Her birthday was in November. He scrutinised the letters. They were by no means a complete set, but they all had the same intensity, and if one paused to look at them in detail there was no reference to an actual face-to-face meeting. This seemed to confirm what everyone had said. According to everyone who knew either of them, Zoë and Sir Ian had never even talked together on the phone or in person. Neither was there any trace of anything written by Sir Ian to Zoë.

The affair seemed to exist only within the confines of Zoë's skull. How had this eighteen-year-old become so immersed in fantasy? How had it become so hard to discard the ideas that she would rather kill than admit them to be false? How has she conceived the obsession that an older cabinet minister could ever be in love with such as she? Perhaps it was easier to destroy, to kill the object of one's desire than face up to admitting such a false love. Easier to kill than know that one's life had been governed by crushing error alone. Power mused over the letters. He'd read ones like them before. He'd talked to murderers who had acted on just such overwhelming passions.

Power flicked through the depositions again. Past the Home Office pathologist's postmortem report on Sir Ian's crisped and blackened body to the transcript of the police interviews. There was a page he had marked especially when he had read them before. There were two voices transcripted; the inquisitorial and confrontational tone of the Detective Inspector and the defensive softness of Zoë Allen. Power could imagine the smoke-ridden interview room, the empty table between them and the tape recorder slowly turning.

> INSPECTOR: Where were you that night . . . the night Sir Ian died?
> ALLEN: I don't know for sure . . . probably at home, watching television.
> INSPECTOR: What did you watch?
> ALLEN: Whatever was on. I don't know.
> INSPECTOR: Was anyone with you?
> ALLEN: No.
> INSPECTOR: You understand that this is an inquiry into a murder? That the fire was started deliberately? That it's important for you to remember . . . in detail?
> ALLEN: Yes. I would have been doing what I do every night . . . my work, eating supper, watching television, maybe listening to a few records. Alone.
> INSPECTOR: No boyfriend?
> ALLEN: Is that relevant?

INSPECTOR: If I think it is. It is. No boyfriend?

ALLEN: No.

INSPECTOR: There are these letters which came into our possession. We feel they're . . . well, threatening.

ALLEN: How did you get hold of them? He kept them safe. Only he and I knew where. How did you . . . ?

INSPECTOR: Tell me about the letters. Why you wrote them.

ALLEN: We were lovers. I wrote them to him, for him only.

INSPECTOR: Lady McWilliam says you weren't lovers. People who've seen these letters think they're crank letters. No-one can confirm you ever met or spoke to Sir Ian. Ever. And there are people who were with him almost every hour of the day. His secretaries, his civil servants, his chauffeur, his servants in London, his wife and family; none of them can say you ever even talked to him on the phone. No-one. I don't think you ever met him. You were just infatuated with him. Every famous person has the problem. Unwanted followers. Obsessed fans with no hope of ever even meeting their idol.

ALLEN: No.

INSPECTOR: No what?

ALLEN: The letters . . . er . . . the letters . . . I'm sorry. The things you've just said. Cruel things.

INSPECTOR: True things. The truth.

ALLEN: No . . . he kept the letters, didn't he. He kept them safe. Kept them to himself.

INSPECTOR: So what?

ALLEN: It means he loved me.

INSPECTOR: You might think so. I don't. He kept them to himself. So? Perhaps he was embarrassed. Didn't want to waste police time. Pity really. If he'd shopped you, perhaps he'd be here today.

ALLEN: But he would have told me to stop if he'd wanted me to. He wouldn't have kept the letters. Wouldn't have kept it from the police; wouldn't have kept it from her.

INSPECTOR: Who?

ALLEN: His wife. She didn't know did she? Not before he was killed. He'd kept the news about us from her. (ALLEN cries)

INSPECTOR: He got loads of crank mail. Couldn't frighten her with all of it. Even if he did keep the letters apart from his other mail, he certainly never met you.

ALLEN: We couldn't meet all the times we wanted to. We were lovers. I know he loved me. I loved him.

INSPECTOR: You're saying you had sex?

ALLEN: I . . . er . . .

INSPECTOR: That's what lovers do, or so I'm told.

ALLEN: We had a truer love than you'd understand.

INSPECTOR: Give one instance, one date of when you met Sir Ian.

ALLEN: My mind doesn't work on dates. I would see him at the weekend. He would come and see me at night. When it was dark, when no-one could see. He would watch me . . . then we would . . .

INSPECTOR: Go upstairs to bed?

ALLEN: You don't understand.

INSPECTOR: I don't think I do. Because I'll tell you what I think. I think it's the other way around. You watched him from a distance. You loved him from a distance. You never even spoke to him. No-one ever remembers you speaking to him. You're not in his diaries at the Ministry, not in his private diaries. Not even your phone number. Nothing. You set the fire. We found the petrol cans at your cottage. When you knew he couldn't give a damn about you, you torched his house. Hell hath no fury, eh.

ALLEN: He kept his private diary . . . his real private diary . . . with him at all times, it would have been burnt with him. (ALLEN cries)

INSPECTOR: It's upsetting to realise you've been living a fiction; that you've just been dreaming about a great man. Writing letters that were never even replied to.

ALLEN: (crying) I burnt his notes. He said I should . . . in case someone found them.

INSPECTOR: Not very convincing. If he did write to you, I'd lay odds that you wouldn't destroy his letters. You'd keep them. You were so infatuated you couldn't bear to burn something he had written and touched. I'll tell you what happened. You wrote all these letters and became frustrated. He didn't answer. Your 'love' or rather infatuation, died when you finally realised he couldn't give a damn about you. Then you decided to have your revenge. So . . . you'd worked out his movements . . . after all you'd been watching him for long enough. When you knew he was at Heaton Hall in Chester you went along. If he'd passed on the letters to us, of course we'd have been able to stop you, but I guess he probably thought you were just a harmless crank. Only you aren't the harmless kind are you? No. You went along to his house, broke in downstairs and set the fire. Maybe you watched as the hall burnt down. Did it give you a thrill to see it burning . . . to know that he was inside, in the flames?

ALLEN: (crying) I didn't kill him. You're wrong. I didn't kill him.

INSPECTOR: No, but the fire you started did.

Power closed the file of depositions, took his black fountain pen from his pocket and arranged his blank paper neatly on the desk in front of him. Now he was ready for her, and just on cue there was a knock at the door. The hospital officer opened the door wide and stood to attention. He announced her rather in the style of a master of ceremonies, "Doctor? Miss Zoë Allen".

She came slowly into the room, like a timid child. Her prison regulation clothes seemed too big for her; perhaps she wasn't eating properly thought Power. She seemed apart from this harsh world of locks and high brick walls. She chanced a glance in Power's direction then looked away again but not before he had glimpsed an undiminished sparkle in her brown eyes; at least something had remained unbowed by the remand regime.

"You've got about an hour-and-a-half, Doctor," said the prison officer. "Then I'll have to take her away again, okay?"

Power nodded. As the door closed, leaving him alone with the accused, he looked up at the clock. Time to focus things and prepare his report for the defence.

"Miss Allen? My name is Dr Carl Power. No doubt just another of many professionals you've had to meet. I'm here in my capacity as a psychiatrist – a doctor who specialises in the mind. I've been asked to provide a report on you by your defence counsel." He smiled at her but she appeared impassive, perhaps even wary. "I'm going to provide an independent report as far as possible. And because I will base it on what you say today, and because the report may be submitted to the court, if there's anything you don't want the court to hear, keep it to yourself. Don't tell me. Do you understand what I am saying? What the report is about?" No reply. Power was beginning to think that she would be mute throughout the interview. "I ... er ... I suppose that I just seem like yet another stranger?" he said. She looked up and shook her head.

"I don't think so," she said slowly, as she gazed up at him. "There's something different about you. Even to the other psychiatrist."

"Professor Anastasi?"

She nodded and Power ventured his first, rather general, question. He asked it automatically, because his mind was elsewhere. Zoë lowered her head. Power watched her lips moving as she spoke, but for a while her words meant nothing to him. He was observing her as if from trance-like remove. Her hair was brown and glossy, though cut short. Power was taken by a slow curl of hair against the soft skin of her neck. Her downcast eyes were correspondingly dark. On first impressions she was a quiet, shy girl, thought Power; no haggard female murderess. Yet from the letters he knew that something more forceful burned in her heart. She sat opposite him, bathed in the sharp morning sunlight from the prison window. The light was harsh, but Power imagined her face as if it were soaked in the honeyed warmth of the Mediterranean sun. He imagined her in a black skirt and a blouse with a generously rounded neckline. In Power's imaginary Mediterranean scenario her slim figure and elegant poise would only contrast with the pear shaped matriarchs who heaved themselves up Spanish steps. He imagined her at a table in the orange groves, laughing; a clear, liquid laugh to refresh your very soul. Her open face seemed to Power to broadcast her honesty. He looked deep into those brown eyes, noted the delicate rings of hazel about the topaz iris, and was disastrously spellbound.

She had soft lips, slightly upturned at the corners. he wondered whether she looked wistful when she was alone. Her delicate and precise movements in front of him now, contrasted with the image of the awkward and rebellious teenager that Power had half expected to see. This person before him had a quality he had not seen before, but she was marred perhaps by the isolated poise of the tragedienne. He had noted her slim figure and had been concerned whether she was eating enough. Now he felt an overwhelming compulsion to help this girl as much as he could.

What was it these soft lips were saying?

He looked down. His moving hand had recorded her answers on the case sheets in front of him as if by automatic writing. He read what she had said whilst she paused for breath. She was just eighteen, a student at the College of Art in Chester. She was researching Russian Art of the Nineteenth Century; specifically the icons of Czarist Russia. How apt, thought Power. She had worshipped at the feet of the unattainable Sir Ian McWilliam as if he were an icon. And Power himself just now felt as if he could just as easily worship at her golden feet. She already wore the tragic scent of Russian fate. She might have been a heroine from Dostoevsky.

Where had she come from? A local girl, born in Chester. Then she hadn't moved far in her short life. Brought up in the village of Heaton. A Russian peasant then, however noble.

"Can you tell me about your family? Your mother perhaps?" asked Power.

Zoë looked away into the blinding sunlight that burned through the frosted glass of the surgery windows. She half-closed her eyelids against the brilliance.

"I was born in the city. In Liverpool. My mother died there when I was four years old. An accident with a car . . . I think it was a car. I, er, don't really know . . . for sure. People don't like talking about death, so you never get to know do you? They wouldn't talk. Not to a child. I think she was having a baby when she was killed. So I'm an only child. I lost my brother in the accident do you see?"

"I think so. You mean she was carrying a son? From the post-mortem'?"

"I don't know about the sex, no . . ." She frowned and looked directly at Power. "It was a fantasy I had at the time. I've always thought it was a boy. But it's just my dream I suppose. Nobody knew whether he was a boy. Don't worry, I'm quite capable of distinguishing fantasy from reality. I liked to feel aggrieved that my other half, my brother, was dead. Sometimes children like to feel sorry for themselves, don't they? Does that sound bizarre?" Power shook his head. "Children sometimes like to put on the agony. I dreamt about my dead brother. What he would have been like when he was two or four, or when he was ten. You know? As if he was there all the time." She paused and looked at this comfortable man opposite her. His eyes seemed infinitely wise, infinitely forgiving, and infinitely understanding. "You know, I've never told anybody about that before. About my fantasy. You've got something there, Dr Power. How did you get that out of me?"

Power ignored the compliment and thought awhile. She seemed quite sure of her grip on reality really. He noted down what she had said.

"People might say," said Power, gauging his words. "On the subject of fantasies, that you weren't so sure about fantasies where Sir Ian was concerned."

"Because they weren't fantasies, Dr Power. He loved me. In every sense of the word."

"And yet people say that you never even met him. That your story about his loving you is a myth."

"One man's myth is another man's gospel."

Sensing he might easily lose her confidence if he challenged her beliefs this early in the relationship; Power changed tack. "So, going back in time. After your mother died . . . who looked after you?"

"We used to live in a terrace. A red bricked terrace . . . in a road that sloped down to the docks. You could see them from the end of the road. All the ships. I remember the smells of the sea. My father couldn't look after me there. I say that because he was a merchant sailor. Away at sea for six months of the year, at home for the other six months. I say he couldn't look after me . . . but perhaps he could of, if he'd wanted to look after me, but he didn't."

"Didn't you get on?"

She looked sharply at him. "He wanted a son, I think. I don't know. He didn't love me in that way. When he was there he shouted at me. I remember his red face over me . . . angry . . . drunk. Standing in my room, shouting at me. I was unhappy all the time he was back from sea, until the time he went away again. Then after a month or so I could forget him, until he got shore leave again."

Power made a note to himself. A suspicion. "And so . . . when you were small who looked after you then?"

"My aunt. My father's elder sister. She could stand up to my father. Stronger than him, always had been. There's my uncle too. He was always kind to me, but kind of distant. He had a smile that faded into the wallpaper."

"Like the Cheshire Cat?"

She laughed. And her laugh was just as Power had hoped it would be, clear and open, and honest.

"Do you remember anything of your mum?"

"As a matter of fact . . . I remember her smile."

"Good."

"I remember her baking in the kitchen. I remember helping; cutting out the pastry: stars and gingerbread men. I remember walking in the park with her. And I remember her fighting with my father. I could hear them from my room upstairs, remember walking onto the landing, down the stairs, remember the carpet under my bare feet. They were standing in the kitchen. Physically fighting with one another. I don't know what about. I feel it had something to do with me. That I was to blame. I never knew why."

"Your father is still alive, I think. How do you get on now?"

"What do you think? I avoid him. I live away on my own. In the cottage where my aunt used to live. I never see him. I never want to."

"And you live in Heaton? Sir Ian's village?" She nodded. "Where you grew up then. You didn't want to move away from there?"

"I think people move around to escape. But they can't escape themselves can they? And anyway, the village is all there is for me. It never changes, so it feels nice and safe, you know?"

Power nodded and asked, "Is it your own house?"

"I rent it from the Heaton Estate. It used to be my aunt's. She used to clean and cook up at the big house and they gave her the use of the cottage as part of her wages I suppose. But after the old lady who owned the Hall died and my aunt moved down south. I wanted to stay on. There was a time when the cottages were meant for the farm labourers, and the servants at the big house. You had to work there to live in Heaton. But there's no work on the Estate now, so the estate manager rents the houses in village out to all comers, including me. But it's the Estate that owns Heaton. All the houses are even painted the same colour. The rents are low enough though ... and I get the bus into Chester for my lectures and tutorials at the College."

"Are you any good at Art?"

"My art teacher at school, Mr Sweet, was very encouraging. I used to spend all my free time in the Art room."

"And you have friends at the Art College?"

"Oh, I don't know. I see a few of the girls for lunch on Thursdays. But they all have more money than I do, you see. Difficult to keep up with. Cars and things. Racy little Renault Clios bought by Daddy, so I couldn't go out with them much..."

"What about boyfriends?" She shook her head. Power went on, "At school ever?" Again she shook her head and pursed her lips. He asked no more. Perhaps, as Professor Anastasi had it in his report, she was a chaste virgin, yearning after the ever-unobtainable Sir Ian. He thought about asking for her fantasies; to explore the possibilities of her other sexual tastes. It was all important, relevant material for his report, but something prevented him from taking the history as he might have done with anybody else.

Instead he asked, "Have you ever seen a psychiatrist before Professor Anastasi and myself?" They smiled at each other.

"As a matter of fact," she said. "I have." Power was surprised. He was surprised that the image he had been assembling of her was wrong. Because he had been attached to that image, the conflict of truth with his fantasy about her vaguely irritated him. She continued. "When I was twelve I saw a child psychiatrist. I'd started to wet the bed again. My aunt was livid because of the extra work. She made me wash the bedding myself. It was always after my father came back from sea. He used to stay with my aunt sometimes you see. Anyway it was after he came back that time that I started wetting the bed." She was watching Power with great care, trying to fathom out what he was thinking. "I saw a kind Welsh doctor at the children's hospital. He was old and quite bald. Looked and moved like a child the way that children's doctors do. There were horrible investigations, 'to make sure the plumbing was all right'. That was what he said; 'plumbing'! Then after he was satisfied there was nothing physically wrong he had me admitted to his children's ward for 'anger therapy' . . . to let out my anger. He supposed I was angry at everyone: my father; my dead mother; my aunt; even him. So that was that. I showed the anger I was meant to have and I got myself back home. I stopped wetting the bed. I didn't want to go back to hospital and so I made sure I stopped, and besides, my father had gone back to sea. Then I saw the same child psychiatrist again when I was fifteen."

"Why?"

She seemed reluctant to say. "I took an overdose. A silly gesture. Dramatic, you know. I regretted it at the time . . . at the instant I swallowed the aspirin. The very instant it slipped down my throat. I thought, "Why sacrifice yourself for . . ."

"For what?"

"I can't remember. Not now."

But Power knew she was covering her tracks. It was unlikely she would forget the reasons for such a crisis in her life, only three years earlier. For the first time in the interview she was back-pedalling to avoid something. And she was back-pedalling furiously. And to his amazement (much later afterwards), he unconsciously colluded with her in avoiding the main issue in her life.

"Have you thought of harming yourself in here? In this place?" Remand suicide was common enough.

"No," she said. "I won't be in here long." Zoë sounded very certain.

"Why not?"

"The jury will acquit me."

And here, for the first time too, her judgment, her insight, seemed unsound. Power had read all the depositions; all the written evidence. He had seen the scene of crime and forensic reports. He had read Professor Anastasi's tightly worded psychiatric report, and though he might disagree with it, he could see that the evidence was highly stacked against Zoë Allen, and he did not share her confidence. Although he noted her sincerity. He coughed a little disconcertedly as he wondered how to reply. "There seems to be quite a body of evidence to overcome before you could be acquitted."

"But I didn't do it. I didn't kill him."

Was she innocent or naive, thought Power? "Can we talk about it?" he asked.

"There's nothing really to talk about."

"You say Sir Ian loved you. How do you know that? Everybody says you never even met him? That his love for you was only in your eyes."

"Either they are lying, or they didn't see what was going on."

"Did you ever talk to him? Face-to-face?"

She looked at him askance. "I don't really want to talk about it."

'Why not?' wondered Power to himself. He had initially believed her, but now he wondered whether Anastasi's opinion was true. Patients were sometimes like this. Was this subject Zoë's Achilles heel? Did her guardedness seek to conceal a system of delusions and madness? He had to probe these ideas. The ideas were central to her guilt or innocence; central to her sanity or insanity. He must press the point to ascertain whether or not she was deluded.

"You never met then?"

"We met regularly."

"Government ministers lead very regulated lives. People must know where they are at all times. It seems unlikely then, doesn't it, that no-one recollects seeing you together."

"You haven't asked them. Haven't tested whether they're lying. You don't believe me. I can see that! Nobody believes me. I told you either people have lied about us, deliberately refused to see or report what was going on, or they were so blindly ignorant as to not see what was going on under their noses. Unless you're going to make the effort to believe me, to entertain the possibility that I might be right, you will think I'm mad. But I know he was with me. I remember him being with me. The others are lying about me." She was almost shouting at Power now, exasperated with everything. Power didn't twitch. He had seen deluded people equally passionate about the most preposterous and bizarre ideas. But could he suspend his own disbelief for an instant, enough to consider what might be happening if she was right? Zoë was carrying on, "He would slip away. Meet me and . . ."

"Where? Where would he meet you? In your cottage?"

"No!"

"It would be logical."

"He didn't want my neighbours to see. If he'd come to my house, they would have seen. We kept it secret."

"So secret that no-one knew? You wrote him letters, tagged around after him, besieged him in his house, his offices . . ."

"Sometimes I needed to speak to him. If not to speak to him, then at least to see him, even in the distance. His wife had him there all the time, but she never appreciated him half as much as I did."

"But his officials say he never spoke to you, not once." She began to cry. And Power felt ashamed of himself. "And of all the letters you sent," he spoke softly. "Do you not have one reply that you could show someone to prove you are right?" Zoë shook her sobbing head.

"We made love," she said, quietly. "He was gentle with me. The first time." She paused. "I shouldn't tell you anymore. It'll all go into the court, into the newspapers. I shouldn't have told you anything." She was still crying, and Power wondered if she was crying because of the weight of his questions or the sudden breakthrough of the reality that she would most probably be convicted. But if it were true that Sir Ian had met her and made love to her then she was sane and possibly quite innocent. And if what was she describing was untrue then it was it all just some somatic hallucination or a fantastic and convoluted delusion about a powerful man? If so, she was psychotic, ill, and maybe she had set the fire of love that killed the object of her desire.

He spoke softly to her and his words came gently to her through her tears. "Without proof that he was with you, made love to you, cherished you in some way . . . without proof, then it all sounds so fantastic. Like you were infatuated, like you were deluded. It does happen. There was a doctor I knew, a GP, who had an elderly spinster for a patient. She was convinced he was in love with her. If he drove past her house on a home visit to another patient she would interpret that he had passed her house as a coded signal of his love. He was plagued by her visits to his house late at night. His wife was appalled and frightened when this stranger would berate her through the letter box. This dear little old lady would call his wife a slag and a whore. And this prim elderly patient was so sucked inside out by this passion that she would, against all her Christian principles, lie down on the doctor's lawn and expose herself to the sky and the suburbs in general. She had what is termed de Clerambault's syndrome. And that is what some psychiatrists would say you've got. They would say that you were obsessed with this phantom love of Sir Ian's and that when you realised it was just a phantom, that you'd wasted everything; you got angry with him and killed him."

"Anger therapy," she said, sniffing and smiling privately.

"And with no hard evidence to the contrary, everyone will think your romance was just a delusion," said Power, softly.

"But it wasn't. People are lying about it."

"Why should they do that?" She stayed silent. "If you could give me anything to go on, perhaps I could help you," said Power. Looking at this beautiful girl, he knew that he was making a genuine offer, but she couldn't or wouldn't tell him what he needed to know.

"I'm not lying to you, Dr Power."

And Power was overwhelmed by surprise to find that somehow he did believe her. And yet his rational mind told him, screamed at him, that she was deluded and probably dangerous. If she could set a fire on the basis of a delusion she could easily set another. By all that was right she should remain behind some high forbidding wall for the rest of her life. And despite all the logic and his experience, in his heart he believed her. He looked at the great wad of paper by his side; the argument against her. The words contained in this document would crush her protests into nothingness. He looked at her tear-stained face and wondered why he wanted to believe her so much. How could he be so ingenuous as to be taken in by such a beautiful face?

"What music do you like?" he asked.

"Is it relevant?"

"Do you have anything to play music on in here?"

"Yes, but..."

"What music do you like?"

"Prokofiev, Tchaikovsky, Stravinsky."

He smiled at her choice. "I'll send you some tapes. Would you like that?"

She paused a while, weighing him up, and then she nodded slowly. He checked his watch. There were some other questions to be asked. He had to complete a mental state examination as well, before he could write his report. He asked them quickly and precisely. Ten minutes later there was a knock on the door as the hospital officer and some female warders came to escort Zoë back to the prison block and what passed for lunch. After the door had closed behind her lithe young figure, Power tried to work out what he could do to help.

Chapter Three

Why must I think of you?
Why must I?
Why should I?
Why should I cry for you?
Why would you want me to?
And what would it mean to say
That loved you in my fashion?
Why should I cry for you?

Sting, 1989.

"So, what made you drag me out to the pub on a summer evening, apart from your obvious thirst?" Superintendent Lynch had been all too pleased that Power had winkled him out of his domestic shell, but he was too canny to think that there was no ulterior motive behind Power's sudden invitation 'to go out for a quick drink, if that won't offend your Christian principles?' It certainly had not offended Lynch's Christian principles. He marshalled the bags of crisps and nuts that the ever-hungry Power had brought to the oak picnic table, and took a swig of a half-pint of real ale. Lynch revelled in the smell of new-mown grass and the warmth of the evening sunlight. There was nothing in his Christian principles against enjoying the good things of life. The beer garden of Power's favourite pub hummed with genial end-of-the-day conversation. In the light of the setting sun a cloud of midges danced over the nearby river. The river moved sluggishly between its summer-dry banks. "You sounded different on the phone," mused Lynch, eyes half-closed in the sun. "Not like you. Kind of excited."

Power laughed. "You're right, something happened to me today. Or perhaps I should say someone happened to me today." Lynch raised an inquisitive eyebrow as Power continued, "Do you remember Sir Ian McWilliam?"

"I couldn't forget him. Couldn't forget such a high-level scandal."

"Scandal?" He pounced on the word.

"Well, I just meant the murder of someone so prominent. And so close, in our backyard, if you like. Well, it was embarrassing for the force."

"But you said scandal."

Lynch sighed; he should have been more circumspect in his choice of words. Power's curiosity seemed almost ferocious. Lynch wondered why Power was so interested in the McWilliam case. "Well, when I said scandal, perhaps I wasn't thinking it out properly, but there was a scandal if you like. The scandal was two things. First there was that girl who loved McWilliam without his ever having so much as talked to her and who set the fire under him and the second piece of scandal concerned the security guards."

"What do you mean?"

"The private security guards at Heaton Hall," said Lynch, taking another sip of ale. He opened a bag of crisps and between sentences began crunching them. "How did the guards manage to perfect their own particular brand of extreme incompetence? To let her wander onto the estate first of all. Secondly to let her break into the house. And thirdly not to notice when she had sprayed petrol about upstairs and down and set a fire big enough to crisp a very senior member of the British Government? What were they doing all that time? That's the scandal."

"I thought you meant something more."

"That's enough isn't it? To let someone torch a cabinet minister to death in his own house? They're almost as culpable as she is. Should almost be on trial with her."

Power had drained his glass dry and was wondering if Lynch would get the next round. "How well do you know the case?"

"It's a colleague's case," said Lynch guardedly, wondering if there was a real danger of saying too much. He comforted himself with the knowledge that Power was as sound a person as he could ever meet.

"I know about it, of course. The Zoë Allen trial. It begins soon I think."

"Within two weeks."

"Aaaah..." Comprehension dawned upon Lynch. "So this is what you want information on is it?" Power nodded. "How do you fit into all this?"

Power took note of the mild disapproval in Lynch's tone. Power lowered his own voice so that the other occupants of the beer garden could not overhear. "I'm being asked for a psychiatric report on her."

"I see why you're interested... but not why you're so interested. After all's said and done everybody accused of murder gets to see at least one psychiatrist. And if they're mad then they can plead 'diminished responsibility'. All this concern to get the conviction and the sentence right . . . a hangover from the days of capital punishment."

"'Hangover'. Very funny," said Power. He smiled in appreciation of his friend's dry humour. "But nowadays there are plenty of people who are convicted for crimes they never committed."

"Maybe," said Lynch. "But this Miss Allen. What is your interest? It's something more than the run-of-the-mill patient."

"She's not my patient," said Power thoughtfully. "I'm not seeing her as her doctor. The solicitors are my client in all this. There's a difference."

For all his principles Lynch had all the cynicism of a police officer too. "She's young. She's pretty. Are you going to tell me that, now she's used her womanly wiles on you, you suddenly believe she's innocent?"

"No." Power was surprised by the acuity of Lynch's insight. "It's just that I don't understand some things about her."

"Of course, it may be all right to succumb to her charms if she's not your patient." said Lynch, teasing Power with a smile.

"I just wanted to ask you about the case – some things I don't understand."

"I know," said Lynch. "Don't mind me. It's just that it's someone else's case, Carl. I don't know it well, and I don't want to say anything that might compromise the case. It all looks quite straightforward though. A young girl gets a crush on an important man. Her crush turns into an obsession. Her love turns to hate. She wants to kill him, but can't do it directly. Can't shoot him, or stab him. Can't face it. So, she kills him by setting a fire. An indirect means of murder. The police find her letters. They're vaguely threatening, especially towards McWilliam's wife. Very jealous letters. Perhaps she thought Lady McWilliam would die too when she set the fire. She might have thought Lady McWilliam was upstairs in bed with him. Perhaps that thought was too much to bear for her. And there's Miss Allen's inability to give any credible alibi, and to top it all a stock of rags and petrol in her garage. Exactly the same kind of petrol can that was found at Heaton Hall at the scene of the fire. And she doesn't have a car or a motor mower, or anything else that she would use that petrol for legitimately. There are witnesses that saw her hanging around the hall day after day after day. Waiting for him. Even when he was in London, or abroad on Government business. She was mad about him. Like all these cranks . . . like who was it . . . the one who tried to kill President Reagan just to impress some actress he thought loved him. He wrote her hundreds of letters too. Dangerous people. You must agree that the case is solidly against her. You can see that, can't you?" Power nodded. "But you're not convinced?"

"No," said Power. "I'm not."

"I think the jury will be."

"If the case is strongly constructed she'll be convicted whether she's innocent or not. And I think she is innocent."

Lynch sighed and opened a bag of plain crisps. "Well, there's not much a psychiatrist can do to help, is there? Except get her off the murder charge by saying she's mad as a hatter."

"She's not mad either. I think that some of what she was saying was true. I need some information to help her. But I've not got much time to get it. The trial is so soon. If we . . ."

Lynch was kind but firm. "I can't go stomping all over some other officer's investigation."

Power decided a strategic pause was needed. He picked up the glasses and asked whether Lynch would like another drink. Lynch nodded. "Something soft though. I'm driving."

"They wouldn't let you off," asked Power. "Old masonic handshake and all?"

"Are you joking? For one thing I'm not the most popular senior officer. I'm not a Freemason." And there were too many colleagues who distrusted his professed Christianity.

"Some soft drink then. Okay . . ." Power did not want to get into an argument with Lynch over the Allen case. He liked Lynch too much to cross swords with him. It was like Lynch's religious nature. Power tolerated this more than anything. He had always appreciated mankind's need for religious experience, but Power could never understand the hatred it caused. He watched the religious with a kind of scientific detachment and yet somehow also yearned to be part of their world; it was a world that seemed closed to him. Inside the white half-timbered pub, Power bought the drinks, a pint of Witches' Pendle Brew for himself and a mineral water for Lynch.

When Power got back to the table he found that the Superintendent had obviously been thinking whilst he had been away. "That girl . . ." he said.

"Zoë Allen?"

"Yes. If she's convicted she'll have a difficult time; whether she's in prison or a security hospital. They won't make things easy for her. And you . . . er . . . you get the feeling she's innocent . . . telling the truth?"

"She was keeping something back, but most of what she said felt sincere."

Lynch had known Power long enough to trust his friend's instincts. "I don't really know why Zoë Allen matters to you. Perhaps you don't even know quite why she matters so much to you. But I guess she does. Maybe there's the challenge of flying in the face of logic." He sipped the mineral water and made a face. The ale that Power had in front of him looked infinitely better. "Will you forgive an old detective's cynicism, eh? Tell me some more."

A casual listener overhearing their conversation might have assumed that the Detective was only half-interested in the Doctor's theories. However, the assumption would have been unwarranted.

The murder of Sir Ian McWilliam had intrigued Lynch from the very start. He had tried to get control of the investigation himself. He had argued against the assignment of another investigating officer. His colleagues, besides recognising Lynch's devout nature, also knew he was an ambitious man, who had seized and solved several important investigations in the past. Lynch was clever politically himself and was clever at using the media to the police's advantage. To be in charge of such a high-level operation as the murder of a cabinet minister and also be successful would be the highlight of any police career. Lynch had been disappointed not to get the case.

If Power's motivation in helping Zoë Allen was clouded, then so was Lynch's. If Power was right and Allen was not the murderer, then it offered Lynch an opportunity to prove himself and confound his critics. He was well aware of his motivation, but comforted himself with the notion that if Zoë Allen could be proved innocent, justice too would be served.

"No," said Power. "Perhaps you're right and perhaps I should let things drop. Why should I start ferreting around in the criminal world? I really don't know why I keep taking these forensic cases on ... they're more trouble than they're worth."

"But I think I've changed my mind, Carl. You've set me a puzzle. A very interesting one ... well, we'd better drink these quickly and get off."

"What?"

"Time's short. You said the trial was only days away. If we're going to stand a chance of helping this girl of yours we'd better start tonight." Power's face registered amazement at Lynch's volte-face. "It's okay," said Lynch. "I've got my own reasons for wanting to help. Not entirely as pure as I would like, but they'll do. The case should have been mine, you see. And it's difficult to forgive when you haven't forgotten. That's always been one of my weaknesses. So, knowing that all we are doing is flying the face of good common sense ... butting in on someone else's case ... well, we shouldn't do it half-heartedly."

"You mean we might as well be hung for a sheep as well as a lamb?"

"Exactly. And since Mrs Lynch has given me parole we'd better use it."

"What are we going to do?"

"We're going to pay a visit; to the scene of the murder."

★ ★ ★

The setting sun gilded the fields and hedgerows of the Cheshire countryside as they drove south. The light was that amber ruddiness that exists just before the pervasive indigo of dusk. Power's car sped gracefully along country lanes towards the late Sir Ian McWilliam's estate.

Power was, by and large, not an eccentric man, but his taste in cars had never been what one might describe as mainstream. He had positively revelled in driving an ancient and untrustworthy green Saab for many years after medical school. He had driven the car long after he could afford something infinitely better. He drove the Saab until eventually it had become such a variegated wreck of rust and green paint that even an impoverished student would not deign to drive it. Power had switched to a more stately, but even older car, a tall and elegant black Rover, beloved of black-and-white British Ealing films, when Britain could just about pretend that it still had a film industry and Harold Macmillan boasted of the British working man's never having had it so good. Lynch, who would not have dared risk his life in the Saab, felt the Rover was an altogether different prospect. After all, he knew and trusted the ex-police mechanic that Power took the Rover to for servicing and repairs, in fact Lynch had recommended him. Lynch even felt confident enough in Power's driving to relax and enjoy the scenery. The light was fading rapidly even so and Lynch turned his attention back inside the car. He leant forward and scrabbled in the glove compartment amongst the maps and bags of mints that Power stored there.

"What are you looking for? Hungry or something?" Hunger was a constant problem as far as Power was concerned. An adequate food supply formed something of an obsession for the doctor. Too many late nights and missed meals as a busy hospital doctor had taken their toll. Nowadays Power and food always had to co-exist. Although as a result Power was something of both a gourmet and a glutton he never seemed to put on weight.

Lynch was continuing his hunt in the glove compartment through mounds of old sweetie papers and packets of paper handkerchiefs. "I'm looking for a torch," he explained. At last he found it; a large, black, rubber torch that Power carried in case the car broke down in the darkness, (a reasonable precaution given the car's longevity). Lynch extracted the torch and tested that it worked, explaining;

"It'll be fully dark by the time we get there."

"Won't the light attract a security guard?" asked Power.

"If an arsonist breaking into the house and a blazing inferno didn't attract them when the minister was here, I hardly think one little torch will now that he's dead," said Lynch. "No, to be quite honest, I don't even think there will be any guards. The Hall is just a blackened shell. There's nothing and no-one to guard anymore."

Power signalled right and turned off the A41 towards Heaton.

"There are people we don't want to alert just yet though," said Lynch. "We don't want to attract the attention of the police. Not just yet. It would be difficult for me. And if you are right about Zoë Allen . . . if we assume that you are right . . . and that she's innocent, then logically, someone else started the fire to kill Sir Ian. And whoever they are, we don't want to alert them to our quest."

The country lanes that led to Heaton village were unlit and dark.

Lynch watched the blur of the car's headlights as it flowed over the tall hedgerows that they passed.

"A fire is an unusual way to kill someone," mused Power in the gloom of the car interior. "It's so indirect. Not like shooting or stabbing someone; both those methods require you to be there – a physical presence acting directly, not indirectly. The murderer has to see his victim, maybe even touch the victim. There's an immediate, dreadful conflict. Setting a fire is different. It's deliberate, calculating and it's indirect. Once the fire is set you can walk away from it and just leave it to do its own work. Like setting a string of dominoes on their edges. You start the first one off falling and the other dominoes fall in sequence. It's like that with fire. You can stand back and watch. You can even pretend the fire is nothing to do with you anymore. As if the fire had a life of its own."

"How do you mean?"

"I once saw a man who had started setting fires when he was twelve. Small ones at first. They would happen after a row with his stepfather. The stepfather would beat the boy and the boy's mother would invariably take the stepfather's side. The boy felt he could never win against this man. So one day he went out with some matches and burnt some kitchen rubbish. He found that he felt better. Watching the fire, his own fire, took the anger and hurt away. So he set some more fires; a plastic rubbish bin on the street, a telephone box, the junction box of the telephone exchange, and after a row with his school teacher he set the school on fire. He developed a love for fire. He even found that fire aroused him sexually. He would hide, watch the fires he had set burning away and masturbate while he watched the flames. He found it even more satisfying to light the fire, call out the fire brigade and then hide and masturbate while he watched the fire men trying to control the flames. He felt very powerful when he did all that . . . like a demi-god. The police who eventually caught him estimated that he must have caused millions of pounds worth of damage."

"How did they catch him?"

"By the time he was eighteen he had graduated to making fire bombs . . . well, Molotov cocktails actually, and these were used in street riots by gangs . . . remember that summer about fifteen years ago? He would stay back behind the front line of the rioters making the bombs for them to throw. Then the rioters would pass his fire bombs forward to hurl at the police. "Lynch scowled in the darkness. "He wouldn't fight directly himself, just use this indirect way of rebelling against authority. Rebelling against the tyranny of his stepfather." Power stopped the Rover by the village inn, where there was a road sign. According to the sign the Hall itself was half-a-mile away. Power noted that the Heaton Arms, looked quite attractive and vowed to try its ale when it was open. As he began driving again, he continued his story. "I had another patient . . . a mentally handicapped lady of twenty; she set fires to kill a social worker who was abusing her. When she was interviewed she admitted setting the fire, but she wouldn't admit to killing the social worker. She said, "Oh no . . . it was the fire killed him, not me. "She treated the fire as if it had a life of its own. Like a spirit or something, that was able to judge the social worker and find him wanting."

Power saw the Hall's open and unlit gates by the side of the road ahead. "What shall I do?" he asked Lynch. "Park here or go on through?"

"Neither," said Lynch. "Follow the road round past the gates and onward to the estate."

"But if we don't go through the gates here, there's a high wall all the way round."

"There is another way," said Lynch confidently. "Follow the road round." Power curved the car round past the open and deserted gates of Heaton Hall. "About half a mile down here is a bridge over a river. Stop on the left just before it."

"You seem to know your way around. How did you know about this place?" asked Power as he parked the Rover in a small, unlit, gravelled lay-by.

"I was born in Cheshire. I grew up here. I suppose I know it like

THE FIRE OF LOVE

the back of my hand," said Lynch, not without a certain amount of pride. "When I was a boy we used to cycle down here, my friends and me. If you climb over the wall here you're right by the river. Good fishing. And if the gamekeeper came by you could just jump back over the wall and scarper on your bike."

"Aha," said Power, amused by this admission of Lynch's lawbreaking. So you're a poacher turned gamekeeper?"

"Well . . ." Lynch smiled.

"And apart from it being a childhood haunt, why did you want to stop here and not go through the gates?"

"Just wanted to see it again."

"It's true then? That the criminal always returns to the scene of the crime?"

"That's enough of that," said Lynch as he got out of the car. "Once we're over the wall we're not far from the big house."

Power locked his car with care and after a backward glance to see that no-one was watching them, followed the Superintendent and the torchlight. Lynch, although he was the older man, seemed to vault the sandstone wall with grace and vigour. He also had the tact to pretend his attention was elsewhere whilst Dr Carl Power, puffing and panting, scrambled clumsily over the wall and dropped leadenly to the ground on the other side. "I always used to hate cross-country runs when I was at school," he said quietly. He remembered the discomfort at school of wheezing his way through the rain and mud to reach the finishing line.

"Pardon?" Lynch's attention really was elsewhere now.

"Nothing," said Power, looking into the darkness of the wood. The tall trees were silhouettes against the deep blue sky.

"Come on," said Lynch, and he moved away into the darkness. Power followed the path marked out by Lynch's light. He hoped his friend knew where they were headed. However, Lynch's adolescent memory of the estate was proved exact when the black skeleton of the old Hall loomed up out of the darkness. Power looked up at the jagged edge of the gable wall, roofless and stark against the stars.

They moved around the edge of the Hall, skirting broken glass and the fallen spars of the roof timbers, twisted and blackened like overgrown spent matchsticks. The ruin seemed preternaturally quiet, like an unvisited country graveyard, forever removed from the bustle of life. And in a way, this was an ideal graveyard: the great house had been the most ornate funeral pyre for Sir Ian McWilliam.

On the south side of the house the French windows to the conservatory had been inexpertly secured after the fire. The rough planks which barricaded the doors were quite superfluous since the conservatory glass had been shattered by the intense heat of the blaze. The metal frame that had supported the panes had been warped and twisted and now entry could easily be gained by simply stepping through the deformed skeleton of metal.

Lynch made his way into the broken conservatory. Glass crunched under the soles of his shoes. He pushed aside some charred wood. It fell noisily to the floor.

"Ssssshh," hissed Power, startled by the sound of the falling planks. Lynch waved his friend's protest aside.

"No-one here to hear us," said Lynch. He played the torch over the sandstone walls of the Hall. He pointed to a doorway from the conservatory into the main building. "Perhaps if we go through here into the house itself." Together the detective and the doctor negotiated the barricades and slipped into the dining saloon, where Sir Ian had dined for the very last time. "Perhaps this might be how the arsonist got into the Hall, unless she was already inside."

Power decided not to challenge Lynch's use of the word 'she', but maybe it just showed how difficult it would be to convince anybody that Zoë Allen did not murder McWilliam. "But before the fire, surely the conservatory would have been locked up tight, with alarms on the doors and what-have-you."

Lynch shrugged. "Alarms can be left off by accident or switched off by design."

The air inside the house was damp and cold. Charred fibres from curtains and carpets still retained the water from the firemen's hoses. The dampness lent the night air a pervasive coldness that quickly penetrated their clothes. Power shivered, but his tremor was born of anxiety as much as the cold. The dark seemed to harbour something else. He did not share the superintendent's assuredness and his senses were tuned as high as they would go to catch the least noise, the least movement in the dark around them. His keen sense of smell was drowned out however by the acrid stench of burnt wood and paint. He sneezed at the unpleasant odour.

"I'll try and get hold of the scene-of-crime reports . . . the forensic stuff," said Lynch. "If somebody's done their job properly, they'll know where the fire was started, whether there were any signs of forced entry."

"Maybe there isn't anything left of the doors. Maybe it all burnt up."

"It's surprising just what does survive a fire," said Lynch. "I heard they found the petrol can that started the fire. That survived."

"Perhaps it was meant to," suggested Power.

"Perhaps," agreed Lynch softly. He was thinking about Allen. If you imagined that Power was right, if you went as far as his idea that she hadn't set the fire, then who had? And if it were not Zoë Allen then the real murderer was free. Was it an individual or an organisation? And if it were the latter, then any attempt to see justice done would not be well received. There was a temptation to drop the whole thing. What was he doing creeping around this place in the dark? What was he thinking about? Why take the risk?

Power was looking at the gloom and mess of the dining room. It was impossible to see anything of significance. "This could have been the library for all we know. Shouldn't we come back in the day?"

"There will be enough details in the scene of crime reports. I wanted to get the feel of the place. Maybe even approach the house like the murderer did. And this isn't the library. It couldn't be next to the conservatory. It would be too humid for the books. Most likely it was the dining room. Can't you see the genteel dinner parties with guests finishing their dessert and trailing into the conservatory for coffee?"

"Perhaps the women withdrew while the men drank port and smoked cigars?"

"Sounds ghastly," said Lynch.

"Oh, I don't know," said Power, mournfully. He rather liked the idea of relaxing after a fine dinner with spirits and the fine smoke of Cuban tobacco, although he did not smoke himself. But even if he disagreed with Lynch's puritan soul he admired the logic of his thoughts. This was most probably the dining room. Weren't those fragments of white china on the floor by the wall?

"Let's go on as far as we can." said Lynch. "Unfortunately I don't think we'll be able to see where he died." This seemed a ghoulish and unwelcome thing to Power. He could imagine a guide perhaps, in the centuries to come, taking a party of tourists around a reconstructed Hall: 'And this room is where Sir Ian McWilliam was horribly murdered by fire. His ghost is said to wander the Hall by night...'

"I don't really want to," said Power.

"Well, he died upstairs in bed. The stairs are either gone or probably too dangerous to climb. And the floors upstairs are in the same way I suppose." They moved through the gap where the dining room doors had once been and into the marble-floored hallway. The marble seemed slippy underfoot, having been coated with a fine layer of greasy ash.

"It would have been the smoke that killed him . . . as it came up the stair well," said Power. "The fire would use up the oxygen, replace it with carbon monoxide. He probably never even realised there was a fire going on. Just slept his life away. Never woke up."

"A comforting thought," said Lynch with a modicum of sarcasm. Even so, he said a silent prayer for the man who had slept his way into death. Lynch prayed for Sir Ian's soul.

They moved carefully amongst the debris of the hall, past the gnarled bulk of the stairs. The thick Victorian stair timbers had just managed to survive the blaze, but as Lynch flashed the light onto them he saw that the stair treads and bannisters had worn perilously thin. Too thin to even attempt a climb. He wondered how they had managed to reclaim Sir Ian's body. Power and Lynch went through the hallway, through an opening and into an echoing void, all that remained of another room. Charred timber lined the walls and the floor was strewn with ash. There were telltale fragments of old leather bindings in the corner of the room. "The Library," declared Lynch. He shone the yellowing torch beam upwards to where the flickering tongues of flame had licked the walls. Above them, where the ornately plastered ceiling, once referred to in Pevsner's architectural guidebook from Cheshire, should have been was a gigantic black hole, which opened up into the floors above. The light from the torch was by now growing too weak to penetrate the darkness above.

There was a sound from the darkened hallway they had come from, as if something had fallen from a height onto the ruined floor. "Piece of wood or plaster," thought Lynch out loud. "The whole place is coming apart. I doubt it could ever be restored." He looked around the ruined walls with awe. "You can imagine the fire running from room-to-room, like some manic animal."

Power looked up into the darkness over his head. "Makes you wonder how safe we are here. The floors might be just as weak." As if to confirm his anxieties about their safety there was a creaking sound from the floor behind him.

Power spun round, frightened by the noise. He half-imagined that his weight was just about to plunge through the weakened floorboards into the cellars below them. He found himself confronted by the brilliant light of another torch, which had just been clicked on. He gasped at the dazzling beam.

Lynch turned round and was equally dazzled by the other's light, so much so that he could only gain the dimmest impression of who was behind it. "Who's that?" he asked.

"You ask me?" It was a woman's voice, thin and strained. "In my own house too."

"Can you lower the torch, please?" Lynch screwed his eyes up against the brilliance. "It's all right. I'm a police superintendent."

"Don't believe you," she said peremptorily. She did not lower the light as he had requested, but only aimed it more deliberately at Lynch's eyes. "You'd better be gone. Nothing for you to steal. Only ghosts here now." As they didn't appear to budge, she added, "I've called the police. I should think they'll be outside soon. You'd better go, if you're going."

Lynch held his warrant card, his identification, out towards the light. "It's genuine," he said. "I am a police officer."

"And him?" She waved the beam onto Power, giving Lynch's eyes some respite. He tried to focus them on the woman's face behind the light. "Who's he? Doesn't look tidy enough to be a policeman."

"I'm a doctor. Dr Power," he said. "I'm a psychiatrist."

"That I can believe," she said. "You look like a psychiatrist. Did my daughter send you to fetch me away?"

"We didn't know you were here," said Power.

"Ah . . . then you're not here to cart me off to the asylum?" There seemed a relaxation of the anxious tone in her voice. Power shook his head in answer to her question. "You're not here to salvage something from the wreckage? Steal a little melted lead from the roof, Dr Power?"

"No," said Lynch. "We're . . . well . . ." It was difficult to explain. "We're on a quest, if you like, to find out the truth."

"That's highly implausible. So implausible in fact it must be true." She dropped the angle of the torch beam and both Power and Lynch could see the frail figure of a woman, her shoulders draped with a woollen shawl against the cold night air. They towered above her. Power fancied that he could have lifted her bird-like body with only one arm.

"We didn't expect to find anybody here," said Lynch. "We would have asked permission, if we'd known . . . er . . ." He wanted her name to finish the apology off properly.

"Lady McWilliam. A widow. The widow. That's how I'd be billed in the cast list of a play. The widow. But not a very merry widow. Not merry at all." Her voice fell to a solemn note of despair.

"I'm sorry to have frightened you, Lady McWilliam," Power struggled to gather the words that would make it right. He suddenly felt very foolish blundering around in the night. The noble quest for justice, that Lynch had alluded to, seemed more like a fool's errand. But even as he felt embarrassment at what had come to pass, he wondered what she was doing in this charred ruin at all. And he remembered her fearful reference to her anxiety about being taken from this place. "We didn't mean to scare you," he said, almost automatically.

"Nothing scares me now." Her voice was flat and distant as if her attention were momentarily elsewhere.

"No, but . . ."

She broke away from the memory that had held her still; "You'd better come along with me. I want to know exactly why you've come here." Lady McWilliam walked back into the hallway, and since their torch had failed altogether, Lynch and Power had little option but to follow her.

"Do you think she called the police?" Power asked Lynch in a whisper. Lynch shook his head and gestured to the doctor to be quiet by putting his finger to his lips. They followed the widow at a discreet distance. She took them across the ruined hall and into a corridor that led gently downwards to some stone steps. A newly erected velvet curtain was draped across their path. She drew the hanging aside. The brass curtain rings clattered along the curtain pole. Behind this a low, but stout oak door, though blackened, had evidently survived the fire.

"The corridor has taken us away from the main house. This is the only part of the Hall that was untouched by fire. This is where I live now." She pushed the door open. Their eyes accustomed to the darkness of the ruins, struggled to adjust to the electric light in the room beyond. "It seems apt somehow," she said. "That this should be my refuge; my sanctuary."

Lynch ducked beneath the low lintel of the door and took in his new surroundings. He looked up. High and broad expanses of whitewashed stone reflected the spotlights that nestled aloft in the pale oak roof trusses. "A chapel," he murmured.

"Built by my husband's aunt in the nineteen-fifties," said Lady McWilliam, closing the door behind her late-night visitors. "Lady Marian was something of a traditionalist. She believed that all great houses should have a chapel for the family and their servants to worship on the Lord's day. By the time she built this there were few servants and no clergy willing to waste their time on such a whim. She worshipped here alone. Sometimes it feels as if she's still here. I imagine her there, kneeling at the altar rail all alone."

"You said she was traditional," said Power. "But the design of the chapel isn't traditional though? I mean it's modern . . . for the fifties I mean."

"You appreciate architecture, Doctor? Lady Marian chose her architect because he was one of the family. She indulged him rather. It's too stark for my tastes. Apart from the stained glass . . . that's more conventional."

Power looked around the chapel. He noted the camp-bed that Lady McWilliam had moved into the centre of the chapel, just in front of the clean, Corbusian lines of pews. She had perched a kettle and a microwave oven on a table nearby. She explained, "There's running water and a water closet in a little office to the right. Perhaps the architect meant it to be a vestry. But I don't think a priest ever set foot here."

"If she worshipped here, the old lady must have had the place consecrated," said Lynch.

"I don't know," said the widow. "I'm just grateful it survived; that there is somewhere I could get peace, find some rest." She closed her green eyes as if even now drawing on some small reserve of inner strength. To Power, Lady McWilliam was a small meek woman with grey hair and rather fine, insignificant features. She didn't look like a forceful politician's wife. But then she was in mourning and it seemed that she would be a broken woman altogether without her inner reserves, bolstered by her faith in the symbol of the chapel. She was a homely person, thought Power, but this might have been the perfect antidote for Sir Ian against the facade of political life. Lady McWilliam might have been his touchstone, just as in her tie of grief Lady McWilliam was using the chapel as her touchstone. She explained herself further, "I had to be close to where he died. Does that make any sense?" Power nodded and she went on grateful that he understood . . . "I feel so guilty that I wasn't here with him at the time." She stumbled in her speech over a difficult idea. "I just think that if I'd been with him . . . I might have saved him."

"The smoke would have killed both of you then," said Lynch bluntly.

"My doctor said that. I don't know that I believed him." She looked at Power's reassuring face. He could be confided in. "I feel so guilty Dr Power." She looked up at his kindly eyes. "I tell myself it makes no sense, but I feel so dreadful when I think of him . . . in pain . . . of the fire . . . burning him." She sank onto the rough woollen blankets that covered her makeshift bed and looked up at Power for reassurance.

"He would have felt nothing, because he was unconscious. He would have simply slept his way into death."

"Yes, yes," she took his words inside herself.

All at once Lady McWilliam stood up and began fussing about to make some tea. "I'm not used to guests here," she said. Lynch offered to get water for the kettle and set off into the vestry to hunt for some.

"You mentioned a daughter," said Power. "It sounds as if she isn't happy about you being here alone?"

"I have two children, Dr Power. One tries too hard to please, and the other doesn't try at all." Power sat down on a pew nearby to listen. "My daughter thinks it's somehow macabre of me . . . to camp out here in this cold chapel. In this discomfort. She doesn't understand why I need to . . . that unless I do . . . I can never forgive myself." She waited for Power to grunt assent and then she continued. "I wasn't always with him, you see. He led such a busy life. Had to. Ministers of State lead such awful lives. I joined him here and there when I could. But I made up my mind early on in his career that I wasn't going to . . . well, I wasn't going to live my life, my one and only life, according to his ambition. He was so ambitious. I could never understand this force inside him, driving him on. I feel guilty, you know. But it was him walking away from me all the time. That's what it felt like. Someone had to keep the family going, and that lot fell to me. That's how I look at it. He had his own path to follow. I joined him on it when I could. Playing the hostess at Constituency events, Ministerial parties, opening Gymkhanas, you know the little wife part. At weekends I sometimes joined him here in this mausoleum of a place." The irony of her words stopped her in mid-flow. She looked down at the floor. "He seemed to want to play at being a country squire," she said. There was bitterness in her voice that Power wondered whether to explore. And as he listened he noticed that she was playing unconsciously with the wedding ring on her finger. "I suppose that I'm paying the price for leading my own life . . . but why . . . why does it feel I'm paying the price for him and me? Why should it be me?"

Lynch returned with the kettle full of water and plugged it in. He set about looking for cups or mugs while Power did the talking.

"You sound angry with him, and I guess that might make you feel more guilty. But sometimes people do get angry with their husbands or wives, for not being there anymore."

"Please don't make me cry, Dr Power." She scrabbled for a handkerchief.

"The feelings are difficult. They can be talked about again. You can talk to me again, or not. I'll leave that with you. But I just want to explain why we're here. That won't be easy either, but I think I should."

"Yes," she sniffed back tears. "I was rather wondering when you would, Dr Power, you and your police . . ."

"Superintendent Lynch," said Power. "We're here unofficially."

She smiled briefly to try and encourage him onwards. "My interest is . . . well, I saw a girl for a report, I think you will know her, Zoë Allen." The widow's expression changed, but she said nothing. Power continued, choosing his words with care. "I wanted to know more about what went on, about her and Sir Ian."

She was adamant. "There was nothing going on. Nothing. Not one blind thing. It was all in her mind."

"Her mind?" said Power. "Yes. I need to find out about her mind. I have to write a court report. I need to know . . ." Power was and had been intent upon gently probing into the widow's collection of emotions, teasing out her regret and angry pain in the hope of finding some memories that would help their quest. Lynch sat down on another of the chapel's pews, bided his time and thought about Sir Ian's murder. He stared at a plate of dried chicken bones that Lady McWilliam had left on a table by her bed. He waited for the moment when she was ready for him to ask the plain questions that would help him create a new, and hopefully correct, hypothesis for the crime. Power was still working on her feelings.

Seated upon her bed with a mug of strong tea that Lynch had placed in her hands, Lady McWilliam's manner almost appeared to alternate between a contumely disdain for those who had invaded her house and a resigned bewilderment. It was the resigned bewilderment which predominated though. Mainly she was only too keen to accept their company and the vague promise that they might bring some relief to her doubting life.

"I never met Sir Ian," said Power. "Of course, I saw him on the television, and I read about him in the papers, but political journalists are not known for their ability to know, really know, people. I always wondered what he was like as a person that you have in your life as a friend or a colleague or a father." Power had always suspected what really lay behind politician's masks.

She looked down and after considering Power's statement, which was really a question, smiled. "I don't know. I really don't. Isn't that odd, Doctor? You look a little surprised. He had a public face, but he was a private man. He was so private, even with me. I think he kept a face for me. I liked what I saw – what he let me see of him. But he only let me see what he thought I wanted to see. He could be very kind. He could be very thoughtful. "Once, I had a car accident. Wrote off the Jaguar he'd bought for me on a country road. It happened when there was an assembly of ministers in Brussels and so he was abroad at the time. I'd had a nasty knock on the head. Concussion. They told him I was in hospital. Of course, he couldn't come back. He had no choice. They told him I was safe and that he must stay. Governments founder if their ministers deviate from the routine. People see any change as a sign of weakness, the pound falls, stock markets slide. Ridiculous. So, there I was ... lying there in that crisp, white bed; wanting him so badly. Some minor civil servant from his Department, an older woman, visited me there to explain where he was. Well, it needed to be explained to me. I had forgotten where he was. Amnesia from the concussion. She explained in words of one syllable. As if I was stupid as well. Well, their solid reasons for wanting him to be politically correct and diplomatic towards some absolute strangers in Brussels couldn't stop me wanting him. Have you ever been to Brussels?"

"Power smiled. "I have as a matter of fact. Good food. And the Trappist beer. Lovely stuff ..."

She interrupted Power's gastronomic recollections. "Brussels is small and grey and dull. Well, Ian must have read my mind, for the next minute he was there, beside me, in my hospital room with flowers and apologies ... showing me the face he only ever showed to me. He jeopardised his career, you see. The civil servants in the ministry were very cross with him, but I think the PM understood. The ministry thought I was well out of danger. The old woman had said so. They couldn't understand his concern. He dropped the whole summit conference to be with me. I've never forgotten." Power mused over what she had said.

Lynch took his cue and moved closer. "Lady McWilliam? Suppose, just suppose, that Zoë Allen didn't kill your husband. Who else would have disliked him enough to kill him?"

The question seemed brutal. She bristled. "But she did kill him. She was obsessed by him. Did you read those letters. Quite mad. There's no doubt about that."

"Is there any truth, any truth at all, in the letters?" asked Lynch. "Mightn't Sir Ian have met her? Just once perhaps?"

"Of course not!"

Lynch toyed with the idea of confronting the widow with the unarguable fact that she had never been with Sir Ian all of the time and so could not justify her certainty. He chose not to. There was a difference between being the officer-in-charge of an inquiry and surgeon unofficially raking though the ashes. Instead he asked again. "But if Zoë Allen didn't set the fire, who else might have done?"

"He was a well-liked man. In politics and outside." She sounded indignant, but there was a defensiveness there as well.

"He was a powerful man," said Lynch softly. "And there are those who fear power or who are jealous of power. He must have attracted enemies just as a ship attracts barnacles as it goes through the seas."

"Well, then, maybe it was the IRA . . . them or some other terrorist," her voice sounded smaller now, weak against the night. As she spoke she was trying to convince herself as much as anybody. "But it was that girl . . . I know it was. I saw her before she did it, you know. Hanging around. Always hanging around on the Heaton road, just around the curve, where the guards at the gate couldn't see her. When I came up to stay she was always somewhere. Like some maddening detail hidden in the background of a painting. We would drive past her in the car. I saw her, looking in through the windows at my husband. Her eyes . . . I can't quite describe them. Appealing perhaps, beseeching him. She looked sad and lost. But he didn't even notice her.

I know he didn't; he just kept looking straight ahead, but I saw her. And . . ."

Her own eyes grew bright and her voice regained its genteel firmness. "She killed him. When she finally, finally realised, after all the letters, and the waiting around in the wet and the cold, with rain streaming down her face and coat, after all the tapping at the windows ... when she finally realised he didn't ... would never give a damn about her ... then she killed him. I suppose it was a kind of revenge. But what had he done? Except for ignoring a mad woman?" She gave a gasp as if she were now about to start crying. She looked at her watch. "If you will forgive me gentlemen ... I am very tired, all of a sudden. I must rest now."

Power nodded. "Thank you for talking to us. I ... we were just interested to see justice done. You have been more than kind ... talking at such a difficult time."

"Sometimes it helps though, doesn't it, Doctor?" She offered him a weak smile, but reserved a disapproving frown for Lynch. "And sometimes it doesn't."

"Might I see you again sometime if a question occurs to me?" Power asked.

"You may," she said, implying that Lynch was less than welcome to come again. They stood up to go. "You can get out through the vestry door. Close it carefully after you leave, please." Power and Lynch said their farewells, but as the doctor passed her by she caught hold of his hand. "I wonder if you have a card, Dr Power. So I can get in touch with you if I need to?"

"Of course," said Power fishing in his jacket pocket for his card.

"Thank you." She waited until they had gone, sitting on her camp-bed for ten minutes or so, still and silent. Power seemed to have woken so many memories in her. With difficulty she got up and toured the chapel making sure the doors and windows were fast then switching off the lights. Finally, exhausted by all that happened she lay down, fully clothed, on her bed before the altar. She looked up at the stained glass window and thought about The Good Shepherd depicted there.

★ ★ ★

After they closed the outside chapel door and had emerged into the suddenly crisp night air, Lynch switched the torch back on. Its weak beam had recovered somewhat. Lynch looked back at the blackened wreckage of the house and the chapel, which had escaped the conflagration. "The Lord tears down the proud man's house, but he keeps the widow's boundaries intact," Lynch quoted. Power said nothing as they passed silently through the woods and clambered back over the wall. Power could see his car in the distance. Lynch broke the silence. "What did you think?"

"I thought you were a bit off-hand with her if you really want to know."

"No," said Lynch quietly. "That's just how I have to be sometimes. I am interested in facts, not how guilty she might be feeling. It's the facts that matter, at the end of the day."

Power wondered if Lynch was teasing him, but he couldn't resist rejoindering, "You're sounding a bit like Dickens's Mr Gradgrind."

"That's unfair, Carl. There's a difference between me and my job. I could have held the widow's hand and comforted her with my faith, maybe with a prayer. I can certainly do that. But to do my job, I need facts. You were concentrating on her feelings, I felt I had to get the facts. She liked you, so I thought I could risk being dislikeable. Okay?"

Power grunted his agreement and they climbed into the car. As the engine coughed into life, Power apologised. As he turned the car round and they started the journey home, he answered Lynch's earlier question. "You wanted to know what I thought? I think she's grieving for him, and on the surface grieving very badly. She's torn herself away from her real home and her society friends to camp here in the ruins of his life. It almost like the old Indian idea of suttee, but not quite. You know, where the widow throws herself on her husband's blazing funeral pyre."

"Except that with Lady McWilliam she waited until the fire went out?"

"Yes . . . well, I wouldn't expect any widow to really kill herself. She's demonstrating something by being here, suffering the privations of living amongst the ruins. But who's she demonstrating it to? Is the sacrifice something she's got to purge her own soul of guilt? Or is it for someone else's benefit?"

"There's no-one here to demonstrate the sacrifice to, is there?"

"She mentioned a daughter. She was worried we'd come to take her away, remember? Perhaps she thinks that the daughter needs a demonstration that her mother did care."

"Why should Lady McWilliam be guilty? It was her husband who led the busy life. The marriage must have been like a correspondence course, all done at a distance."

"Probably suited them both. I'm thinking of those marriages that sailors have . . . months away at a time. Those marriages wouldn't last a year if the arrangement didn't suit both partners.

"Well," said Lynch thoughtfully. "The wives might not have been given the choice."

"No, no, you're right of course. But partners usually choose each other for good reasons, some of them quite unconscious. But Lady McWilliam . . . she's more complex than I thought, and that being so I'll need to talk to her again, and it also means that if partners reflect each other . . . then Sir Ian was more complex than his life time image suggested.

"And things between them were more dangerous than she made out. Beneath her protests that Sir Ian was such a good man, underneath her certainty that he was always faithful, I felt she was angry, resentful in fact. Did you notice the way she kept on pulling and tugging at the wedding ring. Pulling it off and putting it back on. Her movements didn't fit in with what she was saying."

"Maybe she was having an affair?"

"Maybe . . . but what I was trying to say was that she has very mixed feelings about Sir Ian. Couldn't admit them to us . . . yet, and probably finds it difficult to admit them to herself."

"She'd know what they were, surely?"

"You might feel you know yourself through and through, but some people find some of their ideas and feelings unacceptable.

Some people have things they can't accept about themselves or what has happened to them . . . the mind is quite able to screen things off . . . dissociate itself."

"If she's mixed up, maybe it's just because she's a widow. She's had a shock. She's grieving."

"Maybe you're right. Nothing more. Still, I'd like to talk to her again."

"Well," said Lynch. She's got your card. I think she'll probably call you. Especially if she gets any doubts about who killed her husband. 'The widow always seeks justice against her adversary'."

The lights of Chester could just be seen in the distance. Power would drop Lynch off at his suburban home before he set off for his own rambling house in Alderley Edge. He wondered whether Lynch was prepared to help any further with Power's quest. He was surprised by the depth of thought that had gone into Lynch's reply when he gathered up enough courage to ask him.

"Carl, there are some very important things we have to do in the next few days. If we can get some evidence, some real evidence that will put your girl's conviction in doubt then perhaps we can persuade the Crown Prosecution Service to back off. To do that we're going to have to work quickly, within limits. I can help, but it will be your investigation most of the time. But I can help; I can get you information, and I can come with you on some of the way."

"Within limits."

"Yes, Carl. I can't afford to jeopardise the cases I'm already working on, and I can't be seen to be helping you, but with all that in mind, I'm willing."

"Any guidance for your junior detective?"

Lynch smiled, "Yes, the first thing you need to do is see Zoë Allen again. If there's a date or a place she can give you that definitely links her to Sir Ian." Power certainly didn't mind the idea of seeing Zoë again. He would arrange that first thing in the morning. Lynch went on, "I will try and get duplicates of the scene of crime reports, and anything else that's around. Then we also have to see some other people who knew Sir Ian. Anybody who might give us a clue as to who might have needed to kill such a 'complex' man, as you called him." They were drawing up outside Lynch's mock-Tudor house. A breeze was beginning to blow. "Thank you for dragging me out, Carl. A most unusual night's drinking and a visit to a Stately Home to boot. Drive carefully now."

Chapter Four

Of all emotions, none is more violent than love.

Cicero

Power woke in the middle of the night. He lay in the warmth of his bed, gently drifting in the satisfying wake of a dream. The pleasure of the dream permeated everything, running into reality like watercolour runs over the stark whiteness of the page. The vividly coloured fantasy about Zoë Allen easily overcame the lonely darkness of Power's bed. In the dream she had been warm, promising and eminently tangible. Emotions of desire bubbling in Power's unconscious had found form in the dream. Now, lying alone in his bed, Power knew there was no logic to his desire, no logic in seeking any satisfaction with Zoë. He could rationalise it away as fantasy, but his baser mind shrieked out that he should satisfy his desire for Zoë.

In his dream, somewhere on a balcony, maybe on top of a high tower, she had been there. She had been leaning on the parapet, laughing and smiling in an easy, golden way, her face made eternal by the Midas-touch of a setting sun. Her skin, clothed in thin cotton, was as soft and firm as any Power had touched and, best of all, she had yielded with such pleasure. Her lips had tasted of sweet, sweet fruit and her warm cotton dress had slipped from her shoulders with a delicious grace.

If Power's waking mind was unwilling to admit his motivation for helping Zoë Allen, his dreaming mind was keen to betray the self-deception. Power might blather to others about a quest for justice, but he had better come clean with himself about a very real quest for affection. Once dreams begin they will shout until their message is made plain. Power guiltily revelled in the dream. If only it could be like that ... falling together so completely. The dream had been so vivid he had felt her beneath him, enclosing him so tenderly.

His rational mind battled with the fantasy. Was it at all ethical to seek out Zoë Allen? Was it ethical even to relish such a dream about her? Power couldn't help feeling guilty. He would not treat her as a patient ever. His only remit was to provide a report on her. But it still didn't feel right. What if she was freed tomorrow? Was it ethical to consider pursuing her? As the dream receded the waking minutes covered the naked fantasy with argument and self-reproach. The dream had shouted out a message, Power was grateful for that. He would be careful, he thought; careful not to harm. He comforted himself with the thought that it was doctors who denied such feelings who were dangerous. To admit such feelings to the self was to hopefully be able to cope with them. Doctors who denied their feelings were still in their grip. There was another message in the dream, but for now, this other meaning of the dream was obscured. If Power was too busy thinking of Zoë's body to pay attention his unconscious would simply re-package the message into another dream for another night.

Power was wondering what Zoë would really be like? Would she ever yield as easily to him? Would she taste as sweet in reality? She had been obsessed by Sir Ian McWilliam. Whatever she said she had followed him around like a lovesick lamb, traipsing after the brutal carapace of his Ministerial car, watching at his study windows from the shadows of the trees, spending long dreamy hours writing verses and imprecations to the distant old politician. Perhaps she had even chanted spells to make Sir Ian love her. Perhaps she was a witch who enchanted every man who met her. Power laughed at the ludicrous turn his thoughts had taken. A witch? Thou shalt not suffer a witch to live. The phrase had bedevilled women through history who were supposed to have tempted men, men who had used them and abused them, and then thrown them away with such dangerous disparagements. Power thought of the thousands of women, some sane, some insane, who had been burnt alive (as Sir Ian had been). *The Malleus Maleficarum*, (The Witches' Hammer) had been written by two monks to crush those women: the 'immoral' temptresses, the eccentric, the demented, the ugly, and the psychotic.

And if calling a woman a witch was man's misbegotten privilege; perhaps how other men had returned the advances of such as Zoë Allen in past centuries, well then what had Sir Ian done? How had he responded to Zoë's advances? Had he responded as she insisted he had done, or was she just filled with a cruel fantasy that she could not resist, a tempting obsession that coloured her every moment, drove her dreams and possessed her so completely. Her pursuit of the older man appeared to have been so futile.

If Sir Ian really had been attainable, would she have been so infatuated? If Sir Ian had simply wound down the window of his limousine and offered her a ride would the obsession have persisted? If he had touched her knees and felt her flesh against the car's upholstery; if he had spirited her into a hotel bed and ridden out her lust then what? Would her obsession, the fire of her love, been extinguished by the explosion of sexual intercourse? Perhaps it was only his distance, which fuelled the fire. He was far above her in wealth, intelligence, and class. Perhaps she had never wanted an attainable male. Perhaps easy, attainable love terrified her. Would she run a thousand miles from any male who actively pursued her? There was no history of her ever having had a normal sexual relationship. Sir Ian might be so unattainable that he was safe enough for her to pursue. What if her desire had been for something else – for which Sir Ian was only a symbol?

Power mused over the questions one-by-one and thought of all the girls who purported to love rock singers and movie stars. Their fantasies were just as unrealistic. Their idols were unattainable; no matter how many groupies the rock star could bed in swift post-concert couplings, he could only inseminate a small minority of his fans. For almost all his fans the idol would remain unattainable and distant. So what happened to the girls and boys with their fantasies of living with their idols? Mel Gibson and Madonna remained far away. And their fans eventually came to terms with the disappointment of reality; and sought other attainable partners. In time they were glad to forget. Only the fool and the fanatic went on hitting their head against the wall that forever separated the idols from the public.

So perhaps Zoë had suddenly realised after the months of yearning for Sir Ian, of staring at his photographs and hours watching videotapes of his television interviews, of watching achingly for some real sign of his reciprocated desire; perhaps she had boiled over with anger. Perhaps just for a while reality had crept past the armour of her delusion. There would have been a raging anger born of frustration at finally having to admit her error, at having to live with the nasty thought that Sir Ian didn't love her, didn't even lust after her, didn't even know her face from the faceless blur of the crowd. And that bitterness, stored up unacknowledged over the years, might burn so very brightly inside her that she would need to destroy her idol; to smash it like some clay god figurine that one has suddenly lost faith in. Conceivably Zoë might really have set the fire that hungrily consumed Sir Ian.

★ ★ ★

From his study window Power watched the sun rising over the tree tops. The orange glow of day warmed and cheered him as he sipped from a mug of hot, strong, sweet black coffee. After his dream he had not been able to get back to sleep. There were things he had to do to rid his mind of all the questions. He had read books and written for the remainder of the night. The computer on his desk nearby hummed gently. He had written part of his report on Zoë Allen, but re-reading the pages he had dragged out of himself, he realised how insufficient it all was, and how much work he had to do. He saved what he had cobbled together and switched the machine off.

He picked up a copy of Professor Anastasi's report and read:

'Miss Allen showed no regret for what she allegedly had done. When I pointed out the weight of evidence against her, she continued to show no remorse, which of course is the hallmark of the sociopathic personality disorder. Her fanatical obsession with Sir Ian is amply demonstrated by her letters and these would provide ample evidence for what is called erotomania, or what is still being called de Clerambault's syndrome. It is however not a pure psychiatric syndrome, as say Down's syndrome is a purely medical syndrome with clearly defined characteristics, but a description of behaviour as Miss Allen displayed. De Clerambault described women who thought that priests and even King George V were in love with them from afar. Dangerous behaviour has been described from these sufferers, who often have a mental illness such as bipolar affective disorder (manic-depressive illness) underlying the delusion. However, Miss Allen seems free of such illness, and apart from her obsession, which might be counted as a monodelusional idea, is free of functional mental disorder. I believe she is though, personality disordered, and in view of her alleged fire setting and lack of insight into this, highly dangerous to society at large.'

Anastasi couldn't be plainer, but his assertions were based on two assumptions. Firstly, that Sir Ian had always been remote from her (and Zoë was quite clear that they had been lovers), and secondly, that she had set the fire, (which he thought was to do with erotomania – de Clerambault's syndrome or Old Maid's Insanity as it was sometimes cruelly termed by Jacques Ferrand – writing about the subject in 1640 he talked about some doctors, "... who although they are Christians, the most of them, doe notwithstanding prescribe for the cure of this disease, Lust and Fornication.")

Somewhat unsettled by this notion Power, who had tried to lay aside his own fantasy about Zoë, showered, shaved and dressed for the day. He would follow up the case, for he suspected that Zoë had truth on her side, but he would be wary of his motives and keep them in check from now on. Being the good doctor he did not wish to harm anyone, or make a fool out of himself. Knowing how he felt about Zoë gave him some control.

As he was gathering his papers from the hall table for his morning clinic at the hospital, the phone rang.

"Hello?" Power answered rather tetchily. He never gave his name on the phone. It was a case of self-preservation rather than poor telephone manners. Some of the personality disordered patients he treated were not people he would care to see outside the hospital or prison setting. This led to a certain caution on the phone, which others, had they been unaware of the good reasons he had for his behaviour, might have thought was high-handed, aloofness or even arrogance.

The person at the end of the phone was, as strangers usually were, none too impressed by Power's initial greeting.

"Who is that'?" he asked.

"You tell me," said Power cagily.

"I'm Lucinda McWilliam. Is that Dr . . . er . . . Carl Power?"

"It is. How can I help?"

"Well, Dr Power. You came to see my mother. She phoned me from a call box this morning. She gave me your number . . . from your card."

"Okay?"

"Well, can you tell me what you were doing there please? I'm worried about her alone there. I need to know you are who you said you were."

"Your mother said you were worried about her. Listen, Mrs . . . McWilliam . . ."

"I'm not married."

"Well, it's difficult to explain who I am and what I wanted on the phone. Could we meet, perhaps?"

"I don't know. You are a doctor?" She sounded almost as suspicious as Power was. Power was not surprised, this daughter was grieving for a murdered father. The world would look very bleak for her just now. But it sounded as if he had been able to reassure her a little just by being there at the end of a line. His card had not been bogus. He did actually exist. "It would have to be today . . . I'm coming up to see her. To try and persuade her to come home. So it would be today."

Power groaned inwardly, there was his clinic this morning and he had arranged something else for the afternoon. "I tell you what," he said brightening up at the thought. "Let me buy you lunch. There's a good free house I know, which has some decent food at lunch time. And, even better, if we meet first in my office at the hospital then at least you'll know I'm for real. How does that sound?"

"Er . . . all right. I'm driving up this morning. I'll call in on you first then go and see Mum. What time?"

"Twelve thirty?"

"Okay, how do I get there?" Power gave her crisp, precise directions.

When she arrived at the hospital Power was dictating his letters, following the clinic. She sat down in the secretary's office that adjoined Power's and waited, whilst his secretary, Laura, eyed her speculatively. Miss McWilliam, as she had introduced herself, was a slim figure dressed in black. The colour, which was part chosen for its mourning function, was also most flattering to her long, dark hair and hazel eyes. Laura envied Lucinda McWilliam her slim figure, but comforted herself with the thought that perhaps this cool dark woman opposite had eyes that were a little too close together and separated by a rather thin, long nose. Nevertheless she had a striking beauty, and a Southern accent that did not place her as one of Power's NHS patients. A private patient perhaps? Or a publisher's agent? Maybe Power's latest woman? Laura was curious to know exactly who she might be.

"Would you like a coffee, Miss McWilliam? While Dr Power is finishing dictating?"

"No, thank you. I'm sorry if I'm a few minutes early. There was less traffic than I anticipated."

"That's quite all right. I'll offer him a coffee and just see how long he'll be."

"Oh please don't . . ."

"It's all right," Laura smiled winningly. She was not going to be put off. She plunged into Power's office. "Miss McWilliam is outside."

she said.

"I know," said Power looking up from a set of clinical notes. "You said on the phone just now."

"But I couldn't ask you who she was from out there."

"Ah!" said Power, smiling. "Curiosity killed the cat."

"You're not going to tell me are you?" Power shrugged and put the notes down. He handed the finished dictation tape to fair-haired Laura and stood up. He shrugged enigmatically and left the room. It was unusual for Laura to scowl. But she did so now.

Power chose to take Lucinda McWilliam to the The Green Man. It was a free house, with a reputation for good simple food and the added attraction to Power was that it was quiet. He chose a table out of earshot and they settled down to wait for their order. Lucinda looked round the pub rather warily. She had expected somewhere rather more salubrious. Perhaps Power couldn't afford the time to take her to somewhere more . . . elegant. She inquired whether he had a busy afternoon ahead. It appeared that this was not the case. Their order of food arrived, carried by a round and red-faced waitress, who appeared to know Power well. Lucinda privately wondered if Power was an alcoholic. But when she suggested that they might order a bottle of wine, he demurred, "I don't usually drink during the day. But if you would like me to fetch you a glass?"

"Thank you," she said. She had been dreading this meeting. She didn't know why. Perhaps it was because this charming and deceptively affable man was a psychiatrist. "I'll have a glass of claret. If that's possible here."

"Of course," and Power dutifully went over to the bar and ordered.

The landlord winked at him conspiratorially, "Nice lady today, Doctor," he whispered. Power nodded. "You're doing well, my son." Power did not acquaint him with the facts, but returned to the table with the ruby-red glass.

"This chicken is good," she admitted, as he sat down again.

"Of course," said Power. "The cook used to run his own

restaurant. Fallen on hard times. Recession and everything."

"My father says . . ." She checked herself. "I'm sorry." She paused a while. "I . . . suppose you know how hard it is for people to adjust after somebody dies . . . I haven't got used to his not being there."

"It takes a long time. Sometimes years or even never."

She thought about this for some time then said with more than a hint of ambiguity, "I don't think it will take that long to get over Dad. What am I saying? To you, too . . ."

"It makes you nervous?" asked Power. "Talking to me?"

"Yes . . . but you're not quite what I expected of a psychiatrist. You're normal . . . you're nice. That makes it worse in a way. I might be lulled into a false sense of security . . . spill more of the beans."

Power nodded. "Well, take your time. Lots of people who meet me think I'm analysing them all the while they're with me, when I'm not doing anything of the sort. Would you like another glass of claret?" He'd noticed how quickly she had drunk the first glass.

"Are you trying to have your wicked way with me?" She laughed for the first time since they met. "Or are you trying to get me talking?"

"You don't have to have anything you don't want. Coffee instead?"

She shook her head. "More claret. I want to talk. Perhaps this is my opportunity to say some things . . ."

Power had sensed as much. He returned to the bar, endured the landlord's humourless humour and returned with more claret for her and coffee for himself.

"It's good of you to keep such a close eye on your mother," said Power.

"I'm worried about her . . . she's like a recluse, stuck away in that cold chapel. I'm really worried. Do you think she's all right, mentally I mean?"

"I think for now she wants and needs to be where she is. When the pain is a little less, your mother will want to leave the chapel and resume her life. How are you coping though?

"You hinted it wouldn't take you so long to get things together again?"

"I was joking," Lucinda replied. Power shook his head. "Okay. I wasn't. How am I meant to feel about him? For a father who was never there. Not when I started at school and not even when I graduated from University. How should I feel? I don't know. I guess I don't feel the same way as any other daughter . . . I just feel regret that he was never there, and well . . . I wonder if it was because of me . . ."

"Angry perhaps?"

She looked into his eyes. "A bit."

Power shook his head again. "A lot. A real lot." He looked into her eyes and knew he was right. "Tell me, there are two of you. Two children?"

She nodded. "There's Michael. Three years older than me."

"You all spent time at Heaton Hall. Your mother said."

"Not always together. She would have liked that. Would have fitted her fantasy of a cosy family. She has this image of everything being just so . . . the family is everything . . . another one of her myths. She couldn't see what was happening right under her nose."

Power's eyebrows rose a notch or two. "I mean," said Lucinda, "that she would ignore whatever didn't fit in with her way of seeing things. Michael was doing heroin for a while. She let my father deal with all that. Deal with it the way the only way he could. Pulling strings when Michael got done for possession. Sending him money to bail him out. Both of them hoping that the problem would just fade away. Dad's way of helping Michael was like pouring water into the sand. He needed a father's guidance. Some limits. To be frank, he needed a boot up the backside. He would disappear for days, weeks, buying drugs, selling drugs, moving around the country, and when he did get in contact it was always some crisis . . . some drama. As I said, he could have done with a boot up the backside. He might have got that if Dad hadn't kept on getting Michael off the hook."

"What does Michael do now?" asked Power.

"You mean drugwise?"

"If you like."

"A bit of cannabis now and then. I think. I don't really know. You never can tell, can you?"

"Maybe not," said Power. "So your dad was quite supportive of Michael then."

"Only because it didn't cost him anything real, any real emotion. It was easy for him to pull the strings, push the levers and make everything wonderful again. Easy. As long as he didn't have to look at why Michael was the way he was. As long as Dad didn't have to face up to the blame. Oh God . . . I think I'm drunk. How much have I had?"

"Six units," said Power. "You okay? Do you want a breath of fresh air?" She nodded. "Okay, we can walk in the fresh air a bit. There's some good walks round here. We're near the Edge. Alderley Edge. There's a good view over the Cheshire plain."

"Yes, I think I need some air. Clear my head a bit."

They moved outside into the sunlit air. They left the pub car park on foot and crossed the road. Ahead of them was the National Trust woodland that cloaked the sandstone Edge. Power was on home territory here. His house was only a mile or so from the pub. They began walking slowly through the trees. Lucinda took a deep breath to clear her lungs.

"You know," said Power. "I don't remember the press picking up on the story about your brother. They would have had a field day. Your dad was risking a lot when he helped get Michael off. Imagine what the press would have said. He must have put himself in debt to some very powerful people. He would have owed plenty of favours on Michael's behalf. Whatever you think of what he did, he must have cared for Michael."

"He was too late though." She suddenly stopped walking. Lucinda looked down at her sandaled feet against the red sandstone of the escarpment. "I . . . er . . . I hope I haven't made a fool of myself. These things I've been saying about Michael. I've never told anyone. Anyone at all. And, if I thought you were going to blab it all to the press . . . I . . ."

"No," said Power. "But I must be fair, I must tell you exactly why I'm interested in what you're telling me. I have to be honest. I'm writing a psychiatric report . . . for the court . . . on the girl they say set the fire that killed your father, Zoë Allen. I've seen her, and although she wasn't altogether helpful, and although I think she was even lying to me sometimes . . . when she said that she didn't kill your father I believed her. I think she loved him, and as far as her love went I think she genuinely loved him."

"The more fool her then." She looked hard at Power, angry that he had the ulterior motive.

"Your mother said that Zoë's claims were impossible . . . that your father had never met her or spoken to her. That all the letters she sent were ignored by him. But you said your mother had a habit of not seeing . . . or not wanting to see . . . what was happening under her nose. So was it . . . perhaps true . . . that Zoë was seeing your father?"

Lucinda glared at Power. "How old are you, Dr Power?"

"Thirty-something. Why do you ask?"

"I'm twenty-four. My father was more than three times that girl's age. She was infatuated with him, not the other way round."

"It has been known," said Power softly. Lucinda eyed Power covertly. Was he trying to say something else? He returned her look and she blushed. Power noted that her embarrassment was disproportionate to their conversation. He wondered what she had been thinking about. She was blushing like a teenage schoolgirl. He continued,

"If it wasn't Zoë Allen who killed your father . . . just supposing it wasn't . . . in that case, who else might it have been?"

"I remember there was a memorial service at the Abbey. There were speeches by the Prime Minister and the other members of the cabinet. Everybody seemed to . . . said they liked him, all his 'friends' were there, but they've all been pretty shitty since then. They made all their speeches. About how wonderful he was as a friend, a colleague, a politician. How British politics would miss him and mourn his loss etcetera etcetera; but the truth is they were glad to see him out of their way. Mummy hasn't had sight nor sound of those friends since he died."

"I have to ask," said Power. "How do you mean, 'wanted him out of the way'?"

"Well, no more than the way his death opened up a path for them ... for promotion ... politicians like to slip their toes into dead men's shoes." She shuddered.

"Was there any other reason?"

"He was always outspoken. Had some fairly rabid views on what should be done to the IRA; thought women should be chained back to the kitchen stove; thought immigration should be reversed."

Power thought back to what he had seen of Sir Ian on the television. "I would never have thought that he . . ."

"He toned down his views in front of the camera and the press. To survive he had to be 'politically correct'. Of course. But he was beginning to think that he should make a stand on his principles. Say exactly what he thought or had only ever said in private up till then.

That's what he was going on about in the months before his death: his principles. I think he was tired of keeping quiet; wanted to speak out about something."

"What was he planning to do? A set-piece speech? An attack on the PM? What?"

"You'd be better off asking his agent. You'll find him ... in Daddy's old constituency offices . . . he's standing in the by-election. He's taking over Dad's old seat."

"*Le Roi est mort* . . ." thought Power as he mulled over what Lucinda had just said. He had already booked an appointment with the pretender to Sir Ian's crown. He wanted to get to know how the old man had really been, but the old man was proving elusive. The closest people in the world to Sir Ian, his wife and his daughter, might have been expected to know everything about him, but it seemed they each only possessed a fragment of the old man's character.

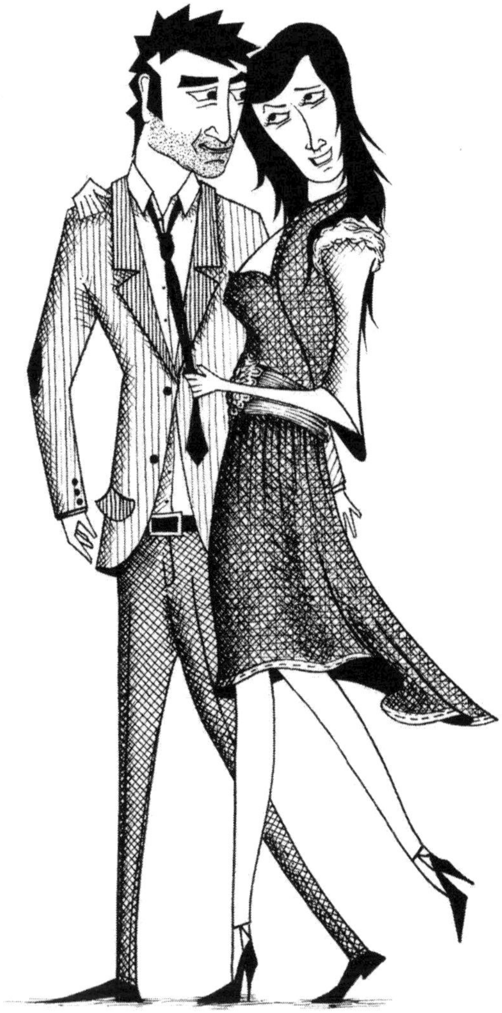

His wife idolised her incomplete picture, and, his daughter bitterly regretted Sir Ian's perpetual absence from her life. Lynch and he needed some other figure in Sir Ian's life to focus upon, to give them some scent of his killer. "So you think his party agent might be a good bet, might know of someone else who bore a grudge against your father?"

"You could try him, or Michael. But my father didn't rate either of them ... not to confide in anyway. Oh, I think I told you that." She closed her eyes and wavered a little unsteadily. "Failing that there are his colleagues in Whitehall. But they'd be busy. Too busy for their own families, probably too busy to see you, and certainly too busy to waste time on a dead man's business." She laughed nervously. "I sound really cynical don't I? To tell you the truth, I don't feel very well. I've had too much to drink. I had some before I even came to the hospital. Some vodka to give me courage."

"Well," said Power. "As a matter of fact, we're very near my house. You could rest there if you like."

"Won't Mrs Power mind?" She smiled and Power thought she was playing with him.

"There is no Mrs Power," he said. "You can rest while I go back and get my car, and when you feel better I'll get you back to your car at the hospital. If you want to phone to let your mother know..."

"You got me drunk," she giggled. "You planned this. 'We're very near my house', you said. Very convenient. Do you want to have me? Is that it?" They had stopped in a clearing close to the wall that ran around Power's property. Power looked at the young woman. There was laughter in her eyes, and he was still haunted by the erotic dream of the night before. "You can have me if you like ... let's go back Carl ..." She caught hold of his arm, partly to draw him closer, partly to steady herself. Power wondered if she was exaggerating her drunkenness.

"No, you don't have to do this. You don't have to pretend. You don't have to do anything. Let's get inside. You can put your feet up and sleep it off."

Her laugh rang round the clearing. She had thought of something else to say, but held her tongue, and wondered if Power knew more about her than he was letting on. Power was relieved to see the drunken act was receding. Lucinda had had too much to drink, but not that much to justify such sexual disinhibition.

They walked to Power's house in silence. He showed her into the living room where she collapsed into the sofa. Lucinda took off her jacket and then her shoes. He put on a recording of Allegri and turned the volume down. Lucinda looked at him with half-closed eyes. She had decided that this man was safe, and good. There was no need to fake anything, and in his healing presence she felt relaxed for the first time in many days.

Power walked down the hill to find his car. He drove it back to his house and let himself quietly back inside. As he stood in the hallway he could hear that in the living room the recording had finished and all was quiet. He wondered whether she had slipped upstairs. Perhaps she was lying naked in his bed. The idea both excited and disturbed him simultaneously. He went into the living room and found her there curled up safely on the sofa, asleep. He found a blanket and gently covered her before writing a note, which he left by her side, telling her to wait; that he would return and give her a lift to her car. Power smiled at himself and closed the door softly behind him. He went off to make some telephone calls before setting off for his afternoon appointment.

★ ★ ★

Sir Ian McWilliam's old constituency was part new-town, part countryside north of the old Roman City of Chester. Sir Ian had been its Member of Parliament for twenty years; from a fresh-faced back bencher fired with ambition to a deliberately cautious cabinet minister in his early sixties.

Carl Power sat in his Rover. He was parked on the street, with his windows open and shirt sleeves rolled up. It had turned out to be a swelteringly hot day. The tarmac on the road ahead shimmered in a heat haze. Most people seemed to be indoors. At a school nearby mothers and grandmothers waited in the shade of a wall to pick their children up from the Church of England primary school. Power caught himself looking at the prettiest of the mothers, dressed in turquoise blue. Her skin was almost copper-coloured. 'Too much sunbathing,' the doctor part of Power thought. He did appreciate the graceful curves of her body and her almost feline grace. He was reminded of the elegant woman, Lucinda McWilliam, that he had left sleeping soundly on the sofa in his living room.

He made a conscious effort not to look at the waiting mother outside the school again. He wondered why he was suddenly looking carefully at every female he saw. Was it the summer heat that made him feel this way? And if he was so keen on seeking a suitable mate, why hadn't he taken up Lucinda McWilliam's offer? It had been a definite offer sure enough and he did think she was attractive. He had the distinct feeling that the offer, made in the woods behind his house, was not an offer to him just then. It wouldn't have mattered who he was, he felt the offer would still have been made. And if that was the case Power wasn't interested, but what Power was focusing upon was the fact that Lucinda could make such offers. Power suspected that it hadn't been the first time she had acted so impulsively. What was it that triggered her to make such offerings of her body? And yet she had been almost relieved when he signalled he was not going to go further with the scenario.

The man Power had come to see was walking down the street. Power saw him stop outside the party headquarters, a new Georgian-style house set back off the road. He saw the man unlock the front door. Power got out of the car and locked it up. His shirt was sticking to his back in the heat, and under the blazing sun he walked across the road to the house. A cherry tree, past its blossom time stood in the neatly kept front garden. Fluffy clouds of alyssum and patriotic blue Lobelia fringed the borders of the lightly-toasted lawn. Power straightened his tie, put on his light jacket and rang the front doorbell.

Power introduced himself and was shown into a suite of large offices at the back of the house. The desks were strewn with papers and documents which sat in stacks by the side of an old word processor. The beige walls were spotted with dabs of old blu-tac where posters had been. Some of the posters had survived removal, for now. Black-and-white photographs of Sir Ian McWilliam's face looked down into the room. Sir Ian had obviously worn his most reassuring expression for the election posters. By the side of the curling election material a framed, signed photograph of the Prime Minister calmly looked out from amidst the disarray.

"We're gearing ourselves up," said Alan Jackson, trying to excuse the mess. "We need to get ready for the by-election band wagon when it arrives. I'm busy co-ordinating volunteers, but you can't presume too much of them. You have to guard their reserves for the fight. You know of course that I'm standing in the election?" Power nodded. "Well, how can I help you, Dr Power?" Alan Jackson sat in his chair with the edgy nervousness of the hitherto perpetual underdog. He looked anxiously through his spectacles at the psychiatrist and ran a hand backwards through his thinning hair. All at once he seemed to check himself and assumed a more assertive air that might just become a potential Member of Parliament. Power noted the change with interest.

"It's about your late colleague, Sir Ian McWilliam."

"Yes?" Jackson spoke slowly and with less certainty than before.

"It's about the fire he died in."

"And probably has ended up in now."

"I'm sorry; I don't quite follow."

"It depends on whether you believe in Hell doesn't it? The night after he died I had a dream about the fire . . . about how the fires of Hell reached up through the earth breaking through the rock and the soil, through the bottom of his house, up to where he lay, to pull him down into the underworld. It was a very vivid dream. I can't forget it." He checked himself. "I'm sorry if it doesn't seem appropriate... I don't know why I mentioned it... well, maybe I was thinking that dreams were your thing, Dr Power."

"They are... very much so. But I hadn't thought of the fire like that... didn't you get on with Sir Ian?"

"You're sure you're not a reporter?"

"No, I'm a doctor. A psychiatrist like I said on the phone."

"Can I be open then? Without the fear of being quoted in some dreadful tabloid?"

"You can talk quite safely."

"Then I can admit that we did not get on. And that is a major admission, I suppose... for a future MP you understand. Don't look surprised, I know the constituency well. McWilliam had a solid majority in the General Election. I'm not giving anything away when I say that I think my campaign will be successful. But my opinion of McWilliam is still not something I could say in public, you understand."

"It sounds as if you already feel you have to guard what you say."

Jackson took his glasses off and looked at the sky beyond the windows. "You can have all sorts of ideas, dreams, and visions as a politician, but you can't voice them all. If some of the ideas were made known, they would lead to your fall, without any doubt. You could despise the Prime Minister in private, oh yes, but to publicise such opinions would be an out-and-out attack. And unless the time was right, you wouldn't survive the counter-attack."

"What private ideas of Sir Ian's did you particularly dislike?"

"Am I that transparent?" Jackson was worried in case he needed to become more opaque. He was finding that there was a difference between being a local party agent and a potential Member of Parliament. The notion that Power could read him so easily disturbed him.

"But there were things you disagreed upon."

"Yes. He believed that society could only afford to subsidise the successful... as a kind of investment for the future. He just couldn't see the point in 'maintaining the underclass' as he put it."

"I never heard him say that though."

"You wouldn't; he kept his beliefs to the coffee cliques of the Commons and sympathetic media friends. But his ideas were getting round. Just before his death he was organising a new backbench committee . . . its aim was to steer the party to the far right. It was beginning to get round that Sir Ian was aiming to take on the PM. If he could have got enough backbench support he might have sought a nomination for the leadership elections. But there were other things he kept secret. Had to keep secret."

"Like what?"

"He always said to me. 'If you have to tell a secret . . . tell it to just one person. And make sure they know that they're the only one that does know. And when they spill the beans you'll know who betrayed you, and who to stick the knife in.' Those were his words. Of course, I think that there were other secrets he told nobody. Nobody at all. He always said how unreliable people were."

"He told you secrets? Did he ever mention a girl called Zoë?"

"Look, what exactly is your interest, your real interest in all this?"

"I'm writing a court report. It's vital for the judge and jury. I need to know for sure whether what she said was true."

"When I started here two years ago . . . I'd been drafted in as a party-funded aide for the Minister you know, to keep his constituency affairs ticking over for him . . . he opened up to me at the beginning. His first impression was that he could trust me. Anyway, he told me about his connections abroad. With other parties, with a German woman who phoned up occasionally. An old woman with a thick accent. He spoke about the European fascist cause once or twice. After heavy lunches . . . you understand? A few drinks? Well, when he told me, when I understood what he meant, he saw my . . . distaste. I couldn't hide what I felt because my wife is Jewish . . . you see?" Power nodded slowly, thinking. "And so he passed it off as a joke. When he'd sobered up he never, ever mentioned it again. And he made sure that none of his phone calls came through here. None of them. And he never confided in me again.

I wasn't to be trusted. After that he was just waiting for a way to get rid of me. The last year here was dreadful."

He looked at Power and wondered how much more he could confide in him. Could he mention his own trip to the GP, his own confession of sadness and anxiety, the prescription of antidepressants? "And er ... since then we didn't really talk about anything important. I just held the fort and prayed I could keep my job. Now he's gone, things are so very different." Jackson smiled innocently. "It's as if night has been replaced by a sunny day."

"But Zoë?"

"Yes, she phoned once or twice, a year or so ago. But he was never here when she phoned. He really wasn't. It wasn't as if I was trying to fend her off. I think she gave up trying this particular number."

"I wonder why she gave up? Did you ever see her?"

Jackson shrugged. "I wouldn't remember."

"Sir Ian never mentioned her?"

"No. He wouldn't. Not to me. He would only tell someone he could trust."

"Like Lady McWilliam?"

Jackson laughed. "He never saw her as far as I could gather. Look ..." he rummaged in one of the piles of papers and took out a thin blue leaflet. He opened it up and showed Power the photographs inside. "That sums it up."

It was a picture of a family group standing around a piano. Sir Ian was seated at the keyboard, smiling widely, as he supposedly played while his daughter looked on and his son stood with a violin, poised to play. His wife hovered on the edge of a group with a tray of tea. It was meant to portray the happy family.

Jackson smiled. "The ad men put that together. To show 'unity and harmony', that was what they said. For one thing, the son wasn't even there. Not in that place, not at that time. The group is assembled from two photos, one old photo of the boy as he was some years ago edited in to the group with computer technology. The happy group never existed at all. And McWilliam couldn't play the bloody piano anyway."

Power looked sadly at the photo. "And they say the camera never lies."

"I designed my own leaflet. I wasn't using any image people. I wanted something honest."

Power smiled at the pretender to the crown. After his thinly veiled hatred of Sir Ian, he was now showing a hint of personal integrity. Power stood up. "So, thank you for talking to me Mr Jackson. I hope your campaign goes well." They shook hands. "Oh, before I go . . . if . . . if Sir Ian wouldn't have confided his secrets in you. Who else would he have confided in?"

"Try his civil servants . . . in the ministry. Most of the time he was as thick as thieves with them."

"Anyone in particular?"

"Yes, there was a very young private secretary called Jacob Tuke. He was with Sir Ian in recent years, until he had to go into a wheelchair. Retired through ill-health months before the fire. Multiple sclerosis, I think. He got close to his new Private Parliamentary secretary and some others, but not as close as he had been with Tuke. And Tuke certainly seemed to like him."

"Is there an address for Tuke?" asked Power. Jackson shrugged again.

"Never mind," said Power. "I'll find him if I need to. Thank you." He made to leave.

"One thing, before you go . . ." said Jackson.

"Yes?"

"Are you on the electoral roll in this constituency?"

"No, I live in Alderley Edge," answered Power.

"Oh well . . ." Jackson sighed and checked himself in his quest for Power's vote. he waved goodbye as Power went out to his sun-hot Rover.

Chapter Five

But you would have felt my soul in a kiss,
And known that once if I loved you well;
And I would have given my soul for this
To Burn Forever in burning hell.

**Les Noyades,
Swinburne.**

Power returned to the village of Alderley Edge in the early evening. He passed the church and the railway station and stopped off at the shops. The shops were about their shutting up for the night. Candy stripe aproned butcher's boys were pushing the shop awnings back into their housings. Florists were taking their fragrant blooms indoors off the streets. Power went into the delicatessen and bought some spit-roast chicken and a bottle of elderflower wine for his supper. He got back into his Rover clutching his purchases. From the window he saw a group of four young people: two boys and two girls in their late teens.

They looked golden and they laughed brightly, unself-consciously. For an instant Power took pleasure in their youthful happiness. Their dreamy body language was redolent of togetherness and shared experience. These were two pairs of lovers moving easily through the summer afternoon. Power got back into his car with a tinge of regret that he could never join them.

He sped away through the village, past the teashops and, turning left, with a minor protest from the car's ancient engine, headed up the steep hill towards the Edge (the escarpment which overlooks the Cheshire plain) and home.

Power's house lay nestled into the woodland that covered the Edge and safe behind a high sandstone wall. The house had been a lucky buy, it afforded enough solitude that he could relax from his work and enjoy his hobbies of writing, walking and cooking, and large enough that he could invite as many friends as he liked to join him whenever he wished.

He opened the arched, stout, oak front door, and placed the bottle of wine and the foil bag of chicken on the hall table. He could still smell heady traces of Lucinda's perfume. Power followed the traces of heavy, fruited scent into his living room.

There was no Lucinda here. He felt the seat where she had been sleeping when he had left that afternoon. Far from being cold the wool upholstery was warm, as if she had only just been there. He frowned. Had he seen her on the road? She hadn't been walking down the hill when he had driven up, and her car was back at the hospital. Unless she had got a taxi (and he couldn't remember being passed by one on the road), she must still be in the house.

He was mindful of the fantasy he had enjoyed earlier, about her being in his bed. All of a sudden he was quite sure that this was what she had done. She had waited until she heard the return of his car. Perhaps she had heard the sound of the wheels grinding through the gravel, then she had jumped up from the sofa and climbed the stairs. By the time Power had come through the door she was nestled expectantly in his bed.

Power hurried out of the living room and ran up the stairs two-at-a-time. Breathless he barged into his bedroom and looked down at the rumpled covers. Lucinda was not there. Power laughed at himself, 'Wishful thinking!' he thought and began to descend the stairs, more slowly this time. He needed someone badly, and he got to thinking how such need, such desires, could distort the thinking processes. He hadn't been sleeping properly. He shook his head to clear his mind. It was Zoë who was supposed to have erotomania, not him. But he could not rationalise his desire away. And it seemed to be focusing on any suitable female that came near. The scent of her perfume . . . that was what had started it . . . the nerve fibres that detect different scents, the olfactory nerve fibres, are one of the most ancient parts of the human brain. They plug directly into the most rudimentary neural circuits, they fuel the emotions of anger, fear and lust. They can stir up emotional memories effortlessly and many times better than pictures or words. The smell of gravy can bring back the comfort of a family Sunday afternoon, or the smell of brick-dust might stir the numbing horror of the bombsite. Lucinda's perfume equated, in Power's mind, with lust. But what was the point of nurturing such desire after Lucinda had flown? Power was partly annoyed at himself for having refused her offer and partly glad that his rational mind had seen the disadvantages of such a dangerous liaison and reigned in his lust. It wouldn't have seemed right to take advantage of her offer. Would it? Power felt he would never know.

He walked through the hall and into the kitchen.

Lucinda McWilliam was standing by the window, looking out onto Power's kitchen garden. She had been chopping carrots, onions and garlic with a sharp knife. The back door was open and the evening sun spread its warm fingers over her back and thighs. She turned as Power opened the door and, seeing his face, laughed. "Did you think I'd gone?" She shook her head. You can't get rid of me that easily. I looked all over your house for you . . . to see if you were hiding from me, but I couldn't find you . . . so I thought I'd wait. And as you took so long I decided to cook something."

"I didn't mean to be so long..." Power apologised. "I should have left you a note . . . or something. I thought perhaps you'd got a taxi back to the hospital and picked up your car."

"You hoped I had, you mean."

"Erm . . . No . . . I went to see your father's party agent Alan Jackson," said Power somewhat lamely, hoping that Lucinda would allow the subject of his discomfort to lapse. Her earlier advances had both excited and disconcerted him. He didn't know how to talk to her now.

"Oh him," said Lucinda, as she efficiently found the right kind of pans and began sweating the vegetables to make a stock. "Dad always said he was a left-wing creep and an armchair critic. I don't know how they could let him take over Daddy's old constituency. Dad would ... well, never mind. Listen, Carl. I made a phone call. I hope you don't mind. I invited my brother Michael over for dinner. I thought you'd want to meet him."

Power sat down at the scrubbed deal table. He was somewhat bemused by Lucinda's ability to use his kitchen as if it were her own. She instinctively seemed to know exactly where everything was. It was as if he had come home to someone else's house. He knew that if it had been anyone else it would have rankled him that they presumed to know what he wanted. He was puzzled to find that he could quite easily accept what Lucinda was doing. He said, "I thought your brother was unreliable ... not the kind of person who's easily contacted."

"Oh, he keeps in contact with the people he wants to, when he wants to. Not Mum or Dad. Others yes, but not family, except me, of course."

"You're more close to him than you suggested before, then."

"Well, Mum and Dad have never been able to fathom him you see."

"And he's coming here?"

"Yes, he's picking up my car and driving it here."

"He must have the keys then?"

"Yes, I told you, we're quite close now. I can trust him with a spare set." She removed the vegetables from the Aga for a moment to add some chopped herbs she'd picked from his garden. "What did you think of Jackson? You didn't say."

"I guess he's always been a back-room boy. Now he's got a chance of being the front man. He looks awkward with his new responsibilities. But that's not to say he doesn't know exactly what he's doing."

"Mm-hum," she agreed and after checking various pots and pans and finding their contents to her satisfaction she sat down opposite Power. "You've got a well-stocked kitchen."

"I like my food."

"I can see that. You're tall enough, but I expect you have to watch your weight."

"A bit," said Power defensively.

"I used to diet a lot," she said. " I got very thin once. But although I tried to stay off food, I got these cravings . . . I used to go out and buy a big packet of chocolate biscuits and gorge myself. Sometimes, afterwards, I'd feel guilty and make myself sick. It was a phase when I was a teenager . . . before I left home. I didn't do it afterwards. You'd call it Bulimia, I suppose."

"Maybe . . ." said Power, pensively. "It doesn't sound too . . . too severe. But things sound better now . . . better away from the family meals?"

"The eating's better, but I binge on other things; sometimes alcohol and sometimes . . . er . . . don't get me wrong. Don't think I can't handle it. It's not a problem for me."

"If you can keep it under control."

She turned slightly away from him, guiltily. "I wonder what you're thinking," she said. "I was wanting to know what you thought of me before . . . in the wood . . . when I . . ."

"Is that why you stayed?"

She glared at him, briefly, before looking down. "You ran out on me. I need to know why . . . ?"

Underneath her capable and proud exterior, there lurked a nagging doubt about herself. Power would have called it low self-esteem. "I'm very pleased you're still here . . . but what you're asking is why . . . er . . . why we didn't go to bed . . ." She nodded and Power felt himself blushing. Real life was so different to the doctor's role. "Because, er . . ."

"Because you didn't want to." Lucinda finished the sentence for him. "You don't like me."

"Lucinda, the time wasn't right. It didn't feel right, then . . . it was too soon. It felt wrong then."

"Oh," she looked away. "I don't know what you're really saying. I feel sort of small again . . . like . . . I don't know. Are you saying there might be a right time then? A right time for us?" She glanced up at him, saw that he was agreeing and looked away again, trying to absorb what they had both communicated in expressions and words. She needed to think it all over. A mosaic of old visual memories flickered in her mind. "How about a drink?" she asked. "A non-alcoholic one?"

"Okay," said Power, feeling rather awkward, but glad at least to be given something to do. "What would you like?"

"Anything," she said. As Power was leaving the kitchen to get the drinks she stopped him. "Wait, I forgot to tell you. A friend of yours rang . . . he said he was a friend . . . a policeman called Lynch. He is a friend, I hope."

"Lynch? Yes, that's right."

"He wanted to talk to you. So I invited him over for dinner too."

Power laughed. "Is there anybody you haven't asked over?" And somehow through all the difficult silences and words the atmosphere had warmed further between them. "I'll get the drinks," he said, and smiling, headed towards the drinks cabinet in the other room. When he returned to the kitchen, Lucinda had floated into the evening sun in the garden outside. Power joined her in the greenery of the garden. He handed her a glass of ginger beer with ice and lemon. She took a gulp with relish.

"Just right for today. It's been absolutely blazing," she said.

"Getting a bit more comfortable now, isn't it'?" said Power.

"Yes, I think you can relax when it's like this. The cool of the evening."

"I'm glad you didn't go Lucinda, but I was wondering whether you would like to let your mother know you're going to be late?"

"We hadn't made any firm arrangements."

"Do you want to use my phone?"

"Er . . . no. I want to keep my options open. Besides, there's not enough time . . . I couldn't stay the night there after all. I think the chapel is rather forbidding. You know how some churches and chapels give you this sense of peace? Well the chapel at Heaton Hall never gave me that feeling. I don't know why. You sit there and all the time you're expecting the door to open and someone to . . ." She shivered; for the sun was no longer burning so hotly in the reddening sky. "So I won't be travelling down there tonight." There was an awkward silence in which Power knew she was inviting him to ask her to stay the night, and he was mustering the courage to do so.

Just as Power was about to say something the front doorbell rang. He went to answer it. Lucinda sighed and continued her preparations for the evening meal.

Power opened the front door. A young man of about medium height stood there. He wore a light canvas jacket and a folded purple flower of dubious age sagged in his lapel. He reminded Power ever so much of a clown. He could imagine the man with white greasepaint, highlighted by black eyebrows and a lurid red grin. The caller affected a jocular air and laughed as Power scrutinised him. "You must be the trick cyclist!"

Power frowned. Behind this young man stood Lucinda's car, recovered from where she had parked it earlier in the day. "And you must be Lucinda's brother?"

"The one and only . . ." He brushed past Power on his way into the house. Power hadn't recalled inviting him in, but Michael McWilliam appeared to assume that he had the right of entry. "Sis in the kitchen? Conning you she's domesticated? Not a good sign that, man." He threaded his way through the darkened hallway to the kitchen door and pushed it open and trumpeted his arrival, "Ta-da!"

Lucinda put down her drink and embraced her brother. She pulled back to look at him. "Well, you have put on a little weight thank goodness. At the funeral you were looking like . . . well . . . you looked, you know."

"Stressful time, Sis."

"Is this the first time you've both met since then," asked Power coming into the kitchen in Michael's wake. Michael affected not to have heard the doctor and spoke only to his sister.

"How long've you been with this one? He's new isn't he?"

"Michael! You're not meant to . . . we've only just met, actually."

"And you're cooking dinner for him?" At last he turned and acknowledged that Power was actually in the room. "She's a quick worker, isn't she? What's your name then?"

"Carl Power," he extended his hand and Michael, after looking at it in surprise for a moment, decided to shake it. McWilliam's hand was anxiously moist. "And it's true," said Power. "I met your sister for the first time today."

"I'll believe you. Thousands wouldn't . . . specially where Lucinda's concerned."

"Michael! Please . . . just calm down."

Power tried to pour oil on troubled waters. "Would you like a drink, Mr McWilliam?"

"Michael, I'm called Michael . . . I'll have a gin and tonic please, Doc." Power left to fetch it.

"Why don't you join him out there, Michael? I'll be along . . ."

"Brrrr . . ." Michael shivered mockingly. "He's chilled-out. An ice man. What does he want Sis?"

"Why don't you ask him?"

He caught hold of her wrist, but only in a half-playful way. "I'm asking you aren't I?"

She pulled her wrist out of his grip. "It's about that girl, Zoë Allen."

As he slipped out of the door he said, "Thank you." He didn't mean it. Power was in the lounge and offered Michael a large tumbler full of ice and gin. McWilliam collapsed into a sofa and extended his long legs. He took a grateful swig of the gin and tonic and then smacked his lips. "The medicine's nice and strong today, Doc."

"Do you usually go out of your way to make people dislike you, or is it a natural talent?" Michael glared at him. Power blinked inquisitively and waited.

"What do you want with us?" Michael asked.

"At last . . . you sound sincere. I prefer it when people are sincere." Power poured himself a refill and sat down opposite the younger man. "It has to do with your father's death." McWilliam nodded, but looked away to the trees outside the window.

"Nice place this. Bit lonely though."

"It has to do with a young girl who is facing a trial which could destroy her life."

"What's your interest in her?" It was a lofty, throwaway line, dismissive of the girl and Power's concern.

"She might be innocent."

"So? Plenty of innocent people in the nick."

"You pretend not to listen to what I am saying. You think this is ... a game."

"Life **is** a game ... or hadn't you noticed yet, Doc?"

"What is it about reality that you don't like?"

Michael frowned at him. Power knew that many people would walk out if he said such things to them, but if he was right about McWilliam, nothing would prise him away from the conversation now. It was just the personality he was.

Power was right. Instead of appearing offended at Power's confrontative style, Michael only smiled. Power had got his undivided attention now. "I live closer to the edge than you, Doctor."

"Mmm? You spend your life running away from reality. Drugs are the definition of your life. They define your reality. They are the boundaries of your life. You needn't pretend to look so surprised ... one only has to look at your eyes, feel your hands, listen to your voice to know."

Michael laughed, "You sound like my Dad."

"Am I as worthy an opponent though?"

"We never fought, physically fought – if that's what you mean."

"Not physically maybe. But your struggle with the father was far more destructive."

"What **do** you mean?" Power's last deliberately obscure comment had finally rankled McWilliam. "Just **what** do you mean?"

"I think that was the doorbell," said Power standing up. "Excuse me. I must answer it." He crossed the room, but hung back at the door and turned to the young man. "Let me just say that now your father is dead, it is time to bury a quarrel with him that has plagued you all your life. If you could bury that argument, you could finally begin to grow."

"Crap!" said McWilliam. "How dare you? What a load of bollocks!"

"Excuse me, please," Power ducked out of the room and opened the front door to his friend, Lynch, who was standing on the threshold. Power could see he was eyeing the extra car in the driveway, which Michael had driven over for his sister.

"A Porsche, Carl. Very nice. I'm looking forward to meeting Miss McWilliam. She sounded very nice on the phone."

"Yes," said Power. "I seem to have gathered the family around me. Although I'm not exactly getting on with her brother..."

"Good. Before I meet them, Carl, could we talk in private?"

"Of course. Let's use my study."

"Good. We'd better do that now."

Power followed Lynch into the book-lined study. Lynch sat by the computer and anxiously began drumming his fingers on the leather desk-top. "Close the door," he said. Power complied without a word and taken by Lynch's tense and conspiratorial attitude seated himself silently in an armchair. "I'll tell you about my researches... and then you can tell me yours."

"Very well," said Power. "What have you found out?"

"Firstly... about the fire. I looked at the reports from the fire service and the scene of crime investigators. There was a fire set in the library... as you thought... it would burn the best. It was started with a can of petrol... splashed liberally about the books. But there was a second fire. An insurance policy in case the first didn't do the job. After all, the Hall was a big place. The second fire had been set upstairs, at the head of the stairs. Preventing escape that way, if Sir Ian had been alerted. As it was he never woke up.

"And the way we got into the Hall... remember? Through the

conservatory? The scene of crime people found that the door had been broken open. Clumsily broken open."

"But the fires had been set well inside the Hall . . . in the library and on the stairs," said Power.

"Yes, all of which implies that whoever it was knew all about Sir Ian's sleeping habits perhaps . . . that he slept soundly, and they also knew the layout of the Hall precisely enough to plan it all out."

"And Zoë wouldn't have known the layout," said Power looking pleased with the information.

"But she could have found out," said Lynch. "Her family worked there didn't they? And some of the Heaton villagers would have known. The layout would have been on public record. Waterhouse was a famous architect of the day. Architectural texts would have it in. *The Buildings of Cheshire* by Pevsner has a section describing the Hall. That's in every library in Cheshire. I even checked in the local library. And Zoë Allen was clearly obsessed with Sir Ian. It's not beyond her wit as an art student to check out the public library like I did."

"Oh," said Power. "I thought you had some good news there."

"And the officers in the initial investigation also found the can used to carry the petrol . . . an old Havoline oil can. Burnt in the fire, but bits of the charred paint still recognisable. It matched another in Zoë's cottage exactly. Remember that?"

"She doesn't have a car or a motorbike, or anything she could use petrol for. The petrol can must have been planted there."

"That's no argument. They'll say she bought the petrol especially to torch the place."

"She said she didn't buy it."

"Well, maybe both petrol cans were planted," said Lynch. "It doesn't seem entirely rational of the arsonist to leave a petrol can behind at Heaton Hall . . . and again the break in . . . they commented upon its clumsiness. And if the girl did set the fire why have two identical cans and keep one behind."

"So what are you saying?" asked Power. "That it was an inside job . . . that perhaps Sir Ian killed himself and framed her?"

"Carl, that's a little too fantastic."

"Well, maybe," Power agreed. "Is that all? Well, let me tell you what I discovered. Sir Ian's party agent, Alan Jackson, referred to McWilliam's intention to stage a bid for the leadership, and mentioned Sir Ian's links to a right wing . . . a very right wing faction in Europe. Perhaps Sir Ian was worried . . . perhaps there was some scandal just about to break . . . like with that publisher, Robert Maxwell, you know. He couldn't face the ignominy; couldn't take the fall and took his own life?"

"No," said Lynch. "If it was suicide he wouldn't frame someone for his murder, would he? The only sense I can make of it is that if someone else, apart from Zoë, killed Sir Ian, then that person, or persons, also wanted Zoë to take the blame. They left the petrol can at Heaton Hall. They ensured that an identical can was at Zoë's house. They knew of her obsession with Sir Ian and that her obsession would be enough to hang her as it were. But all this . . . all of it is just our surmise. We have nothing to take to the Crown Prosecution Service and say 'Hold on, stop the trial going ahead, we've got proof she didn't do it.' It wouldn't work."

"So, we're no further forward?"

"Well, not quite. I've done something the original investigation team in their wisdom didn't do." Lynch allowed himself a small smile of self-congratulation. "It was a memo from Divisional Headquarters that put me in mind of it. The memo was about a series of cash machine frauds in Manchester . . . what the thieves had done was to set up a video camera opposite a bank cash machine. It would record people going up to the machine and drawing money. The video recorded the time and date they went there and also the code they tapped in. They worked that out by watching over the person's shoulder as it were and also they recorded the four tones played by the machine as the person punched in their code. Now this gave them the secret number, the PIN number, and they had the time of the transaction, so that if they could get the receipt if it was thrown away

... and a lot of people do throw them away remember ... they could get the time of the transaction and match it with the video. So then they could match the time with the PIN code and also the bank account number printed on the receipt ... and that's all they needed to make a new card. A blank card with a magnetic strip containing those details. Simple ... and very profitable." Lynch paused to ensure Power had understood and then continued. "And that got me to thinking that, with computer technology, our lives have become so circumscribed. Our every financial transaction is monitored ... the place and the time and what the purchase was and for how much. I often tell any students in the police college that detective work at the scene of a crime often resembles archaeology, well, this idea, looking at credit card and cash card transactions ... is a bit like looking through historical sources."

"I'm sorry," said Power. "But I've lost you completely."

"Well. We need more information on Sir Ian McWilliam, don't we? We're trying his family. We presumably will go on to try his friends and colleagues if need be, but there is a good source of information that nobody has tapped. His credit cards and cheque cards will give us a clue as to his movements in the days and weeks before his murder."

Now Power began to understand. "Ah ..." he said. "Like a diary."

"Yes, well, a skeleton of a diary . . . restaurant bills, theatre bookings, petrol station bills, debits by flower shops, hotel payments, cash withdrawals, and bank addresses ... all there with dates, and luckily often with times too."

"Who do we approach to get this information?"

"I already have his accounts for the last two months. I spoke with a friend at the tax office. They have the details of all his accounts and with a little friendly persuasion and judicious pressure I got an electronic locksmith, as it were, to open up the bank and credit card computers for me. Here it is ... the Cabinet Minister's bank accounts ..." From out of his jacket pocket he took a sheaf of papers, placed them on the desk and pushed them over towards Power. The doctor picked the statements up and began sifting through them. He looked at the balances. "Not a very wealthy man . . . that's odd. You'd have thought he'd got more money than this. His credit card bills are enormous. Look at this . . . a gold Amex card with £15,000 of debt. Do you think he was being blackmailed?"

Lynch raised his eyebrows. "Was a possibility, but most of the payments are to different, quite separate organisations; not to individuals. And although the debts are high he had considerable reserves elsewhere. He only kept a minor amount in his bank accounts. You see there are regulations about the way Government ministers transact their personal portfolios. They have access to privileged information. It wouldn't be ethical if they were to manage their own stocks and shares. They might buy or sell on the basis of private information, or it could open them up to corruption, you know? So what they do is they have independent managers for their portfolios during the time they are ministers. And Sir Ian's portfolio was, and is, considerable. He was a multi-millionaire."

Power nodded and returned to the dense rows of figures that Lynch had provided. "Any donations to right-wing organisations?"

"Sorry, what right-wing organisation?"

"Well, I told you that his party agent implied McWilliam was a closet fascist, with links to European rightwing parties." Lynch nodded his head. "I was wondering if he had financial links to them . . . made donations?"

"If he was involved . . . he would be careful wouldn't he? So he wouldn't make payments from his own accounts. Well, I suppose we've only got the visible accounts here. McWilliam would know the Inland Revenue could access his account if need be . . . so there might just be another account that nobody knows about, but that's pure speculation. We have to work on what we've got . . ."

"Well," said Power, having trawled through all the figures. "I can't see anything. It's just a record of minor things. He bought quite a lot of petrol, I suppose."

"It's not that. It's not what he bought. It's *where* he bought it."

Power looked at the records again. "Nowhere outlandish. No purchases of vodka in Moscow or Red Stripe beer in Jamaica. No diamonds in Amsterdam . . ."

"Well, Sir Ian would spend time around Westminster, around Lady McWilliam's flat in London. We could predict that he would spend around there. He might spend money on the motorways travelling between London and Heaton Hall. He might spend while abroad on ministerial conferences. But there's more spending than you would expect in Chester."

"Heaton isn't far away from Chester."

"No, but there are garages, banks and shops nearer to Heaton and the motorway. If you look carefully you can see that every so often he spent long periods of time in or very near the town centre. There are debits from Boots Chemists, a petrol station, a supermarket, a restaurant . . ."

"But he lived nearby, I don't see . . ."

"The debits are spread out over the days. You and I might go and spend an hour or so in town, then come home. He was in Chester, spending now and then throughout the day . . . sometimes over twelve and forty-eight hour periods. He wasn't going home. Every so often he spent days in Chester. Not at home in Heaton Hall. Look on page two . . . a cash withdrawal at five a.m. on a Monday morning, then he bought some petrol from a garage at five fifteen."

"He was just passing through on his way back down to London."

"No, you're wrong. I looked at the maps. Both the bank and the garage were off course for him. You know that from Heaton you wouldn't go into Chester to get onto the motorway. There are more direct routes. And there are many nearer bank machines and garages he could have gone to."

Power shook his head and sighed. "So why would he spend so much time in Chester?"

Lynch shrugged. "Don't know, but I bet you one thing. If you ask Lady McWilliam she won't be able to tell us."

"I feel guilty about her . . . as if I should be doing something for her ... she seemed rather lost. You know; vulnerable."

"When will you ever learn? She's not your patient, You don't have to let the whole world cry on your shoulder." He smiled. "Shall we go through now and see what your lady friend has cooked for us."

"She's not my lady friend and to tell you the truth ... she's rather taken over my house."

"I rather gathered that on the telephone. You'd better watch out, Carl."

They left the snug confines of Power's study and joined Michael in the large living room. Power introduced Lynch, got him a drink and refreshed everybody else's glasses. In their conversation Michael was intermittently either facile and superficial or noticeably wary. Power's earlier words had struck a chord with him and it was clear to Power that he had pushed McWilliam's son onto unsafe ground. Any topic that might return the conversation to Michael's father was met with a supercilious remark by the young man. Michael was being particularly careful when addressing Power, not when he was talking to Lynch.

Power would have imagined that Lynch, as a policeman, would represent the most threat, but this wasn't borne out by Michael's behaviour.

It was something of a relief all round when Lucinda came in to announce that dinner was ready. She led the party into the oak-panelled dining room. Power waited until his guests and his hostess had seated themselves, then sat down himself, opposite Lynch. Lucinda glanced at her brother and picked up a silver ladle. She had made a simple but nourishing soup to begin with. The taste was so reminiscent of his mother's own lentil soup that Power almost felt like crying. He finished it quickly, greedily and asked for more. The adage 'The way to a man's heart ...' jumped unbidden into his mind. Comfortable memories of nights before the fire, safe in the warmth and light of home with the windswept rainy darkness shut outside; spooning up his mother's heart-warming soup after a long walk across the fields and hills of his boyhood home.

"Not bad," said Michael.

"Not bad?" said Power. "It's delicious. You know what Lucinda? I'm glad you invited yourself for dinner. On the strength of this soup you can invite yourself again." Lynch nodded his agreement, but said nothing and watched how Power was looking at her. From time-to-time he also glanced at Michael, watching the way his jaw muscles worked as he ate his bread, trying to assess how nervous the young man was, and wondering what was making him so anxious. Why had he agreed with his sister to come here? Was it some amateurish attempt on his part to demonstrate his innocence? Whatever his reason for attending the impromptu dinner party Michael did not radiate calm.

"What do you do, Michael?" asked Lynch. "You know, what's your line of work?

Michael looked jumpy. "Oh, you know. Whatever I can get." Lynch wondered about the provisions of Sir Ian's will. As of now Lynch had no mandate to interrogate the son. Perhaps he would have call to do so soon enough. But Michael did not know that Lynch would let the questioning go so easily. Almost panicked, he turned to the doctor at his side and tried to make conversation with him. "And you're a psychiatrist. That must be difficult, understanding . . . well, mad people . . . making sense of what they do."

Power finished his soup and sighed with pleasure. He would rate food as a passion, at least for himself, if not others. He almost appeared not to have heard Michael's question.

He certainly hadn't looked at Michael when he had asked it. His mellow eyes had been regarding the cook, Michael's sister. But he had heard, as he had heard similar comments from others, complacent in their sanity. "The psychotic people, those who the general public would term 'mad', wear their hearts upon their sleeves. The neurotic 'sane' people, the people in the office and the supermarket queue; their hearts are more often than not buried beneath a thin veneer – a mask of sanity. I find the sane endlessly complex and infinitely dangerous; because they have such a poor idea of their own motives and desires. Endless desires. Dangerous desires that sometimes they won't admit, even to themselves, except in their dreams, perhaps. They deny their own selves at the expense of blundering about in their own and others' lives. Like clockwork toys . . . repeating the same old mistakes until they wind down and die."

Lynch buttered some more bread and held his tongue.

"What kind of desires?" asked Lucinda.

"It's not time for such tales," said Power.

"Oh go on, you can't tease us like that," said Lucinda, and for a split-second she looked like a sulking child.

Power considered her eagerness; thought things through. "There are some things I have heard . . . from the mouths of 'ordinary' people that you would not wish to know."

"Oh come on . . . tell us, you can't keep us guessing."

"You couldn't guess. Not these things." said Power. "There are some things so terrible . . . they are best not revealed. Best contained. Best sealed away for ever." Lynch kept silent and looked at Power, wondering whether Power meant what he was saying.

"You mentioned people . . . making mistakes," said Michael. "Repeating mistakes . . . on and on . . . surely there must be some escape?"

"Oh yes," said Lynch, intervening at last. "There is a way."

"We would differ there though," said Power to Lynch. This was well-trodden ground between them. "Andrew would say that the escape is through knowing God. The escape, as far as I am concerned, is through self-knowledge. But exploring the unconscious is seldom pleasant. You notice . . . well, I notice . . . when I'm at a party and someone asks me what I do. When I say I'm a psychiatrist . . . without exception . . . people clam up. They are all afraid you're just going to reach inside them and pluck out something exceptionally unsavoury from their hidden thoughts. And it's the most respectable people who seem to fear themselves most."

"The holy men, the vicars of the world," said Michael with a mocking glance at Lynch.

"Vicars and priests are down to earth people, they seem to have a good knowledge of human weaknesses. Better than most," said Power. "When you get higher up in society though . . . that's where the problems come. You have to be more ruthless to get to the top. More ruthless to others and to yourself."

"You're trying to talk about my father again," said Michael.

"Not particularly," said Power. "Did what I said ring true?"

"What do you want with us, huh? I mean I can see that, for whatever reason, you've won Lucinda over . . . but what . . . what are you really, really interested in?"

Power found an image of Lucinda recurring in his mind's eye. The image distracted him so much that it was Lynch who began his answer before Power could formulate his own. Lucinda began clearing away the plates and started bringing in her pot roast.

"I'm sure that Dr Power explained it before," said Lynch. "We want to see that your father's murderer is caught, rightly convicted and sentenced for the crime he or she did. There's no catch."

"You said 'he or she'," said Michael. "But surely there's no doubt . . . they've caught her haven't they? And she's one of yours, isn't she?" He gestured to the psychiatrist on his left.

"The devil's own?" muttered Power. He was watching Lucinda bringing in the pot roast. He viewed the array of roast potatoes and buttered carrots with a pleased, mouth-watering anticipation.

Lynch moved relentlessly on. "The girl you're referring to, Michael, is due for trial. She may well be found innocent by the jury. She may **be** innocent."

"I very much doubt that. She did it. She's guilty as sin. But she'll get off lightly though, won't she? Unbalanced mind. Diminished responsibility . . . something like that." He sounded glib, but Power detected some relief, however slight, at the notion that Zoë Allen would not suffer the full sentence that the Law could bring to bear.

"The only problem," said Power, ". . . is that I don't think there is evidence of any major mental disorder; so the defence of manslaughter on the basis of diminished responsibility would not apply . . . in my opinion."

"But psychiatrists often disagree, don't they, Dr Power? Look at Peter Sutcliffe for instance . . . some psychiatrist at the trial said he was sane, didn't he?"

Power momentarily busied himself carving the tender meat of Lucinda's pot roast. Whilst he distributed the meat on his guest's plates, he wondered if Sir Ian's son had read Professor Anastasi's report. Had some solicitor, friendly to the family, passed it on to him?

Lynch said, "If we assume that Zoë Allen is guilty and is sentenced appropriately. You'll be relieved, eh?"

"We'd all be relieved," said Lucinda. "Perhaps then Mummy can pick up her life again."

Lynch thought about this. "And so, where were you all up to in your own lives . . . before all this happened? If it was all sorted out tomorrow . . . what pieces would you pick up?"

Michael glared at his sister opposite, clearly resenting the burden inherent in the evening's questions. She was to blame for dragging him here. At the same time he was also torn between evading the questions altogether and unburdening himself freely for once.

Knowing her brother's unpredictability of old, Lucinda spoke quickly, seizing the initiative from Michael. "I graduated two years ago from Cambridge. English if you're interested. And since then I've been working as a trainee director for television drama. It seems to involve too much sitting on the set beside some egotistical young men and some old men who should know better."

"Narcissistic personalities," said Power softly to himself.

"What do you mean, Lucinda?" asked Lynch. ". . . old men who should know better?"

"I mean; if they're not into other men, they expect a free pass to explore my body whenever they feel like it." She glanced at Michael who was frowning at her. "As I hope you might expect . . . I'm not making any friends there, since I usually refuse."

"Please don't ask for credit as a refusal often offends?" suggested Power.

"Exactly," said Lucinda. Lynch had noted Lucinda's use of the qualification 'usually' in her sentence, but he said nothing. "You'd think," said Lucinda warming to her theme. "That after a century of feminism men would have changed their ways, but..."

"Boys will be boys," interrupted Michael. He hadn't eaten much of his meal. He gave his sister a half-smile and poured himself another glass of Power's excellent wine.

She ignored his comment and continued, "So I have three alternatives. One, stick it out and see what kind of work they give me when I'm further on, or two, find Mr Right..."

"Not an easy thing," said Michael draining his glass and pouring himself another, unbidden. "Finding Mr Right. I've tried that. There aren't many... none in fact."

Lynch politely asked Lucinda what her third option was. Power listened and chose not to follow up Michael's ambiguous comment. With the alcohol inside him he was becoming disinhibited. Power suspected that this was not the last of Michael's alcohol-fuelled indiscretions.

"My third option," said Lucinda, her eyes shining now. She had saved the best until last. "Is to give up on the broadcasting company. Form my own independent company. Why not?"

" Good for you," said Lynch. "Sounds a risky thing to do though in a recession..." Lynch's voice trailed away meaningfully.

"People have said that. Dad was one of them."

"I'm one of them too," said Michael.

"A lot of people tell you that all kinds of things are impossible. Most of them are perfectly possible," said Power. "Given a fair wind, you can succeed, I'm sure. You can listen to people's criticisms; accept what is true and act upon it, but reject any criticism which is designed to destroy you. Still, it would be exciting, can you raise the capital?"

"My father had plenty of contacts... whether they might help..."

"They've all gone to ground," said Michael. "Running scared. Waiting till the time is right . . . to come out with their bloody fascist ideas . . ." He yawned suddenly. "The moneybags have gone to ground. Dad was saying what they wanted to hear. As long as he kept on saying it . . . as long as he strung them along . . . then they'd keep coming up with the goods."

"But cabinet ministers are meant to be above being bought . . ." said Lynch. "What are you saying?"

Michael smiled. "Must be drunk. If I'm not making sense then I must be drunk. Mustn't I?"

"But what was it you said . . . about the 'moneybags'?" Lynch pressed Michael for an answer, but the young man just shrugged and smiled haplessly. Lynch knew he wasn't that drunk. The brother and sister were annoying him. They hinted at just so much, but so much was hidden below the surface; they were like a pair of icebergs.

"Anyway Lucinda . . . once the will goes through you'll have your capital . . . ah well, what do I care? What does anyone care? All the time you spend . . . making films and plays . . . it's just a dream world. Play time. You live in as much of a dream as I do . . . or 'Mummy' playing her guilty widow part."

Power had been watching Lucinda whilst Lynch and Michael had been talking. She had bowed her head and focused her gaze on the empty plate in front of her. Although she had created a marvellous meal for everyone, Power had only just realised that, like Michael, she had eaten little; but whereas Michael had picked at his food and drunk a great deal, Lucinda had eaten and drunk virtually nothing. Couldn't she eat in company . . . or was the meal's uncomfortable conversation reminiscent of her family life?

Perhaps she had sat at the family table just as she did now with head hung low while her parents and her spoilt brother seemed to rotate in their own orbits: out of her reach and out of her control. Now Michael had seemingly brought everyone down to his own level, he ate some of his roast, made a face at the cold meat and pushed the plate away from him; rejecting her food.

She looked up reproachfully at her brother. "There's not as much money going to come our way as you think Michael. Not enough for what I want to do, anyway."

"Well, we can't talk about that **here**," said Michael, all at once quite clear in his thought and speech. He had control when he wanted, thought Power. He wondered which aspects of life were most important to Michael McWilliam.

"We've talked about Lucinda's hopes," said Power. "What hopes have you got, Michael?"

"None," said the young man, draining another glass. "None that I'd tell you anyway. And if you're such a brilliant man . . . a psychiatrist . . . how come you . . . how come you . . . well, you tell me." The atmosphere around the dinner-table, was flash-frozen in an instant as Michael goaded Power further, "Go on . . . you tell me. Read my mind!" Under the young man's aggressive, part-drunken stare, Power dropped his gaze to his own hands. His nails needed cutting. The left thumbnail had been bitten down. 'I must have done it inadvertently,' thought Power. 'Must be under more stress than I thought.' He remembered his dreams and their harsh, insistent images driving their way into his consciousness . . . like Michael's voice now, biting into the silence. "I'm waiting." It was Michael's mimicry of an angry father, shouting at his naughty boy child.

Quietly, firmly, Power began to speak. "For a long time . . . for many years, Michael . . . your hope has been to destroy your father. Now that work has been done for you. Your father has been destroyed, I think that the danger for you now is that you must feel suddenly lost."

"Utter crap," Michael snarled at Power.

"It might seem like that to you. Maybe its difficult to accept." Power caught Lucinda's startled glance. Her eyes were filled with tears. "I'm not accusing your brother of actually destroying your father; I am talking about the psychological work that Michael longed to do; the psychological destruction of the father. Put in such terms it might seem glib and unacceptable . . . like crap. The problem is that your father was physically destroyed before you had time ... to realise that you **didn't** need to psychologically destroy your father ... or rather what your father stood for inside yourself. You may feel that you have to perpetuate the cycle of destruction ... destroying yourself and others, but mainly yourself ... with drugs, alcohol ... whatever. But there is hope and there is help."

"Shit," said Michael, varying the expletive. He reached for the wine bottle and for a second Power felt sure that he was going to be hit with it. Michael seemed to hold the neck of the bottle speculatively, on the verge of hefting it against Power's skull and pulping the soft brain inside. In the event he just poured himself another glass of wine.

"I think maybe you've had enough now," said Lynch and reached out to take the glass away. McWilliam snatched it back out of the Superintendent's hands, and as he did so a spray of blood-red droplets flew upwards and then splattered onto the table-cloth.

"Fuck off!" he shouted and then, like a sulky child, pouted his lips. He sipped his wine whilst avoiding everybody's eyes.

"What you said ..." Lucinda turned to Power. Her questioning seemed urgent as if the question could not miss the moment. "About Michael. Did you really mean it?"

"There would be less strife in the world if we all simply obeyed the commandment, 'Honour thy father and mother'," said Lynch.

Power paused, wondering how best to redeem the situation. He had pushed Michael too far and in doing so, probably both made an enemy and alienated the girl to his left? How could he defuse things? There was Lynch's intervention just now. He could address that of course. How appropriate was Lynch's paternalistic comment? Lynch was always quoting from the Bible. It was sometimes comforting and sometimes downright annoying.

"Yes ... but the problem with quoting the Bible ..." said Power, "... isn't there a line about having to hate your father and mother before coming to Christ?" Michael flicked a curious glance at Power, but tried to avoid actively showing any interest.

"Yes, well," said Lynch. "You're right about the dangers of quoting the Bible out of context. Someone always comes along with another quote that seems to prove the opposite. You're referring to a phrase in Luke and elsewhere. Luke was a doctor, like you. The sentence is something like, 'If any one comes to me and does not hate his own father and mother and wife and children and brothers and sisters, yes, and even his own life then he cannot be my disciple.' But it doesn't quite mean . . ."

"Carl," Lucinda was simply unwilling to let Power's comment slip away and interrupted Lynch's digression. "I asked you about Michael."

"Did what I said before strike a chord?"

"About Dad and Michael . . . yes. Could you . . ."

"I don't want to be discussed with me here, thank you," said Michael. He stood up. "If I leave for a few minutes I can clear my head and you can talk about me all you like." Trying to regain some composure and retain some dignity, Michael left the room and wandered into the evening-scented garden. Power hoped he didn't wander. The Edge could be a dangerous place at night.

"I'm sorry," said Lucinda. "He's never usually like that . . . to someone he hardly even knows."

It's my fault," said Power. "I'm sorry. I went too quickly."

"If you want to exorcise a demon you must first find out its name," said Lynch.

"My friend always insists on using a more ancient model of the world," said Power apologetically. "I think he means that if you're going to heal a person's troubled mind, you must first find out what the trouble is. That's what a diagnosis is. Diagnosis means 'from knowledge'. It's a scientific principle rather than a religious model."

"And for us, for Michael and I . . . was our father our problem, our trouble?"

"Lucinda, I don't really know. Not fully, not yet. I've said too much, stirred things up. I don't feel I know what your father was really like. And anyway, it's difficult to say what fathers should be like, most research focuses on mothers and their role. Mothers should be 'good enough', or so they say. But what about fathers? What do you think?"

"They should think ahead, and provide, but they should be caring, and kind, and strong," said Lynch.

"And they should do no harm," added Power.

Lucinda paused. They were looking at her for her contribution. She said simply, "They should be there." All at once she seemed to sag under the cares of the day. She looked at Power. "What do I know about good fathers? Nothing." She sighed. "I don't know whether this meal was a good idea. I don't know what I expected from it . . . I certainly didn't expect it to end as a total mess."

"It hasn't," said Power.

"I don't know," she said, and after further reflection. "You do stir things up inside people. I'm remembering things I'd forgotten from years ago. Dad working in the summer-house when I was a child. Writing some speech on a clapped-out grey typewriter. He had no speech-writers working for him in those days. I adored him. I would have done anything for him. I believed everything he said. I remember there was a kettle in the corner. I remember he used it to make tea while he worked on his papers. I asked him one day, 'Is it hot?' And he said, 'Touch it and see. It'll be all right. Go on.' And so I did. I touched the side. It had only just boiled and it burnt me; and he laughed. I adored him and he just laughed at me. I'm sorry . . ." She looked desolate and Power felt his heart going out to her. He felt like putting his arms around her to comfort her. But she struggled to keep control, "I made a dessert," she said and looked at Power for instructions. "Shall I get it or shall we call the evening to a close?"

Over Lucinda's shoulder Power saw Lynch's mimed request to draw the embarrassing evening to a rapid conclusion. But Power saw Lucinda's question for what it was. Were she and her brother safe with Dr Power or was he about to set them up to burn themselves?

"Lucinda," he said. "I think I have a small corner left that yearns to be filled with dessert. Could you please ask your brother to come back in too?" She smiled, evidently pleased by his reply. She left to fetch bowls, serving spoons and the fruit pudding she had concocted.

"Don't know how you can stand it," Lynch exploded (or explode as much as he could do in a whisper). "They're both so . . . "

"Damaged?" suggested Power.

"I was going to say unstable . . . if not downright odd. I thought he was going to smash that bottle over your head."

"That's interesting," said Power. I thought so too."

"More than 'interesting'," said Lynch. "He's destructive, he . . . "

"If parents can't provide enough care and love; then children will find their suck in the outside world. Both of them are sucking the world dry; sex, alcohol, drugs. And that last story about the father. To set your child up to burn herself and then to laugh. What kind of security, what kind of love does that speak of?"

"They need more internal discipline," said Lynch, not totally convinced by Power's arguments.

"In a way they need discipline," said Power. "But they need stability and consistency more."

"Well anyway, Carl . . . don't go thinking you can change them," Lynch warned. "You go round sometimes trying to heal each and every one."

"A terrible thing has happened in their lives. Now, if that could be used for good in some way. If it could be used to make them stop and think . . . it might turn them around . . . start the healing process inside them . . ."

"You're not God, Carl, you can't be responsible for everyone and everything. Don't start something you cannot finish . . ."

"I can't argue with that advice. You're right of course. If we try to do too much, it all goes wrong. But let me salvage something at least from this evening."

"You can't be doctor to them . . . either of them. Not if the next minute we're going to see the son jailed for his father's murder."

"You think he could do that . . . actually do it in reality?"

"Why not?"

Power had no ready answer. He could not be definite, anyway. If provoked Michael McWilliam could be roused to violence. That much had been clear tonight. But Michael's aggression tonight had been in the heat of the moment, and the fire that killed his father had been coldly and carefully planned. But Power could not easily forget the sudden hatred that had blazed in Michael McWilliam's eyes and the sudden fear that the young man would smash the glass bottle down on his skull. "Yes, why not?" said Power softly.

"You look at the family, down the years, I mean, they've always been a successful, well-to-do sort of family. They're a famous family ... their ancestors' success in the Victorian world of new technologies ... the railways, the cotton industry ... and their father a central figure in the Government ... to come down to Michael ... to end with him ... perhaps there is a price for all their success."

"Isn't that too cruel?" suggested Power. "Rather an unforgiving view of the world ... not what I'd expect of you. You know that Michael might very well make amends. Perhaps with his father gone he can finally come into his own."

"With his father gone Michael can finally get his hands on the family money," said Lynch cynically.

Power sighed, "I know, but what are we basing this all on? Just my assumption that maybe Zoë is innocent. It's all surmise. We've got no proof of anything. We're running hard and getting nowhere."

"When you first came to me you were sure that Zoë was innocent."

"That was just a first impression," said Power defensively.

"I'm still not discarding that Carl. I think first impressions matter. And if you were right – that Zoë is about to be convicted for something she never did ... then our murderer has been wily enough to set Zoë up, let her go down for the murder. Our murderer is running free. And it follows that if we are questioning the case against her, then the key players will know that we are questioning the case. Maybe then we have made the murderer a little less complacent. He or she was secure in the knowledge that a mad woman was going to take the blame ... they can't be so secure, now we've started asking questions."

Power thought it through. "If whoever set the fire ... if we've made them less secure then they'll be frightened of what we'll discover. Fear leads to all sorts of things ..."

"You're worried the murderer might do something even more foolish?"

"Well ... yes, I am. When I treat paranoid people, I'm always a little wary ... fear makes people unstable. Fear makes people strike out at you."

Lynch nodded. "I think we should both be careful then, Carl." He looked at his watch. "I really must be getting back ... Mrs. Lynch will flay me alive if I'm not back soon. Where are they? Where have they both got to?"

"The children who hate their mother and father ... was that the quote from the Bible?"

"Not quite," said Lynch.

"No," said Power. "Well, it wouldn't fit these two. They both love and hate their parents."

"How can anyone do both?"

"No human relationship exists on only one emotion. There is always a mixture of feelings. For a child the mother provides everything; the food, the warmth, the shelter, the love, but she is simultaneously frustrating. She might not provide the food exactly when it is wanted, she may disappear to attend to her own needs, or she may place the needs of other people before the child's. She may have another child to attend to, work to go to. Then the child has to balance his needs and love for his mother against the resentment he feels for this denial of food or care or whatever. That's the first difficult lesson to learn ... and it's not at all easy to reconcile love with hate."

"So maybe our murderer both loves and hates? Like Michael?" asked Lynch. Power nodded agreement, half-heartedly. The thought crossed his mind that Sir Ian's extremist political views might conceivably have enraged someone to hate him so thoroughly that pure loathing and political expediency had provoked his murderer. But he and Lynch had studiously avoided the paranoid theories of political intrigue and conspiracy until now. But Lynch was still toying with the idea of ambivalent emotions.

And on cue, here was Sir Ian's heir, returned from his time out. He came in silently and meekly resumed his seat. He darted a glance in both Power and Lynch's directions. "I er . . . I . . . went into the garden for a while. I feel calmer now . . . I climbed over the wall and walked through the woods, over the sandstone rocks beyond the trees. There's a sudden cliff. The ground just drops away from you, doesn't it?"

"Yes," said Power. "That's the Edge. You can see for miles over the Cheshire plain. It's a very special place."

"I looked over the Edge. It must be hundreds of feet down . . . I felt a bit dizzy, like falling. I don't like heights. I had to step back."

"It often affects people that way," said Power thoughtfully. "I walk them down to the Edge, and some can stand right on the brink and others have to move right back."

"There are pagan legends about the place," said Lynch. "The police have to try and keep the New Age travellers away in the summer. Some of them set up camp in the caves and old mine workings."

"They say they're looking for King Arthur," added Power. "He's said to be buried in a hidden cave, with his mighty army with him. They're all of them meant to be just asleep, waiting for when England's need is greatest, and then they will re-awake and fight the good fight."

"Superstition," said Lynch. "Too much of it about these days. Everything's going to pot."

"Well," said Michael. "I certainly felt it was a special place . . . like to meditate or something . . . you know, a holy place or something like that. You're lucky to live here . . ." He sighed, and tried a placatory smile. "I want to apologise . . . to you both. Will you accept my apologies for my behaviour before?" The smile blossomed most charmingly. Neither Power nor Lynch had expected such an apology. Power wondered if Michael might eventually extend the charm into a career like politics as his father had done? 'Probably not,' he thought. There were too many past peccadilloes in his life for him to be rehabilitated into public life.

"Okay," said Lynch, grudgingly accepting Michael's apology. "Whatever you're taking; it doesn't suit you. Stay off it."

Michael tried to suppress a scowl at Lynch's response. Power did things differently to his old friend. He said, "I don't accept your apology, Michael. Not yet anyway."

"Why not?

"Because it's as if you want to brush what did happen under the carpet. You need to forget just how angry you were with me. As if it had never happened. It did happen. I was afraid you were going to brain me with that bottle."

Michael seemed a little taken aback, "I did think about doing that actually."

"Yes," said Power. "Now it is known." Lucinda appeared carrying a tray of fruit compote, made from the soft fruits: raspberries; strawberries and blackberries that were growing in Power's kitchen garden. The tray also bore biscuits and sour cream. Power spoke to Lucinda, "We were just saying how angry Michael was with me. How he felt like hitting me. Did you guess he was that angry?"

"I've never seen him that angry before." She looked at Power and raised an eyebrow and spoke reproachfully, "Maybe you stirred too much up?"

"Sorry, Michael," Power said and ate his compote hungrily as if his appetite had been sharpened by the conflict earlier. Lucinda followed his example, but Michael and Lynch did not. Lynch had the sense that the doctor inside Power was in top gear and Lynch was watching the doctor at work minutely. Michael seemed caught up in his own memories."Delicious," said Power as he scraped the last of the brilliant red syrup from his dish. "Lovely, crisp flavour – cuts through everything. Thank you for making the food, Lucinda. I feel a lot better."

"So do I," she said. "I don't really know why, though." She smiled honestly.

"Well," she said. "I think it's time to go. I feel it's the right time, don't you Michael?"

"What did you say? Oh . . . yeah. Yeah. Home time." The diners stood up and Power led his guests out of the dining room. Lynch was left alone. He resumed his seat and contemplated his untouched fruit compote. After a moment's further hesitation he began to eat it.

At the front door, Power bade them both goodbye. Brother and sister hovered on the doorstep however; both wanting to speak. "About before," said Michael. "About the anger. I didn't really want to hurt you, you know. I am sorry."

"That's okay, Michael. Thank you for coming." The doctor watched as Michael walked into the night to the passenger door of Lucinda's car.

And suddenly, Lucinda was leaning forward, out of the cold darkness and into the warmth of his house again; she kissed him lightly on the lips. "Good night, Carl."

She got into the driving seat and closed the door behind her. She started the car and slowly inched it down the drive towards the road. In the rear view mirror she could still see Power's silhouette against the light. The outlined figure raised its right hand above its head in a gesture of farewell as she slipped into the night with her car headlights blazing.

By her side in the privacy of the car her wine-soaked brother drowsily intoned, "I quite like him, actually. The witch-doctor man."

"Hands off," she said. "He's not for you. If he's anybody's, he's mine."

Inside the great house, Power returned to the dining room with two mugs of black coffee. Lynch had finished his sweet and was wiping his lips on a napkin. "Thank you," he said as he took a swig of the strong coffee. "Just what I needed." He was beginning to relax again, now he was alone in his friend's company. "They're a mixed-up pair aren't they? On the surface they can manage quite good manners when they want, but underneath . . . they're like a long scream. All uneven and awkward. Uncomfortable with themselves and the world. Capable of being quite charming though. Still, I've met some very charming murderers in my time. People you'd trust any day of the week. I wonder how they both got so messed up."

"They're a reflection of their father," said Power. "He's a man we'll never get to meet . . . and all we'll ever see of him are facets of him . . . his reflections in other people."

"Well," said Lynch. "Even though I've only seen reflections of him . . . I don't like what I've seen of Sir Ian McWilliam. To think that he was in the Government."

"You don't get to the top without a degree of ruthlessness. And that's ruthlessness towards people all round: to colleagues, wives, mistresses, children and your own self."

"And to your own soul," added Lynch. "Take my advice, Carl. Don't get mixed up with these McWilliam children. Either of them could be . . . just don't get close to them."

"Of course," said Power, but he deliberately didn't mention the kiss. "When I was making coffee just now I noticed that there was a call left on the kitchen answering machine. It must have been while we were having dinner. I'm surprised Lucinda didn't mention it. She must have been in the kitchen. The call came in about nine o'clock."

"I presume you're going to tell me about it?" said Lynch.

"Yes . . . it was a call from Zoë's solicitor. He'd been trying to reach me all day, but of course I was out most of the time. It's Zoë, she wants to speak to me again."

"What about?"

"She wouldn't tell him. Said she only wanted to talk to me."

"You must be flattered. When are you seeing her, Carl?"

"Well, it'll have to be tomorrow morning."

"Have to be? You are getting wrapped up in this."

119

"I think you're laughing at me," Power smiled and laughed at himself.

"Guilty on all charges, my friend. Listen, I must get back to my wife. She'll be worrying about me. When you see Zoë don't forget what I said earlier." He stood up to leave. "Seriously, Carl. I can say this because you're a friend; use your head in all this . . . not your heart. 'Be self-controlled and alert. Your enemy the devil prowls around like a roaring lion looking for someone to devour'."

Chapter Six

The desires of the heart are as crooked as corkscrews.

**W H Auden,
Death's Echo**

Carl Power lay in his early-morning bed, restlessly dreaming. He was swimming underwater. He felt his breathing was forced, artificially supported by unseen valves and an air supply upon his back. The facemask was tight about his face and his vision was impaired, almost dulled. There were things to his right and his left that he wished to see, but could not. The mask was one problem and, in addition, he could not move his head. He sucked in another laboured breath. He was just managing to control his sense of panic at being denied all the oxygen he wanted. The air he breathed was in some way rationed. He could inspire as vigorously as he liked, he could strain to draw in every cubic centimetre of air he could, but his efforts would meet with an uncompromising vacuum. And this frightened him.

The dream shifted. Now he was in a narrow passage underwater, which he knew he must get past, and through. He seemed to half-float, half-walk (he did not know which), forwards along the corridor, to where steps began. To his surprise, his feet felt as if they had firm contact with the steps. Here he was no longer floating as he had been in the corridor. He climbed a few steps, and found the corridor was beginning to curve round, and the stairway began to assume the shape of a spiral staircase. He tried to look down. The stairs were narrow and steep as they curled round. They were made of some wood. He could see the holes made by giant worms within the wood itself. Elsewhere barnacles encrusted the handrail. He could feel them with his hands. His hands looked pale, swollen, like the lifeless white hands of an underwater corpse. He shivered. The air he was breathing was beginning to get stale. He had to press on. Where was he? Was this the stairway of a submerged ship, a wreck on the ocean bed. How old was the wreck? The stairway was intricately carved. No twentieth-century cargo vessel. Some ancient Armada vessel ruined by the storm, or one of the King's ships ... the Mary Rose, lost with all hands in front of Henry's very eyes on a Summer's day? The stair treads seemed impossibly narrow. Weren't they like that on ships? Under the cold water, the only sound was of his breathing. The dream mask was gone, but the water was still about him. The breathing tanks had gone. Fallen away? Pulled off by unseen hands? Vanished. He struggled under the water feeling the fingers of water trying to creep their way into his mouth, his nose, his lungs. Suppressing his panic he tried to climb faster. Above him there seemed to be light ... the promise of the surface and God-given air. He scrabbled at the staircase with all four limbs, aware that he was drowning, striving for air and allowed only the murky waters of the deep, green sea.

Somehow, by some unknown miracle he was above the surface of the water and the stairwell ahead of him was flooded with sunlight, he sagged against the spiral stairs and drank the fresh air into his starved and painful lungs. There was the sound of a catch being thrown and the stairs snapped flat. Where the stair angles had been was now a smooth, spiralling descent of wood. Power began his helter-skelter descent into the dark waters that lapped at the wood beneath him.

Power awoke. He lay in the soft white cotton sheets of his bed and felt a swell of relief shiver through his body. He was suddenly and gloriously awake, and glad to be full of life. The morning sun blazed against the red-velvet curtains and shot through the cracks between the material to dance on the wall opposite. For a second or so Power exulted in the thrill of being alive, then leapt from his bed and half-ran into his bathroom to shower under needle-hot streams of water. He dried himself with fluffy white towels and, wrapped in a bathrobe, sauntered downstairs for a breakfast of eggs, buttered toast and strong, aromatic coffee.

He had nearly finished dressing, and had contemplated the meanings of his dream, when he was suddenly struck by the guilty feeling that he should have contacted McWilliam's widow. He couldn't understand his own guilt. He knew she was grieving, had seen her distress, but wondered why he was suddenly concerned about her. She wasn't a relative, a friend or a patient, so why did he feel that he should be in some way responsible for her? Lady McWilliams was at risk . . . she had altered her lifestyle so dramatically after her husband's death. Perhaps her distress wasn't within normal limits. As a psychiatrist didn't he have some responsibility for her . . . if he suspected that she was ill . . . depressed? The dilemma made him uncomfortable. In the end the phone rang and he was glad to be able to push the sudden concern about Lady McWilliam to the back of his mind, where it was to stay for only a short while. For now, Lady McWilliam, the hermit widow alone in the ruin of her husband's beloved hall, could wait her turn. The phone was ringing.

Power detested the phone. Its insistent ring never brought him welcome news. It summoned him to the hospital to see the sick, it gave him bad news about his friends and relatives, it bade him do its wishes whenever other saw fit to command it, and thereby Power. He despised the phone, the bleep and all the 'conveniences' of modern life and wished they could be swopped for uninterrupted and heavenly peace. Unlike the old he did not see the phone as a lifeline, or as a friend. He would quite happily pull the necessary evil from the wall and never replace it.

He reached the phone on its fifth insistent ring. Although he hated phones, he was such a slave to them that he could never bear to leave one ringing longer than was absolutely necessary. He put the receiver to his ear. "Hello?"

"Is that Dr Power?" It was a quiet voice. The voice of an old man who had lived in the country for a long time, but who had not quite lost a Mediterranean accent.

"Who's speaking please?" asked Power as cagey as ever.

"This is Professor Anastasi. Please could you ask Dr Power to come to the phone? Tell him it is most important."

Power paused. He did not relish the idea of a conversation with Anastasi. He had read the Professor's psychiatric report on Zoë Allen and disagreed with it. He knew his report would clash with it and that the disagreement would be exposed to cross-examination in the court. Given that this confrontation was certain in the future Power had no wish to argue now with Anastasi. He toyed with the idea of saying that 'Dr Power is not at home', but could not bring himself to lie. "I am Dr Power," he said. "What can I do for you?"

Professor Anastasi's thickly accented voice sounded against a background of gently splashing water. Power imagined the Professor to be perhaps at breakfast, alfresco next to a fountain in his sunlit garden. "I'm speaking from the bathroom," said the Professor. "Hold on, let me turn the bath off. There. I tried to reach you yesterday. Your secretary said you were out." He made it sound like a crime and Power felt guilty. "So I thought I'd call you early at home. Let me sit down . . . ah, that's better. I'm calling you from the bathroom on one of these portable phones."

"So I gathered," said Power. "What can I do for you?"

Now that he had him at his mercy, Professor Anastasi showed no sign of letting him go with a quick conversation, he was evidently settling down for a major discussion. "I wanted to talk over the Allen case with you. You are writing a report, I hear?"

"Yes . . ." said Power, with some hesitation.

"I believe that you've had the opportunity to read my own report. I was rather hoping that you might extend me the courtesy of seeing your report before it is finalised."

Power was dumbfounded by the suggestion. Before he could say anything the Professor went on. "You see," he said. "It's not an easy case. I wouldn't like you to get the wrong idea about the girl. She can be very convincing..."

"Should we really be discussing the case?" asked Power. "I mean we don't want it to look as if we had cooked something up between ourselves."

There was a time, a year or so ago, when they were going to offer you a chair of psychiatry down south. Did you know that?"

"No," said Power quietly. "No-one ever said..." For a time Power had been a Lecturer and had nursed dreams of being in academia.

"Oh yes," said Anastasi. "We liked your publications. The word was out that you would do very well as a Professor."

"What happened?" said Power, feeling vaguely astonished at this news.

"Well," said Anastasi. "You know how things are. It must be odd for you, suddenly being told how things might have been if you'd taken a different path from the one you chose. Time and tide and all that. I gather you must have been at a crossroads in your life. You chose to be a consultant in the hurly-burly of hospital life. It was you who forsook the groves of academe, not the other way round. If you ever wanted to go for a chair, I think you could you know. A little more up-to-date research might be needed on your curriculum vitae, but... you could do it you know."

Power thought. The academic life had been an interesting mix of University intrigue, lectures and tutorials as well, and research and some clinical work. He missed the pursuit of the idea, rather than the NHS management pursuit of targets and budgets and the whole depressing round of hospital bureaucracy. Anastasi's phone call had suddenly taken on a whole new and tempting dimension.

"But..." Anastasi continued. "... it wouldn't go down at all well if you were seen to be disagreeing with mainstream psychiatry in such a case as this. It seems a basic issue to me, Dr Power, the girl is sadly very ill, very deluded. She will say whatever she thinks will convince you, but she will not be forced into giving away anything which can or cannot be verified. The media will be very interested indeed in this story. Very interested. If we disagree in public... well, it wouldn't be good for either of us, but then I'm an old man, and I am where I am, and I am not about to be moved, for I am happy enough where I am, but you may wish to move in the future and people have long memories for this kind of case."

Power wondered if the Professor was threatening him. He had found that academics never used blunt language. They were circumspect, genteel and excruciatingly polite in the conduct of their backstabbing. But academic backstabbing, though polite, was as fatal as any other kind.

"Well, thank you for your opinions," Power said. "I'll bear what you've said in mind when I speak to Miss Allen. She is though very convincing."

"A tissue of lies," said Anastasi confidently. "She is a sexually starved, frigid girl, with incredible fantasies . . . all sublimated lust and wishful thinking."

"I see." Power looked at his watch anxiously. He wanted to get as much time with Zoë as he could today. "Thank you for calling. And that news . . . about the chair in London . . . I'm very surprised. I never knew . . ."

"Would you have taken it?"

"I would have preferred a chair at the University of Chester, but . . . yes, of course I would have taken it if it had been offered."

"Well, think about what I said." There was a groan as Anastasi bent down to test the temperature of his bath. "Damn," he said. "It's gone cold. I'll have to take a shower instead. Goodbye, Power." The line went dead with a click and Power left with several things to ponder. He tried not to let the belated news about his once having been considered for a Chair dominate his thoughts What intrigued Power was the fact that Anastasi had gone so far out of his way to discuss the case with him and had so wanted Power's report to concur with his own that he was prepared to pressure Power with a story of lost ambition. And anyway, what truth was there in Anastasi's recollections of some mythical selection committee for a University Chair. It was all so much flattering flummery, designed to put him off his immediate goal. Crossly, Power locked up the house and drove off, back to the grim prison which housed the remanded Zoë Allen.

★ ★ ★

The journey into the hospital wing of the prison was no less depressing and the wait for Zoë to be escorted from the female remand wing no shorter than before. But this time Power had secured a longer interview with her and he was eager to hear what she had summoned him for.

When she came into the room Power was again struck by the grace of her lithely moving body, and her eyes were as seductive as ever, but she was somehow thinner and more pallid. There was the trace of a frown-line on her smooth forehead. When he asked her about her cares she replied, "It's the people in here . . . they say I'll get life, no matter what. They won't let me be found innocent. Not now. Not after they've gone to so much trouble. There are plenty of innocent people in jail after all . . . and if I'm found guilty . . . well, they come down 'specially hard on arsonists don't they, because there's a chance they'll do it again and there are so many lives at risk. I'm really scared, Dr Power. Really scared."

The composure that she had shown the last time he had seen her had almost totally gone. Only vestiges of the reserved elegance remained to remind Power of the sensual woman she had appeared to be before. He wondered why she should appear so very different now? There was the worry of the forthcoming trial, but also there was the possibility of a change in the eye of the beholder. He struggled with doubts of his that had been fuelled by Professor Anastasi's phone call. It seemed possible, sitting here now, before this worried girl, that maybe the true nature of her crime was tearing away the curtain of denial that she had hidden behind. And then again there was the advent of Lucinda in the last few days. Had Power merely transferred his attentions elsewhere? Was he as fickle as he suddenly felt? Sitting in front of her he no longer had the feelings of desire he had had before.

Anastasi's words buzzed irritatingly around in his head, 'a sexually starved, frigid girl, with incredible fantasies . . . all sublimated lust and wishful thinking'. He shook his head.

These thoughts would do him and Zoë a disservice. He had been convinced of her innocence the first time he had seen her. Surely that judgement had been based on more than her obvious attractions. There had been sincerity in her voice, and a striking lack of mental illness symptoms. He must continue to believe in her if he was to help her. He must trust her enough to let her tell her story. "You look anxious," he said. "Are you sleeping all right?"

"Not these last few days," she said. "Hardly at all I'm afraid."

"Eating?"

"I don't feel like food."

"You need to keep your strength up." He paused, listening to the words he had just said. "I'm sorry, I'm beginning to sound like my mother!" She smiled, but her smile was a thin, watery reminder of her usually bright expression. "There's something you wanted very much to talk about."

"I need to," she said. "I tried to keep it to myself. I'd promised, you see. Made him all sorts of promises."

"Him?"

"Ian."

"Go on," Power urged.

"It's what they're saying you see . . . the other prisoners. About what happens to arsonists. I didn't think I would tell anyone, but now the trial seems so much nearer and so much more real. She retched. Sudden fear made her abdomen contract in a rictus of anxiety. "There are things I . . . need to tell someone but . . . they're so difficult to say. I thought about it all last night . . . lying there in my cell. I listened to the sounds of the prison at night and I thought it all out. What I was going to say. I could only tell you. I thought you'd listen you see. Thought you might believe me. I thought it all out and what order to tell you in and what words to use. And I sit here looking at you looking at me and it's all gone . . . I can't bring myself to look at you and tell you about these things. They're so personal. The secrets . . . the kind of things that you never tell anybody."

"The kind of things that some people can tell me about."

"I know, but what do you think about them after they've told you?"

"You're worried what I'll think about you after you've told me?"

"Yes," she said softly and looked away.

"Perhaps," suggested Power, carefully choosing his words. "If you can be more relaxed about telling me . . . if you turned you chair around so I wasn't in your view . . . so that your words could just go into space. That might be more comfortable."

"Yes," she said, and as if she had made the choice to tell him she turned her chair around and faced the wall. It was like the confessional. Now she could spill everything out to him. If she could just get that far . . . perhaps everything would flow from that point. There was a moment of silence between them as she sat facing the open window. She was collecting her thoughts as she watched the dust motes dancing in the sunlight. She could hear his easy, measured breathing, like the tide gently breaking on the shore. "I met Ian some months before his death. I'd been writing to him for almost a year, I think. My letters were getting more desperate. Do you know how overwhelming love can be? How it sucks your life inside out?" Power was taking notes, every now and then he looked up at the back of Zoë's head.

He could just see a fraction of her cheek, how her head moved as she talked, but he could not see her eyes, or her strawberry lips as she spoke. There was just her soft, hesitant voice, beginning to unburden herself of her secrets. This removing oneself from the patient's line of sight was one of Freud's techniques to overcome his patients' resistance. Power thought of the prim Viennese girls and men lying on Freud's cushion covered couch, sometimes under a thin woollen blanket. They would meet him five times a week, sometimes their meetings would be filled with silence. The unseen Freud would perch out of sight at the head of the couch and do what? What did he think about in the silences? Occasionally there would be a catharsis as perhaps there promised to be with Zoë. And Freud's 'hysterical' female patients would tell him of the abusive fathers and uncles of Vienna, and of what went on behind the nursery doors. Freud published his findings to the opprobrium of the Viennese medical establishment, and later to his discredit, labelled his patient's laboured unburdening as fantasy, denying reality and shifting the blame back on to the victim. Power wondered why the situation had made him go back and think about Freud?

"This is difficult." Zoë was saying.

'I hope I don't let you down,' Power thought to himself.

"He'd seen me, I think. Watching from his car as he drove past me as I waited."

'He must have been curious,' thought Power. 'To see what kind of girl was sending him such messages of desire. The curiosity must have been burning away inside him.'

"One day. A Saturday. He passed me in his Land Rover . . . I'd seen him look at me."

'Or had she just imagined it,' wondered Power. Like the poor lovesick woman who stood outside Buckingham Palace and every time the curtains twitched somewhere in the Palace, assumed that it was a message from Edward the Seventh.

"He went up to the gates of the Hall and drove down the drive, but he didn't go far before he stopped the car and waited. He got out. Something I'd never seen him do. And he looked back down the road at me. Then he walked off, onto the grass beside the drive and into the trees behind the wall. You know, the high wall that surrounds the Hall.

I didn't know what to do, but he'd looked at me. Actually looked at me. And I wondered what he was doing, so I went down the road to the gates. And there were no guards. Why? I don't know, but at that moment there were none about. Had he arranged it? I don't know. So I went through the gateway, past the lodge to where his car was, and I too went into the trees. The way he must have gone. And there he was in front of me. Standing only a few feet away from me. He looked me up and down and asked me if I was Zoë Allen, the girl who'd been sending him the letters. I had sent him a photograph so he knew it was me, but I suppose it was a way of starting talking to me. He explained that he couldn't be seen talking to me. He'd seen me waiting as he'd driven past, and knowing the guards weren't on duty till after two, he thought he might talk to me. I asked him if he'd got all my letters. For a while I had been wondering whether or not they reached him. Perhaps they were being screened out by some dragon of a secretary. Perhaps they'd never reached him at all. He said he'd received every one and kept them too. That pleased me. I can't say how much it pleased me. I felt as if I was in a dream. I was no longer in a wet cold forest on a damp dark afternoon; it was as if I was in bright sunlight. But he was frowning and I was suddenly afraid that I'd got the wrong end of the stick. That he didn't want to see me, but just needed to speak with me. He said that once he'd seen a few of my letters, he'd always tried to keep my letters to him secret. There was something about them, he said. But it wasn't easy to get his mail first and pick them out before others saw them. And he apologised for never responding. Nothing could be written down by him. If it fell into the wrong hands . . . and he couldn't be seen talking to me. He couldn't phone because the telephone system wasn't safe. He said he was glad to meet me at last. But he was clear that other people wouldn't understand. He suggested that if I wrote again I should write in a special way so that his secretary would think the letters were personal ones from his family and automatically channel them separately to him, unopened. Ministers have this system you see, for their closest family and friends."

"How did you feel?" asked Power. "Did you think he was classifying you as his closest family?"

"I couldn't quite believe it. You want something so much. Then when it starts happening to you ... you can't quite believe it. You're sounding sceptical ... Dr Power?"

"I'm trying not to." Power was thinking about what Anastasi had said she would say. He thought about Freud disbelieving the young girls who told him about their nursery nightmares. 'Screen memories', thought Power.

"Trying not to. That says a lot..." But Zoë wasn't that easily put off. "I'll carry on anyway. If you can suspend your disbelief a little longer, I'd be grateful." She listened out but Power said nothing. He was deep in thought. "He asked about me. He knew where I lived. Did I live with my parents? No, I lived alone. That interested him. You could see that, and I felt this warmth growing inside me. I can remember beginning to feel very ... aroused by his interest. He asked me to describe my cottage. You could see he was disappointed. The cottage is right in the centre of the village. Too close to home. Too close by far. He couldn't afford to have anything 'irregular' in the press or for his colleagues to know. He said, 'A politician's worst enemies are his friends.'"

"Mrs Thatcher had hundreds of friends, or so she said," said Power. He wondered about the words she had used: 'anything irregular in the press'. They sounded as if they were someone else's words. Was this a genuine reminiscence of hers? Let it run and see where things led.

"He was interested in my age. He pressed me on it. He couldn't believe that I was as old as I said I was."

"He was worried that you were too young?" Power sought clarification. Had McWilliam been keen to limit any damage should the affair break into the national consciousness? An affair with an under-age girl would destroy his career, whereas affairs with actresses and others might only entail a period of career recuperation.

"You're a bit cynical aren't you, Dr Power? You don't think in romantic terms." Power kept his counsel of silence and she continued. "He asked me whether I meant what I had written to him.

Did I mean every word? And I did. I could tell he was looking at me; appraising me. In my letters I'd said I was willing to do anything; so would I do anything, absolutely anything for him? I hesitated. I considered what I'd written in passion . . . did I hold to it here . . . actually standing in front of him? Now that the idea had become real? I think I nodded yes, I don't remember saying yes, but he said good and then he asked me whether I could keep a secret. It was most important I was able to. I mustn't tell a soul, not anyone. Ever. Could I keep a secret? I said I could, and I must have been in a kind of frenzy at that point, because I remember jabbering on about how I would do anything for him, only please . . . please . . . what? I don't know. I was so desperate for him. I was willing to give up everything to him. I wanted to be his possession. It was a most strange feeling . . . like wanting to give up my . . . identity . . . myself . . . like dissolving. Does it make any sense?"

"I understand," said Power.

"He moved away. To think. Away from my mumbling desire. He stood by a tree and leant against it resting his head on his forearm. I think he was deciding whether he could trust me. I stood there silently watching him. I was so anxious, because I didn't want him to reject me. Not now. It felt like I had been through some great ordeal. Well, I had been writing to him, wanting him, for months. After a moment he turned round, but he did not smile. I was waiting for a smile . . . some sign that he was pleased with me or . . . . He just came over to me and stood there. He didn't say anything. I was frozen like a rabbit. It wasn't fear. It was just that I was so . . . fascinated. I couldn't move. It was like I was a million miles away. I was only vaguely aware that he was lifting my skirt. I couldn't look down. I felt his hands about my thighs, pulling down my panties. I remember stepping out of them automatically. His fingers probing me. Then he pulled away and I felt my skirt dropping back into place. His face was flushed, but there was no expression of joy or disgust or anything . . . I felt so ashamed as if I'd done something terribly wrong. My panties were lying on the wet grass. I bent down to pick them up. He stopped me. Told me I was to leave them there. He wanted me to walk back home without them now. I felt I had displeased him. That he never wanted to see me again . . . that I had failed his trust. I felt puzzled."

"Angry too?" asked Power.

"No," she said. "Dismayed. I remember saying that I wanted him. I wanted him to do it to me there and then. How I'd been waiting for him and if this . . . but he told me to be quiet. He knew what he was doing. He would make arrangements. I didn't need to know anything. All I had to do was fall into place. He would be in Chester most weekends. Each night of the weekend . . . Friday, Saturday, Sunday. I was to leave my house and meet him. I asked him whether I would be allowed past the guards and he laughed at me. He said we would meet elsewhere. I was to wait on one of the country roads, at a junction . . . you know one of these tiny triangles of grass where three winding roads meet. There was a wooden bus shelter there, next to a milk churn stand. There would be shelter if it rained. He said the waiting would make it more fun for us both. I was to wait an hour each night . . . from eight o'clock to nine o'clock. If he didn't come by then I was to go home, but that I must be there every night without fail. He had to know I would be there. Would I promise? I had after all, been prepared to wait in the pouring rain outside Heaton Hall for hours on end before. So I agreed. I think he liked to have the control over me. To know that I would be there for him. Every night of the weekend. I agreed. I'm wondering what you think of me now, Dr Power, but I don't want to ask you. I don't really want to know. I'm afraid."

"I would like to hear more . . . what else is there you can tell me?"

"He watched me while I walked away, out of the wood. Out of the gates. And all the time I couldn't quite believe what had happened. It seemed too awful and also too marvellous. I was ashamed and brilliantly enlightened at the same time. It was like exploding. You might have thought that meeting him like that . . . that it would prick the balloon . . . that my need for him would vanish. It didn't. I found I was thinking of him every moment. I would sit down to do some studying and I would daydream about him, what I wanted him to do, and then suddenly I would find it was hours later. I hadn't studied a thing. I'd even missed lunch by hours. So I got down to the serious business of waiting. I waited. In the fading sun, at the end of every day, every weekend. I waited for the golden hour that he would come. I waited in that shelter for two weekends on the run, for six nights, and he didn't come. One of the nights I thought that there was someone there, unseen. But nothing happened. The third week after we'd met in the woods. I wasn't sure that we had ever actually met at all. I wondered if I'd dreamed the first meeting up . . . that it was a delusion or a hallucination or something like that. I was wondering if it was a good idea at all to go down to that lonely spot and wait like I was doing. I was getting a bit afraid you see. Afraid that I might be physically attacked, but also afraid that I was losing my hold on things. It was a very dark time for me. I'd virtually stopped sleeping altogether. There was just this need inside me, as if I'd been reduced to this one desire.

"Then the next weekend, on the Friday . . . I'd waited for the whole hour almost. It was nearly nine o'clock. I was tired. I was at the end of my tether. I felt worth less than nothing. I was so tired I could hardly care whether I could walk back home or not. I couldn't have cared if I'd died there and then. There was a car. I didn't recognise it. I'd watched cars go up and down the lane. I knew everyone by now . . . all the regular users, the farmers and the stockbrokers and . . . this one was different. It didn't swoop on by, it stopped across the way on the verge. I looked at it stupidly. It was getting dark. I'd had the feeling that someone had been watching me again just a few minutes before and I knew this car was for me in some way. All I knew was it wasn't Sir Ian's Land Rover. I felt afraid again. Like I was staring death in the face. And I went rigid with fear. The horn on the car blared. It blared twice more, angrily. Then the door opened and it was him. He looked really angry. He looked up and down the road and walked over to me. 'Come on!' he said, 'Don't mess me about. We can't be seen together. Get in.' He was angry because he was afraid. He had to pull at my arm before I would move though. I walked to the car. The ground felt squashy beneath my feet like it was a dream. He told me to get into the back and lie down. There was a blanket there. He told me to cover myself with it. I think he thought I was cold after my wait."

'Or he wanted to make sure you weren't seen,' thought Power.

"I lay down on the back seat and he got into the front. The car was new. It smelt new."

"What kind was it?"

"It was white. A big car. A Ford. I think it might have been a hire car. He started driving, then he swore and stopped the car. He fished something black out of his pocket and told me to put it on. I couldn't see what it was. He swore at me and came round to the back of the car, opened the door and put it round my head. It was a blindfold. He tied it tightly. It had two pads inside that pressed on your eyes. He tied it so tight I could see colours where it pressed on my eyes. He told me to stay quiet and keep as still as I could. Then he covered me up and we set off again."

"So you didn't know where you were going?" Power was astounded at the danger she had put herself in.

"We drove for about half-an-hour. The roads were busy. I could hear other cars passing us, people talking on the streets. Then eventually we slowed, turned right and came to a halt. He told me to stay where I was. Not to move. Not to do anything. He got out and I heard him closing a sliding garage door behind the car, so I knew then that he'd driven straight into an open garage. He opened the door and helped me out. I couldn't see what I was doing. He led me around the front of the car. He said he was going to ask an important question. That there would be no going back after this. He asked me to think carefully. Was I really willing for him to do anything to me? He said he would give me time to think; so behind my blindfold I thought as quickly as I could. I remember biting my cheek and wondering if he was watching my hesitation. I said I wondered if I could trust him. He replied that I had trusted him with all my letters. I told him I was worried in case he harmed me in some way. He said that what he needed to do to me might be uncomfortable, but that it would not harm me. He seemed sure he knew what I wanted. I was not to worry. Did I agree or not? I felt I had to say 'yes': firstly because I wanted to be his; and secondly because I thought I would lose him forever if I did not.

"After I had agreed, he said we would not talk about the matter again, but that whatever happened now I had already consented and no longer had the right to refuse. I had given that up. I had to trust him. I remember nodding and do you know how it felt?"

"No," said Power. He imagined it might be profoundly frightening. He wondered, if her story was true, what would have happened if, having got as far as the garage, Zoë had panicked and refused her consent. What would McWilliam have done then?

"It felt like a relief. That all decisions had been taken from me. There was no struggle between right and wrong anymore. I could just give myself up and enjoy. He told me that from then on I could ask no questions. I could say nothing unless he asked me something. I nodded. I felt his hand on my left wrist. He lifted it up and took off my watch. Then he told me to slip off my shoes. The garage floor was cold rough concrete under my feet. I could smell old grass, thinners, paint ... I don't know ... something in the garage anyway. I allowed him to take off my coat and my blouse. It was cold without them. With the cold and the excitement my flesh was covered in goose pimples. He removed my bra and skirt. I remembered shivering naked in front of him. He felt my breasts and I was grateful his hands were so warm and dry. I wondered whether he would take me there and then. He took hold of my hand and led me forward a few steps to a door."

"You couldn't see though," Power tried to clarify.

"Don't you believe me? I could hear him unlocking it."

"Carry on then."

"He led me into the main part of the house. I listened out for other voices, the sounds of a television or a radio. It was quiet. From outside came the noise of traffic on the road. The silent house had no carpet. His footsteps echoed because he had shoes on. I could feel the uneven floorboards under my feet. He pushed me forwards and I found my toes were up against something. He told me to climb the stairs that were in front of me. I got hold of the banister and stepped upwards. I was a little too confident and I stumbled on the half-landing. I had expected the stairs to go on. I fell forward on to my face. I remember grazing my shin against the top step. It felt unworldly, like a dream. I remember the smell of the new wood from the stairboards and realising slowly as I lay there that his fingers were exploring between my legs, uninvited. He told me not to move, but it was as if I'd lost the will to do so. It was as if I was floating – a very familiar feeling from long ago. I remember wondering how incredible it was . . . that his fingers could get so far into me . . . that I had become so wonderfully open to him. I lay there forever. Did I pass out? Can you pass out if something is too wonderful? After, I don't know how long, he helped me up. I remember staggering. He was very firm, very strong . . . he almost lifted me to my feet. He guided me up the steps to the landing. Bare boards again. He pushed me into a bathroom. 'You can make yourself comfortable in here,' he said. 'You won't have the chance again for some time, so make the most of the opportunity. You can take your blindfold off inside, but before you come out put the blindfold back on. When you want to come out, knock on the door.' And he closed the door and he locked it."

"Bathroom doors lock from the inside usually."

"Once I took the blindfold off I could see that the bolt inside had been taken off. Remember this was the only room in the house that I ever saw. I must have been in them all I think, but never without my blindfold on. I remember looking at myself in the mirror. I could see the flush of excitement over my face and neck. My legs felt so weak like they would just give way. I sat down on the toilet and looked around. The bathroom was clean. There was a white suite:

basin; bath; bidet; toilet. There was purple soap from Bodyshop; a new Oral-B toothbrush in its wrapper; Aquafresh toothpaste unopened; soft, white towels made in England. I looked at everything. Really to make sure that it wasn't a dream."

"What about a window?" asked Power, seeking more detail to help try and corroborate this story.

"There was a large window over the bath."

"What could you see?"

"It was special glass ... the kind you can't see through."

Anastasi had said there would be no verifiable detail. Power felt his heart sinking. "So this could have been any bathroom, anywhere."

"It had orange, flowery curtains," she said. Behind her back, Power was frowning. "And there was a small window – one that opens outwards. All the windows had window-locks except this one, which was open. Before you ask, I did look through it."

"And?"

"I saw a featureless end brick wall ... of the house next door."

"So it was a detached house?" asked Power.

"I think so. It was so quiet. You never heard the neighbours. And if you looked obliquely you could see the next door back garden, but there was never anybody in it. It had a pond I think."

"No-one to see you arrive or when you left?"

"Never. It was always night when we arrived."

"So this all happened several times? You went back again?"

"You sound a bit incredulous. I did go back. I went back for more again and again."

"Through the window," asked Power. "Can you remember seeing anything else in the garden?"

"No, but if I looked the other way, towards the front of the house I could see the road."

"Right," said Power. This was exactly the kind of detail he was seeking. Did you recognise the street?"

"No." It seemed she had defeated him again.

"Any street signs or advertising hoardings?"

"No."

Power sighed. "Any buildings opposite?"

"No. Countryside. Hedges. Cow pasture. It was a main road though. Lots of cars."

"None parked nearby? No registration numbers of cars in the drive of the next door house?"

"No. No parked cars. But there was a petrol station. I could just see the edge of a forecourt carved out of the field opposite."

"Name of the garage?" Somehow Power knew the question was futile; he just knew there wouldn't be a name.

"I couldn't see it. It was an Esso station. I remember that."

"All right," he said, unable to cudgel his brains for any more questions. He estimated there must be thousands of such petrol stations in the country, "Go on. Tell me what happened next." It seemed the least troublesome thing to say given that there was plenty of time for the interview to run.

"I finished in the bathroom. Washed my hands and face and put the blindfold back on. I put it on as tightly as he had done before."

"Why? Didn't you want to see?" Power was frustrated with the story's lack of useful objective detail. He realised his questioning was sounding judgemental. He was implying that she should have cheated and looked around her. If her story was true why had she played along with McWilliam? He realised how angry he was with her. Was she making him jealous? Was she teasing him with her fantasies?

"I didn't want to see," she said. I trusted him. After I was sure I couldn't see, I knocked on the door. He took some time in opening it. I think he was training me in what he wanted from me. He wanted unquestioning submission. He wanted control and I wanted him to have control." She stopped her narrative. "Do you want to know any more?"Power wondered why she asked. Did she want him to take control?

"Tell me as much as you need to," he said. "As much as you can."

He led me into one of the rooms at the back of the house. I felt carpet under my feet. This was the one room that had carpet. I knew this was the room that he'd brought me here for, and I began to tremble, you know, with excitement. He pushed me forward a little way and I was standing on some soft rug. It was all cool and furry under my feet. He shut the door behind us. He was watching me as I rubbed my feet on the rug. 'You like that,' he said, but before I could answer he laid a hand on the small of my back and told me that I was to be quiet. He pushed me forward and my feet and shins came up against something covered in material. It was the edge of a bed. He turned me round so that I was facing him then he pushed me back and down on to the bed. I could feel that it was covered by a sheet, nothing else. A hand was placed between my thighs and he pulled me open. The next moment he was rubbing the silky rug between my legs. It felt exquisite. So exquisite it was almost painful, you know?" Power didn't say anything.

"Then he rolled me over on my front and told me to move up the bed. I knelt up and moved forward until I came to a metal headboard, then I lay down again on my front as he directed me. He got hold of one wrist and tied a thin rope to it and then did the same with the other. He pulled on both ropes and tied them somewhere, beyond the bed. He pulled my arms out till they were as taut as they would go. Then he tied my legs together and that rope was secured somewhere else. The effort needed to do all this made him pant, like an animal or something. He didn't like what he'd done though. He untied my legs and tied rope around each ankle, then he drew each leg out to the side and secured them. All the time he asked me to pull against the knots, to make sure they were tight. Twice he untied them and stretched my legs wider apart. When he was satisfied, I could not move my legs any closer together nor could I move them further apart. I lay there spreadeagled and waited. He wanted me to wait, but he could not resist one more exploration of my secret parts. It was as if I'd given myself up. I no longer existed. It was . . . like shedding all my cares and responsibilities. I don't know if that makes sense. He was in control. He could direct two bodies, his own and mine too. He left the room. I heard him closing the door and going downstairs. Downstairs in the kitchen I could hear him making a cup of tea or something. He waited a short time then returned. He said, 'I will come back. You must wait quietly. Not a sound.' And he left. I heard him start the car and drive off."

"Weren't you frightened?"

"Should I have been? I didn't feel frightened. I felt incredibly relieved. I was uncomfortable, I know that, but my body didn't seem to be me anymore. It wasn't as if I was in it much. I was somewhere else. I drifted far away. When I came to again there was someone in the room with me, watching. Then he went away again. I heard the front door slam. Sometime later. I don't know how long I heard someone climbing the stairs and coming into the bedroom. There was an intake of breath and then something was unwrapped and taken out of its box. There was a click and a crackle, and whirring sound. This happened ten times. I counted. Then a drawer was opened somewhere in the room and something was put away, and the door was opened and closed, the stairs were climbed down and the front door banged to.

"I drifted in and out of sleep. When I woke up, I would revel in my situation. The protracted desire seemed to beat in my brain. It seemed to possess my every stretched muscle fibre and every frayed nerve. It was cold on my bed. I presumed it was early morning when I fell asleep again. When I awoke there was sun on my skin, so I guessed the curtains in this room must be open, but I couldn't see. My eyes made up patterns where the blindfold pressed. That was all I could see. My mind made up other pictures. Then I heard the car again and he was there in the room with me. He pushed a kind of nozzle in my mouth and squirted orange juice into my mouth. I sucked it, like a greedy baby. Then he pulled it away, just before my thirst was satisfied and he apologised for being away so long. I felt his hands on my buttocks, cupping them with his palms. Then without warning he had climbed between my legs and his penis was on me, then in me, then up me. Time seemed distorted and lying there for so long, it seemed as if I was infinitely small and this thing that dilated me was infinitely huge, that it filled my entire body. He came quickly that first time, and as I received his... seed, I felt quite uplifted... like I knew that I'd trapped him. I'd attracted him like an open flower, you know that just sits there, waiting to be pollinated. He was my bumble bee." She laughed and Power saw that her reservations about telling her story had gone. She gloried in it. He shivered.

"He repeated it all that first weekend. Other times we used other rooms. When he left me I wondered what anyone would think if they walked in and found me there. I wondered what they'd do, or if they saw through the windows. I think he always closed the downstairs curtains. He stuffed me full of his seed. I wanted it. I wanted to be used by him as a receptacle; whatever he wanted to do, I acquiesced. If he wanted to burn me with a cigarette I would willingly endure and enjoy it. Every weekend, whenever he could manage I would wait for him and be driven to his house, and wait for him there and let him possess me as he wanted. He would come and go, but I would be there for him all weekend. And afterwards, in the darkness of Monday morning he would untie me and dress me and stow me away in his car and drive me through the darkness to the country lane we met in and he would leave me there to find my way home." She stopped and turned round for the first time to look Power in the eye. "You don't believe me, do you?"

"I... er... I..."

Power was taken aback by the directness of her question.

"You don't," she seemed to sag. The red thrill of telling the story fled from her face. "And if you don't, then no-one else will."

There was a knock on the door. "I think that's the end of the interview," said Power. "They've come to pick you up."

"You think I'm mad then, do you? Perhaps I am. It all seemed real enough to me. We both enjoyed ourselves... I think we did." She frowned and stood up.

"It's just I was hoping for your sake that there would be some detail that could be checked out. There's no proof that I can see there," said Power apologetically. "No dates, no places, no witnesses."

"There were photographs taken. I heard them being taken. I told you about that."

Power thought about the clicking and whirring noises she had mentioned. Had these noises been photographs being taken? "But where are these photographs?" he asked.

She shrugged and there was another polite knock at the door in case they hadn't heard the first time.

"All right!" Power called out. "Nearly finished." He turned back to her ". . . and another thing, you're not on the pill are you?" She shook her head. "And you didn't mention any other form of contraception did you? Or did I miss that bit?" She shook her head again and looked into the middle distance. The prison world outside the door beckoned her.

"Intercourse and no contraception equals pregnancy as far as I'm concerned," said Power, as if this was the final nail in the coffin of her fantasy. He sat back and wondered what his report would say now. What could he say to Lynch to make amends for involving him in such a futile quest?

The door was starting to open. The female prison officers stood outside ready for Zoë. Power followed his own inexorable logic to its conclusion, "And, since you're not pregnant . . ."

Zoë smiled a real smile at last and pushing the roundness of her belly out in an exaggerated way, patted her abdomen. "Oh, but I am, Dr Power."

Chapter Seven

*Come, Holy Ghost, our souls inspire
And lighten with celestial fire,
Though the anointing spirit art,
Who dost they seven-fold gifts impart,
Thy blessed Unction from above,
In Comfort, life, and the fire of love.
Enable with perpetual light
The dullness of our blinded sight.*

**The Ordering of Priests,
The Book of Common Prayer.**

"And is she?" asked Lynch, who had just been told of the results of Power's trip to see Zoë Allen.

Sitting in Lynch's back garden with a glass of mint tea in his hands, a disheartened Dr Power looked at Lynch and shrugged his shoulders. "I don't know," he said. "I asked the Prison Medical Officer to send a urine sample for testing. She didn't look pregnant."

"But then, women don't in the first few months, do they?"

"No," said Power. "And she has been losing weight, because she's just not eating."

"So, why are you so down yourself?"

Power sighed and looked up at the copper beech tree that dominated the lawn. "Well . . . I just realised that I must have been wrong all the time. I'm sorry to have dragged you into it. I thought that there was a chance she was telling the truth, but listening to her yesterday I just kept thinking about what Anastasi had said."

"Which was?"

"That there would be no detail. He said that she would spin me a yarn based on her own erotic fantasies and . . . he was right. I suppose he draws on more experience than I do, but I'm annoyed with myself for being taken in, for being sucked in to her delusional world. You warned me to keep my head. You warned me."

Lynch said no more than "Ah."

Power paused and let the evening sun warm him. He closed his eyes and felt himself drifting. "I've been ignoring my work. I suppose I was enchanted by her or something. Spellbound by her. Sex really is a problem isn't it? Messes up our lives. You need it. Or you think you need it – so badly. The drive is so very strong, but it's a snare. Sex is . . . is . . . like death. It sometimes feels like death. I mean it's meant to be about life, making new life, but sometimes it gets all twisted up and pain becomes pleasure and pleasure becomes pain and . . . sometimes when the drive becomes too much, it takes over, like the smell of death. If sex had a colour it would be black."

"You really have got sucked into this case," said Lynch. "I think you're seeing it from the inside out. These ideas are ideas from inside the case, not your ideas."

"I'm sorry," said Power. "I'm turning you into my therapist. I'll shut up . . ."

Lynch poured himself another glass of tea from the jug his wife had carefully left on the table by their chairs. He waved a cloud of midges away and went on. "When you talked about death and sex I suddenly had this image of Sir Ian and the girl . . . and she is a girl. He must have been over three times her age. Three times. An old man stealing life back from a child. I think he was trying to evade death by trying to get as much power over sex, over her young life as he possibly could."

"When I was listening to her, I felt confused, " said Power. As she told me the story I was aroused by her telling it. She was aroused by the telling of it. But I didn't know whose story it was. It didn't feel right. Felt creepy . . . like it was the old man speaking through her. And I felt guilty for enjoying any part of it – like I was a voyeur. I was repelled and fascinated at the same time."

"Evil is fascinating and corrupting at the same time," said Lynch. "That is why I told you to stand clear. And at the end of the day you have done. Haven't you?"

"Yes," said Power. "I have, but I was drawn close to the edge. "

"But you stepped back," said Lynch gently, so his words were a statement and hardly even a question.

Power was deep in thought. He hadn't told Lynch about Lucinda and what had or rather had not happened between them. He was not sure whether he should tell him. After all, he had been phoned by Lucinda just before coming out to see Lynch. They had arranged to meet in Manchester for an evening at the theatre the following night. Why did it feel like a secret he could not tell Lynch? Lucinda and Power were both consenting adults after all.

"What you are saying to me," said Lynch. "Is that from the inside this case is all about sex. When you look at the outside of someone or something, the inside is not visible. We keep our sensual nature well under wraps. And as a detective observing a case, that is something that is often most deeply buried. When you were sucked in you got a glimpse of what the case was like for those on the inside. There is a lack of definition, of boundaries being blurred, of excesses of sex and drugs and alcohol and everything happening in a chaotic way. Horrible things happen and people have things done against them and don't know whether they wanted it or whether someone else wanted it and everything is washed over, soothed away, diluted by a comforting haze of alcohol. As though they were all players in a play seeking an end, seeking oblivion, seeking a dark end-of-show curtain."

Power groaned, "Oh God, that's too deep." Lynch frowned at the miss-use of God's name. "It makes me feel even more inadequate and foolish."

"Wallowing in self-pity won't help anyone," said Lynch bluntly. He picked up Power's notes from his two visits to see Zoë. "Yes," he said as he read through. "The story doesn't sound right, it sounds far-fetched that a cabinet minister might do all this, but that's just looking at the surface of the package, it doesn't mean it's untrue. It may be true. You've had a glimpse of what's underneath Sir Ian

McWilliam's wrappings and you've found it a very confused world. A world we can only pick out pieces from."

"It's her own psychosis. It's all her," said Power harshly. "Anastasi was right. She's a little witch."

"But you didn't think so before she told you her story," said Lynch. "You're casting her in the role of sinner, when perhaps she's been sinned against."

"I don't understand you," said Power. "You've got the papers there. She avoided giving me anything we could test. There's nothing there."

"On the contrary," said Lynch.

"What!" Power couldn't believe his ears. He exclaimed so loudly that Mrs Lynch popped her head out of the bedroom window. It was unusual for the two friends to raise their voices at each other and she was intrigued to find out what was going on.

"There are facts in her account. They met at weekends. That would fit with his trips up north."

"But no dates!"

"Just listen, Carl. There are no dates yet. He drives her in a hire car to a house within a thirty-minute radius of Chester. From what she said, we know it's on a busy main road. It's a detached house; a new, unfurnished house. The wood smelt new, remember? Opposite is farmland and an Esso garage."

"She was making up general facts that could fit anywhere. It's too vague."

"It would be," said Lynch. "I told you not to forget what I told you the other evening. Do you remember?" From her vantage point above them Mrs Lynch thought there would not be an escalation in the argument. Things seemed to be simmering down and a fight looked highly unlikely. Amused, she put her head back in and turned up the television she had been watching.

Power sighed and attempted to recall what had been said. "You mentioned the fire report. That fires had been set upstairs and downstairs and in my lady's chamber." Lynch raised his eyebrows.

"Well, you also talked about Sir Ian's cheques and credit cards."

"Yes! That's it. You put his information together with her information and I think . . . I'm pretty sure that they'll fit."

"Do you really think so?" Power regarded Lynch with a healthy scepticism. He was less than willing to invest his hope again.

"I've got some free time tomorrow," said Lynch. "I promise you I'll find that house."

"I don't want to waste anymore of your time you know . . ."

"It won't be wasted," said Lynch.

"I'm surprised you're suddenly so sure. I'm spending tomorrow trying to catch up at work. I've got to do a mammoth ward round. I've been neglecting my registrar and my real patients."

"It's okay," said Lynch. "I'll work more quickly on my own. I should be able to phone you tomorrow night."

"Oh...oh . . . yes . . ." Tomorrow night Power was taking Lucinda out.

"If you can get the results of Zoë's pregnancy test?"

Power nodded and swiftly changed the subject. He did not want to tell Lynch about Lucinda. He might only receive another lecture about keeping his heart out of the case. And Power didn't like facing the uncomfortable truth that Lynch was right in this matter.

★ ★ ★

Superintendent Lynch drove a more up-to-date Rover than Carl Power. Lynch was an efficient, mildly obsessional man and the thought of unscheduled breakdowns in a classic car from the 1950s was not his idea of an appropriate car. He liked reliability, comfort and safety, with the emphasis on the latter. He was a cautious individual, usually. The investigation that he had embarked on with Power was an exception to his usual cautious nature. Sometimes he felt compelled to break out of his cautious mode of life, and his detective work was one means of doing this. He had had more than one run-in with his superiors over occasionally unorthodox methods of police work. So far his methods had always paid off. But one day they would not and Lynch knew he would then be held to account for all the other times he had broken the rules. Interfering in another investigation was one such rule and here he was breaking it wholeheartedly. And the flouting of the rules gave him a thrill, rather like gambling against the odds. He was a just man, a religious man, but he was no absolute saint.

Clutching a sheaf of photocopied credit card receipts Lynch had visited three of the four petrol stations that Sir Ian McWilliam appeared to have bought petrol from. One of them had been only two miles from Heaton Hall, the now burnt-out wreck in which Lady McWilliam eked out her penance of an existence. The garage hand remembered Sir Ian driving a metallic blue Land Rover Discovery, but never anything else. Sir Ian had always bought the petrol himself. Only occasionally had Sir Ian been seen to drive others in his Land Rover and they had always been males. The garage attendant remembered that Sir Ian always checked under the car before driving off. He'd once told the garage attendant he was checking for bombs. He did it automatically, every time he approached the car, as regularly as putting on his seat belt. The garage attendant had once seen a wheelchair in the back of the Land Rover, was that any help? Lynch thanked him for his help and drove on.

As Lynch drove to the fourth garage along the A540 out of Chester he felt a sense of triumphant *deja vu*. Here was a busy main road, with houses built on one side. On the hill behind them was the Deva hospital. In front of them rolling Cheshire countryside that ran down to the River Dee. Ahead on the left was a filling station with a blue and red oval Esso sign. Lynch drove onto the block paviered forecourt and parked. He introduced himself to the cashier, but she was new and didn't even recognise the photograph of Sir Ian McWilliam that he showed her. 'Fame is a brief, frail thing,' Lynch thought. If Sir Ian had bought petrol here he had not been remembered. But his credit card records placed him here at the 24-hour station late at night and in the early hours of the morning, mainly at weekends. The station was out of his way and about thirty minutes drive from Chester. A journey here would have taken McWilliam through Chester's Georgian faced city streets. Zoë had remembered those.

He left the forecourt cashier and crossed the road. There was a row of three to four bedroomed modern houses, built with red brick. Zoë had described a red brick end wall. All of the houses were within sight of the garage. Which one? He went up the path of one. It had suburban net curtains and a garden full of flame-red asters and a neatly kept lawn. He peered around the back to see if there was a pond. The occupant opened the front door, a small, dumpy woman with wild, frizzy, grey hair and horn-rimmed spectacles. Lynch was caught by the sight of her dimpled Spam-like arms, folded crossly over her ample chest.

"What do you want? Are you from the council tax people? I don't want any double glazing. We've had that done."

"I'm sorry to intrude, Ma'am. My name is Detective Superintendent Lynch, of the Cheshire Police. He offered her his warrant card for her inspection, and she was taken aback by his status.

"We did pay the council tax. A bit late, but we did pay. They over-rated the place, but we did pay. Norman complained..."

"It's not about that. I'm on an investigation. I'm looking for a house in this road with a pond at the back. I know it sounds bizarre, but it is important. It's to do with information we've received about the murder of Sir Ian McWilliam."

"Ooooh," she gasped. "Nothing like that round here." She said the words as if they were a talisman or a mantra to ward off evil. If the phrase was repeated often enough you could believe that home was a safe place, apart from the horrors of the world.

"Is there a pond nearby, perhaps?"

"Nothing like that round here," she seemed to be stuck in a groove. "Oh wait though, two doors down has an ornamental fish pond, with a heron to stop the birds getting the goldfish. What about the cats though, that's what I wondered."

"Two doors down?"

She nodded and pointed, and her hair nodded with her after a slight time-delay. "Thank you," said Lynch, and smiling, turned on his heel. Two doors down he found a similar house, this time with a bed of purple and blue heather instead of the more florid asters. He peeped around the side of the building. He could just see the dark-green surface of a pond. A small fountain threw a weedy spray of water up a few inches from the surface. He returned down the path and approached the next house further on. 'This must be it,' he thought. The vague details Zoë had given Power were adding up to a significance beyond mere coincidence.

He opened the thin rolled-steel gate, closed it behind him and walked up the path to the front door. This house had no keen gardener as an owner. The lawn was overgrown and there were weeds in the flowerbed. The garden had signs of being periodically attacked, but no evidence of on-going loving care. He pushed the front door bell and waited. He noted that the front room curtains sagged where there were insufficient curtain hooks to hold them up. A glance through the window revealed the room to be cleared of any furniture. Inside there was no carpet or underlay covering the yellow pine floorboards. He rang the doorbell again, but there was no sign that anybody would be coming to answer.

The temptation to get inside was too strong for Lynch and locks had never presented a problem to him. He carried a set of master keys and a set of fine picks made for him by an ex-convict he had helped rehabilitate at the local church. 'Mysterious ways,' he thought to himself as he opened the front door. He pushed it open against a small mountain of free papers and circular letters. Once inside he smelt the vaguely musty aroma of an unlived-in house. It was musty, but he was pleased that there was no more sinister smell. The smell of decomposition haunted him. Lynch closed the front door behind him and reaching into his pocket took out and put on a pair of fine white cotton gloves. For all Lynch knew he might have been the first person in the house since the late Sir Ian and he didn't want to disturb fingerprints. He made a tour of the downstairs. It was empty except for a kettle in the kitchen with teabags, powdered milk and a solitary mug. The fridge was not switched on, and a stale carton of orange juice gave off a sickly smell when he opened the door. There was a quarter-pound of melted rancid butter beside the carton. He shut the fridge hurriedly and sought to open the kitchen window. The window lock defeated him. In the pedal bin was a green mould-furred piece of sliced bread from a breakfast of toast long ago.

The other rooms in the downstairs were unremarkable. The telephone in the hall had been disconnected. Lynch patted his breast pocket where he carried a slim cell-phone, just in case he needed it. From the hallway there was a door, which Lynch tried. A mortise-lock and a security bolt delayed him for a few seconds. He stepped down into a gloomy garage.

The temperature was lower than the rest of the house. He imagined Zoë standing naked and shivering in here. But it was in here that he was to find what might be a conclusive proof of Zoë's tale. Standing in the middle of the garage was a white K-registered Ford Granada. Lynch guessed that McWilliam had parked his Land Rover elsewhere and driven this to blur any link that would identify him with the house or Zoë. McWilliam must have died before he could sever that link. This was a hire car though surely. But there was no record of a hire car on the credit card receipts.

Lynch looked through the side window. There was a sticker for Chester Wheelhire on the windscreen. He didn't want to touch the car, even to open the door. The fingerprint record on the doorjamb and the window glass would be important links. He could, though, just make out the Chester Wheelhire's phone number on the reverse of the tax disc. He pulled the cellphone out of his pocket and dialled the number.

"Good morning, Chester Wheelhire. Diana speaking. How may I help you?"

"Can I speak to the duty manager please?"

"That's me, Diana. Who's calling?"

"Detective Superintendent Lynch. I'm phoning about one of your cars. You might have reported it missing actually. I guess some time ago."

"Well, we're not a large firm . . . things do happen to our cars, naturally, clients are never as careful with our cars as they would be with their own, but there has only been one car that didn't come back. Let me see, from memory it was a K registered Ford Granada."

"White?"

"Yes. Have you found it?"

"In a private garage, yes."

"Can we come and pick it up?" she asked.

"No, I'm afraid not. Not yet, anyway. There will need to be some forensic tests. Actually, it may be some time before it can be returned."

"Oh, I see. Has the car been involved in some crime, is that what you're saying?"

"Not directly involved in any crime," said Lynch. "but it may be important in solving one. Can you tell me who rented the car last?"

"I can't remember. The paperwork isn't here now. It was taken by one of your detectives the other day."

Lynch swallowed hard. "The other day? But when did you report the lost car?"

"It was overdue two or three months ago. I can't be precise. Your colleague will have all the details now."

"It seems an odd time to take all the paperwork away, that's all," said Lynch. "You can't remember any more about the hiring of the car?"

"No, it was months ago. You don't think these things are important at the time. But I do remember it was supposed to be hired out for over a month, and the hirer paid in cash. Quite a large sum. A bit unusual, but not dramatically so. We're usually more worried about rubber cheques. We took all his details, but of course they were fake."

"Thank you," said Lynch. "I'll send someone round to take a further statement." He ended the call and stared at the car. The link was almost established, Zoë's story almost verified, but not quite. He knew that he must involve the proper McWilliam murder inquiry team now. This was no time for more solo detective work. He needed all the forensic resources available to analyse the house. If they did so, their findings might just avert Zoë's conviction. He would phone, he promised himself, just after he had looked upstairs.

His shoes made a resounding creaking noise as he climbed the bare board stairs. At the top of the stairs was the bathroom door. He noted the lock on the outside with satisfaction. Inside was just as she had described: a white bathroom suite, orange curtains, even down to the purple soap. Lynch passed now to the small bedroom. There was a sky-blue carpet, a white fur rug. A grand and massive metal bedstead with a thick mattress and a single, stained and grubby sheet covering it. The stains would bear analysing, he thought. By the side of the bed were coiled lengths of thin, nylon rope, each tethered to thick hooks set into the brickwork of the walls. He could see where the holes had been clumsily drilled through the plaster-work to house the shafts of the hooks. He pulled at one of the hooks. It was rock-solid. On the skirting-board below there was a minute pile of fine white and red brick-dust. Old curtains had been crudely hung at the window. A purely functional room, thought Lynch. And the function had been the acting-out of a mutual sex fantasy. He looked around as intently as he could, but his intellect could barely dispel his distaste for what he had discovered. In the light of day, to Lynch's eyes, the lovers' excitement seemed a bad dream, if not a hung-over nightmare.

The only other piece of furniture in the barren house was a small chest of drawers. He opened it from the bottom drawer upwards. It was empty except for the top drawer. Here there was a single Polaroid photograph. He didn't pick it up. In the sunlight he could see two clear fingerprints on its glossy surface, and he didn't want to ruin them. This was something Zoë had never seen, but Lynch remembered from her description that she had heard it being taken. Ten photographs had been taken of her naked body, stretched apart upon the bed. This was one of them. For the right person, in the right place, at the right time, it would have been an erotic image. But this was the wrong time and the wrong place and the wrong person. Lynch closed the drawer on the photograph and surveyed the room once more before descending the stairs and making his phone call. He spoke carefully and clearly, mindful that his discovery would make a great difference to the lives of many different people.

★ ★ ★

Lucinda had driven her car into the wide drive in front of Power's home soon after six o'clock, and they had travelled together, with her driving, into the centre of Manchester. There had been tickets to see The Tempest at the Royal Exchange Theatre and a booking for an evening meal in Chinatown. The evening went well, and for most of it Power had enjoyed a deliciously easy conversation with her. The play, performed in the round, had combined the best of balances between clarity and mysticism, and so entrancing was the performance that both Power and Lucinda had felt themselves transported as if by magic carpet to Prospero' s isle. A short walk through the evening's busy city streets, between Victorian office blocks and shops had brought them to Albert Square and the Town Hall, a design by the architect Waterhouse who had also planned Heaton Hall. At this spot in the City, Power had asked about Lucinda's mother. He was told that she was much the same, and Power made a mental note that he must visit her again. 'Why do I keep putting it off?' he asked himself. Lucinda didn't seem to wish to talk more about the widow or about her errant brother and so they talked about far-off islands and tropical waters as they drifted into Chinatown, where a new restaurant had opened in the marbled splendour of a Victorian banking hall. There they dined on duck and beef and fish and drank Tsingtao beer and Jasmine tea. At the end of the perfect evening, Power felt somewhat bowled over by the ease of it all. Lucinda and he had been so at ease with each other. The feeling was unusual to him. There was almost a tacit agreement between them. It felt as if they were riding on smooth rails down a delicious gradient that would lead inexorably into a crisply white-sheeted double bed.

In the car on the way home, passing through the city streets, between their lights and sleeping buildings, Power was gradually more aware that he must say something, even if it spoilt the ease between them. She had just been laughing at one of his gentle jokes. He paused, thinking twice before going on. "There's something I've been wanting to say," said Power, and felt guilty when he saw her bright and smiling face glance up from the road to him. "It isn't easy . . ."

"Oh," she said softly, and you could see her pulling ever so slightly away in her seat, and composing her face against disappointment.

"It's about your father."

"Not about us?"

Power shook his head, "Well . . . er, I suppose it does affect us, but it's not particularly about you and me. You know we were investigating Zoë Allen? And everybody thought she had murdered your father because she was driven by some deluded infatuation? My friend, Superintendent Lynch, and I investigated some of the things she was saying a little more carefully than anybody had done before. We think she was right. I'm afraid that there was some truth in her story of an affair with your father. It seems to have happened. The case against her seems very much weakened. Lynch has been talking to the Crown Prosecution Service this afternoon. The trial may not go ahead, and probably the investigation will start all over again."

"Oh no . . . it's all starting over? Wait," she said. "Hold on . . . I . . . don't quite follow. You said she was having an affair with Daddy?" Power nodded. "But there was no evidence for that. Absolutely none."

"I don't think he wanted to hurt anybody," said Power, putting things in a more than generous light. For her sake. "He kept it all very secret. So secret that nobody believed her."

"I just can't believe it," said Lucinda. "Her? A girl from the village? No . . ."

"Well yes," said Power. "I'm very sorry, but I'm afraid so. And the investigation will re-open. At least that's what Lynch is banking on."

"Oh please no," said Lucinda. "Mummy couldn't stand the news. She mustn't be told."

"Mustn't be told what?"

"Any of it . . . she mustn't get to know. It would kill her, simply finish her off."

"It will be difficult to keep it from her. She'll be re-questioned by the police for a start. And no-one would tell the press deliberately, but they will get to know. You can't shelter your mother from the truth any longer."

"Any longer . . . what do you mean?"

"Just that she will get to know eventually. It might be best if you or your brother were to talk to her first."

"Oh no . . ." She paused, and failed to finish what she was going to say. "How does this affect us?"

"I . . . erm. I just felt that while things are so uncertain . . . with me being linked into the police investigation too . . . that it wouldn't be . . . er . . . for the best, for us to accelerate our relationship. Put things on hold maybe, until happier times perhaps?"

She stared at him. "I see," she said. "No, don't say anymore. I get the picture. You can't trust me . . . it might be me that set the fire or something like that . . . maybe I was jealous of the village girl who slept with my Dad so I burnt the place down? Come on, Carl. Don't freeze me just when I . . ." She started to cry and Power felt guilt-ridden and small. "Just when I need some . . . some support." She sobbed. He reached for and pulled her into his comforting shoulder. He cursed himself for being pragmatic, and for listening to Lynch's words of caution. He could cope with the tears his patients shed, but these tears in front of him were 'his' tears, caused by him and shed on his account. 'Damn', he thought. 'What do I say now? Where are you when you're really needed, Lynch?'

She sobbed her heart out. She cried for herself, for her mother, for Power, and finally for her dead father, and the floods of tears felt suddenly like letting go of everything that troubled her soul. At length she sniffed a final tear away and dried her eyes on his shoulder. Mustering as much dignity as she could she pulled away from him. "I'm sorry. It won't happen again. I promise." Power tried to say something, but he was struck by a profound inarticulacy for once. "Don't worry," she said. She fished in her jacket pocket for a handkerchief and dabbed ineffectually at his shoulder. " 's wet," she said. "All those tears."

"The material's shrink resistant. It's okay."

She laughed a snuffling, moist kind of laugh. "You're okay too," she said. "But I can't quite work you out. It's almost like you're a bit afraid of me. I get that feeling ... like you're afraid I'll eat you up ... like a praying mantis or ..."

"I don't ... it's just that I'm saying our timing isn't right."

"When is the timing ever right? When will the timing ever be right for you to trust me? Or does the trust have to come before the time is right?"

They were passing out from the concrete suburban sprawl that surrounded the city of Manchester like a coral reef surrounds an island. Power thought of all the people safe and warm in their well-lit homes, making tea and settling down to the late-night news, or taking their baths and going to bed. Living their routine and comfortable lives, cheek-by-jowl and yet peaceably intent upon their own existence, on their own small islands of family and home. He would like to be like them, to be like Lynch, with his wife and his daughter. 'Maybe,' he thought. 'Given time ...'

He said, "Can we ... will you wait?"

She looked at him again, "It's usually the other way round. That should be my line."

"Well, we're in the middle of a storm ... the middle of a Tempest. Let's wait until the seas are calmer. At the moment it feels like I've got to keep my head, hang on to the ship, steer it as best I can through difficult waters ..."

She said nothing, but stared out into the darkness ahead of them. Their speed had fallen. They were driving up the hill towards Alderley Edge and Power's home. "I'm going to suggest something," she said. "It might sound a bit different, but I want you to think about it carefully, and, please, don't ... don't refuse me this."

"Go on ..." he said.

"I don't want to ... I can't go home tonight." She had been staying alternately with her brother or on a spare camp bed in the cold smoke damaged chapel with her mother. "Can you ... please let me sleep with you. Just sleep with you. In your bed? I don't want to be alone tonight. I can't face things alone tonight." She risked a look at his face. "Nothing need happen. I just want to feel your warmth, beside me, that's all . . ." They were driving into his drive. The infra-red passive detectors picked up the heat of her engine and the outdoor floodlight switched on bathing them with light. "Can I?" she asked.

"Come on," said Power, as he opened the door. "I've got an old nightshirt you could wear. I'll make some hot cocoa and we can put our nightcaps and nightshirts on and climb the old wooden hill. How about that?"

There were tears in her eyes, but either he couldn't see them, or he was pretending not to. They got out, and he held out his arm in a gesture of welcome and they went into the warmth indoors. Outside the house, the night air was becoming chill. The security lights, detecting that there was no-one outside, blinked off, and the drive once again was blanketed with darkness. After half-an-hour the golden light that beamed out into the darkness from the bedroom windows was extinguished and all was still.

Chapter Eight

I will not choose what many men desire, because I will not jump with common spirits and rank me with the barbarous multitude.

**Merchant of Venice,
Shakespeare.**

Power and Lynch had been walking for fifteen minutes or so along the top of the bare, sandstone ridge of Alderley Edge, in the evening sunlight. After a light meal of salad and fresh strawberries from Power's kitchen garden, Lynch was in a talkative mood. Power had drunk the wine that Lynch so assiduously eschewed, and after a long day's work the wine had a soporific effect. At Power's suggestion they climbed down a conveniently graded slope and sat on the sun-warmed rock. The distant farms and houses below the Edge were spread out under the setting sun like food on a green tablecloth at some picnic of the gods. If Power had been alone he would have stretched out upon the warm red sandstone, shut his eyes, and luxuriated in the embers of the day.

But Lynch was talking and his words were insistent. "I wanted to tell you about the forensic laboratory's preliminary results."

Power nodded, but his mind still dwelt on a different theme, "I'm still struggling with the fact that I was so wrong," he said. "I mean I had been sure last time I saw Zoë, that she was either deluded or lying through her teeth. I mean . . . it is as if somebody had told me that aliens from the star Betelgeuse were outside and I had dismissed it as a delusion only to find out that the aliens were indeed standing there when I opened the door. That's how I feel. Well, that's not just how I feel . . . I'm angry . . . I can't seem to get away from the fact."

Lynch wondered how to respond, "I think you want Zoë to be something she's not. When all is said and done she has been honest.

That's the way it seems. It's the outside world that has expectations of her. You're angry because she didn't meet up to your expectations, but they were your expectations, not hers."

Power winced slightly. Lynch's counsel could sometimes sting, but then the truth often did. "It didn't help when I phoned the prison medical officer. They got the pregnancy test back today."

"And?"

"She's pregnant all right. The vaginal examination revealed a pregnant uterus . . . Zoë's just about four month's pregnant. Presumably with Sir Ian's baby. Oh . . ." he wondered about how he was going to break that news to Lucinda.

"It was ironic wasn't it . . . don't you think? That this man should spend so much time and effort keeping the whole affair secret: night-time liaisons, renting a halfway-house, hiring cars . . . and he should forget the most obvious, the most basic precaution."

"Perhaps, unconsciously, they both wanted a child . . ." Power shrugged. "Why do all our idols have to fall?"

"That's the nature of idols," said Lynch. "And all graven images for that matter. But you don't worship at their feet do you?"

"I don't worship. Full stop."

"I pray that sometimes, one day, you might. It would ease your cynicism a little," said Lynch. "Faith in something greater than the sum of humankind is a great comfort . . . 'Though they go mad they shall be sane, Though they sink through the sea they shall rise again; Though lovers be lost love shall not; And death shall have no dominion.'"

Power smiled at his friend. He hadn't the heart to argue with him anymore. And if Power himself could not believe, he somehow found his friend's faith a comfort. "And the Crown Prosecution do they still have dominion over Zoë Allen?"

"For a little while longer, yes. But something will happen in a few days . . . and she will be released."

Power chuckled. "I wonder what Professor Anastasi will say!"

"Well the more evidence we get back from the house suggests

that her statement to you was right. That is, her version of the truth seems to be right."

He reached in his pocket for a copy of the Polaroid he had found in the house. He wondered whether he should show it to Power. He took the picture out of his pocket, but for a moment he just kept his palm around the image. Lynch asked, "Shall I tell you about the results now?" Power nodded. "The car in the garage had been hired out some five months ago. The hirer paid cash, and enough of it to secure the car for two months. The hirer used a false name and false identification to get his hands on the car. There were photocopies of all these documents at the hire firm, but someone, someone unknown, removed those files from the hire firm only a few days ago."

"Who'd do that?"

Lynch shrugged. "Whoever took the files explained that they were CID. I suspect that they were removed by someone pretending to be a police officer."

"But what you're saying is that to hire the car McWilliam used false names, false identification . . . it was a very elaborate deception, wasn't it?"

"McWilliam was almost paranoid that he might be found out . . . the discrepancy between his age and Zoë's . . . his right-wing political stance on moral values . . . if he had been found out he would have been finished as a politician. No, he couldn't afford not to use such an elaborate subterfuge. He'd probably never dared to have an affair before because of all these factors, but when Zoë Allen came along, passive, that she would submit herself to any of his demands . . . well, temptation was too much for him."

"It was his secrecy that made her look like a liar . . . made her look mad to everybody."

"But she was protecting him, she really did care for him."

"He was using her, but I don't think Zoë would ever, ever accept that he was using her. Was he ever interested in her, the real her?" Power wondered whether she represented Sir Ian's chance to snatch something good before he got too old. "How did he get his forged documents?"

"Well, that's where things get even more complicated. Whoever went in there originally to hire the car, pretending to be this non-existent person, with a non-existent driving licence ... it wasn't Sir Ian McWilliam. None of the staff at the hire company recall his face. He used someone else."

"Well, I suppose he'd have to," said Power. "It's obvious when you think of it. As a cabinet minister his face was all over the newspapers and the television."

"You'd be surprised by how little interest people take in current affairs," said Lynch. "But that still doesn't tell us who did the hiring for him, and who got the forged documents? Who was prepared to act illegally on McWilliam's behalf?"

"These European organisations of fascists he had links with?"

"Possibly," said Lynch. "Although the answer may be closer to home. Best exclude those people closest to McWilliam first, then work outwards." Some children were running about the foot of the slope. Power and Lynch watched them shouting and running and chasing each other, waving branches about their heads like spears. Eventually they climbed the slope and, gasping for breath, ran into the depths of the cave near Power and Lynch. In a moment the boys and girls emerged and like the Neolithic people they were pretending to be, ran up into the forest screaming incoherently in a made-up language. Lynch waited until they had gone. "We tested sets of fingerprints on the car, around the driver and passenger doors.

"There were good prints for Zoë Allen over the back of the car. Some definite prints from a second individual around the driver's side and another, third set, quite indistinct, useless really, but certainly different to the other two."

"A third set?"

"Well, the car is a hire car, and therefore has many users, but it is cleaned after each hirer. The third set could be the phantom hirer and the better set of prints could be Sir Ian's. He drove the car according to Zoë. The only problem being that we don't have a set of prints anywhere on record for Sir Ian. Unlike his son, Sir Ian had no criminal record and was a minister of the Crown."

"What's that in your hand?" asked Power. He was looking at what seemed like a piece of card that Lynch was holding. "You're holding it very guiltily."

"It's a copy of something I found upstairs in the bedroom of the house. It links in with the statement Zoë made to you. I didn't know whether to show you." He passed it over to Power. Lynch looked away at the sunset, tactfully ignoring his friend's reaction.

Power looked at the image of Zoë splayed on Sir Ian's bed. He looked at her body with an uncomfortable mixture of feelings. He felt like a voyeur. He even looked over his shoulder in case anybody was watching him as he looked at the photograph. He could just make out the thin black blindfold on her face. And it was her face. He was sure of that. He passed it back to Lynch without a word.

"I'm sorry," said Lynch. "The photograph I found was a Polaroid, slipped into one of the drawers."

With some distaste, Power said, "McWilliam probably took it to gloat over."

"Maybe," said Lynch. "She actually refers to the photographs being taken in her statement. Do you remember? I read the notes you'd taken over again. Zoë mentions being alone in the house and someone coming up the stairs whilst she was blindfold. Remember? Something was unwrapped and then ten mechanical noises. Clicks and whirrs. Polaroid cameras are noisy things. Every time a picture is taken a motor inside the camera spits the photo out of the front. There was probably a flash, but the blindfold was so tight, she didn't see it."

"So?" said Power sullenly. He was glad to have saved Zoë Allen, but was dismayed at having his ideas about her destroyed. Lynch might have pointed out that at some level he was just jealous, but that was too blunt even for the forthright Lynch. Power said, "It just means that McWilliam wanted dirty pictures of her. He degraded her without her even knowing about it."

"No," said Lynch. "I don't think so. You see, I noticed that there were prints on the glossy surface of the Polaroid. And they didn't match the fingerprints . . . the good set of fingerprints . . . on the car. They were probably off a different person to McWilliam altogether."

"Oh," said Power. "Oh dear . . . he goes down even further in my estimation. So McWilliam went round showing the photographs, bragging about his conquest, bragging about the girl that he could do what he liked with . . . ugh."

"No," said Lynch carefully; aware that Power's feelings were clouding his judgement. "McWilliam wouldn't go to all that trouble to hide his affair away and then brag about her would he? It just doesn't make sense. I don't think McWilliam took the photograph. Someone else took it. Zoë describes times when the door of the bedroom opened . . . and maybe it was McWilliam come to check on her in his cage, but what if it was someone else? She would know the difference if this other person touched her, or if the other person spoke, but otherwise, how was she to know the difference between McWilliam and someone else?"

Lynch's assessment seemed feasible to Power. "She would be drifting in and out of consciousness . . . probably quite disorientated . . ."

"And this person who visited the house when McWilliam left, well, this person who might have come to see Zoë just once or ten times. But this person brought a camera, maybe bought specially for the purpose in Chester, and unwrapped it there and then in the bedroom. The photographs were taken of her as she lay there. She was unaware that this was not Sir Ian, and unaware that she was being recorded in any way."

Power shuddered. "The sun is losing its warmth. Let's go back indoors." Even though it was a summer evening it was growing cool and Power thought he might light a wood fire when he got back home. 'To keep the night at bay,' he thought. They began walking back through the trees to Power's house. "There are two things you haven't mentioned," Power said.

"Yes?"

"I remember Zoë counted the machine noises. There were ten. That means ten photographs. We only have one. Where are the others? I don't suppose you have the answer to that?" Lynch shook his head. "And the house. It was a rented house. Who rented it?"

"That I do know," said Lynch. "The house was rented in the same name as the car. However, there were false references too, and so we see the hand of the fixer at work again."

"The hand, yes. And it's fingerprints too?"

"I've asked for all the family and friends to be fingerprinted," said Lynch matter-of-factly. "Including the children and their mother."

"The mother? Lucinda didn't want her told . . ."

"Do you think we can afford to cut corners this time? This time it has to be right. We don't want another victim to end up as the accused. We'll fingerprint everybody we can. And I'll tell you this, the first person on my list is Michael McWilliam. The only problem is, he has gone missing."

The security lights came on in welcome as they climbed up the gravel drive. Lynch bade his friend good bye on the doorstep. After waving Lynch's latter-day Rover off, Power lit the oak fire in his living room and comforted himself with a warming glass of port. He sank into the deep recesses of his favourite wingback chair and switched on the remainder of the News at Ten. He was surprised to see a piece of footage from earlier in the day. A crowd of reporters were bustling about a tall, well-mannered policeman, who bore more than a passing likeness to Lynch. The caption beneath his close-up confirmed that it was indeed the Superintendent recorded earlier that same day. He was saying: "It seems likely that there will need to be an urgent review of the case against Miss Zoë Allen. I have brought certain facts to the attention of the Crown Prosecution Service today regarding Miss Allen's allegations that she was having an affair with Sir Ian McWilliam in the weeks before his death.

Depending on their decision, we may need to re-open the McWilliam murder enquiry."

The reporters' numerous questions merged into one another, "Is there a suspicion that the IRA had anything to do with . . . is she innocent then? . . . isn't she mad? . . . were they lovers? . . . what about the security implications? . . . any reaction from Government sources?"

Lynch smiled gently, "A further statement will be issued later."

"Will you be in charge of the new investigation?"

"I cannot say," said Lynch, but the smile on his face, and his expert public fronting of the statement indicated to Power that Lynch's command of the new McWilliam investigation was almost guaranteed. Power sipped his port amusedly; Lynch had been able to tell the world but he had been too modest to tell his old friend.

He sighed contentedly and felt his whole body relaxing at last. The comments that Lynch had made earlier about Power and his feelings for Zoë had been direct, uncomfortable, but true. Alone and at the end of the day, Power finally acknowledged to himself that he had been jealous all along. At one time he had wanted Zoë for himself; now he saw the folly of it all. Who was he to judge Zoë Allen? His judgement had been based upon anger and regret that she was not the partner for him. The realisation that he could stop judging Zoë and her relationship with Sir Ian made Power easier in his mind. He could not reverse what they had done together; so why worry? One of his aims had been to see Zoë exonerated. By various means Power had achieved just this aim. This should clear his mind, just as Zoë's love for Sir Ian redeemed her unusual relationship with him. Surely he, Power, could now put his life back on an even keel for hadn't he achieved all he had set out to do?

However, a doubt surfaced in his mind, because there was still unfinished business. The quest would not be over until the true murderer was found and punished and McWilliam's family healed.

A wave of sleep washed over him. Power was wondering what Lucinda was doing at this moment, puzzling where Michael

McWilliam had disappeared to. A second, greater wave of sleep engulfed Power and his cares were washed temporarily away. In his wingback chair, a half-finished glass of port by his side, and in front of the glowing TV screen, Dr Power rested with his head back, gently snoring.

★ ★ ★

Power was dictating a reference for his registrar amongst the debris of a sandwich lunch. The reference, for a Senior Registrar appointment committee, had been on his mind all day. He was trying to formulate a reference that toed the fine line between unconvincing eulogy and damnation by faint praise. Deciding upon a policy of sincerity Power had embarked on the dictation with gusto, but now halfway through he was stuck. He was fishing around in a packet of crisps for a morsel to inspire him when his telephone rang. It was Laura. He was secretly rather pleased to have been interrupted; he enjoyed Laura's company. "Are you busy?" she asked. "I need to talk to you about a letter."

"I'll come and see you out there. Is there any coffee?" He planned on at least ten minutes of gossip to lighten his spirits before a return to his registrar's lengthy *curriculum vitae.*

"No," said Laura hurriedly, to forestall him. "I'll bring the letter in to you now." And fair-haired Laura was in his adjoining room in a trice. She closed the door firmly behind her firm figure.

"What's the matter?" asked Power, having divined that all was not well."

"It's her," said Laura. "She's back to see you."

"Who? The wicked witch of the West?"

"Well . . ." said Laura. "No, it's your friend, Miss McWilliam."

"Oh," said Power slightly relieved. "I wasn't expecting a visit."

"No," said Laura. "It looks like a spur of the moment thing. She's crying. I should think she's finished a whole box of my tissues by now."

"Ah," said Power, as a stopgap, while he tried to think of something more cogent to say.

"Shall I wheel her in?"

"Erm . . ." Power dithered.

Laura took charge. "I'll bring her in then. You can cope, Carl, I know you can." She paused by the door. "Two cups of strong, hot, sweet tea?" Power nodded automatically at the suggestion. Laura smiled. She wondered if Power would ever get round to asking her out. Up to now, she felt that his choice in women had been sorely wanting.

After Laura had closed the door, Power cleared his desk of crisp packets and sandwich crumbs. He stood up as Laura escorted Lucinda into the room. Power put his arm about Lucinda's shoulders (to Laura's unseen disapproval), and guided her to an armchair. He could see that she had been crying, but had made an attempt to disguise the fact. Laura left silently.

"Your secretary is very kind," said Lucinda.

"She's bringing some tea, I hope. I think she said tea anyway. What's wrong?"

Lucinda essayed a smile, but the attempt was without conviction.

"I had a phone call from mother. I've never heard her that way. She . . ." Laura entered, carrying a small tray of biscuits and cups of tea which she placed on the table. She left wordlessly. Lucinda continued, "She heard about the Allen trial being suspended. She bought a newspaper when she was buying food in a supermarket. She read all about the reasons why the trial . . . she heard about the affair. There's a rumour that the girl is pregnant. Mummy couldn't bear it. She just couldn't take that . . ."

Power wasn't going to confirm the pregnancy . . . he felt he couldn't. "How did she sound?"

"Bitter," said Lucinda. "Bitter I hadn't told her. Bitter that it had all got out. She'd tried so hard to keep all of her suspicions at bay. Tried to think the best of him for so many years. Keep his memory alive and . . . well . . . keep her memory of him . . . the way she wanted him when he was alive. Mum sounded so hurt and so sad. I should have told her first. You said that, didn't you? I should have . . ."

"Never mind," said Power. "Don't blame yourself. She knows now. What is she going to do?"

"I told her to come and stay with me. I thought we'd take a holiday. Find somewhere pretty and deserted. But she didn't want to . . . and the detectives and the reporters will be buzzing round us like flies again. I know it. I'm sure I'm being followed by reporters. I think of them listening in to my phone calls . . . and Mummy is on her own. She can't cope. She was crying and she said she'd seen somebody outside the chapel, in the grounds of the Hall. She sounded a bit confused, but she refused to leave the Hall even with this man walking about."

"Can I help?"

"Carl, would you come with me to see her? Perhaps she'd listen to you. She liked you. Perhaps you could persuade her to come home with me?"

Power had been meaning to contact Lady McWilliam again for some time. "Of course," he said. "I'll come along. Do you want to go now?" She nodded gratefully. "Okay,"

"We'll take my car," said Lucinda. "It'll be quicker."

"I think I should drive though," said Power firmly. He believed that those in the grip of strong emotion should not drive. She handed over the keys to her car without protest. Power was somewhat taken aback that she had acquiesced so easily. He had half-intended to drive his own car after her expected refusal to hand over the keys to her powerful Porsche. Now here he was presented with the temptation of driving a fast, new car. He held the keys in the palm of his hand and tried to suppress any anxiety that he might have had about experimenting with a car forty years younger than his own.

"One thing," said Power as he prepared to leave his office. "Where is your brother?"

"Oh, he'd be no good at a thing like this . . . Mother would never take his advice."

"No," said Power. "I meant where is he in the geographical sense?"

"Oh," she understood now. "I thought you meant it should be him . . . I should be asking him for help first before coming to you."

"No," said Power.

"I don't know." Lucinda said. "That's what makes it worse. I don't know where Michael is. I really don't. Sometime he just does this. Goes away for days at a time. He says . . . he has to find himself."

Power wondered whether this was code for a few days' binge of alcohol or drugs, but he couldn't face asking Lucinda at that moment. He merely collected his things together and put his jacket on. "Ready now?" He asked.

Power had not sat behind the wheel in control of such a powerful engine for years. The initial part of their journey was not, therefore, without event. The leaving of the car park was somewhat fraught. Power soon found that the minutest touch on the accelerator could propel the car forwards like a freshly launched rocket. After two miles fitful driving on the A41, Power was keen to cede defeat. Both he and Lucinda were relieved when she resumed her seat at the wheel. Power chuckled at his inability to 'ride the rocket' as he called it and gladly nestled his way back into the passenger seat. Lucinda drove quickly but carefully. She took no risks, for which the generally cautious Dr Power was grateful.

He rootled in his pocket to see if there was a packet of mints. At moments of stress he would often reach for the sweet rations he stored there. Although he searched each and every pocket he could not find even a single stray mint, which might have rolled out of a tube. He did however find a nomad ten-pound note which he gladly returned to his wallet. He toyed with the idea of asking Lucinda to stop at a garage so that he could buy some sweets, but a sense of some foreboding prevented him. He couldn't stop thinking about the lonely widow in the chapel. He turned to look at Lucinda. There was a distinct tension about her mouth. There was a steady determination about her. There was nobility in the arch of her eyebrow and the delicate fineness of her nose. She would be successful, he thought, at whatever she decided to do, unlike her brother, Michael. Lucinda had an inner fire, an inner strength that Michael had never had. He wondered which of her parents she was most like.

"When you were younger," said Power. "Who did you like to spend most of your time with?"

She shot a sideways look at him. "Is that question from a friend or from a doctor?"

"I don't know," said Power. "These days sometimes it's difficult to tell. I want to know more about you, that's all."

"Is that a good sign?"

"I hope so," he said. "But it depends on your point-of-view."

"Oh I don't know," said Lucinda. "It sounds like you're trying to make a diagnosis."

Power wondered about her unease. It reflected how uneasy they both felt. It was as if they were both lost in a fog, waiting for the cloud to lift, so that they could see where they were going. "I don't know," he said. "I'm just interested. Tell me about your mother."

"Why do psychiatrists always concentrate on the mother?" She smiled. "My mother was an orphan," said Lucinda. "I don't think she knew much about love. There were always the things we wanted; food, clothes, toys, books. She never stinted on providing those things, but when you ask about the times we had . . . I can't remember. I remember times with my nanny and some of the au pairs. Since we grew up she said how much she regrets not having been . . . easier with us. I mean she took us on outings – the zoo, the beach, the family holiday . . . but each outing was structured so tightly. There was no time to be spontaneous . . . to run free . . . if I did I just felt guilty. She would look at me so reproachfully. I shouldn't be moving so fast or laughing so loud. I was terrified she would get too embarrassed, grow tired of me and just walk away. I lay awake at night listening to her moving about downstairs, waiting for her to come to bed. Then when she was asleep I would open her bedroom door and tiptoe in to see her – to make sure she was there, that she was asleep . . . that she was breathing. And only then could I get some rest."

"Sounds like you were caring for her rather than the other way round."

Lucinda nodded sadly, but there was something proud in the expression of her face, as if she had done her duty well. "When she held me . . . she held me close you know, but I was never safe . . . you know, sure that she really loved me. She just held me tightly in her arms, but there was no warmth there. It's difficult to explain." They were taking the motorway exit off the M53 for Chester. Lucinda momentarily slowed the car then accelerated into the fast lane. "When I was fourteen I rebelled . . . I fought my way out of her hold as hard as I could. I went down on to the streets of London and I submerged myself in them. I talked to anyone. Everyone. I spent hours in bars, in theatres, in clubs, and in . . ."

"At fourteen?" Power was surprised.

"Men are hopeless at telling what your age really is."

Power wanted to know about the men, but now seemed too early. Perhaps he would never be able to ask that question. Instead he asked, "What did your mother make of all this?"

"She went crazy. She was left to cope with all of it. Dad just wasn't around . . . and I was never where I was meant to be. Instead of being in my bed I was with a gang of boys on the streets. When I came back in she would be waiting, wrapped up in a quilt at the bottom of the stairs. She would slap my face, shout at me for ten minutes and then she would break down and cry. There would be no consoling her. And when Father eventually came back from his travels and from sittings at the House . . . he would play the Grand Inquisitor. Then we would have these silent meals where no one spoke. You could hear him breathing . . . sort of snorting or wheezing . . . and you'd think, 'God, can't you stop that noise?' There was a kind of energy taking over the house. I felt like I was a whirlwind spinning through the family, blasting everything apart . . . whirling from out of the empty desert and sandblasting the cobwebs away. It was as if I was charged with this energy or desire . . . and I was excited because I never knew whether I'd be able to contain it . . . like a horse that's about to run away under you. It felt a bit like gambling. You didn't know whether you'd win or lose, and there was a thrill in the risk of destroying everything. I'd fight with my mother and it felt like I was on a winning streak. I was in charge now. I felt I was in charge of the world. There were no secrets and no taboos any more.

"One day I had this argument with her and I grabbed these scissors and lunged at her with them . . . I was so angry with her . . . as if the anger had become me, taken me over. I missed or maybe I scratched her arm a bit – I don't know. She has never forgiven me. Never. She felt I could have killed her . . . and I suppose that I could have done. I was that angry. I sort of came to my senses after that. I'd nearly lost everything. Things felt as if they had nearly slipped away from me forever. I had to get some kind of control back."

They turned off the motorway and swung around the roundabout that took them on to the A roads that led towards Heaton village and the Hall.

"I dreamt about my brother and my mother last night. They were shouting at each other. I remember that. Shouting about money and love. Love and money. It all seemed the same. They always argue about money. It's always been the same. He's very bad at sorting out his affairs. Always taking out loans. He always owes a lot of money. It's got so that good people, reputable firms, won't lend him anything. He has to go to anyone he can. And then he gets to the stage where he comes home demanding instant help. Most people plan carefully . . . it's not easy to lay your hands on money just like that if it's invested. He had some furious rows with Dad. Mum is rather too soft on him . . . tries to help too often."

"But what happens one day when the cupboard is bare?" asked Power, but he did not expect an answer. "So tell me what happened in the dream?"

"In the dream Mum sat Michael down on a couch in our old living room and then she got her sewing kit out. She threaded this big gold needle with thick black thread. Very quickly... her hand moved like a machine... she sewed his lips together. Then he couldn't shout at her anymore."

Power looked out of the car window. The sky was clouded over and the leaves on the trees were turned about by the blustering wind. The weather was changing. The leaves seemed redder as if the autumn days were stealing into the summer weeks ahead of their time.

"Dreams always mean something," he said. "And they often work at different levels of meaning. It's a disturbing dream. Did it frighten you?"

"Yes," said Lucinda. "It was a different kind of mother. One I'd never seen before. As if she'd suddenly had enough of him, had enough of everything and was at the end of her tether..."

"Umm..." said Power thoughtfully. The dream worried him. And he also felt uneasy because he had up until now avoided confirming that Zoë Allen was pregnant. He didn't want to have to break the bad news that the rumours in the press were true. The tests all confirmed Zoë's story. And furthermore on gynaecological examination the number of weeks' gestation matched the time when Zoë had said Sir Ian was having an affair with her.

The car sped through the gateposts of Heaton Hall, past the deserted Lodge where once Sir Ian's security guards had watched television, and drunk and diced their nights away. Bright green weeds were growing up through the pebbles of the drive. The verges were uncut and through the long grass poked the yellow and white-furred heads of dandelions. The evidence of neglect only added to the desolation of the Hall's ruins. The singed walls of the chapel stood by the charcoaled stumps of timbers and jagged remnants of the Hall's brickwork. Lucinda parked her car by the chapel door and turned off the engine. "Thank you for coming with me. Thank you for listening to me, Carl."

Power got out of the low car and stretched himself slowly. He looked around him at the trees and the wilderness that the garden was fast becoming. It reminded him of the forest of thorns that grew up around the castle where Sleeping Beauty slept her hundred year sleep. Perhaps all Heaton Hall could do was sleep now. Who would build it up again? Neither Michael nor Lucinda appeared to have inherited their ancestors ability to build business empires or had acquired their father's ability to influence people.

"Carl?" She was standing at the chapel's outer door. "You seem far away?"

He smiled and apologised. "I was just wondering if the Hall would ever be re-built."

She opened the door. "Who needs to live in a palace these days?" Power noticed that although the door had been closed to, it had not been locked. He thought to comment upon the fact, but decided to hold his tongue.

The small vestry had been recently used to prepare food. Power was sure he could smell fried bacon and mushrooms. His stomach rumbled in response to the thought of temptation. A small collection of washing-up stood on a table near a small sink. A small Belling electric oven with two pan rings rested on the stone floor near a plug socket. A frying pan lay on the unheated ring. The fat in the pan hot, not yet congealed.

They passed through the Southeast door into the chapel. There was a portable radio on the floor near the doorway. The volume was turned down low, but Power could discern the voices of Radio 4. Next to the radio was a plate of untouched food – mushrooms and bacon, as Power had suspected. But by now the fried food was grown cold.

Lucinda crouched down to turn the radio off. The chapel was silenced, except for one sound; a quiet and rhythmic creaking noise.

Lucinda did not scream. Power saw her face fade and become pale. Her eyes opened saucer-wide. Her lips parted slightly. She sucked in a sharp breath. Then Power himself turned to face what Lucinda had been staring at.

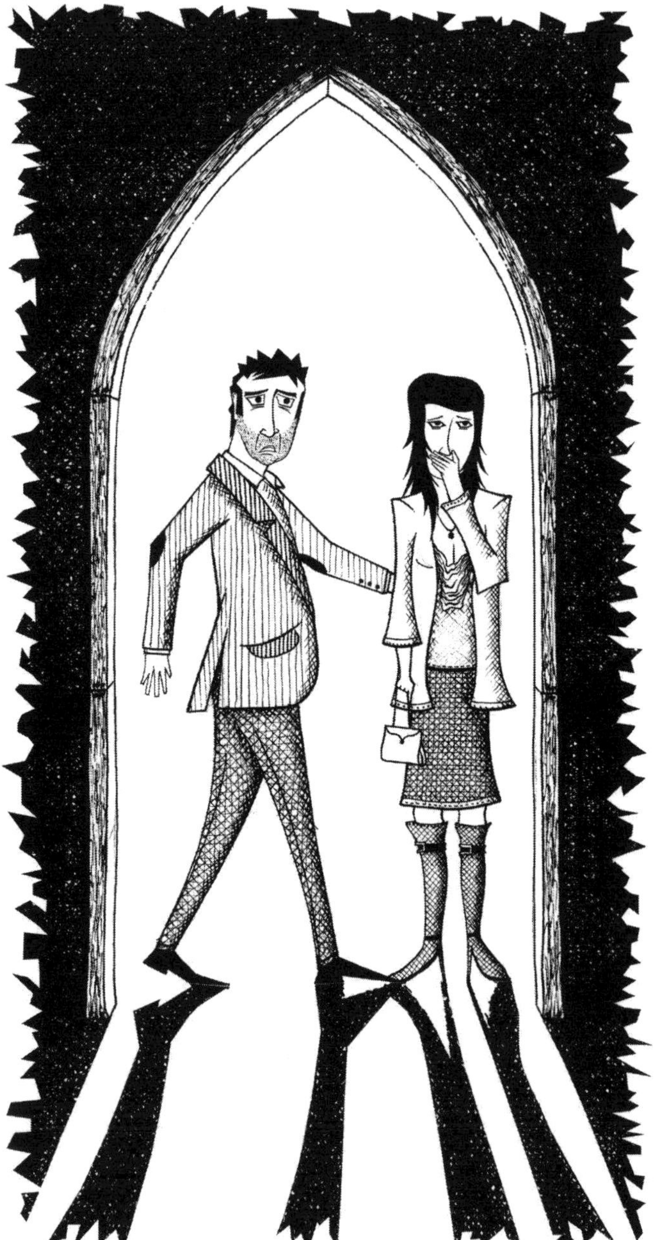

The body of her mother swung gently round-and-round, suspended by its neck. A long rope had been slung over a beam in the roof above and anchored to a fixing on the stone floor, so that there were two taut strands of rope: one leading up to the beam and the other stretched tight from the beam to the swinging body. The face, thought Power, was slightly cyanosed and the hands hung limply by the body's sides. The body looked like a puppet hung from a hook after the puppet master had been called away.

Power's mind went into over-drive. Whilst one part of his attention was focusing on each and every macabre detail, another part was urging him to act and berating him for failing to prevent this death. He ran to the slowly swinging body and forced himself to touch its hand. It felt warm, not cold as he had expected. Lucinda watched from the corner of the chapel. For her, time had slowed to a numbing crawl. Power seemed to move leadenly to her, although he had run to the body. He was shouting something, but she couldn't hear across the distance of her thoughts. It was like watching a silent film. She half-expected subtitles.

She said slowly, almost so that she could herself understand, "She's hung herself."

Power realised that Lucinda wouldn't hear him. After another look at the body and its stretched neck he bent down and struggled with the knot that anchored the rope, but the rope was hauled taut and the knot had been brutally tightened. He ran into the kitchen and brought back a knife to cut, to slash, to hack at the rope. The many twisted fibres of the rope proved to be difficult to sever. When at last the frayed fibres eventually parted company, Power had to drop the knife to the floor with a clatter and grab and snatch at the rope as it slipped away upwards. The rope snatched back pulling his arms upwards. Gaining control over the rope, he gently lowered the puppet body back to the floor, surprised at its dead weight. The body seemed to crumple like a rag doll as it sagged onto the stone floor by the altar. Power felt sick as at last its head audibly bumped onto the stone floor.

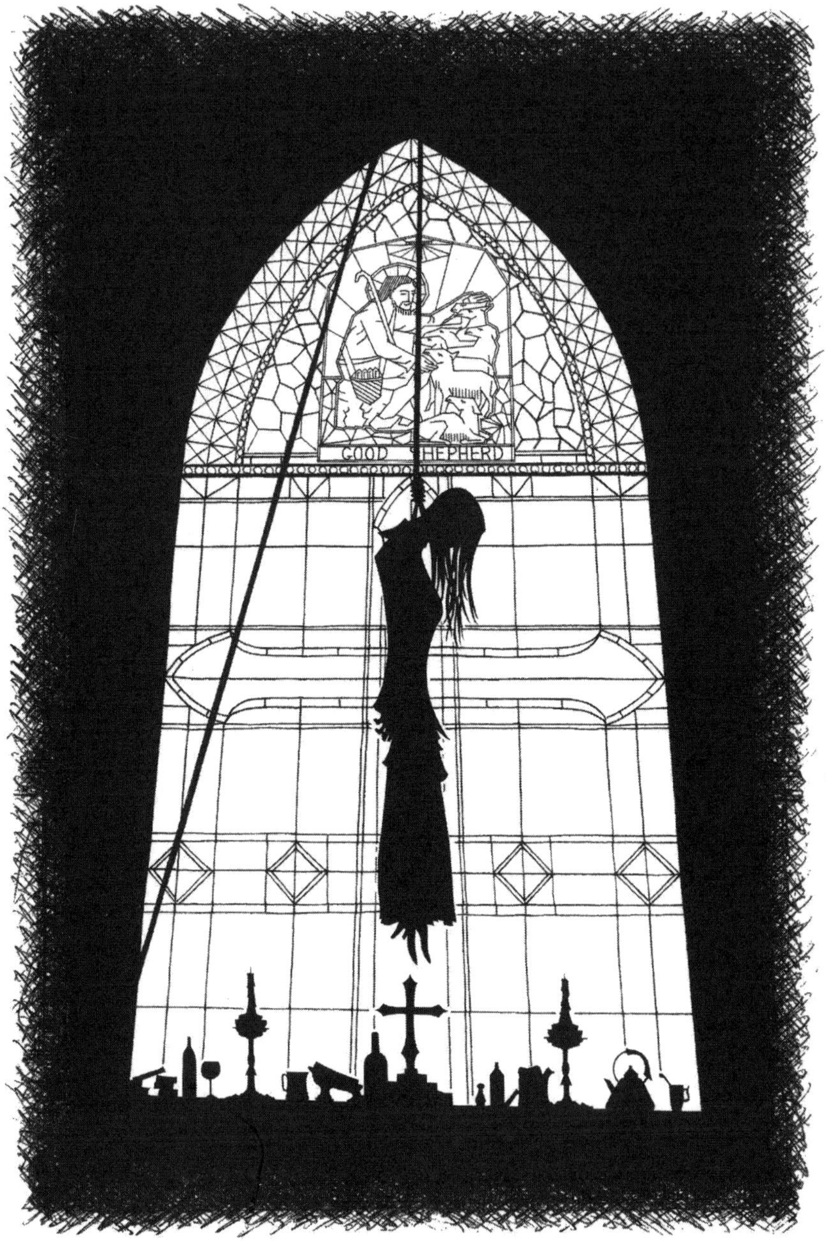
GOOD SHEPHERD

Then he was loosening the rope, untying the noose around her neck. The dilated eyes stared up at him reproachfully.

Mustering his remaining courage and remembering his days as a junior house physician, he began the resuscitation procedure he had learnt on the busy hospital wards. He tilted the head back and then put his warm lips to the cooling, open mouth and blew his life breath into the dead lungs. He pulled away and thumped the thorax, trying to re-start the arrested pulse. He felt for the carotid artery. No response. He began external cardiac massage, pushing down five times on the rib cage; then he breathed in deeply and blew into the mouth again. He didn't feel at all professional. He wanted to retch, but he forced himself on, repeating the same grisly procedure again and again.

He felt he had to go on, even though whenever he checked there was no sign of a returning heartbeat. The pulse was stilled forever now, but he went on in the faint hope of success, denying what he knew to be true.

Power was hit from behind. Two blows. One to his back, an ineffectual glancing blow, and a second strike with a clenched fist against the side of his head. His ear burned under the stinging blow. He turned and half-fell against the corpse. When he looked up Lucinda was standing over him. "Stop it! She's dead. You can't do anything for her. Just stop it!"

He looked back at the body. He took in as if for the first time the fixed, dilated pupils; and the tiny blotchy red haemorrhages, called petechiae, in the skin and corneal tissue. "Yes," he said. "You're right. I should stop ... I just thought ... " He got to his feet, slowly, brokenly. "I thought ..."

"Why did she do it? Why did she? Why did she kill herself?"

Power moved aside and walked to the chapel door. He felt compelled to get out into the open, as if he were suffocating. He had to get out. He walked out into the fresh air, leaving the chapel behind. There was the comfort of the earth outside; no people; no noise except the wind and the rain, which fell against the skin of his face.

He welcomed the cool, wet droplets and breathed the clean air deep inside his aching lungs.

When he felt restored he went back into the chapel. Lucinda McWilliam was bent over her mother placing an awkward hug about the body's still lifeless arms. Power noticed that there was a telephone in the corner of the room. He crossed over to it and began dialling.

Chapter Nine

Lynch looked over at Lucinda McWilliam. She was sitting at the back of the chapel, a blanket around her shoulders. She was staring blankly out into space. "Ask someone to escort her home please," he said to one of the sergeants in the chapel. "She's been here long enough now." He looked at the body near the altar. "In such a place as this..." he said. Then he turned to Power, "I'm sorry I couldn't get here earlier, Carl, I was in London, but I see you made them wait for me. They tell me you wouldn't let them touch anything without me being here."

"If they want to be annoyed, let them be", said Power, without remorse.

Lynch looked up at the rope. It had once hung tautly, now it was simply draped around the chapel roof-beams. He thought it possible that the widow had, by trial and error, managed to throw the end of the rope up and over the beam. Perhaps she had weighted the end to control its trajectory better. Lynch noted the proximity of the body to the altar. Had she perhaps stood on the altar before jumping off into oblivion? The thought of the lonely and bereft Lady McWilliam dying in this way was hard to bear. Lynch pitied her, but could not forgive her desecration of the chapel. "In this place..." he said softly.

Power prepared himself. He had been waiting tensely for Lynch to arrive.

"I didn't want to tell anybody but you. I wanted you to be the first to know. It was difficult to make them understand."

"About the suicide?" Lynch knew his friend must be feeling bad. Power spent his working days as a psychiatrist trying to prevent just this. And Lynch knew that Power had let himself get too involved with the family. The suicide must have shaken him.

"It's not that," said Power. "I . . . I had a look . . . at her neck. At the marks on her neck. I'm not absolutely sure, it's been a long time since I did any pathology, but this is no suicide."

"So that's why you made them wait for me." He looked at Lucinda McWilliam again. A woman police officer had her arm about Lucinda's shoulders and was coaxing her to leave the cold chapel. "Does she know?"

"No," said Power. "I wanted to make sure first before I told her. It's been a long time since medical school."

"Tell me, then, Carl. Why isn't this suicide? Lady McWilliam had been taking her bereavement badly. She'd isolated herself from all her friends and family, was living out here in the ruins of her husband's funeral pyre. She felt guilty that he was dead and that she was still alive. Maybe she was very depressed. Suicide might seem a natural way out to someone in such an unbalanced state. As you know."

"I know," said Power. "I know. At first I felt very guilty. I felt I should have known better. I'd seen she was depressed. I knew the risks and I just kept putting off seeing her again."

"Blaming yourself for any sins of omission?"

Power nodded. He looked down at the corpse and shuddered momentarily. "I want to get out of here now," he said.

"We'll go," said Lynch. He had already planned what orders to give his officers.

After that he would take his friend away from the scene of destruction. He would return alone later. "But while we're both here, Carl, tell me what you know."

Power watched as Lucinda left the chapel. He was waiting to see if she would look at him. She did not, and Power felt guilty that he was not with her, but at that moment he was acutely aware that he could not bear her grief. When he felt stronger perhaps he could face her. He turned to Lynch, "When I took the body down I saw the back of the neck. When someone hangs themselves there are always marks on the neck. Well, the rope in this case had caused marks . . . the marks of the rope fibres . . . in the skin where it had pulled upwards. And there were marks around the back of the neck too, where the rope had been pulled up into an inverted 'V', you know, at the knot. The V in the rope makes a corresponding mark on the neck."

"Yes," said Lynch. "I follow, but . . . "

"Well, there was another mark on the neck. A fine red line that ran all the way around the neck in a complete circle. And where the inverted 'V' of the rope was, the fine red line was even more obvious."

"So?"

"When someone hangs themselves the mark usually follows the noose, so it always produces an inverted 'V' mark at the time of the hanging. Now the fine red line on her isn't consistent with that. It doesn't follow the pattern. It goes straight round the neck. Like a collar, or a necklace. The fine red line was produced earlier than the noose mark. Around the front of the neck the cartilage of the trachea has been broken under the line. Whatever caused the line killed Lady McWilliam . . . something like a tight wire or a tight cord . . . pulled tight to asphyxiate her. Which would fit with the small haemorrhages in the sclera of her eyes."

"You seem to know about these things . . ."

"I once saw a man in a high security hospital who had tried to take his life by using the flex from a hi-fi speaker. The marks were the same. He tried to strangle himself, but was found by the nurses. Just in time. When I saw him he tried to deny that he'd tried to harm himself, but under his collar there was this ugly red line."

"So, Lady McWilliam couldn't very well have strangled herself and then decided to arrange a hanging, could she?" Power shook his head. "I see," said the Superintendent. "So, somebody else came into the widow's sanctuary. And this . . ." He gestured vaguely in the direction of the rope and the body. ". . . is no suicide, but another murder."

"I think so," said Power as Lynch bent low over the body and inspected the neck for himself. "Of course, you would need a Home Office pathologist to do a post-mortem. I may be wrong."

"I'm sure you're right. We'll need to follow the Home Office guidelines, but you've convinced me." Lynch got to his feet. He felt like swearing, but restrained himself as always. "I need to give some orders. Can you wait here a minute?"

Power stepped back from the body and shivered in the coolness of the chapel. "I'll wait outside for you," he said, and left the way Lucinda had done, through the vestry and out into the open again. The drive was, by now, clogged with police cars and vans. Disembodied police voices crackled on police radios, and there was an air of intense activity, of something new just begun. White-suited scene of crime officers were climbing out of van doors, clutching clipboards and tape. Carl Power ached to get away from the Hall whilst Lynch spoke to his junior officers. His stomach let out a squealing rumble of hunger and Power suddenly realised that he was famished. In this place of death and destruction his body seemed anxious to remind him that he was alive, quick and needy.

Lynch had sensed Power's need to change scene, and after he had made temporary arrangements with his officers, spoken to the Assistant Chief Constable on a car phone and argued for more resources for the widening investigation, he joined his friend outside. "Come on," he said. "Let's get you away from here. You look like you could do with something to cheer you up. Are you hungry?"

"Yes," said Power. "How did you guess?"

"Not difficult," said Lynch. "Years of experience have taught me that these things only serve to make some people very hungry. And I know you inside out, Power." Lynch led Power to his own car. "Come on, I'll drive."

"It's strange," said Power as he settled into the passenger seat with some relief at the prospect of getting away from Heaton Hall. "You'd think it'd take your appetite away."

"Sometimes," said Lynch. "But knowing how you like your food

..." It felt good to Power to be understood. Lynch drove swiftly and carefully through the village and out onto the main roads. He sought out the nearest cafe with a keen sense of determination. It turned out to be a garish red brick single storey Little Chef. They breezed in and took a non-smoking table by the window. "Comfort food is what we want," said Lynch, glancing down the large laminated plastic menu at the lurid photographs of grilled meals that had been christened with appetizing clean-sounding names by the copywriters. He ordered pots of tea and gammon platters for them both, and for Power a Jubilee Pancake (a concoction of pancake, cherries and ice cream) – comfort food indeed.

Power drank the hot, sweet tea and felt his body coming back to life. He was, by now, afflicted by a voracious appetite. "Better than brandy," he said. "Hot, sweet tea – it's not a myth. It really does help." He let out a sigh of relief. "It's so good to get warm. There was such a cold feeling in the chapel . . ."

The food arrived, sizzling from the grill. Power waited patiently, and without embarrassment whilst Lynch closed his eyes and said grace. The waitresses and other customers looked at the praying man with curiosity. Such behaviour was unusual in this plastic place. As Lynch murmured his 'Amen' Power dived into the food, with the words "Just what the doctor ordered."

Lynch looked around and tried to judge whether the other diners were sufficiently far away so that they could not hear their conversation. Although they had stared at him in prayer the other diners were unwilling to look Lynch in the eye. He judged it safe to proceed with any conversation. "Zoë was released this afternoon, Carl. Did you know that?"

"I was expecting her release, but not today."

"Yes, in front of all the television cameras and the microphones."

"She could hardly have made it to Heaton Hall with the press on her tail, could she?" asked Power as he cut into the pink gammon steak.

"It would be difficult," said Lynch. "But then . . . what happened this afternoon . . . if you're thinking whether anybody suspects Zoë, well . . . she wouldn't have the strength would she? I mean to haul the body up. To make it look like a hanging. Even though Lady McWilliam was as light as a sparrow, it would take strength, agility, and youth. Zoë has the youth, but not the strength. Not on her own."

"And there should have been people round her since her release," said Power. "There must be people round her, full time, mustn't there?"

"There was a safe house booked for a few days, to give her some kind of buffer, but soon enough she'll have to try and sort out her own life. Try and pick up the pieces. This murder won't make that any easier."

Power shook some salt over the French fries and began to crunch them thoughtfully. He conjured up the image he had of her, elegant, slim and vulnerable. He had it in mind to seek her out. Perhaps it would be for the best if he did not. He had helped her. He had facilitated her release. He had almost certainly prevented her false conviction. But it would be unfair to impose himself on her. No, he would not seek her out. "It's an unfortunate coincidence, though," said Power. "That she should be released on the same day as Sir Ian's widow is killed."

Lynch's mind was whirling through all the things that he needed to do. Here he was in a roadside cafe, with an old friend, when there was the task force to co-ordinate and a press conference to face. And yet he knew that this doctor was somehow central to the solution of everything. Power had helped him in the past. Could Power help now? Lynch felt confused. The events of this afternoon had thrown him off balance. Perhaps he needed this time out in a plastic world of comfort food for himself as much as Power needed ministering to.

He put his cup down, suddenly aware of his own outraged feelings. "People don't believe anymore," he said bitterly. "They don't believe in God, in Jesus, in anything. They have no more hope of salvation than a hope of winning the football pools, and given the choice they would prefer to take the money and take their chances on the Devil. Can't they see the hand of the devil everywhere in this modern world? Can't they see it? Aren't they afraid?" Power looked up, slightly puzzled by Lynch's outburst. He wondered what the detective could have been thinking of. Lynch had been seething gently ever since the discovery of Lady McWilliam's body. "In a holy place," he muttered. "In the sanctuary of God's house. How could anyone do this to a widow in such a place?"

"I doubt that the fact it was a chapel was the first thing on the murderer's mind," said Power. "Whatever emotion that drove the murderer on was probably enough to blot out almost everything. When you talk to murderers afterwards . . . they seem to remember very little except this blinding rage . . . as if they were someone else. And, to them, sometimes it feels as if it was someone else. It takes a long time for them to come to terms with what they've done. Sometimes they can't accept they did anything for many years. I mean there are parts of ourselves which we don't always own. The dark thoughts we get in the darkest night. How do we fuse them with the light of day? The answer is that we usually don't. The brain holds both sets of thoughts apart. Like two computers each working on their own, completely dissociated from one another. But sometimes the communications break through. The murderer will get flashes of what he has done, details he thought he had forgotten long ago come back . . ."

". . . to haunt him?" said Lynch. "You make it sound like some people have two separate lives . . . it makes me think of Sir Ian McWilliam. He had the public face of the ideal family man and the senior statesman. And he hid a very different private face . . . an abuser, a liar, a cheat. Like two different men. Strange that murderers should think in the same dissociated way."

"Politicians are creative psychopaths. They have to split their thoughts in order to survive. So many faces for so many people. Oh, but don't we all do it?" said Power. Lynch raised his eyebrows in surprise at being lumped in with McWilliam and his murderer.

Power went on, "Who can say that they are content with everything they have said or done or thought, so content they wouldn't mind their whole being exposed?"

"I suppose it would be difficult for anyone to be so free of guilt," conceded Lynch. "But wouldn't it be a joy to be so . . . free, don't you think so?" He smiled at the thought. "Shall I tell you of my trip today? I went to see some very secret people. People who would never like any things they say exposed to anyone . . . people who talk in unattributable riddles." Power nodded and Lynch continued. "I sent myself down to London . . . to a building on the Thames . . . where some very secret people told me all they knew about Sir Ian. I wanted to make sure what we were dealing with. I'm sure the thought might have crossed your mind that, er . . . well, perhaps Sir Ian was treading on too many people's toes? That perhaps there was a group of people that would have benefited by his death?"

"You're not being any clearer," complained Power.

"How can I put it? Sir Ian was becoming a liability to his party. No matter how discreet he was trying to be, the secret services had plenty of files on his links with fascist groups in East Germany and France. And whereas the organisations were open enough in Europe, the links were secret here in the UK, because they would have been embarrassing to Sir Ian and his party. You can see how dangerous it would be if a Government with a small majority lost support because of a minister's strange bed-fellows – in both senses of the word. I wanted some assurances that he wasn't . . . erm . . . that he wasn't assassinated. Like Kennedy was when he offended one too many . . . I was checking out the conspiracy theory."

"And did you get any reassurances, from these very secret people?"

"As much as they could reassure anyone. It seems the Establishment genuinely believed Zoë Allen was the murderer. Now that she seems unlikely to be the guilty party . . . they've reviewed their evidence, their secret evidence, and they assured me that, in their opinion, 'the murder was unlikely to have been a covert operation by legitimate or terrorist bodies.' And so... we're thrown back on our own resources. The murderer's unseen hand is not moved by the IRA or MI5 or any other secret society. We're looking for a private individual or individuals. Just as before..."

"So the trip to London yielded no positive clues?"

"I think it was an important negative, don't you? And these secret ladies and gentlemen promised to send on any information they could. After all they are the protectors of the State. Most of the time anyway. I was asking them about McWilliam. It seems he kept himself a very private person. He revealed a little to each person, like each person he knew had a piece of the jigsaw."

"And some people," said Power. "Had nicer pieces than others. Some people had pieces of sunny blue heavens, and others had pieces of the dark night sky."

"Poetic," said Lynch as he poured himself another cup of strong tea. "I'd like to find someone who had seen the whole jigsaw."

"Maybe there was only Lady McWilliam. Perhaps that's why someone killed her."

"You're suggesting that she knew more than she ever told us?" Power nodded. "Maybe," said Lynch. "But would she have pressed the case against Zoë Allen, released all those letters if she'd known where it was all going to lead? If she had known of Sir Ian's true involvement with Zoë Allen... then would she have taken the risk of it becoming public knowledge and gone along with everything without a word. We thought before that she only ever saw the face that Sir Ian wanted her to see. And nothing has really changed."

"So why kill her?"

"I don't know," said Lynch. The waitress cleared their main course plates away and returned with a large pancake, dusted with sugar, for the Doctor. "But someone must know more about Sir Ian"

"When I went to see the Party agent, Alan Jackson... the one that's standing in the by-election next month..."

"We interviewed him," said Lynch. "He didn't strike me as a likely murderer, even though he clearly hated McWilliam. He has his sights set on starting his career in Her Majesty's Government, not ending it in Her Majesty's nick."

"No . . . I don't think he had any major role in all this . . . it was just that he mentioned someone, a private secretary or something who had to retire through ill-health. Now what was his name? He was close to McWilliam. Sounded more like a friend than a civil servant . . . his name was something like Tuke. Something like that."

"He will have been interviewed," said Lynch, without any enthusiasm.

"Perhaps if he knew Sir Ian better than we thought," suggested Power. Lynch shook his head. A day spent trying to get any useful information out of the secret service had undermined his confidence in civil servants as conduits of help or knowledge. It had been so difficult pinning them down on anything. This Tuke would be another blind alley, Lynch was sure of that. "Well, said Power. "Perhaps I could go and see him, if you won't."

"Feel free," said Lynch. "I can get you the address. But we've interviewed all these types before . . ."

Power sighed. His appetite was beginning to flag. Finishing the pancake seemed an uphill task. "Okay . . . I'll take the address and think about it. But what now then? I mean where do we go from here?"

"There will be the usual procedures in any murder enquiry . . . an autopsy . . . the scene of crime forensic investigation . . . a suspect list and statements taken from each of them. Where were they when Lady McWilliam died? Most important of all, where was Michael McWilliam? And since we can't contact him he has to be our prime suspect. Don't you think?"

"Before we got here, Lucinda was telling me about her brother's debts."

"Hmmm," said Lynch. "Of course his absence could mean something else . . . something entirely innocent, but he's our prime suspect. He hated his parents. He hates himself enough to pump drugs into himself and he covets his parents' wealth. He wants more than the world can ever give him. Maybe he had one last, cataclysmic argument with first his father and then his mother. Perhaps both had to die when finally they became exhausted by his demands. Perhaps when they said their final 'No' to him he just decided they were no use to him anymore. Not alive anyway. They were worth more to him dead, and so perhaps he killed them both, setting a fire under his sleeping father and faking his widowed mother's suicide. The arrest of Zoë Allen must have been a godsend to him. Perhaps he directed the police to those letters of hers. I'll have to check who prompted the police to look at all the letters. Perhaps he planted the fire-making equipment in Zoë's cottage. He could have got away with his father's murder if Zoë had been convicted. And as for the suicide of his mother, it would have seemed logical. She'd been acting strangely, hiding away in the ruins of the Hall. On her own. You said she was depressed."

"When I saw her this afternoon I felt so guilty. It was like being punched in the stomach... you know, winded. I felt I was to blame. That I hadn't cared enough to treat her depression."

"Did you ever mention to Lucinda that you were worried about her mother's state of mind?"

"I made it clear that she was depressed, but not more than that."

"And Michael? Did he know you thought she was depressed; that you were worried about her as a suicide risk?" Power went pale. He had felt almost relieved that Lady McWilliam's death had not been a preventable suicide. He had been comforting himself with the thought that he had not been to blame for her death. Now here was Lynch putting his guilt on trial again. Had Michael McWilliam heard Power talking about his concerns about Lady McWilliam's mental health, or had Lucinda spoken to him about it? Either way, had Power inadvertently suggested to the murderer that they should fake Lady McWilliam's suicide?

"Oh God," sighed Power. "I don't know, maybe."

Lynch's eyebrows flickered briefly at the casual way Power had mentioned his God, but he said nothing. "Well anyway," said Lynch remorselessly. "There might be another theory to explain Michael McWilliam's absence."

"Like what?"

"He might not be the murderer, of course. And unless we find him first he might just turn out to be the murderer's next victim."

Chapter Ten

There had been a terse phone call from her. She had meant it to be a brittle leave-taking with just a mixture of apology and anger. She had wanted to keep the conversation brief and to avoid breaking into tears. Sensing that the conversation might be ended at any moment Power asked her for her whereabouts and extracted a promise to stay there until he arrived.

Lucinda had been staying at her brother's house in Lymm. Michael's house had once been a doctor's home and surgery in the nineteen-thirties. Power parked his Rover in the driveway and noticed that all the curtains were drawn tightly shut. The arched front door was open and Lucinda was standing there, dressed soberly in well-made, but sombre, fawn and olive clothing by Ralph Lauren. She was pale and the tears she had shed before he arrived reddened her eyes. He bent to hug and kiss her. She let him do so, but he felt a tension in her body and saw reluctance in her smile. "I'm sorry," he said.

"For what?" said Lucinda, but Power didn't know quite what she meant. "You'd better come in," she said. Power could detect no alcohol on her breath. He had been worried that she would seek solace in the bottle. She went on, "I'm beginning to think there are journalists hiding in the bushes and swinging from the trees." Power looked around. He could see no-one. "They've been phoning all morning," she explained.

He followed her inside and took in the atmosphere of the house. The air smelt close and smoky-sweet. He listened to the sounds of the house, and besides the gurgling of a water cistern upstairs, there was no other sound besides their own breathing. There was no noise that might betray Lucinda's brother. "You'd better go into the front room. I'll get some coffee." She left him to wander into the darkened lounge. He switched the lights on.

In the corner of the room was a telephone answering machine. It silently added another call to its collection of three. Power wondered whether these were indeed journalists hunting after some reaction to the double tragedy of Sir Ian and Lady McWilliams' deaths, or whether one of them might be a call from Michael. Was the line secure now? Perhaps Michael McWilliam would not phone his sister because he suspected that the police would have the line tapped. Power looked around the rest of the room which was in considerable disarray. A heavy and rather ancient suite bought from a junk-yard sat in the middle of the room. It smelled fusty and was damp to the touch. The moquette was badly worn and torn in places. A potted plant had lived and died in an earthenware pot by the curtained window. There was pile of partially opened and unopened bills on the coffee table. A pile of books, some of them rare first editions and some of them torn comic books, sat near the wall where once a book shelf had been. Power picked one up, a first edition of Gray's *Elegy Written in a Country Churchyard*. Power could see grooved marks in the carpet pile where once the shelves had stood. Perhaps the original furnishings had had to be sold to repay debts? If so, had Michael McWilliam decided to keep the valuable first editions through sentiment, or because he was ignorant of their true value? Power imagined that Michael had bought the old suite as a replacement for something pawned or repossessed. He wandered over to the coffee table. There were some opened bills on it. They were printed in red. There was ample evidence here of Michael McWilliam's singular lack of talent in managing money. But where was he?

When Lucinda entered with a tray of coffee, Power was pleased to notice that it was good, heavily aromatic, fresh coffee. There were fresh butter biscuits too. The combination could almost banish the squalor of the house. "I'm sorry about the place," she said. "I was only staying here while I was seeing Mummy... I tried to clear it up, but he's got it into such a state. You should see the kitchen. I had to buy industrial strength cleaners. Don't worry," she added. "All this is fresh stuff," she pointed to the tray of coffee. "I bought it myself."

"I didn't realise that Michael lived life so close to the brink."

"Believe me, this is all a step up from where he has been in the past."

"How large are his debts?"

She looked at Power suspiciously. "I... I can't say exactly." Power wondered if it was because she didn't know or because she didn't want to say. "But these," she said pointing to the utility bills on the table. "These are the small fry. There are nastier people involved. There have been some unpleasant phone calls. From the people who lent him money. I shouldn't say too much, should I?"

Power picked up a mug of coffee. He eschewed the chance to sit on the settee, and with the pair of them standing on ceremony the atmosphere between them could hardly relax. Power had noted the distrust in her voice. "Don't you trust me?" he asked mournfully.

"Carl... who can I trust? I don't really know. The world doesn't feel a very stable place. You're too close to that policeman, Lynch. I feel that anything I say could go back to him."

"You mean about your brother?"

"Yes. Exactly."

"Have you seen him?"

"He won't come here. Not while they're looking for him."

"Isn't he courting police suspicion? By hiding away doesn't he make things worse?"

"You saw what happened to Zoë Allen. You were always concerned about her, weren't you? They crucified her when she was innocent, they'd crucify Michael just as easily. He won't come out of hiding until they've caught who really... who really... I'm sorry." She moved over to the window and stood staring out into the garden, fighting back her tears. "He's all I've got left," she said. "And I won't give him up."

"You're sure he's innocent?"

"Of course I am! I have to be. He's my brother, Carl."

Power wondered if Michael McWilliam might be cynically using his sister's loyalty. Certainly Michael had systematically and cynically sucked all the money he could from his parents to feed his addictions and his chaotic life. He had used his parents when they were alive. He had jeopardised his father's career. Sir Ian, despite his many faults had seen fit to support his son by using all the influence he could muster, and had thereby put himself in danger. But if Michael had found his parents resisting him . . . would his rage have overwhelmed him? What would Michael do if his parents ceased to be of use to him? What if Michael had sucked his parents dry and then spat them out like useless pips? Michael would have been without a reason to keep them alive. Now after years of frustration, he could let himself go and unleash his fury. Power's mind forged ahead. Sir Ian might have been confronted in the Heaton Hall dining room by his son, a final row after a fruitless argument about money. Seething with humiliated rage and conscious of the value of his father's will, might not Michael have returned later when his father was asleep. In the darkness Michael could have soaked the library books in petrol and then climbed the stairs to his father's bedroom. There he could pour more petrol on the landing carpet. Would he have lit the upstairs fire first? And after he had set the fire, perhaps he had lingered in the wood to watch the flames gathering force. Maybe he had experienced the thrill of ultimate domination over his father as the funeral pyre of Heaton Hall exploded into the night sky.

Weeks later he had confronted his mother, the main beneficiary of the will, in the same way as he had confronted his father. Maybe she had resisted his demands too, or since Zoë's innocence had been established, perhaps now Lady McWilliam had guessed that Michael had orchestrated her husband's death. She might have confronted him with his guilt. She could have found some evidence, and Michael could have realised, perhaps with a kind of sorrow, that she had to die too.

Was it just an absurd idea of Power's? How could a son do these things to his parents? Power remembered a report he had once written on a patient from a special hospital. The man had been a physics undergraduate, a brilliant young man at Cambridge. At his work he had achieved the highest grades in his college for a decade, but he had been curiously aloof. His name had been Cole. He had not joined in with the parties on his staircase. He had carefully avoided talking to his fellow students on the very same staircase. He tended to eat on his own at table, placing himself far away from the others in the refectory and judging his entry to lectures to the time when he would meet least people. He performed well in tutorials, but tended to out-perform his fellow students in a dismissive and contemptuous way. His tutors found him a challenge, for he often knew the subjects discussed, better than they. They nick-named him 'The Genius', but they grudgingly meant it. Cole spent most of his time closeted in his room, emerging only for food, or to scurry to the quiet of a room in the library.

Cole had never been seen to show any emotion, besides an unpleasant sneering contempt for brains less good than he. He could see no merit in Music or the Arts, or value in friendship. There had never been a girlfriend. His desires were secret ones, and acted out in private.

The only emotional outburst came one night when he was on the phone on the stairwell. The students unfortunate enough to be in the nearby rooms were both disturbed and surprised to hear him shouting, even ranting, in a most uncontrolled way. At last he slammed the receiver down, and returned to his room. The door closed and no more was seen of him at the College. He shut the door on the world and began planning what to do with parents he felt had never really cared for him. He emerged only once more to go into the centre of Cambridge, only to return to the seclusion of his room. Two nights later in the early hours of the morning, he emerged from his study. The night was quiet, and there was no-one about. He was adept at avoiding people, and the porters never saw him crossing the quad under the light of a full moon. He had to take a taxi to the village near his parents. The taxi-driver remembered him, even though Cole took great care to get the driver to stop several miles away from his parents' cottage. The taxi driver had remembered the fare, and remembered the heavy bag that Cole had been carrying.

Cole had walked up to the front door of the cottage and in the moonlight he had let himself in to the hallway. As he climbed the stairs Cole was careful to make no noise. He went first to his father's room. He paused outside to open his bag. Taking the heavy felling axe out, he pushed open the bedroom door and smashed his father's skull with a single blow. As the pillow soaked up the dark cerebral blood, Cole took out a knife and stabbed his father's chest over and over again. Disturbed by the sound of this frenzy his mother woke and nervously called out for her husband. 'It's only me,' Cole had reassured her, before taking the axe next door to use in his mother's room. After stabbing her body numerous times, Cole had stripped himself naked, showered, and with the moisture still beading his bare skin, had gone downstairs to make a cup of tea for himself. He watched an hour's worth of night-time television and then gathered together the axe and the knife. He packed a suitcase of his favourite clothes from his old bedroom, and gently laid his old threadbare teddy bear on the top of the clothes before closing the lid. Downstairs he switched on an electric fire in the lounge, then soaked one of his mother's dresses in methylated spirits before throwing it over the electric fire. On the Monday after the fire he walked into a Cambridge police station and challenged them to prove he was guilty. Power had written in his report that Cole was 'utterly without remorse, and so unable to judge personal relationships that he is and will continue to be most dangerous'. Power had felt that this flawed genius had been one of the most dangerous men he had ever met. The prosecution had asked Power whether he felt, as a psychiatrist, that the full moon had had an influence over Cole. It had been an attempt to discredit him. 'You mean do I think he's a lunatic?' Power had asked. The barrister affected intense interest. 'No, he is a psychopath, a very dangerous psychopath.' At that moment, Cole who had been sitting all this time in the dock, avoiding everybody's eyes, suddenly looked up. His cold eyes met Power's and held his gaze across the packed courtroom.

"Do you know his heart, Doctor?" The barrister had asked, but Power had barely heard him, the gaze from Cole's eyes was so full of hatred.

Power was wondering if Michael was the same as or worse than Cole? Power felt suddenly tired, as if the burden of his knowledge of men's inner world had acutely overwhelmed him.

He looked over at Lucinda. She was still as brittle as thin ice stretched over cold, dark water. Once upon a time it might have been different between them, but now she was rendered untouchable by her grief and her silent rage.

"What now?" she asked. There were layers to the question Power chose to ignore.

"I have to interview someone else," said Power.

"Who? Who is there left to interview? Who else matters anymore?"

"A friend of your father."

"There were no real friends, I told you. Only contacts. People to be used. People owed and owing favours. No friends like you or I might like and love . . . Bitterness oozed out of her like dark, heavy blood.

"This was a close colleague," said Power. "A contemporary. Jacob Tuke. His private secretary . . ."

Lucinda looked quizzically at Power. "You haven't done your research," she said. "Jacob is no contemporary. My father was in his sixties. Tuke was at least thirty years his junior. A bright, young thing."

"But he had a senior post in the Ministry."

"Yes, Tuke was . . . is . . . a brilliant young man. They fast-tracked him through the civil service. He found promotion through the grades as easy as a red-hot knife moving through butter. I often wondered how or why he was so brilliant. He burned very brightly . . . and maybe too fast as well. Multiple sclerosis started on him in his twenties and very soon he was in a wheelchair. He had to retire on health grounds. All of a sudden he wanted out and that was it. I remember him though, when he was with Dad at the Ministry. Always running about, always around Dad, trying to please, pulling out the best ideas. He was imaginative in policy terms. He got Dad out of some difficult corners with the press. He was a fixer in the best sense of the word."

"But?"

". . . but . . . I didn't like him."

"Do you know why?" asked Power.

"He was like a rival I suppose. Yes, a rival. He felt like a brother or something. We competed for Dad's time. I mean he was like a younger brother, who kept pulling off these wonderful tricks. He could make my father laugh with his brilliant ideas."

"So they were close then. Closer than you liked?"

"I know this is horrid of me, but I remember being pleased when I heard he was going. That he wouldn't be around anymore. I was almost glad he'd got multiple sclerosis. That he would soon be gone. Isn't that dreadful? And I was disappointed when I heard he was going to settle in North Wales. I thought; 'that's not far enough away, he wants to stay close to Dad'. I resented Jacob. I hadn't got rid of him after all. But we didn't see much of him. He was too ill. He exists there even now in splendid isolation, I believe, with only his nurse for company. I'm not being fair. I could have liked him. There was something very pleasing about him. Very charming, but maybe too much so. You know what I mean? Erring towards being a Uriah Heep. Ingratiating. And my father was too kind to him. They first met when my father taught in Cambridge as an honorary tutor. Tuke was one of his protégés from that time."

"I didn't know your father was anything to do with a University?"

"Oh yes. These contacts. You keep them all your days, especially politicians. They keep up with the journalists they were at University with. They keep up with the academics who taught them. These people... contacts... were always floating in and out of our London house. When I was little I remember he would have his tutorial students to stay. Entertain them in the grand manner. Our dinner-table was always full. Politicians have to entertain all sorts of media people and business men. There were some ferociously right-wing academics that Dad used to butter up. Tuke enjoyed those evenings when he was a student. He'd come with his borrowed tuxedo and his borrowed bow tie. He'd sit by my father's right hand and lap up these crazy ideas like some toy dog. You didn't know if he really agreed with them, but he played with the ideas, though, and improved them for my father's use. There were dinners when these right-wingers would meet and there would be dinners when the mainstream great and the good would meet. Daddy kept them separate, of course, but Tuke could go anywhere he pleased."

"You didn't like him, did you?"

"I try to forget him as much as I can," she said. "His rapid rise in the civil service was because of Dad. But I have to admit Tuke was clever, he'd have got there himself, only it would have taken more time. But then again, with the multiple sclerosis, time wasn't something Jacob had much of."

"He's an important figure then. Someone I should see."

She looked at Power out of the corner of her eye. "What good will it do? He's a cripple in a wheelchair. His nurse has to put him on the toilet. He can't even stand. His speech is slurred. Hardly understandable. He can't do anything."

"He might know something."

"It would be from a while ago. He'd have lost touch over the last few years," she said.

"It sounds as if you don't want me to see him."

"Old jealousies never die," she said. "The thought of him getting any attention, from anyone I know or care about upsets me."

Power thought about what she had just said. He stood up slowly, thinking what to say, but ready to go.

"You're off then," she said in a clipped tone, but stopped herself from saying something worse.

"Yes," said Power, "I'm wondering, whether . . . when you said just now . . . about people you care about. When things are easier perhaps we . . ."

"Things . . . " she said softly, looking away from him. She stood aside so that he could leave. "Things, Carl?" She wondered about all the things he might mean. He said some more words. Expressions of hope, of concern. He was worried about her brother. He even thought Michael might be a danger to her. His awkward words faltered and she was left to say, lamely, "You know where I am." There was a long silence filled with their unspoken words, and then Power left, filled with uncertainty and a longing that he knew would last for a long time. He didn't look back at the house as he walked to the car. He heard the front door closing softly behind him.

Although Mrs Lynch believed in God she did not share her husband's fervour for all things religious. On a Sunday morning she liked nothing better than to curl up in her bed with the papers and a tray of tea and toast. Lynch would rise early. He would make his wife's breakfast and dutifully carry it upstairs with the Sunday newspapers tucked under his arm. Having done this ritual penance he was allowed to escape to the parish church for Holy Communion. On this particular Sunday he had made an extra special breakfast because he planned to prolong his absence from home. He was having lunch with Power. Today therefore, his wife's breakfast tray also carried a small vase of flowers and a cooked breakfast.

After the church service Lynch drove his way through the sunny lanes of Cheshire to Power's house in Alderley Edge. Power had made a simple enough lunch: honey-roast ham, crisp roast potatoes, and succulent broad beans served with chilled Chablis. After lunch they walked on the sandstone plateau behind the house and sat in the sun by the mouth of the old Roman mines.

"So," said Lynch. "She wouldn't tell you where her brother was?"

Power shook his head. "I had the feeling he was upstairs, listening to us talking in the living room below."

"He couldn't have been," said Lynch. "I'll tell you for why. His credit card has been used to buy food in Amsterdam in the last few days. Unless the card has been stolen, of course. That's a possibility. But then again the card hasn't been reported stolen. So . . . he's probably abroad. But anyway he's staying well away from us. Unless he has a large supply of cash, he'll use his card again before long and then we'll have another trace on him."

"If Michael murdered his father, then he must have made it look like Zoë was guilty. He must have planted the petrol cans in her house. He must have known about his father's relationship with her, he must have brought the letters to the police's attention. He must have manipulated everything to make it seem like Zoë killed his father.

"I wonder how much Michael knew about his father's relationship with her. If he had evidence that he was having an affair with her . . . he could have blackmailed his father. That would have solved his money problems. Michael is riddled with debt."

"Exactly," said Lynch, whose thought processes had got there long before Power. "And the evidence he used to blackmail his father might have included her letters to Sir Ian. Perhaps he'd got hold of those. But there might have been something else, some other proof he was using . . ." Lynch thought about the matter of proof. "We need to search his house," he said. "And search it quickly too."

"What for?" asked Power.

"Michael wouldn't take any evidence with him in case he was stopped by us. He wouldn't want any links to a motive like blackmail would he? He must have hidden any evidence somewhere. And the house seems the most likely. And by evidence I mean letters . . . and photographs."

"I don't understand," said Power who had partially blanked out the memory of the photographs.

"The Polaroids," said Lynch. Power suddenly remembered the

blurred photograph of Zoë's splayed, naked body. The image had upset him and he had tried to forget. "We imagined that Sir Ian might have taken the photographs for his own satisfaction. What if they fell into Michael's hands?"

"How do we know there were others? Perhaps Sir Ian just had the one, kept in the drawer in the rented house. And what do they prove? Just pictures of a naked body."

"No," said Lynch. "But Sir Ian would. And that's where the power of the photo lies. Because Sir Ian knows who the photograph is of. With the letters and the photographs Michael had all the power he needed to make his hated father do whatever he wanted. And when his father was dead, the photos could be used on his mother to the same effect."

"Could any son be so cruel?" Power looked doubtful, but he knew that both of them had met men crueller still (and they had all been sons too).

"I need to organise the search," said Lynch, suddenly standing up. "That sister of his is in the house. She could be disposing of the evidence right now."

"Oh," said Power. "I'm sure not." Lynch began to stride away through the trees towards Power's house and his car. Power had no option but to follow. He protested as they hurried. "But Lucinda..."

"She could be just as guilty as him. She'd help him rather than give him up. You know that. You can't trust anyone in an investigation." He paused in his stride for a moment. "The McWilliam family had a flat in Knightsbridge on Cadogan Road. I'll need to arrange a search there too." He began sailing onwards again with Power in tow. "There must be at least nine other photographs floating about. They must be somewhere." Power still found it difficult to accept that the girl on the Polaroid was the one he had interviewed and found so pleasantly attractive. Why did it matter so much to him? Was it that he had simply misjudged her? Was he angry at her, or angry at Sir Ian's abuse of her dependency, or angry at himself for finding her attractive? He tramped along behind Lynch feeling dejected. The fact that it was turning to Autumn and that it was also beginning to rain did not help matters.

Back at the house, Power watched as Lynch unlocked his car. Power wanted to talk about something else, but with Lynch suddenly spurred into action there seemed to be no real opportunity. He tried to catch Lynch's attention as he was getting into the driver's seat. "Er . . . I'm going to see Tuke."

"Tuke?"

"We talked about him. He used to be McWilliam's private secretary."

"He's been out of action for a while, hasn't he though?" asked Lynch.

"Yes," agreed Power softly. "But . . ."

"I can't see why you're interested in him. He might have known McWilliam in the past, but all this is a problem of the present. Some very active, fit young man killed Sir Ian and Lady McWilliam. But," he conceded. "Tuke might be able to throw some light on the past. After all, Sir Ian seems to have led many lives." He shut the car door and wound down the window as a thought suddenly occurred to him. "You could ask Tuke about the fascist connection. We haven't really explored that." Power's mind entertained an image of a brown-shirted storm trooper kicking down Sir Ian's door and spraying petrol everywhere, before setting light to the funeral pyre in a recreation of the arson of the German Rathaus. Except the image didn't fit, because it was Sir Ian, apparently, who had right-wing sympathies. McWilliam had been a friend, not a foe, of the European right-wing movements.

Lynch's car took off smoothly and disappeared out of the drive. Perhaps Lynch was right, thought Power, all Tuke would be good for was to talk over the past. From Lucinda's description of his clinical state, Tuke might resent talking about the future.

Power went inside out of the wind and the rain and began planning his route to Tuke's home in North Wales. He was looking at an Ordnance Survey map of Denbighshire when the doorbell rang.

He put down the cup of tea he had just made and went into the hall.

She stared up at him with her dark, brown eyes. Her face looked pale in the daylight and her hair had been slicked down by the rain. The security lights, tricked by the dullness of the day, had switched on as she approached the house. Power could see the raindrops glinting as they fell on the wet grass. He looked about. There was no car outside and her shoes were soaked. Drips from her sodden jacket fell onto the floor of the porch.

"Zoë!" Power was so astonished to see her that he could not manage an adequate welcome. "How did you get here?"

"Found your address in the library," she said.

"No, I didn't mean that. I mean did you get a taxi or . . ."

"I walked from the station."

Power was surprised, "That's miles away."

"I wanted to see you," she said determinedly.

Power thought of how Zoë had waited outside Heaton Hall in all weathers for Sir Ian McWilliam. She had tracked Power down just as she had pursued the Minister. The thought of her waiting and watching him was uncomfortable. How long had she been outside?

Had she been waiting in the trees? Had she seen Lynch? Had she waited until he had gone, before ringing the front doorbell? Being tracked down to his own lair frightened him.

"How can I help you?" He stood unmoving on the doorstep, reluctant to admit this potential source of trouble to his home.

She, for her part, found his manner somewhat harsh, not like the times they had met before. "Can't I come in? I can't talk on the doorstep . . . it's too cold and too wet."

Grudgingly, Power moved aside to let her come in. He was aware that his sudden discomfort was irrational. Zoë had never been deluded. Power had proved that himself. Sir Ian had, in the end, pursued her and made use of her, far more than she had pursued him.

It was he who had been so pathological in their relationship. There was no basis for the foreboding that Power felt. After all, it was Power who had been initially attracted to her and not the other way about.

Having chastised himself inwardly for his churlishness, he offered to take her coat.

He offered her tea and a seat in his lounge and went off to dry her coat by the Aga stove. He made strong tea and unwrapped a cake. He arrived back carrying everything on a tray. She had taken the liberty of lighting a fire in the grate and was kneeling on the hearth rug. He noticed how comfortable she was making herself as he poured a cup of tea. He hoped she hadn't got the wrong idea, that she wouldn't get too comfortable. He handed her the tea and tried to make conversation. "The summer's over," he said. "At least there are lights to turn on and fires to sit by," he offered her some currant cake. "We can always keep the night at bay." He sat down across the room from her, in his high, wingback chair.

"If only the nights didn't keep coming back. I don't like my dreams. When I wake up from them, it's always so dark. If only it could stay day time forever."

"What brings you here today, Zoë?"

"Right in like that? Straight to the point? No time for polite conversation over tea and cake? No 'How was prison, Zoë? It must have been awful...'"

"Well this isn't a vicarage tea party, and I'm curious..." Power was more than curious, he was desperate to know what this young woman wanted.

"It's difficult," she said. "When you've been living inside somewhere like that. Living according to other people's rules. On remand, you're there... locked up all day. You haven't done anything wrong, but you're still locked up. And even though you're innocent you get to feel... I must have done something wrong, or else I wouldn't be in prison. You wonder if you did do what they accused you of and you just forgot doing it. As if you can't quite remember. You get to feel responsible for what you haven't done.

"You helped me get out of there, Dr Power. I know you did. You did that for me. You believed me, when no-one else did. When I said that Sir Ian loved me, you believed me..." Whatever Sir Ian had done to her she had to believe that he had loved her. Power did not feel like dispelling the idea. "So I needed to see you. I wanted to say thank you." Her voice trailed away.

"You wanted to say thank you, but..."

"I sort of set out with that intention. To say thank you. But... and I know it sounds odd... I feel sort of cross with you."

"Yes?"

Her eyes flashed angrily at him. "Because when you made me tell my story about the house and about what Ian and I did together ... I felt you didn't believe me or that you disapproved. You changed towards me and I had to come here... I had to know why."

Power had once seen a patient who had shouted at him for an hour and then left, and as she left she had calmly put a loaded gun on the table in front of Power. 'I was going to kill you with that', she had said, before putting on her coat and vanishing from his life forever. Power wondered if Zoë might attack him.

He looked at Zoë and tried to quell any irrational panic he might be feeling. "What did you want to know?"

"I had to know what gives you the right to judge me? To judge us?" Power shifted uncomfortably in his chair. "Did you disapprove of us?"

"It sounds as if you want to know what I think?"

"Yes! Of course I do. Don't play any patient games with me. 'It sounds like this...' and 'It sounds like that...' I'm not your patient. You made that clear enough..."

Power reflected her red-faced emotion back. "You are very angry."

"Tell me," she demanded. "You felt he used me didn't you? Or rather that he abused me..."

Power could not meet her eyes. "They are your words, Zoë." He spoke with quiet reticence. "If you want to know how I felt. I felt angry with him for what he had done."

"So you did think it was wrong," she said it almost to herself, as if to confirm her fears. She paused and for a few minutes neither of them could meet each other's glances. At last she spoke, "I'm going to have his child. I always knew I should go through with it. I never really had any choice, but if things were to happen over again, I still wouldn't change anything." She sighed. "But . . . if you were right about the way he treated me . . . just supposing you were right . . . I never felt that I was being used by him. It was never like that."

"No?" asked Power quietly.

"No. It all felt all right. But if . . . if you were right, then I'm wrong somehow . . . wrong through and through . . . and in that case does it all make the baby wrong too?"

"Do you want me to judge . . . to judge that things are right? To reassure you." he paused, thinking, "Has the baby moved inside you? It's often then – that's when the baby becomes real."

"The 'kick inside'? I don't think so. Not yet."

"How do you think you'll feel when the baby moves inside you? Are you looking forward to it?" Power asked.

She smiled at last, "I'm hopeful."

"That's good enough for anyone," said Power.

"You look relieved I said that," Zoë said.

"I am," said Power, and laughed.

She stood up, "I've got to go."

"Is the train due?"

"No," she said. "I don't want to say anymore – that's what it is. I want to be on my own now. We've talked enough. I've said all I wanted to."

"Okay," said Power.

"Just one thing," she said. "I need to know if I can talk to you again. Sometime . . . maybe in a few years. Just to see how things are." Zoë needed to know there was an open door.

"Yes," said Power knowing full well that she might never want to talk again. He showed her to the front door, held it open wide and watched her walk away and out of his drive. Power hoped he might have helped her for the better, but he could never know for sure. If he had been Lynch he would have prayed for her. Being Dr Power all he could do was hope. He went inside to finish his tea.

★ ★ ★

The late Sunday afternoon was passing easily and gently into the evening. The rain had cleared and a bright needle of sunlight shone through the purple-grey clouds. The wet road glistened beneath the wheels of Power's car. As Power drove through the villages of Cheshire and North Wales, the bells could be heard inviting worshippers to evensong.

Power was thinking about two women: Lucinda and Zoë. Both of them had seemed special and attractive to him, and both of their lives had been touched by Sir Ian. Power knew that Sir Ian's touch had been far from golden. Lucinda had resented her father's frequent self-seeking absences, and had hinted at darker reasons for disliking her father. Zoë had adored him, and had been so enamoured that she allowed herself to be controlled by him as if he had been an omnipotent satyr. For all Sir Ian's objective exterior charm, Power was repelled by the desires which had crawled just beneath Sir Ian's skin. Power was also perplexed. He could have so easily fallen for either Zoë or Lucinda, but in the last few days both had slipped out of his life, apparently forever. He thought about them ruefully and couldn't understand whether his anger was towards Sir Ian because of Sir Ian's effects on both women, or whether the anger was with himself for failing to hold on to either woman.

There was a squeal from the brakes as he stopped just short of the boot of the car in front. Power had been so immersed in thought that he had not realised that the traffic lights were red ahead. The line of cars in front had halted. Power was thus jolted back to the present.

He had arranged an evening appointment to see Tuke, Sir Ian's old private secretary. Jacob Tuke had bought a large bungalow on a hillside, west of the village of Penrhyn on the North Wales coast. The village was not blessed with much seashore to speak of, and to the west were hills and high windy cliffs of granite, which overlooked a cold and forbidding sea. To the north-east was the Wirral peninsula, and further north still the Lancashire coast.

Tuke's newly-built bungalow was part of a new development on the site of an old hillside farm. The bungalow sat in the lee of a headland called the Little Orme. A hedge of evergreens kept the bungalow out of sight from the road. On three sides, however, the house was surrounded by fields. Across the fields was an uninterrupted view of the sea.

He walked across the concrete drive between elevated troughs of flowers and shrubs. Small juniper and japonica bushes were planted defiantly in the lee of windbreaks that gave shelter from the salt sea breeze. Once upon a time Tuke could have gardened here from the fastness of his wheelchair. His knees would have been able to fit under the ledges of the planting troughs. The garden looked somewhat untended now. Tuke's illness had progressed so much that he was unable to garden even from his wheelchair. Even so, here and there some blooms remained from high summer.

The curtains were drawn, but at their edges light shone out like a miniature beacon into the night. Power imagined the light being visible far out to sea. He paused at the front door. From inside there were sounds of an opera being played. He recognised the sounds of Britten's *Peter Grimes.*

Power looked down at his feet in the porch light. A sea-mist was already beginning to curl about his ankles. The cold, damp air made him cough asthmatically. He pushed the doorbell and looked forward to getting into the light and warmth of Tuke's home. Power shuffled his feet and waited.

A figure appeared, silhouetted onto the frosted glass of the front door. She opened it wide and greeted Power with a smile of courtesy. "Dr Power?" she asked. "Come in."

Power took a welcome step into the dry warmth of the hall,

leaving the night and the mist behind him. "Do come inside and get warm," she said. "I think we spoke earlier on the phone." She shook his hand in a formal way. "Jacob calls me Sister, because I am his nurse. I'd prefer it if he'd call me Megan or Meg, but I think it reassures him to realise that I'm a trained nurse, not a companion." She locked the front door behind Power. "Before I let you see him, Dr Power. I wanted to ask you again what you hoped to gain from seeing him. Although he might not like it to be known, he is very ill now."

"It was his involvement with the McWilliam family," said Power. "If he could just tell me a little about them."

"Surely there are other people. I wouldn't like Jacob to be stressed for no reason."

"At one time he was probably one of the closest people to Sir Ian," said Power, feeling that she was intent on dissuading him from seeing Tuke. "I don't think my questioning would harm him."

Megan Driver looked sceptical. Power himself had always retained a vague fear of ward sisters ever since his days as a medical student. He found them difficult to stand up to, and especially difficult to thwart. Sister Driver eyed him thoughtfully. Despite her old school manner she was a young woman. Her brown hair was cut short and randomly streaked with grey. Power imagined she must have given up a hospital career to nurse Tuke. He wondered why. Her left hand bore no wedding ring. Her accent did not suggest she had ever been a local girl. There was no Welsh lilt to her voice. He therefore concluded that she was probably working only for Tuke, and out of her own choice.

She had given some thought to Power's assertion that questioning Tuke wouldn't harm him. She had noted a mild desperation in Power's voice and decided to press him further by stressing how ill Tuke had become. Perhaps Power would bow to her pressure and leave without disturbing her patient. "He was very upset by Sir Ian's death," she said. "It seemed to age him. I thought twice before I told him about Lady McWilliam. I thought I had to tell him though, because he would have heard it sooner or later on the news or some other programme. He's addicted to the radio, you see. I couldn't have kept it a secret." Power was uncomfortable. He didn't like being held at bay in Tuke's hallway, but clearly the nurse was not yet satisfied. "You're a psychiatrist then," she said. She had changed tack in her enquiries. "Working for the police?"

"Working with the police," Power corrected her. He didn't want to specify any more than this. He had the feeling she was thinking of asking him to leave.

"It seems unusual," she said.

"It's ethical enough," said Power defensively. "As long as I make it clear that I am not Jacob Tuke's doctor, and as long as he freely consents to talk to me, there's no problem. It's as if the police were my clients, not the individual."

She frowned. "Still, it seems unusual."

Power was tempted to agree, but refrained from doing so. "Psychiatrists are often asked for their opinion in court. In court cases the client is the defence or the prosecution, not the individual ... now, if I've reassured you about those things..."

"He might be worried if he knows you're a psychiatrist," said Nurse Driver. "He might think that I've got you in to see him specially. He might think he's going mad. Don't tell him you're a psychiatrist."

"I will be careful not to give the wrong idea," said Power, who was equally careful not to agree to deceive Tuke in any way. If Power was a psychiatrist he would not pretend otherwise. "I want to interview him to ... build up a picture of Sir Ian, that's all. He was a complicated character. I'm interested in Sir Ian McWilliam, not Jacob Tuke. Mr Tuke might be able to throw some new light on his character. I shall make that clear enough."

"I suppose a psychiatrist would be interested in character ... more than a policeman, perhaps." She was clearly suspicious of Power and his motives. "All right," she said reluctantly. "But don't tax him. It's late." She was keen to put Tuke to bed early. She had already prepared a tray of milk and biscuits. All she had to do was heat the milk in the microwave. She had even put a single tablet of Temazepam ready by the digestive biscuits. He slept poorly without Temazepam.

"You care about him a lot, don't you?" commented Power.

"Yes," she said and was surprised by the honesty of her own reply.

"Don't worry," said Power. "If necessary I can do the interview in two halves, on different days. May I see him now?"

She nodded and Power stifled a sigh of relief. It was as if he had withstood the questions of a dragon. Although he had passed the test and was to be admitted, however, he had not yet won her trust. She still regarded him with a degree of scepticism. She did though offer him a cup of tea. "Jacob usually has something to drink about this time. I'll tell him you're here." She disappeared into the living room. Alone in the hall Power listened to the indistinct sounds of talking over the music.

Jacob Tuke looked up from his wheelchair as Carl Power was shown in. He reached out holding a remote-control and with a trembling aim switched the music off. He put the remote control back down on the rug that covered his knees and held out his right hand for the doctor to shake.

He was a thin, gaunt man with a surprisingly youthful face. His ginger hair was cut tightly about his head and his pale, blue eyes regarded Power with a lucid curiosity. His alert and steady gaze was spoilt only by two involuntary neck movements. Tuke ignored the spasms and spoke. His voice was measured; almost rationed. The syllables were carefully, painfully enunciated. Tuke was desperate to retain all the control he could. Only towards the end of each sentence was there the merest hint of slurring. "Dr Power is it? Please come in." His hand was shaken. Tuke's grip was no stronger than Power had anticipated from his thin and pale appearance. "Please sit down on the sofa over there. I shall come over to you."

'I'll get some hot drinks for you both," said Megan and left them alone.

Power seated himself on the sofa and watched a little guiltily as Tuke made his slow way over, propelling the wheelchair with his weakened arms. Tuke was having some difficulty in making his hand grip the wheel rim. Once his fingers had found the wheel he clung onto it for grim death. Power restrained himself from offering to help, but felt tense until Tuke was by his side at last. Tuke panted from the effort. Power looked at his profile. He had seen him before somewhere, but he couldn't remember the context. He tried to locate the memory. Was it recently he had seen him, or years ago? Perhaps it had been some television programme where Tuke had been a ministry spokesman or a silent alter ego to his minister? Power wondered if the feeling of recognition was important or not. Nowadays he seemed to recognise more and more people only because they looked like people he had once known. Who did Tuke look like? Van Gogh maybe? No-one else he could think of.

Tuke was talking. "You found us. I wondered whether you would ... be coming. You were a little late." Power apologised. The journey had taken longer than he had imagined. He noticed that Tuke chose only short sentences to say. "I was listening to Peter Grimes. Do you know it?"

"I do," said Power. "Is it a favourite of yours?"

"It is," said Tuke. "I like everything about it. Except the waste of the young boys' lives. You know: Grimes' apprentices. Lost by their master. Through his neglect. The boys' lives taken by the sea." he paused to see if Power understood his speech. "When I listen I open the curtains. I can watch the sea from here. You listen to the great wash of operatic sound. You look out there. And at the same time as Britten's music you can see the power of the sea. It is inevitable. So arbitrary in its power."

"The cruel sea?" suggested Power.

"No," said Tuke. "There is no intent in the actions of the sea, just something so great, so overwhelming. Like a great grey judge of men. Taking lives with impartiality ... with no regard for a man's good deeds or his sins."

"But if it has no intent how can it judge?"

"It is like a machine, a mindless equation. We match ourselves against the equation. We pit our strength and our wits against its power. If we are not equal, then we are overwhelmed. Drowned." Power looked out at the grim night and shivered. Tuke continued, "Grimes the fisherman knows his boys are unequal to the sea. Still he pitches them against it. He gambled with their lives. Like they were dice. Like he was gambling with the sea for the boys' souls. When the opera ends I listen to the sea. Sometimes the wind sounds like voices. Calling. Lost souls, calling out from the seabed."

"It sounds . . . bleak," said Power.

"Realistically bleak. No-one can control the sea. We have to take whatever it throws at us. The raging wind. The waves as high as houses. We must accept its judgement. That's realistic."

Power had to agree, reluctantly. "Did your nurse say why I wanted to see you?" Tuke nodded. Power went on, "I am a medical doctor working with the police in this instance. A psychiatrist."

"I know," said Tuke.

"Oh," said Power, surprised since Megan had warned him to be careful about this.

"I thought you might not know."

"Sister Driver said who you were."

"Oh," said Power. He was vaguely puzzled by this exchange, but he saw no merit in arguing. He accepted that he, Power, must have been wrong.

"Me? Help you?" He gestured to the wheelchair. "I can't help myself. I would be intrigued . . . to know how I can help you."

"I wanted to talk about Sir Ian and Lady McWilliam," said Power, and he looked for some emotional response after the nurse's comment about Tuke's sensitivity.

"Yes?" Tuke asked blankly. He showed no outward emotion. Power wondered if Tuke prided himself on the control of every aspect of his life. He would resist physical help as much as he could in order to remain as independent as possible, and it seemed as if he would go to any lengths to remain emotionally detached too.

"I believe that you knew Sir Ian for a long time."

"Yes. I was like the apprentice to his Sorcerer. He was my College tutor and then he was my minister. So for about a dozen years or so our lives ran in parallel." Tuke paused. "Why, exactly, have you come to see me?"

"What was he like when you were his student?"

Tuke frowned. Surely this wasn't what Power really wanted to know? "I have a different perspective on things now," said Tuke. "I look back. I judge what happened to me. I judge the roles certain people played in my life. I sit in judgement in my wheelchair. I can be as critical or as kind as I like. None of them will be bothered by what I think of them now. They forgot me long ago. Out of sight and out of mind. But really all that is left me is my mind. So I range back and forth through the years. Then you turn up wanting a replay. As if I'd been waiting for just this moment. It's as if I'm already a piece of history." The nurse came in with a tray of tea, hot milk, buttered toast and biscuits. She put the tray on a table by Tuke and left. Tuke determinedly picked up Power's full teacup and tried to pass it to him. The cup wobbled and rattled in its saucer. Power shot forward and caught the cup just as the tremulous Tuke was about to drop it. As it was, a wave of boiling, brown tea sloshed over the rim of the teacup and splashed over Power's wrist. Power hissed with pain. Tuke affected not to notice this consequence of his infirmity. Power was too polite to complain and surreptitiously wrapped a handkerchief about his scalded wrist.

"Well," said Tuke, using both hands to steer a mug of warm milk to his lips. "Since you've come all this way what can I tell you? I went to school in Chester. Do you know Chester?" Power nodded. "It was a small town then. Almost the same as it had been in the Middle Ages. Filled with honest, thrifty people. Typical English middle class. Kindly, but fiercely conservative. The women were staid snobs in tweed skirts. Repressive. It was such as change to get away to University."

"Surely Cambridge was little different to Chester? Both Cambridge and Chester are small towns burdened by tradition."

"I felt free. It was being away from home. Cambridge was an escape for me. I loved my mother, but she smothered me. You know? Smothered me till I hated her. I'd been ill as a child and I don't think she ever believed I could survive away from her. McWilliam was my first tutor. He opened up my eyes and my mind. Yes, at least I must give him that. He painted a picture of what was possible. He seemed full of promise and he made his students feel that they were full of the same sort of promise too. Good politicians are like that. They fill you with optimism, not realism. He was a young man then. Unmarried. With a full head of thick, black hair. There were a few bespectacled girls at Cambridge then. They adored him. He always liked that. He would get them to do research for him. They would spend hours in the library ferreting out information for him. They'd do all that work, just for a smile from him and a glass of sherry in his study. I'm not saying he had sex with them. At least I don't think so." He paused and set the milk mug back down carefully on the tray. "He'd hold tutorials in his rooms. His students would never miss them. And it wasn't just the endless flow of dry sherry and even drier wit. The conversation would soar like an eagle. Those were the days when anything seemed possible. Anything could be achieved. You just had to imagine it. If it could be imagined it was possible. Any goal could be achieved. Well, I know now that Ian was only talking for the rich and the influential and the healthy, not for the poor, not for the intelligent or for the wise, and certainly not for the sick. I never understood that I was a fool, because for so long I believed it all. I swallowed every myth that Ian cared to pedal."

"It sounds as if you felt betrayed by him."

"When I realised it wasn't true . . . yes. I wondered how I could have believed it all for so long. I followed him for so long. I trailed round him at the College. Listened to his opinions at art galleries and dinner parties. I watched in wonder as he scored points against the academic hierarchy. You know, he always wanted to go back there.

To Cambridge. He wanted to be Master of Queens." Tuke smiled almost privately to himself. "I suppose he could have done. He was getting rather distinguished."

"What did he do then? What was it that made you change your mind about him?"

Tuke pulled the blanket up ever so slightly over his legs. "He was working me hard at the Ministry. He'd invited me in to the civil service, pushed me as high as I could decently go. He wanted me to work out a complete re-vamp of Government policy in secret. Incorporating his favourite ideas. I was his logical choice. I'd played along for so many years. It had got so that I knew what he was thinking before he said it. There were the usual ideas he had. Giving power back to the individual. A deconstruction of the state health system. A re-arming policy. A change in foreign policy. Use third world economies as manufacturing bases. Run their governments by proxy. He wanted to thin our population down. The underclass were no longer worth anything. They had ceased to be economically viable. He was intent on turning the clock back seventy years. His main idea was to carve up Europe and Asia between Britain and Germany." Tuke paused and smiled at Power. "You look surprised Dr Power."

"I ... never thought ... it sounds a bit ... unusual."

"You never thought he was so ambitious? Sir Ian's plans were wide-ranging, I'll give you that. He was putting together an alternative agenda. He saw himself as the next Prime Minister. He wanted me to help formulate his plans so that they would be ready to put in place when he got to Number 10. He was having regular meetings in Europe. At least he was when I was working with him. He would tell me then. After I became ill ... I was not to be trusted anymore. I don't know what happened to his plans. He didn't want too many people to know. There would have come a time when the current Prime Minister looked weak. Then he would have seized his chance. But after I left, what happened to his dreams? What happened to his secret flights to Bonn and Munich? I don't know.

"I knew I was becoming ill. For a time I walked the corridors of power with a limp."

For some reason my right leg just wouldn't work the way it wanted to. There were times when it felt as if it was changing: tingling and swelling up like a balloon. I'd be chairing a meeting and I'd have to reach down and check to see whether my leg was still there. I'd go and see the doctor and he'd look at me with a glum expression and shake his head. He wouldn't say what was wrong. But he knew what it was. I'm sure he did. And I knew it was serious stuff. Did I mention I was ill as a child?" Tuke looked to see if there was any recognition.

"You did mention it, I think," said Power.

"Well," said Tuke, trying to ignore an involuntary twitch of his right arm. "Since that time I've always dreading being ill. Like a phobia. But the way the doctor looked when he examined my reflexes. I knew then that something was very wrong. Things were very busy at work. Ian was demanding more and more information before his flights abroad. And when he returned there would be endless revisions of his plans. I was feeling incredibly tired. I struggled as well as I could with my legs. It was getting difficult to walk. I had to drag my right leg behind me. One day I could struggle as much as I liked, but I couldn't get out of bed. My legs had just given up altogether. The doctor couldn't hide the multiple sclerosis from me anymore. After that day I never went back to the Ministry. There came a time when they sent a courier to my home with the things from my desk. The box they came in said 'Jacob Tuke's effects'. As if I was dead."

"Did you ever see Sir Ian again?"

There was a pause. Tuke gave Power a piercing stare. At last he dragged the words out of himself. "No. And then I had to learn that what he'd sold me . . . that anything was possible . . . was a heap of shit. Since then I've only learnt that more and more is impossible." Tuke looked hard at Power with his blue eyes. "Am I very bitter?"

"You sound hurt more than anything," said Power.

"Well," Tuke sighed. "Ian was not Mephistopheles, but he was damn close. I always wondered how much my first at Cambridge was due to him, and how much was due to his magic." He paused. "I think I can tell you that I worshipped him. I was pleased for him. Pleased by his success. He made you feel that his success was your success. Or rather that your success depended upon his succeeding. I was pleased when he met Helen, Lady McWilliam, you know? I introduced them at a party I held in Knightsbridge. I had a small flat in Sloane Street. It was the early seventies. I'd been down from Cambridge for a couple of years. Climbing the civil service ladder, with a little help from Ian. Helen was the daughter of a family I had known from my early days. Her parents knew my parents. My mother entertained the notion that we, Helen and I, would fall in love one day. Get married even. I watched them at this dinner party. They sat so close at the table. Their eyes seemed to lock. And I thought to myself 'he's taking her away from you and you can't even do anything'. That's the kind of thing my mother would have said, 'don't let him take advantage of you . . . be strong . . . stand up for yourself.' But you know, I was glad. I watched them go off hand-in-hand . . . well, they swopped addresses anyway. And I was glad they were together. They kind of matched. She adored him, and he needed that. Having said that, Helen was a doormat. I mean, she had a strong character, but her destiny was always to come second. He became her *raison d'etre*. When he died, she had nothing to live for. So she killed herself."

"No," said Power. "She was murdered. Just as Sir Ian was."

Tuke didn't blink. "I knew her, Doctor. And she was exactly the kind of person who would kill herself. She would have wanted to die. Even if she was killed . . . she would have been grateful. As a psychiatrist you will be familiar with the death drive, *Thanatos*. She would have been consumed with guilt that Ian was dead. What does a doormat do when there's nobody to walk all over it?" Power tried to conceal his frown of disapproval. Tuke noticed it however. "I don't care what people think, Dr Power."

"I always used to think that civil servants were more . . ."

"Civil? Believe me it's good to take the diplomatic flannel out of one's mouth. To say what you really mean. It's one of the few luxuries I can enjoy these days."

"But to use your phraseology, and to contradict you, there were others who wanted to use her as a doormat. There was Michael, for instance, he would suck her for her money. He was probably asking for more and more even in the days before she was killed."

"Michael?" Tuke paused. "A crude version of his father. A frustrated Oedipus don't you think, Dr Power?"

"That's the second reference you've made to Freud, Mr Tuke. If you recall, Oedipus killed his father unawares, and then equally unawares married his mother. Do you think Michael would have killed his father?"

"Well, Michael did hate him."

"It seems that Sir Ian aroused strong feelings in those around him."

"Transference would you say, Dr Power?" Tuke's clipped tone was mocking and derisive.

"You're well up on the jargon."

"I'm good at languages. And the language you psychiatrists use is called Psychobabble."

Was Tuke trying to destroy the interview by deliberately making him angry? Power returned doggedly to his line of questioning. "McWilliam's political rivals hated him. Even his political agent hated him. His son hates him, according to you, and you yourself give no sign of really . . . loving the man." Tuke seemed surprised at the choice of the word 'love'. The word threw him. "No," said Power. "And at the other end of the spectrum from hate we have intense love – his wife (a 'doormat', according to you), his daughter, Lucinda, and his mistress, Zoë. Do you think anybody who loved him could kill him?"

Tuke seemed almost to choke. He coughed until he was red in the face. Power got up and patted Tuke's back. Tuke waved him angrily away with his hand. Regaining some composure he took a sip of his milk.

"Are you all right?" asked Dr Power, showing his concern.

"My throat goes into spasm. Occasionally. Due to the MS. I can't control it."

"It must be frightening when that happens."

"It is," said Tuke.

"I've noticed your legs sometimes move too."

"Involuntary," said Tuke, glaring at Power. "All involuntary. I have no control."

"I know," said Power. "It happens in multiple sclerosis."

"And it's worse when I'm tired," said Tuke pointedly.

Power took the hint. "We can postpone the rest of the interview, if you like."

Tuke looked as if he did not relish the thought of postponement. A complete cancellation would have been more welcome to him. "Perhaps just one or two more questions then?"

"You were close to Sir Ian for so very long. Surely you would know if Sir Ian was in the habit of taking mistresses?"

Tuke appeared mildly horrified. "No . . . no . . . that was the one thing he didn't do. And so Zoë was a new departure for him. I saw the letters she sent. I tried to keep them from him. She was mad."

"Or madly in love."

"Mad," said Tuke. "She was determined to get him. She would have done any perverted thing he asked her to, just to get him. She tempted him beyond endurance. And he was only human. He couldn't resist what she offered."

"What did she offer?"

Tuke paused, whether through prudishness or some other motive Power found it difficult to tell. "The letters were graphic enough for me to guess, Doctor. You will have seen them, I suppose?" Power nodded and waited for Tuke to say something more. On this subject though Tuke was not going to be as outspoken as before. "My knowledge of such things is pretty scant, Doctor. I have never

225

married. Matters of the flesh have never concerned me."

"Never?"

Tuke did not look him in the eye. "Never," he said. "I have never had the slightest inclination. The human form is essentially imperfect. We are trapped inside what is essentially a hunk of meat. It is ironic, because my body has become more imperfect than others."

"You didn't like Zoë then?"

"I . . . never met her."

"But from her letters?"

"I warned him. I warned that she was unstable. That if he took what she offered . . . he could be destroyed. He agreed at first. He could resist her then at first. But when she went on . . . and on . . . and on. He couldn't remain aloof. He gave in . . ."

"I'm confused," said Power. "Can you help me? You were at the Ministry when Sir Ian started getting these letters?" Tuke nodded.

"And you advised Sir Ian to have nothing to do with Zoë?"

"That was appropriate, don't you think?"

"It's not that, it's just that you implied you were still advising him when he started seeing Zoë, but surely that was after you left the Ministry. After you stopped walking."

"Yes. That is what I said."

"So you advised him after you left the Ministry. But you said that you didn't see him after you left work."

"Did I?" said Tuke. "Perhaps I just gave the wrong impression. We talked occasionally on the phone. But you know how things are. I felt he'd let me down. I had thought we were very close friends. Very close. And then there was no contact. Or so it seemed to me. But perhaps he felt I'd betrayed him. That might be right, mightn't it? He might construe my illness as a betrayal. He'd invested so much in me you see. I knew so much about his politics, you see. To not be there when he needed me. Wasn't that a betrayal?"

"He might see it like that."

"You know, I really hadn't seen it in quite that way," said Tuke;

"It makes more sense to me now. Why he was so cold to me . . . well, maybe there's more to this psychobabble than I thought. I must thank you, Dr Power, for helping me see that."

"I'm not aware I did anything, Mr Tuke."

"Will you excuse me?" said Tuke. "I'm tired now." And it seemed true. Tuke was paler than before. Power could see the effort of the conversation had etched itself into his face. Power had been surprised by Tuke's fluency and facility with words, but now the efforts of the evening had had their effect. Tuke's words seemed more slurred, less carefully chosen. Silences and consonants merged into one another, as if Tuke was drunk. Tuke picked up the small tablet of Temazepam that his nurse had put by his plate. He'd saved a mouthful of milk to wash it down with. He swallowed the sleeping tablet in front of Power. "Do these stop dreams, Dr Power?"

"It looked like a Temazepam tablet," said Power. Tuke nodded. "Well, Temazepam does suppress dreams."

"Good," said Tuke cryptically. "Goodnight, then. Let yourself out." Tuke seemed to slump, but Power knew it was too early for the drug to have acted.

"I'll make an appointment for another time," said Power. He offered his hand, but Tuke seemed not to notice. "Well. Good night. And if you have any dreams I hope that they're peaceful ones."

Megan Driver was hovering outside the room. "I hope you didn't wear him out," she said as Power emerged.

"I don't know," said Power. "There was no sign of him flagging and then all of a sudden he started slurring his speech and slowing down just like his battery was fading."

"Oh dear," she said. "You shouldn't have taxed him." She made a move to go and check on Tuke.

Power gently caught hold of her arm. "He's all right. He's just taken his sleeping tablet. Fast asleep now."

"Oh," she said.

"Can I ask you . . . how long have you been with Mr Tuke?"

"Nearly two years."

"And has he always been the same?"

"The same as what?"

"I mean has he deteriorated rapidly, or has he always been able to do about the same amount for himself."

"He tried to struggle on sticks when I first knew him, but he used the wheelchair mainly. Now he only uses the wheelchair. He's got gradually worse. I have to help him transfer from the bed to the chair. Perhaps the multiple sclerosis has been accelerating these last few months."

"His mood. Is that stable? He seems very bitter."

"He doesn't like the way he's been left high and dry by his former friends. They've cast him off like dead skin. That hurts him. I'm his only contact with the world."

"Do you live in with him . . . sleep here?"

"He bought me a cottage in the village. I sleep there. At nine or ten o'clock, after he's in bed, I go home. I come back in at nine in the morning to get him up and stay until two o'clock. I have some free time until six and then I make him his dinner and get him ready for bed. It's a fixed routine. I haven't taken a holiday yet, but we would get an agency nurse to stand in if I did want to go. And when he needs me to I will stay overnight – when things get worse and the disease progresses. After he dies I have two months in which I can stay on in the house, then I have to find somewhere else and move on. He's leaving all his estate to a society researching into MS. So my prime motive, if I want to keep my house and my job, is to keep him fit and well."

"That seems very . . . er . . . clear," said Power. "His idea or yours?"

"His I think. Jacob is very logical and very practical. His affairs are all perfectly sorted out. My salary is paid automatically by the bank. He's a great organiser."

"I expect that Sir Ian missed having that skill available to him."

"Oh, I think Sir Ian missed him all round. Once or twice he came here in the afternoons and took Jacob out for a drive in his Land Rover."

Power didn't think that Tuke had mentioned that point. "Was that often?"

"I don't know," said Megan. "I'm sometimes not here in the afternoons."

"No," said Power. "No, you're not . . . but Mr Tuke implied he never saw Sir Ian."

"Jacob sometimes exaggerates. To gain sympathy, I expect. And why shouldn't he? But he wouldn't lie. He's never lied to me." Power nodded. He thought that given a Minister's busy schedule the effort required to take time out to see Jacob Tuke, here in the back of beyond, must have been considerable on Sir Ian's part. That Sir Ian managed it even once was, perhaps, an admirable achievement.

Power told her how Tuke had agreed (albeit tacitly) to speak with him again. The nurse clearly disapproved, but she did not voice her disapproval this time. In a way, Power felt she had begun to trust him. As she bustled into the other room to get Tuke ready for bed Power let himself out of the front door.

Outside the mist had grown thicker and the moon in the night sky was a dull and diffuse glow. Power held his coat tightly about his chest and coughed because of the damp, cold air. Near-silence accompanied him as he walked carefully through the mist to his car. Only if he strained to hear could he just discern the sound of waves breaking on the nearby shore. The mist made the sounds seem muffled and deceptively distant. As he climbed into the cold car Power imagined that safe in the warm house, the sounds of the sea could be a soothing sound to fall asleep to on a balmy night. But when the rain came in torrents and the wind roared about the chimneys, Power did not wonder that Tuke would need a drug to help him sleep against the clamour of the ocean.

Chapter Eleven

A police car was waiting in the driveway of Power's home. The constables inside the car had the lights on and were reading the evening paper and eating a Chinese takeaway from the village. They gave all the signs of having waited some time for him. As Power's headlights came into the drive, one of the officers finished her mouthful of duck in oyster sauce and climbed out of the new Rover. She surreptitiously brushed a few stray grains of rice off her tunic. Power was just locking his car door. He was not surprised to see the police car, nor to hear that she had been dispatched to fetch him by Lynch.

"I'm PC Wilson, Dr Power. I'm sorry to call on you at this late hour. Mr Michael McWilliam has been returned from Holland ... he's in police custody," she explained. "Superintendent Lynch would welcome your interviewing him, Doctor. We're to accompany you."

"Oh," said Power, who had been looking forward to a soak in a hot bath after the long journey back from Tuke's place of exile. Images of comfort such as a glass of strong beer and a relax in front of the television evaporated. "Well," he said, "if you don't mind. I'll just let myself into the house. I need to make myself comfortable before the journey ... if you understand that is." She nodded.

"Actually," she said. "If we could come in and do the same ..."

"Ah ..." said Power. "Of course. If you need to – do come in."

And so, later, when they had finished and the house had been locked up again, Power sat in the back of the police car and they began their journey back down the country roads he had just been on. Although his house stood in splendid isolation, Power wondered about what any neighbours might think. Police cars often came and went in the night... any neighbours would assume that Power was 'always helping the police with their enquiries'. They might have imagined him to be a shady character forever on the wrong side of the law, but never proven guilty (at least not yet).

Power asked for more information about Michael McWilliam's surrender or capture, but the constables did not know. They were more interested in Power himself and were clearly intrigued by Power's status as a psychiatrist. "They said at HQ that you were an expert in dreams, Dr Power." Power grunted from the dark recesses of the back seat. "Can you interpret them, then?"

Power stirred himself grudgingly. "Only if I know the person. You have to know the person to interpret the dream." He half-expected that from the question there was some dream that she wanted him to interpret. He was tired, but a sudden curiosity about her dreams had been awakened inside him. He needed to know. Wanted to be able to help. And it was something about all doctors, all healers. He reflected on his profession as a healer. They all had a need to heal, much as artists have a compulsion to paint or write or sculpt. In the same way Power needed to be in this car now, trying to heal the wounds caused by the murders of Sir Ian and Lady McWilliam. It was as if he was trying to repair something, like a rip in a curtain or a veil. To make things better.

"Dr Power? Are you all right?"

"Uh?"

"I said 'are you all right'?"

"I'm sorry," said Power. "I was miles away. I'm sorry. What were you saying?" The real world of the police car re-visited itself upon him.

PC Wilson was looking at him over the back of her seat. Power noticed her fine, fair hair in the headlights of passing cars. She stared at him. He was not an unattractive man, she thought. Perhaps his manner was a little more vague than she was used to. "We were talking about dreams. I never seem to have any."

"Oh," said Power. "You must have dreams. Everybody dreams,

it's just that sometimes we just don't seem to see them or fail to listen to them. It's like we're not listening to ourselves. As if what our unconscious mind says to us is not important. You know . . ." He did not know her name.

"Angela." She said.

"Angela, it's a funny thing. After people have met me they start to dream. After they hear me or read about me, they start to have the most important dreams. I don't know why, I tell people 'you can dream' and they can."

"Oh," she said.

Her colleague, who was driving the Rover, was more interested in other things. "They say you know Superintendent Lynch inside out. What's he like?"

"Why do you want to know?"

"He's distant. Not like the rest of us. They say he's really religious."

"He makes no secret of his faith," said Power. "I'm beginning to believe we all need a faith."

The lights of Chester were in the distance. "I'm not religious. Don't believe in religions. They just divide the world, and anything that divides the world causes war."

"Perhaps you believe in yourself," said Power. "That's a different kind of faith."

"You're a friend of Lynch," said Angela. "Are you religious too?"

"I wish I could believe in something," said Power, looking out at the night sky. One of the brightest stars seemed to be moving.

Angela Wilson watched the wistful doctor as he stared out into the dark sky. She could get to like him if she saw more of him. She turned round and sat back in her seat as they drove up to the floodlit police headquarters, overlooking the River Dee.

Lynch welcomed Power into his office on the fourth floor. The weary Doctor sank gratefully into one of the deep leather chairs that Lynch had once rescued from the old police headquarters. Lynch was smiling broadly. "We've caught him," he beamed. "Trying to get money using his sister's credit card in Amsterdam. I knew it wouldn't be long before he turned up. Michael McWilliam isn't the kind of person who can survive without money."

"He's been in Amsterdam, has he been using anything?" asked Power.

"Of course," said Lynch. "Michael McWilliam wouldn't last ten minutes in Amsterdam before he got stuck into whatever muck was on sale. I should think he's been pushing the crap into his veins since he first got there. His sister gave him over two thousand pounds in cash. It was to see him through a few weeks. I guess it only saw him through a few days. He likes to buy very pure stuff. So, after going hungry for a few days and starting to withdraw, he needed to get some more cash. He had his sister's credit card details and tried those. A bank assistant was curious about him and ran the necessary checks. A computer trace alerted us. That's how we got hold of him. For the last few days he'd been squatting in a houseboat on the river. That's if you can squat on a boat." Lynch seemed pleased with himself.

"A computer trace?" It seemed to Power that no-one could hide anymore, that sooner or later all human activity was registered as a brief, bright spark of electricity in some dark memory bank. "And he was trying to raid her credit account? He's not got much family feeling has he?" Power felt angered on Lucinda's behalf. She must have given Michael the money to help him, as his father and mother had done before her. Michael has abused their love.

"It all fits," said Lynch. "He only loves himself. As long as he feeds his habit he's all right. Anything, anyone, can be sacrificed as long as he's fixed. People hardly matter to him as people. They're just a means to an end. Just there to be used.

"And what's even better . . . we have a witness that saw him driving the white car. You remember the white car we found at the house that Sir Ian used? We have a villager in Heaton who swears that she saw that car racing through the village the night of the fire . . . when the Hall was burnt down. She says Michael was driving it."

"But if the car was racing through the village how could she see his face?"

"He had to stop for another car at a T-junction. Our witness lives on the corner of the T-junction in the village. She looked out of her front room window to see what all the noise was about, and there was Michael McWilliam in the driving seat. She even took the car's number on the back of a telephone bill. The next day she had forgotten all about the car. Forgot to mention it, and of course nobody asked any of the villagers about a white car because at that stage we didn't know anything about the white car. To our great and good fortune she stuck the telephone bill at the back of a drawer, and when we went round questioning everybody after Lady McWilliam's death she remembered the piece of paper and brought it forward. Her evidence links Michael with the house fire, with the white car, and with the house his father kept, and ultimately with Zoë Allen."

"And if he is linked in," said Power. "All our ideas about his getting photographs of Zoë and blackmailing his father and mother become possible at last."

"We'd like a confession from him. That would be the icing on the cake," said Lynch.

"Is that why you've asked me here?"

"Well, Carl. I'd like your opinion on him . . . on how he is . . ."

On the ground floor of the building there was a suite of interview rooms. Once upon a time they had been carefully furnished in the then fashionable, warm colours of brown and maroon. Time had rendered the colours unfashionable and heavy wear had taken its toll on the tables, chairs and carpet. The table was scratched, burnt by neglected cigarette ends, and ringed by leaking plastic coffee cups. The carpet was matted with chewing gum and black burns from carelessly discarded cigarettes. The room smelt fusty, reeking of stale cigarette smoke and the sweat of fearful anxiety.

Michael McWilliam sat dejectedly by the wall. On the table by him was the official tape recorder that would record all Lynch's interviews with him. Lynch was a pedant where the use of the tape recorder was concerned. He would record every exchange if he could. No sooner had he and Power entered the room than Lynch put fresh cassette tapes into the machine. As he formally introduced himself and Dr Power he watched Michael's responses carefully. Nothing about him had changed since Lynch had tried, abortively, to interview McWilliam before. McWilliam did not look up as Lynch spoke. No movement indicated that he was even aware of the others in the room.

"When the Dutch police found you, you offered to come back to this country. Is that right?" asked Lynch. No response. "Why was that? They told me that you had been trying to get money out of your sister's credit account. Is that right? Was it easier to come back here now you've run out of money? Or did you want to put us straight about one or two things?" Silence. "I was wondering why you'd left the country all of a sudden like that? It looked suspicious you see? Some people might have thought the worse . . . that you were responsible for your parents' deaths. You might want to set the matter straight about that mightn't you? That might be why you agreed to come back to us."

Michael looked at his fingers intently. He had a scrap of silver paper between his forefinger and thumb. The reflections of light from its shiny surface seemed to be an endless wonder to him. "Some people might read things into your silence, Michael. They might suggest that your silence indicated guilt rather than innocence. A good prosecutor might just do that. And then what role did your sister play in all this spiriting you out of the country? Was she an accessory to the crimes?" Lynch felt Power stirring uncomfortably at his elbow. Clearly the thought that Lucinda was more deeply involved in the affair unsettled him. Lynch had warned Power about getting too attached . . . however, if mentioning his sister was designed to provoke Michael into some defence of her it had failed as a mechanism. Michael said nothing. Whether this was through a selfish lack of brotherly feeling, or something else was not clear.

235

Power indicated silently that he would like to ask something. Lynch nodded his assent. "Michael, I'm Dr Power. Do you remember me? You drove Lucinda's car to my house. You ate with us. Do you remember?" Power's voice caught Michael's attention. He looked up and stopped fiddling with the silver foil. His eyes were unearthly, because their pupils were so tightly constricted. They stared at Power unwaveringly. Power felt uncomfortable at such close scrutiny. Although the scrutiny was close it also seemed uncomprehending, for McWilliam's face was as blank as snow. "What did you take in Amsterdam? What drug?" No response. "What day do you think it is?" Nothing. "Where do you think you are? Holland or Britain?" Beyond the shift in attention that he had made, Michael McWilliam seemed as unlikely to talk as ever. Power stood up and moved around the table. McWilliam's head did not move to follow the doctor. Power touched McWilliam's shoulder and arm. Michael did not move. Power lifted up Michael's arm. It felt heavy and when Power tried to bend it at the elbow, the muscle tone was increased, as if all the muscles in his arm were tautened by anxiety. Power lifted the arm up and then let it go. For a moment the arm remained high in the air, its posture preserved as if Michael were an animator's doll. Only slowly did the arm gradually return to the table top. Power resumed his seat. "We might as well conclude the interview," he said. He beckoned to Lynch to follow him. Outside in the corridor Power spoke, "He's not in a fit state to interview. Whether it's from the drugs he's been taking, or from great anxiety I don't know, but he's practically catatonic. You could fire questions at him all day, and he won't respond. Only when he comes out of the catatonic stupor will he begin to answer you."

"Do you think he's putting it on? I mean we asked the police surgeon to see him and he wasn't sure. He advised us to get a psychiatric opinion. That's why I thought of you."

Power nodded. "Did the police surgeon take blood samples?"

"I don't think so."

Power frowned. "I'll take them then. We need urine samples too.

I want to find out what he's been taking. I don't think he's putting this on. No doubt you've seen people who feign mental illness. They call it the Ganser syndrome, where prisoners say what they think will make you believe they're mad. You'll ask them a simple question and they'll give you what they think is a wrong answer. Like you ask them how many legs a camel has and they'll say three. But their conception of what madness is, is usually wrong. Michael McWilliam isn't faking, though. For one thing the constriction of pupils is involuntary. I think he's probably been on some opiate, like heroin, but he's been mixing it with something else. MDMA, acid or amphetamines, I can't tell. So, until all that's out of his system you won't be able to make any sense of him. It's possible that even when the drugs have worn off he may have some underlying mental illness. People who have been through a lot of stress . . . and he has been whichever way you look at it . . . the stress can precipitate mental illness."

"Or he may have been mentally ill for some time. He may have killed his parents when he was ill."

"It's possible," conceded Power. "Children with schizophrenia may rarely kill their parents, especially if they are a focus for their delusions. But here, in this case, that wouldn't be my first bet."

"Does he need to be in hospital?"

"Things will be very different in a few hours when the drugs have worn off. I'd be reluctant to admit him to my ward," said Power. "Especially if you decide to charge him. If he's charged you'd need somewhere more secure than my general hospital ward. The Regional Secure Unit might help."

Lynch groaned. "Just when you think life is getting simple. I don't want to charge him until I've spoken to him. And I can't speak to him until he's better. And the places that could make him better won't take him until they know what they're dealing with. It goes round in circles."

"It could be different in an hour or so."

"Right," said Lynch. "May I call you again, if he doesn't settle? To arrange the secure bed?"

"Of course," said Power wearily. He ached to get back to his home and his bed. He managed a smile though and his friend patted him on the back.

"Oh . . . I pray that I'm doing the right thing. If Michael isn't the murderer, he's still out there. Waiting for me." Lynch sighed. He had set his course when he sought Zoë Allen's release. And it had been Dr Power who had instigated it all. Was it any wonder that Lynch should now want Power here to share in the ending of it all. He had the errant son in his grasp, he had the good beginnings of a case that might convict Michael McWilliam of his parents' murder. So what was wrong? It was that Lynch's own self-doubt was matched by Power's doubts about Michael's guilt. Lynch wanted to be alone now, to pray and to think. Lynch felt that more than ever only his faith could help him steer the right course through these waters. He smiled reassuringly at his friend, but the smile of reassurance was more for himself. "Thank you for coming, Carl. I'll get someone to run you home."

Chapter Twelve

Somnia a Deo missa

Power reached home at one o'clock in the morning. He collapsed into his bed and, although apprehensive about the possibility of being woken by Lynch seeking a secure psychiatric placement for Michael McWilliam, Power fell into a deep and solid sleep. Even if Lynch had rung, it was doubtful that the telephone could have woken him, but in the event, Lynch did not ring. Power hurtled downwards into a vivid underworld of dreams. Every so often he dreamt a dream of such intense colour and sound that it surpassed even reality. This was such a dream. And when he awoke just before dawn he was drenched in perspiration. Never before had he woken with such a clear plan of action in his mind. He switched the lights on and busied himself getting up. After a cursory shower he dressed hurriedly and without regard to colour or style. His mind kept on running through the dream. He did not pause to eat (an unusual thing for Power), and ran out of the house to the car. As he drove through the darkened village streets towards the motorway his mind kept playing through images from the dream.

There had been a magical place, a place of great joy and great comfort. There had been music and laughter and smiling faces. He remembered looking at all the dream children that were thronging what seemed to be a great hall. At one end a group of the children were playing party games, a game of blind man's bluff. The blindfolded boy in the centre was close to a roaring fire in a huge, gothic fireplace that occupied the whole of one end of the hall. The blindfolded boy was able to find the other children around him, but he could not hold onto them. All the children that came within his grasp broke free. They fought and struggled like mad to get away from him. One such child was so vigorous in his attempts to escape that when he did so, the hoodwinked child fell backwards and into the flames. He seemed to exist for only a second before he disappeared, like a tissue of paper exploding into a brief scintillation of fire. A girl on the edge of the crowd began to cry. She hadn't joined in this game of blind man's bluff, she had been too afraid. Now her fears seemed justified. The dream Power looked around, wondering where the adults were to comfort the children, but someone said that they had gone a long time ago.

The girl's tears melted away her face, and she cried so much that her entire body had dissolved. The children were quiet for a second and then they began to play again. Power tried to protest that things were not right, that whoever was in charge of the hall should be found. But his sensible words were drowned out in another party game. The game seemed to go on around Power. He felt distant, because he could not participate. The laughter passed by him and over him, like a bright wave of sound.

The sound of laughter was then replaced by the sound of a flute. The flute became louder. Its tone changed so that each note sounded like a bell chiming. Power tried to look around, but he couldn't. He looked down and saw that his feet and body were encased in glass, like an insect frozen forever in amber. He could not see who was playing the flute. The children around him started to leave the hall through the two doors by the fireplace. Gradually there were fewer and fewer children in the hall, and Power was in danger of being left alone. He tried to follow, but his legs would not work. The last children to leave seemed to be in a panic to do so. They pushed the children in front of them so that they might hurry all the quicker out of the hall. At first the dream child that Power had become wondered if this was like The Pied Piper of Hamelin, where the children are piped away by the Piper to a magic realm under the hill, and where only the lame boy fails to reach the Promised Land. But the dream Power was disabused of this notion by the fear evident on the faces of the children as they scrambled to leave the hall. They were looking behind them in terror to where Power was. Power wondered if they were frightened of him. As the last child left and the doors boomed shut at the other end of the hall Power was uncomfortably aware that the flute/bell music had come much closer. He managed to turn his head slightly and his eyes met those of an old man. The old man's eyes twinkled as he played, but there was no delight in those eyes, only a mischievous glee. The music that the old man played with his wizened lips was not designed to attract the children. The notes began to squeak and squawk, making awkward high-pitched sounds. The dream child Power began to feel afraid of what might be to come. He wondered if he might break the glass, but he was held fast and could not move nor rock the glass block that imprisoned him. Then behind him he heard the scrabble of tiny claws against the wooden floor. The scrabbling became a rumble and then hundreds of rats scattered across the floor. They crawled over the old man, who became festooned with their furry brown bodies and pink tails, so that no part of him could be seen. The music continued unaffected. At first the rats could not climb the glass walls of the block that held Power. Their claws made no purchase upon the hard sheer sides. But then the rats took to jumping. And with each jump they seemed to be able to jump higher the next time, until at last one managed to jump on to the top of the glass block. It sat there for a moment cleaning its whiskers. Then it turned to Power's face and looked him in the eye.

    Power had woken at that point and been catapulted into a flurry of activity even though it was still dark. Now, driving through the final last hours of the night his adrenalin levels were so high that he did not feel tired at all, despite having lost hours of sleep from either end of the night.

    As the sun began to rise he was entering the outskirts of the city to the children's hospital where he had once worked. He prayed that someone there could help him in this sudden quest.

    Power parked in the hospital car park, under the glow of an

orange sodium light. He stepped out into the morning air. He could hear the birds beginning to sing as he crossed the dew-moistened tarmac to the main entrance. He almost walked into the plate-glass doors, expecting them to slide open as he approached. But there was no 'open-sesame' to be had at this time of the morning. He pressed the emergency bell by the entrance. He waited whilst the lone telephonist on duty looked up from the glass booth where she worked. Behind her head a bank of video screens glowed, showing various views of the car park and hospital entrances. She looked at Power suspiciously. He did not look the type to press the emergency bell late at night. He didn't look like an anxious parent visiting his sick child, and without a child with him, he was evidently not some anguished parent bringing their child as an emergency to casualty. He was dressed well enough, but he was not any of the doctors she recognised from the paediatric hospital's staff. She pressed the intercom and spoke to him, "Hello, can I help you?"

"My name's Dr Power, I'm a Consultant Psychiatrist. I'm wanting to get hold of some records, please."

He could see the explanation did not impress her. She thought about it for a while.

"The records office is closed," she said. "You'll have to come back in the morning, I'm sorry."

"It's an emergency," said Power. "There must be some contingency . . . other doctors must be able to get hold of notes in an emergency." She frowned, because that was so. But she still did not want to admit this stranger.

"I don't know," she said. "You don't work here do you?" It was a statement, more than a question.

"No," said Power. "But I used to . . . when I was a Registrar." She pursed her lips. "I used to work with Dr Jones." He had clearly long retired for there was no flicker of recognition on the receptionist's face. The mention of another unfamiliar name did not help his case.

"I'm sorry." she said. "Have you any identification?" This set Power riffling through his pockets whilst she looked on guardedly, unsure of whether she could grant this stranger access even if he was a bona fide consultant. A call came through on the console to divert her. Whilst she was taking the telephone call and putting the caller through to the cardiology ward Power found his identity card. It had always looked like a prison mug shot. He waved it at the glass, but the telephonist's attention was elsewhere. Just then, when Power's nocturnal quest seemed doomed to failure and he was thinking of finding somewhere to breakfast and eat away his sorrows, a familiar figure sauntered into view.

The figure, pushing a heated food trolley (shaped like Thomas the Tank Engine) for one of the wards, paused at the reception desk and leant in a relaxed way against the glass, about to make some bantering comment to the telephonist. He was alerted by her glance at Power and he straightened up immediately, his jovial expression replaced by alertness. He stared at Power for a moment, and then he remembered. His moustachioed face split into a broad grin. His eyes laughed. He said something to the receptionist and the hospital doors opened as if by magic. Power hadn't heard what Roly the porter had said but it had worked like an 'open sesame' anyway.

Power stepped into the warmth and light of the hospital. Roly came out from behind the breakfast-laden food trolley and slapped his hand into Power's. "Dr Power, you old bastard, what brings you back to wonderland?" Power smiled at Roly's effortless scouseness. Roly had the ability to talk how he liked to whoever he liked and get away with it. Roly was Roly and nobody would change him. He was brutally frank, but he was kind; he was irreverent, but he was good-hearted. The children in the hospital loved him and he loved them. Like the cartoon characters depicted on the hospital corridor's walls, Roly was larger than life. He was loud and he was brash, but he could just as easily be softly spoken and tender to a child being wheeled to the operating theatre. He was a one-off.

"It's been a long time," said Power.

"Too right," said Roly. "Come with me, I've got to shift this trolley to C ward."

"What's it got in it?" asked Power as Roly set off pushing the trolley down the long and deserted corridor. "Eggs and bacon and baked beans?"

Roly looked at Power as though he was from outer space. "Where have you been, Doc? This is the NHS."

"They used to have eggs and bacon on the wards when I was a Registrar."

"Porridge, that's what, Doc. There are some dry bread rolls and jam and a little bit of toast that you wouldn't give your Rottweiler. This wagon-train's not worth hijacking."

"I seem to remember there was always a spare bit of bacon when I worked here, I used to have a bacon butty when I came on to the ward at eight o'clock."

"There ain't none of that. The managers are tighter than a duck's arse. No bacon for the kids let alone wasters like doctors. Tell me, doc, it's years since I clapped eyes on you. What happened to you?"

"I'm a consultant in Cheshire, now."

"You always were a no-good. Working over there in Manchester are you? Manchester's full of scumbags." He pulled up outside the ward and plugged the heated trolley into the wall outside the door. "Got to be quiet here Doc. Whisper. Sick kids in there, Doc. Break your heart to see them. Kids born with hepatitis or HIV, no immune system. You know?" Power nodded. "Break your heart. Still . . ." Roly looked closely at Power. "You didn't come here for Roly's chat. If you don't mind me saying it you look . . ." He looked around to make sure no one was near. "Well, to be frank, you look shagged-out."

"I couldn't sleep. Bad dreams."

"Oh . . . like that is it . . . all this psycho stuff. I went to a hypnotist once, to cure me smokin'. He went on about me dreams. Told him to mind his own . . ." Roly saw a nurse approaching and moderated his language. His accent became more respectable as she passed. He even spoke a little louder so she could hear. "You were saying Dr Power?" As they passed he instinctively looked backwards at her disappearing figure. "I like her," he confided. "Go on, what do you want? Can I help?"

"I'm working on a case . . . after this dream that I had I remembered something. I need to look up something in some case notes. A patient I once saw here. A teenager when I saw him. The notes are very important."

"Life and death important?"

"Life and death" said Power.

"Oh well," said Roly. "If it's **that** important you can't see them, you'll have to fill in a request to the Hospital Trust in triplicate and wait three weeks for some manager to think it over and see whether it's in their business int'rests . . ."

"I haven't got that time," said Power.

"I know," said Roly. "That's why you've come to the main man. The man at the very eye of the needle. Roly can get you anything and everything. Roly can get you anywhere and everywhere. There is nothing I can't go, get or do." He leant confidentially towards Power. "I have a bit of difficulty with the computer system, but I'm getting the hang of it. Hacking, Doc. That's what I do in the long night hours. Tapping away at the keyboard. Huntin' an' ferretin' an' nosin' about."

It was outrageous talk. How much was exaggeration and how much truth Power didn't like to imagine, but he did need those notes and he wasn't going to challenge Roly's grandiose assertions. If Roly could get him the notes Power wasn't going to argue. Roly took Power past the closed doors of the wards and down to the old outpatient unit. "They've re-vamped most of this for the managers. The managers always have the best offices, the best desks, the best computers."

"They all have offices?" said Power sadly, remembering the battle he had had to get his own small space to see patients in.

"Ay," said Roly. "I think they sometimes forget that the hospital's for the kids, not for them to line their purses." Power fell silent. Roly was unlocking a stout wooden door. "You remember this, Doc?"

"The old child psychiatry ward," said Power.

"Yeah," said Roly. "It's closed now though . . . after all, what's a hospital for..." He opened the door wide and Power looked into the chaos of the abandoned ward. As he walked in, he walked into his own past. Where the discarded beds and trolleys now stood as sentinels to the past, Power could see the children running about, screaming with laughter. He remembered the cheeky ones running up to him with grins and insults that they used to try and hide their respect for the young doctor. He remembered more withdrawn children, quiet and pale, nestled under the ample wings of the ward sister as they all sat on the couch watching Neighbours on the television. And he remembered the others. There was the girl who wouldn't come out of her bedroom to talk to him, so abused had she been by the men in her past. There in the corner was a dust-covered pool table. Power remembered the boys clustered about it fighting over the rules. On their periphery had been a small boy, small for his years, rejected by his mother because he soiled his pants day-in and day-out. He remembered his smell, and the toothless grin he had made. All his teeth had been rotted by the cola his mother had fed to him in his baby bottle.

Power looked at the dining tables and could see in his mind's eye, an eight-year-old anorexic boy, colouring in a cartoon with painstaking accuracy. Every now and then he would stand up and wobble on matchstick legs to his bedroom to get another crayon. He deliberately made as many trips as he could to burn as many calories off as he could: from the minimal amounts he ate.

All of these children that Power remembered had recovered with care and with love. The memory of his short time there as a Registrar was warm within his heart. Standing in the broken ward now he remembered another boy on the ward, who sat by the television and called out smart insults and wisecracks to the other children, who tried as much as he could to hurt with his tongue, because he couldn't hurt with his hands or his legs. The boy had been in a wheelchair.

"The notes," said Power looking about the desolation with panic in his heart. "What did they do with the notes? Is there anything left on microfiche or . . . ?"

Roly laughed. "They're not that organised! They told me to burn them, when they closed the unit. Can you believe it? I thought it was a daft idea at the time, so Roly found a place for them. Come on." He led Power into what had been the children's dormitory. The child size beds had been stacked into a corner and against the cubicle walls were piles of notes all tied up with string. "If you put 'em into a single pile," said Roly. "There'd be a pile a hundred foot high." Power groaned at the mountains of paper work. "Don't worry, Doc, they're all in alphabetical order. I'm not that daft."

Power seated himself on one of the battered old chairs and began sifting through the pile of notes, which looked most promising. Pleased by his own ability to help, Roly went on his own way, whistling happily to himself. Morning sun was beaming through the old ward windows when Power finally came across the single set of case notes that he had wanted so much.

He put the unwanted case notes back on their pile and then settled down to look at the pink cardboard folder of notes he had selected. The notes were thick and crammed full of letters and investigation sheets. Power had wondered whether his recollection of what these notes contained was just a wishful fantasy. He had wondered if his mind had merely dreamed their existence. But here they were. The name on the cover was the same as he had imagined it to be. His memory had not been playing him tricks.

As he opened the notes he caught sight of a glimpse of his own black fountain-penned script. He looked at the dates and was sobered by the passage of time. He had written these at the start of his career . . . in the previous decade, but personally he didn't feel a day older. He must have seen thousands of patients since this one child. He read through his own meticulous entries. The first time he had clerked this patient he had written eleven pages of notes on him. He remembered the patient better with the notes in front of him. The boy had been brought to the psychiatry ward from the orthopaedic department.

The teenage boy had been unable to walk for three months after an accident in a school rugby match. Despite his continuing insistence that he was in great pain and unable to walk, the surgeons could find not find a single shred of evidence that there was anything wrong with the young man. His many X-rays, nerve conduction tests and brain scans were all normal. There was no evidence of malignancy or infection. Physically he was well, but although this had been explained time after time after time to the boy and to his anxious mother, still the boy would not give up his wheelchair. When Power had seen him as a junior doctor all those years ago, he had sat there solidly, answering the junior psychiatrist's questions with polite detachment. He had said, "I know they think it's all in my mind, but from where I'm sitting my legs just will not work, and they can't rule everything out, can they? It's impossible to have a medical test for everything. Even if they can rule out 99% of all things there's still the 1% they don't know about."

Power had documented the strictly religious school. The boy had stressed his faith and in the same way had described his parents with almost reverential tones. His father was a great man, an international businessman and a pillar of the community. He didn't have much time for the boy when he was home, which was rarely, his time was spent on the golf course or sailing. But the young man made it clear that his father was not to be blamed. His father had a stressful life and could not be burdened. His father needed time to relax. It was vital for his health. His mother had seemed an anxious woman, according to Power's notes. She was particularly anxious about the boy's schoolwork. They had such plans for him. Power had noted that the mother had wanted the boy to be a doctor. He remembered that her ambitions for her son had angered him. Medicine was no career to follow unless it was your own choice of profession! Power had written down in the notes about a younger brother and a sister too, but the young man had spoken of them in derogatory terms. They were 'no marks', his brother was 'retarded' and his sister was a 'nymphomaniac', whilst the young man piously boasted on his own intelligence, taste and virginity. Although he hadn't noted it down, Power now recalled how irritated he had been at the boy's egocentric view of the world.

It had seemed to Power at the time that the young man was desperately trying to escape something; either some problem at school or a problem with his distant father, or some internal clash between his own drives and the suffocating demands of his mother and father. Power hadn't recorded it, but he remembered thinking that the boy didn't seem master of his destiny, that there was rebellion in his young heart, borne out by his obstinate refusal to walk, and a disturbing lack of insight into his own denial.

They had kept him on the ward for two months and no progress had been made, until a promise was made to him by his grandmother that if he could progress sufficiently well with his physiotherapy to dance with her at her eighty-fifth birthday, then she would buy him a car when he was eighteen. The improvement in his condition was not so dramatic as to prove that he was faking his inability to walk, but there was a noticeable improvement in terms of his effort in physiotherapy. After another month he was standing and walking short steps. He was discharged a week before the grand party and danced with his grandmother at this family event. There was no note of any contact with the hospital after this time.

Power had offered psychotherapy to try and unravel the dilemmas that had driven the young man to adopt the wheelchair as his shield or as some kind of revenge against his family, but the offer was never taken up. And the record might have stood there with the boy's regained ability to walk as one of the successes of the hospital, except that here now was Dr Power, many years later re-visiting the hospital and with the certain knowledge that the boy's fate had been altogether different.

Power put the case notes back into the folder that they had spent the last decade or so in. He made his way out of the ward and back towards the main hospital entrance. On his way he stopped to say 'goodbye' to Roly, but Roly had gone off shift an hour before. Power smuggled the notes out inside his coat and drove himself to a fast food restaurant to reward himself for his discovery. He sat in the car park of the drive-in munching a decidedly unhealthy breakfast of scrambled eggs and bacon from a plastic tray and swigging hot sweet black coffee. As he breakfasted, Power listened to an old recording of Peter Grimes that he had unearthed from of his collection. He glanced occasionally at the case notes sitting on the passenger seat and wondered how best he might use this final clue. Eventually, replete and cheered by the sun Power drove off, his mind made up.

★ ★ ★

Power stopped the car near the post office in the village of Penrhyn. It was still only early morning. A few elderly early birds were pottering between the butchers and the greengrocers. Power made a phone call from the High Street telephone box. The line was poor, but the Police receptionist's voice was clear enough. Superintendent Lynch was not in the office and his secretary could not tell the caller where he was. Power had tried to make his case to be allowed an urgent message to the Superintendent, but the stonewalling skills of the receptionist were admirable. Power went to the village post office and bought a copy of *The Independent* and waited. He phoned the police headquarters in Chester ten minutes later, hoping that the response might be different. Since he merely encountered the same receptionist the result was equally frustrating.

"Has he gone to the Cathedral?" asked Power. Power knew that Lynch usually liked to attend the morning service if he could, particularly if a case was proving extra difficult. Prayer helped Lynch. However, the receptionist would not be drawn on the piety or otherwise of any senior officer. Shrugging off the rebuff Power left a message for Lynch's secretary, thanked her for her help and put the phone down. He had tried to get help, and if that help was not immediately forthcoming Power was not one to hold back, not when his interest was so strongly aroused. He got back in the car and set today's newspaper down on the pink cardboard-bound notes on the passenger seat.

The sun beamed down on Power as he drove the short distance up the hill from the coastal village to Tuke's bungalow on the Little Orme. Had he but known it Power passed the nurse's cottage on the way. He parked his car on the drive way of Tuke's bungalow. A cool breeze was blowing inland off the sea although the warm, morning sun was some protection against the wind. Power's jacket flapped about him as he got out. He reached over and took the notes off the passenger seat. He paused for a moment then picked up *The Independent* too and wrapped the notes discreetly inside the folded newspaper. His mind was full of memories and his heart was filled with a controlled anger. He did not have the attention to spare to notice the sun sparkling on the heavy blue sea, nor the time to see the horizon's darkening sky. Towering columns of cloud were building up far out over the restless ocean, like an army massing on the crest of a hill.

Power shut his car door softly and walked over to the front door, passing the garage on his way. For a moment he paused, his finger suspended over the doorbell, then he turned and walked back to the garage. He peered through the window. It might have been reasonable for Tuke to have sold his car, but the dark garage housed a modern, white Toyota Carina. Power thought that perhaps Tuke could not bear to acknowledge his final disability by selling his car. But he noticed from the windscreen tax disc that the car was taxed for the current year.

Curiosity satisfied, Power returned to the front door and lifted his hand to ring the doorbell. At that very moment the front door opened. He came face-to-face with Tuke's nurse, Megan Driver. She had not been expecting anybody to be there and consequently was as startled by him as he was by her. It took her a few seconds to recognise him, "What do you want?" It was hardly a welcome of any sort.

"I wanted to see him, please."

"He's in bed," she said. "He took to his bed after you left. He can hardly move his head off the pillow. I have to transfer him from the bed to the commode. He's lost his will to survive . . . as if you'd just destroyed him . . ." She stood firmly in the doorway, barring any entrance. "Have you come back to finish him off!"

Power thought about the notes that he carried hidden under his arm. "I'm sorry to hear this . . . perhaps I can help . . . talk to him about it and sort things out."

"He was worried about you . . . that you were a fraud . . . nothing to do with the police at all. Just someone with a grudge or something. He phoned up the police in Chester and then he sent me out to the Library to look you up in the Medical Directory. He wanted your address."

"And I trust that your researches confirmed my story?"

She nodded. "And is that why you've come back to hound him? More police business? He was devastated by the news of the deaths. He was very upset by you. Felt that you didn't believe that he was upset."

"It sounds as if he wanted to convince me he was upset."

"There you go," she said in triumph. "That was as sceptical a comment as I've ever heard. You should be ashamed of yourself, calling yourself a psychiatrist."

"I must talk with Mr Tuke," said Power.

"He's in bed," she said. She folded her arms and did not move an inch.

"I have to talk with him. Either here or in the police cells," and so saying he pushed past her. There was something of an unseemly struggle as he squeezed through the doorway.

"You're no gentleman," she said angrily as Power succeeded in barging his way into the house.

"I know it seems that way," said Power as he disappeared down the hallway. "But I have good reasons. You'll see that in the end . . ."

She did not follow him. Power was struck by how she had silently vanished like a conquered monster disappearing off screen in a computer game. He put his hand to Tuke's door and pushed it open.

At one end of the room, a single divan had been set up near the window. The strong morning sunlight fell on the crisp white pillow. Dust from the bed danced in the sunbeam. Tuke's yellowish face seemed to recede into the pillow as if bleached out by the sun. All at once a cloud obscured the sun and Tuke's features became wholly visible to Power.

"I thought it would be you," said Tuke. His voice was fractured and weak. "What can a dead husk ... of a man ... do for the living?"

"Your car is brand new and taxed for the current year," said Power. "Hardly consistent with a 'dead husk of a man'."

Tuke frowned. "No pleasantries? No 'and how are you today'?"

"No," said Power, fully aware of how confrontative he must seem. Despite Power's simmering anger with the man, he knew that Tuke would seek out any self-doubt that Power had and exploit it as best he could. Tuke would play on this if he let him. Power couldn't allow himself to be deflected anymore. "Tell me about the car."

"It's there in the garage. You know I can't use it, but I like to know it's there. And Megan could use it if she wanted to ..."

"But it must be expensive to keep it going," said Power. "You've only just renewed the road tax. An unnecessary expense."

"My money will last me out," said Tuke. "Are you trying to rub my nose ... in the shit, Doctor?" He chose his words with care to provoke and disturb the doctor.

"It sounds like you want me to feel sorry for you," said Power.

"I'm talking about my independence," said Tuke. "My rights as a person. I don't want, and would never court, your sympathy Doctor."

"So you keep the car on, because you can't bear the idea that giving it up is one step nearer the grave."

Tuke coughed. "You're a blunt bastard aren't you?"

"Sometimes," said Power. "When people cling onto false ideas, you have to confront them with the truth. Because people will do all kinds of things to avoid the truth. They'll lie through their teeth to deceive others, but even worse, they'll lie to themselves ... deceive themselves unconsciously as well as consciously."

"I know I'm going to die soon, Doctor. You don't have to confront me with that."

"That's not the truth I meant," said Power. "In the last few weeks I've encountered more deceptions and half-truths than I've ever done before. I've had a glimpse into the world of the politicians and found that in the world of politics nothing is what it seems. Strange that you should find your way into that world, where truth has a very short half-life."

"What do you mean?"

"Politicians seem to be paradoxes. Like Sir Ian McWilliam, your mentor. The man who you followed like a disciple for so many years, and the man who you ... loved? And at the same time you loved him he was the man who you think betrayed you, and whom you hated. He was at the same time a respected cabinet minister, and someone who was courting European extremists. All along I've had to reconcile the different faces of Sir Ian McWilliam. I've had to learn how to seek out both parts of a paradox. Sir Ian was neither a very good man (as he would like to be remembered I have no doubt), nor a very bad man. And Zoë Allen was neither a sweet innocent virgin, nor an sex-obsessed murderer. I've had to reconcile my impressions of all these people."

"So," said Tuke. "So what? People are more complex than the stereotypes we're fed on TV? So you have to make an effort to understand ... so what?"

"I'm saying it must have been difficult for you ... to realise that Sir Ian McWilliam was not the great white hope you imagined him to be. When he was your tutor at University and you became enamoured with him as a student ... he must have seemed like a god, and you expected him to be the same. It was clear that he expected you to behave in a certain way too ... he began to trust you with secrets. He must have thought you were good with secrets, mustn't he?"

"He was thinking of resigning as a minister," said Tuke.

Power sat down at the bedside. The statement had been thrown out as bait. What was Tuke trying to do? What was he trying to say? "Why would a politician give up power?" Power asked, struggling to keep control of the conversation.

"To get more power," said Tuke shortly. "He was opening up the way to take up a part in European politics. 'Fortress Europe', that's what he wanted. A strong Europe, looking inwards, trading within itself, ignoring the rest of the world, expelling non-Europeans. There were certain Europeans who spotted his leadership potential."

Power noted that Tuke was becoming more fluent now he had control of the conversation. He was adeptly steering it away from where Power was heading, but at the same time making his points interesting enough so that Power would follow him. "So . . . what would happen to you . . . if McWilliam went European . . . what did he have planned for you?"

"Nothing," said Tuke.

"Why not?"

"I was already weak in his eyes."

"The illness?"

Tuke looked at Power, there was a hesitancy about him, as if he did want to say something, as if he burned to confess something. Something honest about himself. "I don't know how to put this," said Tuke. "You mentioned love . . . implied that . . ." he faltered in his explanation, then found his way again. "I was weak . . . to be dominated by him . . . he could never see, or know what to do with the love that people gave him . . . he counted their affection and their loyalty, but I don't think he knew why he did . . . because when he had their loyalty, when he'd led them to a point where they would give their everything to him . . . he would shit on them. He crapped on his wife. She adored him. He ignored her. He had affairs. I knew about them all." There was real pain in his voice. The knowledge had hurt him personally in some way. Power wondered whether Tuke had been jealous.

"And I mistook his confidence in me for some kind of affection or trust. He saw my loyalty as a weakness really. He liked other people's weakness, weakness was to be exploited."

Quietly, so as to minimise the threat as far as was possible, Power said "You mentioned love this time."

Despite Power's care with his words Tuke was exquisitely sensitive about the subject, "Well you would love to interpret that wouldn't you, I bet you would like to read all kinds of things into the word love wouldn't you?" He sneered at Power. "You'd think the worst. Wouldn't you? Like all of them. One day I was stupid. I told Ian how much I cared for him too. I did, you know. You couldn't begin to believe how much I cared for him. He used to be everything to me for years and years. I don't know whether he understood me the right way. He took it the same way as you. Just like you've obviously twisted things in your mind, Doctor . . . made them dirty and squalid . . . and . . ." Tuke swallowed hard. Now he had begun to tell Power he felt he must continue. He had wanted to tell someone for so long.

"When I told him, Ian, he laughed and said something awfully polite. I don't even know whether he understood me properly. It was shortly after this that I learnt he was contemplating leaving the British Government. He had had plans to take me with him, and now these plans had gone. I had frightened him away. He started being . . . I think he was being . . . cruel. The girl that had been writing to him . . . Zoë . . . he started seeing her. He flaunted her in front of me . . . to spite me. And I was becoming ill at that time too."

"In a way then," said Power. "The illness served both of you. It meant that McWilliam couldn't make further use of you, and it saved you any further embarrassment." Tuke looked sideways at Power. This was very dangerous ground.

"Well," said Tuke,"I didn't want to keep on working at the Department after he had gone. But the multiple sclerosis was affected by the stress. The stress made it much more aggressive. Without all the stress I might still be working."

"'It's possible," said Power. He paused. What Tuke had said confirmed all his theories. Power was gathering confidence. And with the confidence his sympathy for Tuke was lessened, and replaced in equal amounts by anger. Power would confront Tuke again. "So you were privy to all McWilliam's secrets? He had trusted you. And. from what you've just said it's clear that you knew more about Zoë than everybody else." And it was clear that Tuke had known all this without disclosing it to anyone before Zoë's trial. "McWilliam trusted you with that knowledge ... about the letters?"

"I didn't want to be trusted with that ... I didn't ask to be trusted with that."

"It hurt you?"

"It hurt me. He wanted it to hurt me," said Tuke, and his pain was almost palpable. It had taken great courage to tell McWilliam of his feelings for him. And McWilliam had laughed, as if it was some bad joke.

"If McWilliam was going to cut himself off from you, why would he let you know such sensitive things? He was careful about his secrets, he would have known that these were things that you could use against him. Surely he would have done everything in his power to keep you on his side. He wouldn't have tried to alienate you." Power doubted some of Tuke's account of events.

Tuke sighed, "He was a careful judge of men. He knew how much I would take. I sit here nowadays and wonder if he always knew what my feelings were for him. He might have known since University. He knew how much he could trust me. He never saw me using secrets against him. He saw me as completely dependent on him. Completely trustworthy.

"And maybe also if he was leaving British politics . . . well, the secrets would lose their dangerousness. It's the British who are so screwed up about sex. In Britain any news of his affairs would destroy his political life. The tabloids would roast him alive. But in European politics the affairs would be . . . less of a problem. He wanted to culture the male image after all. An affair or two would only emphasise his masculinity. He knew what he was doing."

"So you were angry with him. He betrayed your feelings for him. He taunted you with his lust for Zoë. He dropped you unceremoniously from his future plans."

"But I was ill," protested Tuke. "It all made no difference anyway. I didn't have any role anymore."

"What came first?" asked Power. "The illness or the rejection?"

Tuke glared at him. "The illness, of course, what else?"

Power slowly shook his head at the figure in the bed. Tuke slumped weakly against the pillows and stared up at the ceiling, as the doctor began to speak. "Since you're in bed, Jacob, let me tell you a bedtime story . . . about a child I met a long time ago." Power unwrapped the notes he had taken from the hospital. He opened the notes and stared at his own writing. "Once upon a time there was a boy who was doing well at school. He was good at sports and he was good in class. In fact, he excelled at everything. Every year he won a school prize. But although this success would have made some people happy, it didn't help this boy. Every time he succeeded it just made it more impossible to fail the next time. His parents kept on raising their expectations, and then he just didn't dare fail them. I guess, looking back, that there was some other pressure on him as well. A secret maybe? Something someone asked him to hide. That's been a pattern all the way through his life. So many secrets. Well, it all got so bad, such a heavy burden, that one day after what was in reality only a trivial sports injury this boy suddenly found he couldn't walk. His legs just wouldn't work for him. He went to the hospital. And over the weeks they ran lots of tests on him, scans of his spine, and scans of his brain, but the doctors scratched their own heads and they couldn't see what was wrong. There were no damaged bones, or muscles or nerves. Everything was in working order. It seemed as if it was just that this boy would not walk, rather than could not. His parents couldn't believe the doctors. They felt the doctors had got it wrong, and they brought in many specialists for second, third and fourth opinions, and the tests were repeated in different hospitals throughout the country. But they all came up with one finding; that there was nothing physically wrong with this boy. And so they asked the psychiatrists to help. The consultant admitted the boy to the ward, 'for rehabilitation' it says here, but it was an attempt to get the boy to gradually give up his wheelchair and walk again. The boy never told the doctors what had driven him into the wheelchair, but it must have been something quite awful, worse even than parents who pressured him to succeed. As a registrar, I was his doctor. It seems a long, long time ago. I suppose he was one of many patients that I treated and I suppose I was one of many doctors he saw. It's really not so surprising I couldn't recognise him when he was older.

"Secrets are dangerous things, they gain a hold over you, don't they, Jacob? In order to stay in the wheelchair you had to lie to yourself, you had to make yourself believe that you couldn't walk. It takes some doing to stop moving your legs for months. Only now you've elevated it to an art form, now you've grown up, you've managed it for years.

"See this," Power held up the notes so that Tuke could see the front cover. Written in large black capitals on the pink front was a patient identification number and below it, 'Jacob Tuke'. "Only chance stopped these notes of mine from being destroyed. And I only remembered you because of a dream. You were one of thousands of patients I've seen and treated and forgotten. It was the dream which helped me remember you."

"I don't know why you're telling me this. That wasn't me."

"This is pointless, Jacob. There aren't many people with your name," said Power. "It's pointless to deny it. People who would have known you then could verify that you were one and the same."

"My parents and all my relatives are dead." Power felt uneasy at this news. What could have happened to wipe out any living contact with the past? Despite the warm invalid's room, the doctor felt chilled. Tuke went on, "You're mistaken, Dr Power."

"I know you're expert at denying the truth, but you can't keep on doing it, Jacob. You can't split yourself off from the past . . . it's reaching out to you. There are these notes. There will be school photographs of you as a boy. You can't re-write what really happened."

Tuke looked carefully at Power's face, wondering if Power had told anybody else about his theory before blundering into his room. He decided to protest again, "My multiple sclerosis was diagnosed by a doctor."

"Doctors can be fooled," said Power. "The boy's name was Tuke, Jacob Tuke."

"It was not me," said Tuke. "You said it yourself, 'Doctors can be fooled'; they can be mistaken. And you are making a mistake. I am not the same person as you think. Before a few days ago I had never, never, met you. You are spinning a wild, wild tale. It is all fantasy. A delusion on your part."

Power laughed. "I know what the truth is."

"Even if you were right," said Tuke. "Even if you had seen me before, you must have been a bad doctor, mustn't you? All those doctors you say I saw, they must have missed my multiple sclerosis. That's why I can't walk now. All this crap about psychology . . . I'm a sick man. I don't have time for it. I'll be dead before the year's out . . . or is death all in the mind too . . . like with the illness of the poor boy whose notes you've got there . . . who you betrayed when you were his doctor all those years ago, by getting his diagnosis wrong."

"Are you admitting that the boy I saw was you?" asked Power.

"It doesn't matter does it? Either way you're professionally incompetent . . . and either way, I'm nearly dead with multiple sclerosis. So what does it all matter?"

The attack on Power's professionalism had stung him, but he reasoned that Tuke's best line of defence now was such an attack. "I didn't get the diagnosis wrong," said Power. "And I am sure you haven't got multiple sclerosis. But I wonder if after playing ill for so long whether even you have convinced yourself that you have the illness." Power stood up and wandered about the room.

"I want you to go," said Tuke from his sick bed. "I want you to go now."

Power looked at the thin figure in the bed. He saw the thin, bony knees that poked up through the bedspread. He felt a mild twinge of doubt. What if he were wrong, disastrously wrong and about to compound his error by accusing Tuke? He looked at the stick-like arms, withered by dis-use. He knew that, for whatever reason, if Tuke didn't use his limbs, they would get thinner and thinner without the exercise of everyday use. "I'm not going to go," said Power. "And if you want me to go, you can get up and make me."

"You bastard," said Tuke, weeping. "You cruel bastard. You're torturing me. You know I can't move. You cruel bastard . . ."

"Let's talk about the way it really is, Jacob." He paused and drew up a chair to Tuke's desk. He leant his elbows on the desk and stared across at the sobbing figure in the bed. "You might have been used by McWilliam, even been exploited by him. If he knew how you felt about him and used you all those years, then perhaps you would feel angry with him. He abused you, just as he abused the wishful fantasies of Zoë Allen. He flaunted his lust for her in your face. He got you to make his arrangements for him . . . or did you offer to do all that in your passive, adoring way? Did you willingly make the arrangements for the secret house, as McWilliam's friend . . . for old time's sake? I know you were no longer his civil servant, but did you kept in contact with McWilliam, want to stay close to him somehow, pay him back for all those wasted years as his adoring slave? I think you found the house in Chester, paid the rent for Sir Ian, hired the car for Sir Ian, and made sure that he could indulge himself to his heart's content without the risk of being caught out by the media. But in protecting him from the press and the embarrassment of their attention, you were gaining more power over him, weren't you? Sir Ian fell for your multiple sclerosis story, like everyone else, he probably wrote you off as a dying man, someone he could trust forever, but he didn't know about your past. When he was exploiting you for one last time he couldn't know that your illness was a psychological one not a physical one. He couldn't have appreciated the danger he was in." Power opened the notes of the child in front of him and read out his own writing. 'During the session this afternoon, Jacob became very angry. We were talking about a schoolmaster and his father. He started to shake with anger. He said he could murder someone. I wondered if this was a transference phenomenon, or whether he was really very angry with his father. He said he would pour petrol on the teacher and light it. It seemed to be a fantasy of his.' I thought those ideas would have gone away with time," said Power. "But the anger has been there all through your life, burning away inside you. You focused it on Sir Ian didn't you? You planned it all to the smallest detail. You would gain control of him forever. When he had Zoë there, when he was playing along with your plan, he was in your power, wasn't he. And to keep that hold over him you visited the house while she was there. You took some polaroid photographs of her, to keep and show to McWilliam. So you would always have something over him. Isn't that right? Where do you keep them?" Power looked around the room for likely places. "Did you enjoy seeing her like that, stretched out on the bed for your master. Did you relish the thought of gaining control over the master and his mistress? Did you want money . . . or just the power? Did her naked body do anything for you, or did she seem like a meaningless lump of flesh? What are people to you anyway?"

Tuke seemed to recede into the soft whiteness of his bed, he said miserably, "I can't even stand by myself. What you're saying is ludicrous. I can't walk, I can't drive. I haven't been out of the house in months. I'm dying."

"McWilliam took you out in his Land Rover," said Power. "So you have been out. You have time on your hands. You could make phone calls on McWilliam's behalf. Act as his agent, his unseen go-between in his affair with Zoë."

No," said Tuke. "Stop torturing me. I can't even move my legs.''

It was difficult to keep on confronting the pathetic figure in the bed.

Power felt doubt creeping into his heart. What if he was wrong? "I think you can do anything you want," he said. "It's like when you were a boy. Not walking is a good way of getting out of things, it's a

THE FIRE OF LOVE

method of getting what you want. It's a defence."

Tuke shut his eyes.

"Your car outside is fully taxed. I bet if I were to get in the driving seat and try to start it the engine would start first time."

Tuke said, "My nurse will confirm that I have been here, in my wheelchair or my bed all the time. Every hour of the day, every day of the week, every week of the year. I will be dead soon."

"I don't know when you planned on walking again, but you'll walk again, perhaps move abroad where people don't know you. Start a new life again. But you won't be able to do that, because you've been found out."

"I haven't left the house on my own. I couldn't. She'll tell you."

"Of course your nurse would," said Power. "You've deceived her like everyone else. When she arrives in the morning you're stuck in bed, she gets you up and washes you and takes you to the toilet and wipes your bottom for you, she dresses you and feeds you. Perhaps she leaves you listening to your music after lunch. Then she goes home, and when she comes back she gets your evening meal and she reverses the process and puts you back to bed. Then she goes home. She's here for some hours in the morning and evening, but for most of the day and all of the night, you are alone. You could get into your car and drive anywhere. Chester would take an hour at the most in that car of yours. It was you who arranged the safe house for McWilliam. You visited it while Zoë was there and you took photographs of her on the bed didn't you?"

Tuke did not stir, he seemed to be asleep. Power tried to take no notice. "You kept the photos to yourself then maybe late one night you took them to Sir Ian. He'd have been surprised, wouldn't he? Surprised to see you walking and talking normally and surprised at what you had to say and surprised at the photographs. After all you'd completely turned the tables on him, hadn't you? Suddenly you thought you were the powerful one. You'd kept some incriminating letters of hers and what with all the other information about Sir Ian, and the car, with his fingerprints on (and yours as well), and the photographs. You had him cornered. One of the most powerful men in the country. What did you want from him? You showed him the photos of her naked body, all tied up, abused by McWilliam and what did you ask him for? A job? Money? Love?" Tuke pulled the bed covers round himself for comfort.

Power ploughed relentlessly on. "I know what Sir Ian did though . . . he refused you. He probably even laughed at you. Laughed at you again. All that effort to trap him and he just laughed. He was used to blackmail. His son used emotional blackmail. He wanted money from his father for drugs . . . if he didn't get it he might cause a scandal, commit some crime . . . but Sir Ian had long ago decided that he wasn't going to keep on bailing out his son. He kept on loving him, but he wouldn't give him money to fill his veins with drugs. He'd refused his only son, it wouldn't be difficult to refuse you. If you give in to the blackmailer's demands there's no end to the blackmail. You just refuse to play the game right at the beginning. Sir Ian refused to play the game with his son. He'd refuse to play it with you. He did, didn't he?" Tuke's only sign of life was his steady breathing. "So one night, when McWilliam was alone you drove to his house, and you crept through the grounds, avoiding the inefficient guards. You broke in and set a fire. Did you watch it? Did you watch the small flame growing? How long did you wait for? Did you wait until it was so hot you couldn't stand there anymore, until the smoke made your throat raw? I expect you waited to make sure the fire wouldn't go out. You set another fire on the first floor just to make sure, didn't you? You wanted to make absolutely sure . . . You were so bitterly angry, so enraged that you wanted McWilliam dead, you wanted him destroyed. Your love, if ever it was, had wholly fumed to hate. If he wouldn't play you wanted him dead. The fire was to cauterise all the things that were denied you. And after he was dead you still hated him. You wanted to destroy everything that McWilliam had touched or liked. For whatever reason he liked Zoë. You could revenge yourself on her, by manipulating things so that she was accused of the murder and the arson."

Power paused for breath. The accusations had come tumbling out of his mouth. He felt excited, but very anxious that he should be right. He wondered where Lynch was at this moment. What would Lynch have done in his place? Would he have played his cards all at once and so breathlessly? More thoughts clamoured in Power's mind, trying to escape into the void between the doctor and the accused. "Did you get Lady McWilliam to release Zoë's letters to the police? Did you plant the petrol cans in Zoë's house? Of course you did. You knew more than anybody about McWilliam's affair. You were the only outsider who knew it was real. The police saw Zoë as a mad woman, deluded that Sir Ian had even met her. You could have phoned the police months ago, and defused the situation. When everyone was saying that Sir Ian had never talked to her, never seen her, never written to her, you were hiding in your wheelchair knowing all that you know about the use he made of her ... and you said nothing. You wanted her to go down. Wanted to destroy her, because he wanted her, not you. You can't deny that. You might say you can't walk, but you could have picked up the phone and said that Zoë had been McWilliam's mistress. You wanted everyone to think her mad."

Whether it was the sight of dust motes dancing in the air or not, Power suddenly felt the urge to sneeze. He fumbled in his pocket for a handkerchief. His pockets had loose change in them, but no handkerchief. He looked on the desktop for a box of tissues, but there was none. Power was used to having tissues on his desk for his patients. Automatically, as if the desk was his own he pulled open the drawers and was rewarded by the sight of a box of Kleenex. He picked one out and blew his nose with relief. At the noise Tuke opened his eyes and propped himself up in bed. He looked impassively at Power. Power took the box of tissues out and put it on the desktop. Tuke tried to crane his neck to see what Power was doing at the desk. Power was so wrapped up in his story that he didn't notice Tuke had become more animated than before.

Power continued with his argument, "And after you set the fire and killed Sir Ian and organised it so that the blame should fall on Zoë then you visited Lady McWilliam. She still loved her husband. She was trying to expiate her guilt by living out her life in the chapel in penance. You were so cruel to her. More cruel than you would know. You showed her the photographs of the girl didn't you? You explained about her husband, to destroy the image she had of him. You burn with hate, don't you?"

"How could I get there?" said Tuke, and his voice was a pitiful bleating, repeating the same old litany of helplessness. "I can't walk."

"You got there," said Power. "And I don't know whether you meant to blackmail her . . . did you need her money? I doubt it. You just wanted to destroy her. Showing her the photos destroyed her peace of mind and then you killed her physically. You strangled her with those not so weak hands and then you hung her. You'd carefully planned it too, because you brought the rope with you. You were lucky, because you might have been discovered. We arrived very soon afterwards. And I assume that since it was the afternoon, you must have slipped out to see Lady McWilliam as soon as your nurse had left the house after lunch. The timing was very close all round. You had to get back to the house before she got back to put you to bed . . . "

"I can't walk," said Tuke. "I keep having to remind you, Doctor, it's all just a fantasy of yours. I am not the same boy you saw all those years ago. I have multiple sclerosis. I am dying of it. I haven't the strength to kill a fly. My nurse and my doctors will confirm it."

"You might have convinced your own doctors to believe you, but you are a convincing liar. You have lied so much in your life, you even believe your own lies. But there are tests you cannot fake – nerve conduction tests and NMR scans of your brain. I know they would show a very healthy nervous system, and a very healthy brain. Unfortunately the healthy brain doesn't house a very healthy mind."

Power had another thought. He looked down at the rows of drawers in Tuke's desk. He tried the drawers one by one. Only one was locked. "Is this it?" asked Power. "Is this where you keep the car keys? Or is this where you keep the photos of Zoë? Do you take them out and gloat over them at night?"

"I need the toilet," said Tuke urgently. He struggled to get up. Supporting himself with one hand, he reached out and tugged at the wheelchair near his bed, trying to bring it nearer. With an effort he pushed and pulled it so that it was by the bed. "Can't you help me?" he asked Power angrily. "I need to get into the wheelchair to get to the toilet."

"I think you're more than capable of doing that yourself." Power looked over the desktop in search of a key for the drawer.

"You shit," said Tuke and began to transfer himself from the bed to the wheelchair. He was unsteady though and he appeared unused to such an effort. When he reached out to the wheelchair with his arm he was attempting to shift part of his weight onto the wheelchair seat. The wheelchair brakes were unlocked however, and just as he started to transfer his weight from the very edge of the bed, the wheelchair shifted backward and away from the bed. For a moment Tuke teetered on the edge of the bed, then he fell like a tree crashing to the forest floor. He fell awkwardly between the chair and the bed. He fell heavily onto his shoulder. He cried out in pain, and then lay helpless on the floor, stunned and gasping.

Power watched the man falling to the floor with a cynical disbelief. But then, as Tuke lay there moaning in pain, Power's scepticism was converted to a genuine concern. It was impossible for him to shrug off his doctor's mantle. Here was someone in real need. Power felt ashamed of himself. The logic of his argument seemed worthless against the suffering of this man as he lay twisted on the floor. "Get me to the toilet, please," said Tuke: "I don't want to mess myself." Power got up from the desk and walked over to the bedside. Power chided himself. What could he have been thinking of! Anyone could see that Tuke was a broken, dying man, to be cared for, and not accused of things he could never commit.

Stung into action by his own self-criticism, Power hurried over to the bedside. Tuke was making ineffectual flapping movements with his arms to try and right himself. Power reached down to Tuke and tried to grip the man's shoulders. They felt almost skeletal, like bone covered with paper. He rolled Tuke over onto his back. The invalid looked hatefully up at him. Tuke gripped Power's forearm to try and pull himself up. The grip was surprisingly strong. He could feel the bony fingers pressing and digging hard into his arm. Just as Power was managing to lift him off the floor Tuke's strength seemed to desert him. The considerable strength of his grip evaporated and he slumped heavily back to the floor. The back of his skull hit the floor with an unhealthy thump. Tuke cursed him. "You're useless," he said. "Get the nurse, quickly. I don't want to pee myself."

"It's all right," said Power. "We almost managed . . ."

"I don't want your help. You're a fool who can't see what's in front of his eyes. Get her!" He closed his eyes and lay back on the floor, moaning in agony. Power straightened up and looked down at the anguished man. He took in the man's stick-like limbs, his wasted muscles and he doubted his earlier judgements. Tuke even had the sickly-sweet smell of the invalid. He smelt ill. Power cursed his lack of judgment and turned on his heel. He opened the door and left the broken man groaning on the floor.

"Nurse?" He called out, feeling as foolish as he had when he had been a junior house officer, freshly qualified and set loose on the wards for the first time. The nurses had seen his awkwardness, knew his newness and had gently (and sometimes not so gently) taken him in hand. He felt now as he had done then, lost and ashamed at his own ineptitude, like a lost sheep searching for a shepherd. He must find Megan Driver. The door behind him closed and he moved through the hall. The house was quiet. He wondered if the nurse was still here. Should he go on or go back to Tuke? He pushed open a door which opened into the kitchen. A set of pans was simmering on the stove in readiness for lunchtime. An ironing-board had been set up near the window. The iron was hot and in the warmth of the kitchen there was the smell of freshly-pressed clothes. The nurse, though, was nowhere to be seen. Power tried the next room downstairs, an elegant dining room with a marble fireplace and an antique oval dining-table. The room was clean, but it had the air of dis-use. There was a bathroom next door that had been modified for Tuke's needs. He went out again into the hallway and called out again. This time there was a response from the kitchen. When he went in she was standing by the ironing-board, with a pile of folded washing in her hands. "Did you want me?" she asked in a surprised tone.

"Where were you?"

"Getting the washing in," she said. "It's dried so nicely in the sun, I thought I'd get on and iron it this morning." She thought Power looked guilty. "What's wrong?"

"He wanted to get to the toilet," said Power. "He's fallen out of bed."

"Oh, you doctors . . . you're useless . . ." she scolded and pushed past him in a panic. "He'll be mortified if he wets himself." She hurried down the corridor with Power following. He saw her push open the door to the living room and stop. She was staring into the room. Behind the desk the curtains were flapping about in the breeze. She turned to Power with a silently accusing look in her eye. Power caught up with her and she moved aside so that he could get into the room. "What have you done with him?" she asked.

So strange was the nurse's reaction that Power imagined to see Tuke dead upon the floor, but when he had eased past her into the room he looked at the floor by the bed. Tuke was no longer there. Nor was he in the bed. In fact, Tuke was no longer in the room. The doctor and the nurse stared at the carpet around the bed as if staring at it would cause it to yield up the invalid.

"What have you done with him?" she asked again.

Power moved further into the room and swore. From where he stood he could see the desk drawers. He observed that the previously locked drawer was now open, as was a large window. "He fooled me like he's fooled everyone else," said Power. "He's made a run for it."

The nurse gaped at him in astonishment. "He can't even walk.

He must be here."

"I'm not wasting any time looking for him here. He's running for sure."

"But . . . but . . ." The news that her invalid patient was neither invalid nor ill confronted the nurse with a mental *volte face* which for now she was unable to make. She gaped at the empty room with the astonishment that Lazarus's friends must have felt when he was risen from the tomb. "What have you done?" she asked over and over.

Power caught hold of her by the shoulders, "Call the police," he said. "Ask them to contact Superintendent Lynch of Chester. Can you do that?" She gaped at him. "Just call the police then. We must catch him."

"Catch him?" She looked at Power as if he was raving.

"Yes," said Power. "Catch Tuke."

He left her standing alone and staring at the empty bed, he couldn't waste any more time on her. He must find Tuke. He wrenched the front door open and ran into the drive. His own car stood in the driveway like a silent sentinel. Tuke could not have got his car out of the garage and past Power's Rover. Power reasoned that Tuke must be on foot. He turned, scanning the road way beyond for some sight of Tuke. He hadn't had time to dress, had he?

Power tried the garage door. It was fast. He peered in through the garage window; the car was still there. He held his hand over his eyes against the glass trying to fathom whether Tuke was hiding in the shadows. Power moved around the house, checking each door and window for sight of Tuke. Like a child playing hide-and-seek he peered behind every shrub and hedge in the garden. He called out, "Tuke, there's no point in running away. You can't get far." Power imagined that Tuke had run without clothes, without money, and without the means of supporting himself . . . but what if he had prepared himself for such a visit as Power's. What if he had secreted all he needed to survive in the desk drawer? Power had no way of knowing what Tuke had hidden there. Enough money to get anywhere in the country; essential documents; the keys of a safe house like the one he'd arranged for McWilliam; a weapon maybe? The thought that Tuke might now be armed made Power halt. Power had never thought himself a hero, and now he suddenly realised the extent of the danger he was in.

Tuke's escape confirmed his guilt as far as Power was concerned. Power was now sure that Tuke had killed at least twice. He had killed for revenge and for jealousy. He had shown great skill at planning his murders. He had killed before and would kill again if it suited. Everyone had believed Tuke. No-one had ever thought him capable of any crime. The knowledge that Tuke had faked his illness (consciously or unconsciously) and how he had used this defence in the past was the only threat to Tuke. And Power personified this knowledge. No-one else knew the truth, except Power. And if Tuke had guessed this too . . . .

He shrank back against the protection of the wall. "Oh God," prayed Power. "Help me, please." Then he wondered about how Tuke must be feeling. He had been living his life as an invalid, hiding his real self, and his real abilities from everybody, even his nurse. He must have felt trapped by Power. He must have lain there tortured by the truth that Power had heaped upon him. What if the truth about him and his past had been too much to bear? After all, mused Power, some things cannot be lived with.

It was just at that moment that Power's attention was taken out across the fields below Tuke's house, towards the rolling sea. It was there, in the distance, that Power saw him. He was running awkwardly, as those with lack of practice do. Power could just see Tuke's red dressing gown flapping absurdly in the sea-breeze, Tuke was attempting to clamber over the remains of a dry stone wall. Power started to run after him. At that moment he didn't know why he was running. Was it to catch Tuke and stop him escaping the truth, or was it to save Tuke from himself?

Power was not a fitness fanatic. Even moderate exertion usually rendered him wheezily breathless. Now though, his mind was too full to entertain such infirmities and he ran as fast as he was able, but Tuke had a head start, and his turn of speed was remarkably good for one who spent most of his days in bed.

The long grass of the fields was wet. Power felt the moisture penetrating his shoes and trousers. Tuke was running barefoot over the grass and between the yellow gorse. Power stumbled on some uneven ground, but regained his balance to see Tuke almost at the interface between land and sea and sky. Land, sea and sky were three horizontal bands of green, blue and grey cloud in the distance. The band of sea visible just above the cliff top was narrow, though, and it was almost as if the green grass of the fields merged with the sky. Tuke had only a few yards to go before he reached this bridge between earth and heaven. Power called out, "Jacob! Wait!" but the wind blew the words back into his mouth. The cold breeze made him gulp his own words down. He screamed out again as loud as his lungs would let him. "Stop!"

Something of the cry must have reached Tuke because he turned, for a fraction of a second. He had just reached the edge of the earth though. Power watched helplessly as Tuke hesitated on the cliff top and then fell. Tuke disappeared from view as if by witchcraft. Power was stunned. He stood looking at the empty horizon and his stomach felt as if it were plummeting downward off the cliff edge with Tuke. His stomach's fall seemed endless.

Power wondered what to do. Should he go back to the house and summon an ambulance to pick up the remains of Tuke's body smashed on the rocks? Perhaps Tuke had fallen into the frigid arms of the sea? Power wondered if he should go and see what had become of the body? The thought that he, a doctor, had driven Tuke to take his own life was particularly distasteful. He reproached himself until he felt like running away.

Power summoned all his courage, and walked the last hundred metres to the cliff top. The dark band of blue sea widened as he approached the cliff top. He looked at the rolling sea with white crested waves and shuddered. The water looked steely grey and very cold. He could hear it churning and smashing on the rocks below. Perhaps the waves were throwing Tuke about in their arms like a sodden rag doll, pounding his broken body against the rocks like a washerwoman pounds her washing against a stone to get it clean. Power reached the spot where he thought he had seen Tuke last. He stood tentatively on the edge. He could see the marks in the grass where Tuke had been. Had he slipped off the edge then or had he deliberately jumped? There was reason enough for him to want to end his own life.

Tuke had spent his whole life trying to escape the truth. Power tried to get as near the edge as he could without falling himself.

The edge of the cliff was steep, but it was convex. It was impossible to see the bottom of the cliff from where Power stood at the top. It could only be seen if he were to climb down the slope some way, and to do this would be to risk himself. Indeed Power could see the tracks that Tuke's body had made in the wet grass as it had slithered towards the visible edge some way down. Power could only see a few hand or footholds. A few bedraggled bushes were trying to grow unsuccessfully in such an exposed spot. A few roots of such plants stuck out from cuts in the coastal earth where land had slipped away into the sea. These offered some kind of purchase, but as Power looked at the straight and sudden path that Tuke's body had made through the grass to the drop beyond, Power fought shy of following him, even calculating his way using handholds and stealth. He would return to the house, call the police and the coastguard. They were the experts and the time had come for him to stop meddling in things, which he was untrained for. He was a doctor, trained to heal the sick, not a detective, he chided himself. He turned to go back.

There was a sound, all of a sudden. A sound which Power, as a doctor, was at least familiar with, a sound he could not ignore. The sound was a human cry of pain. The cry came from the cliff top in front of him, from somewhere just out of view and was something between a wail and a moan. And try as he might Power could not ignore the pain. He had to help.

The sky had turned a glowering grey without a hint of sun, and from the north a keen breeze was beginning whipping the sea into white-peaked waves. Power looked unenthusiastically down at the sea some fifty feet below. He bent down close to the grass and began to edge down the slope towards the cry of pain. He grabbed at a nearby bush to steady himself as he reached down with his foot. He remembered climbing Borrowdale in the Lakes when he was a boy. He recalled the panic that he had felt scaling a difficult rock face. His fear of heights had started then. It was only a moment of panic, but for a moment he was back there, clinging to the rock face, whimpering through clenched teeth as he hung there, eyes tightly shut, unable to move forward, unable to move back. Power tried to shake off the memory, but the fear stuck in his belly like a knife. The grass was slippery. Power slithered his way to the safety offered by a root, which protruded from the clay. The root felt rough in his palm. The slope of the cliff edge became sheerer and Power had to rest his whole body against the earth. Ahead of him Power could only see grey cloud, behind him only the churning, heaving sea. By his exercises Power had squirmed and wormed his way to the track that Tuke's body had made in the wet grass as it shot downwards. Power reasoned that Tuke must be somewhere below him. Power was hanging onto a clump of coarse grass with one hand and with one foot resting on a tussock to his left. He looked desperately about and behind him. It was difficult to get his bearings; there was only earth below, sky above and sea behind him. And yet he knew he was much closer to Tuke, for his moaning sob was the loudest it had been.

"Tuke?" Power called out into the space around him. "Is that you? The groaning stopped. There was a long pause. Power's voice had obviously not been expected, and such was the surprise that even pain was momentarily suppressed.

Power struggled to see if there was any other handhold nearby that he could use to lower himself still further. "Tuke? Are you there?"

Where a portion of the cliff face had given way and sheered off into the sea there was a root dangling out of the earth. Power grabbed it and inched himself further down the cliff. Without warning, the earth abruptly fell away from under his feet.

He tried waving his feet about to make a purchase, but there was no purchase to be made in free air. He allowed himself to fall back a few more feet. His legs swung down from the hips, and the tips of his shoes came up against the granite cliff face. His right foot found purchase on a small ledge and he tested it with his weight. The rock held. Scrabbling at the grass around him to get a grip he turned to look over the edge behind him. To his right there was nothing but a sheer drop to the rocks below. He could see hear and see the sea swirling through the jagged rocks, like saliva washing around teeth. The sight made him retch with fear. He began to feel that even if he wanted to he could not reverse the experiment. He could not climb back up the cliff face. Power moved his left foot around in urgent exploration. He could not feel anything.

Power looked over his left shoulder to see a thin ledge. If he stretched his left leg as far as it could go he might just reach it. But to do so he would have to leave go of his existing handholds. The waves crashed below him. It would be a leap of faith, and faith alone. Fighting with incipient panic, Power heaved his body to the left. His left foot found a stable footing just as the rock that had supported his right foot gave way. He watched the rock fall towards the sea, dwindling in size until it disappeared into the cold and raging waters. Power inched his way sideways, putting all his trust in the ledge he had found. The ledge seemed to widen under his feet. His knees found that now he had moved sideways, the cliff face had become concave. The ledge had opened up, and became a shallow concavity in the cliff wall, perhaps some six foot wide, and four foot deep. Here was a temporary refuge, and here was Tuke. The ledge that his body had fallen onto was a lip that pouted outwards from the sheer face of the cliff. Had Tuke's fall not led him exactly here then he would certainly have plummeted to the sea below.

Power found that he could take his arms away from the cliff face

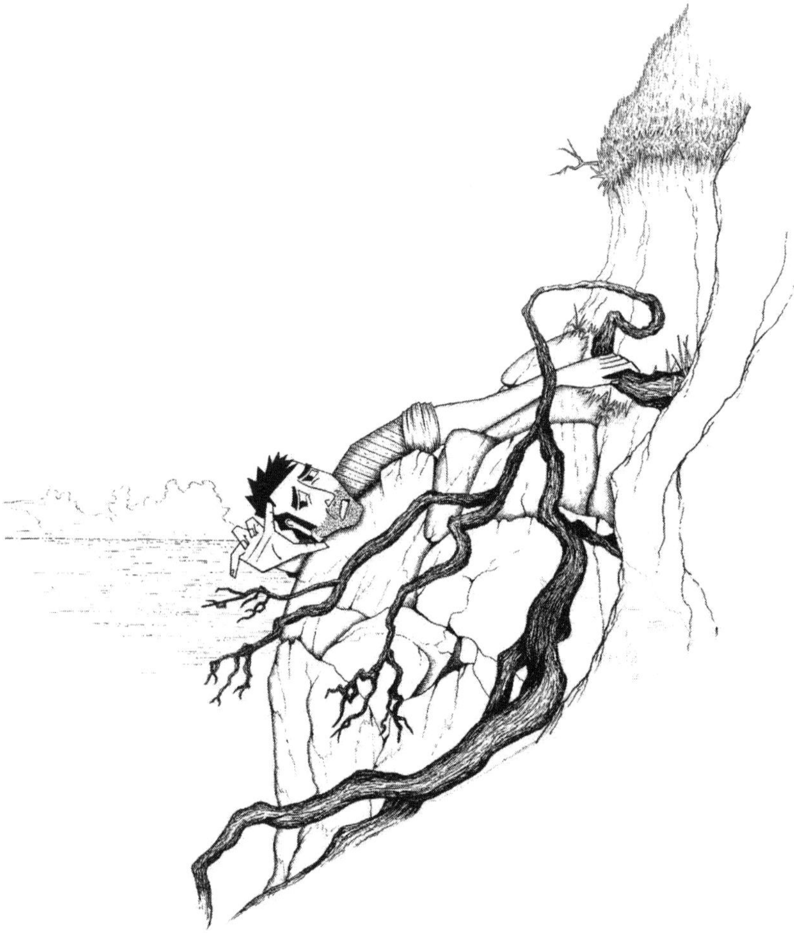

now. His feet could support him here and provided he leaned inward away from the edge, he could lull himself into some kind of security. He took in his situation. The only conceivable way of getting off the ledge was to reverse his climb exactly, because the cliff wall soared above the ledge for at least twenty feet in all directions except to the right, which was the direction he had come from. To the right the sheer cliff wall was only five feet or so high, and above that was the steeply curving grass-covered headland that he had clambered down.

Tuke was slumped at the eastern edge of the ledge. His eyes were closed and he appeared to have lost consciousness. Power looked at the fallen figure. There looked to be something wrong with his right arm. It seemed twisted round, as if his shoulder began in the wrong place. Power thought it likely that Tuke's collarbone had been broken in the fall.

"Tuke," he said. "It's Dr Power."

Power edged towards the collapsed figure. He noticed a thin stream of blood running from a cut on Tuke's forehead. "Tuke?" Slowly, painfully, the figure raised his head and looked up at Power. "Don't move," said Power.

"Why not?" Tuke struggled to get up. The movement of his right arm caused him to flinch with pain. Before he could get to his feet he seemed about to faint. Power stepped forward and gripped Tuke's left arm. He pulled Tuke into the middle of the ledge, to its widest safe point, and propped him up against the cliff wall.

"Why did you run?" asked Power.

Tuke gave Power a disdainful look. The question was not worth answering. "I didn't expect you to follow me."

"Did you mean to kill yourself?"

"Are you the only one who knows?" asked Tuke slyly. Power stared at him, but said nothing. "Of course," said Tuke. "I don't expect you to say anything . . . because I know you're here alone. Why did you come down here after me?"

"To save you," said Power edging into a more secure position on the ledge himself. "And if I'm going to do that I'd better get some help. You can't climb back up yourself. You've broken some bones."

"Why'd you want to save me?"

"I don't know, is the honest answer," said Power. "Look. I'll climb back up, and get the coastguard. It'll need a proper rescue operation. I couldn't try to get you up alone . . ."

"If you save me," said Tuke. ". . .if you go up there and get help then some weeks later I go on trial and you give your evidence and then . . . I spend the rest of my life in some institution. Do you really think I want that?" Power shook his head. Tuke struggled to stand and winced at the shoulder pain. He reached into the pocket of his dressing gown with his left hand. "It seems to me that you're the one, the only one, who has put the whole case together."

"I've let people know what I'm doing," said Power defensively. "They know where I am."

Tuke looked sceptical. "I don't see anybody else," he said. "They don't know you're here, on this ledge, with me." The hairs on the back of Power's head rose in fear. Tuke straightened himself up.

"Well, if your cleverness has brought you here, I suppose you'd like to know all the details wouldn't you?" He pulled something out of his pocket. "When I was younger and you were my doctor, you seemed to be so mighty. You seemed to know everything." His eyes were full of cunning. "Did you like Zoë? You seemed to be rather attached to her, to me."

"I liked her, yes."

"You liked her . . . but do you like her now. Now you know what she did for him, for McWilliam? You always wanted to know too much it seemed to me. Do you really like it when you find out the truth?" He looked down at the pile of Polaroid photographs he had in his hand. "They're all here," he said. "You were right about them. I stood over her as she lay naked on the bed and I took all the photographs I wanted to have. I wanted them as proof, and I wanted them for . . . myself. Does that make you feel better? Does the truth help you?"

"The truth is the truth," said Power. "It's you who has always run away from the truth, not me."

Tuke snarled at him, "If you like truth so much you can have it!" And he hurled the nine photographs up into the air and into Power's face. The photographs fluttered round him like confetti. As a reflex Power tried to catch at the cloud of photographs that was falling on his right and on his left. He clawed ineffectually at the air, grabbing first one and then another of the glossy Polaroids. To his left he saw one of these pieces of evidence falling, out of reach, down towards the restless sea. Tuke lunged forward. Power was too distracted by the fall of photographs to even notice. Tuke's weight slammed into the doctor. Power reeled backwards off-balance. He fell heavily backwards onto the ledge. The fall knocked the wind out of his ribcage. Tuke was leaning over him, and with his good left arm, Tuke tried to push him out over the edge. Power was again struck by how strong Tuke was despite his wiry frame. Dazed by the blow he could feel himself slipping sideways. His own left shoulder was already over the edge and in free space. If he didn't resist with all his strength ... if he didn't fight now ...

The ledge had been gouged out of the cliff face by the wind, and rain and waves. The cliff face was a temporary thing, as changeable as the make-up on a human face. A new face only lasted so long until it was next washed away. The ledge was therefore a temporary feature anyway, and unused to anything more than the weight of a passing seagull.

Power was pushing upward with his right arm, against the weight of Tuke's assault. The earth beneath Power's left thigh slipped downwards. Alarmed, Power tried to throw his weight over to the right. His right hand clawed at the cliff. He could feel his nails scrabbling in the dirt for some hold.

From a distance out to sea, an observer of the duel, if there had been one, would have seen a heavy lumpen mass of clay and rock falling downwards as it was shed by the cliff face. The mass of earth and stone smashed against the rocks as it descended, shattering into a cascading shower that peppered the agitated face of the waters.

And following the shower of earth there was a single flailing piece of flesh. The body hit the cliff face twice as it fell. Each time there was a soft thud as the torso or head bounced off the rock face. After the second time it hit the cliff, the body stopped moving. The arms and legs were already flaccid as the body plunged into the shifting grey tide. Foam washed over and extinguished the fire of life in the staring eyes and the face disappeared under the waves forever.

Lynch will return in The Good Shepherd.

The Fire of Love

Music for Dr Power

A set of music has been suggested by readers; these suggestions accompany some of the music that inspired the author, Hugh Greene, whilst writing the original novels

If you would like to suggest additions to this list please email the author via www.hughgreene.com

For The Darkening Sky

Darkening Sky (Peter Bradley Adams)

Leylines (Aes Dana)

Alignments (Aes Dana)

Sky Quest (Toby Langton Gilks)

Sky Strikeforce (David Hughes, John Murphy)

Sky Dark Orchestral Hardcore (David Hughes, John Murphy)

For The Fire of Love

The Fire of Love (The Gun Club)

4 Sea Interludes by Benjamin Britten

For The Good Shepherd

The Dreamscape by Chad Setter

Symphony No. 6 by Vaughan Williams

Mosquito by Yeah Yeah Yeahs

Mosquito by Flexness

Infra 2 Max Richter

Recomposed: Vivaldi Four Seasons by Max Richter - Spring 0, Spring 1, Shadow 2, Winter 2, Winter 3

The Lord is my Shepherd (John Rutter)

Shepherd of Fire (Avenged Sevenfold)

Shepherd's Chorus (Contenti N'andremo) (Respighi)

Good Shepherd (Wovenhand)

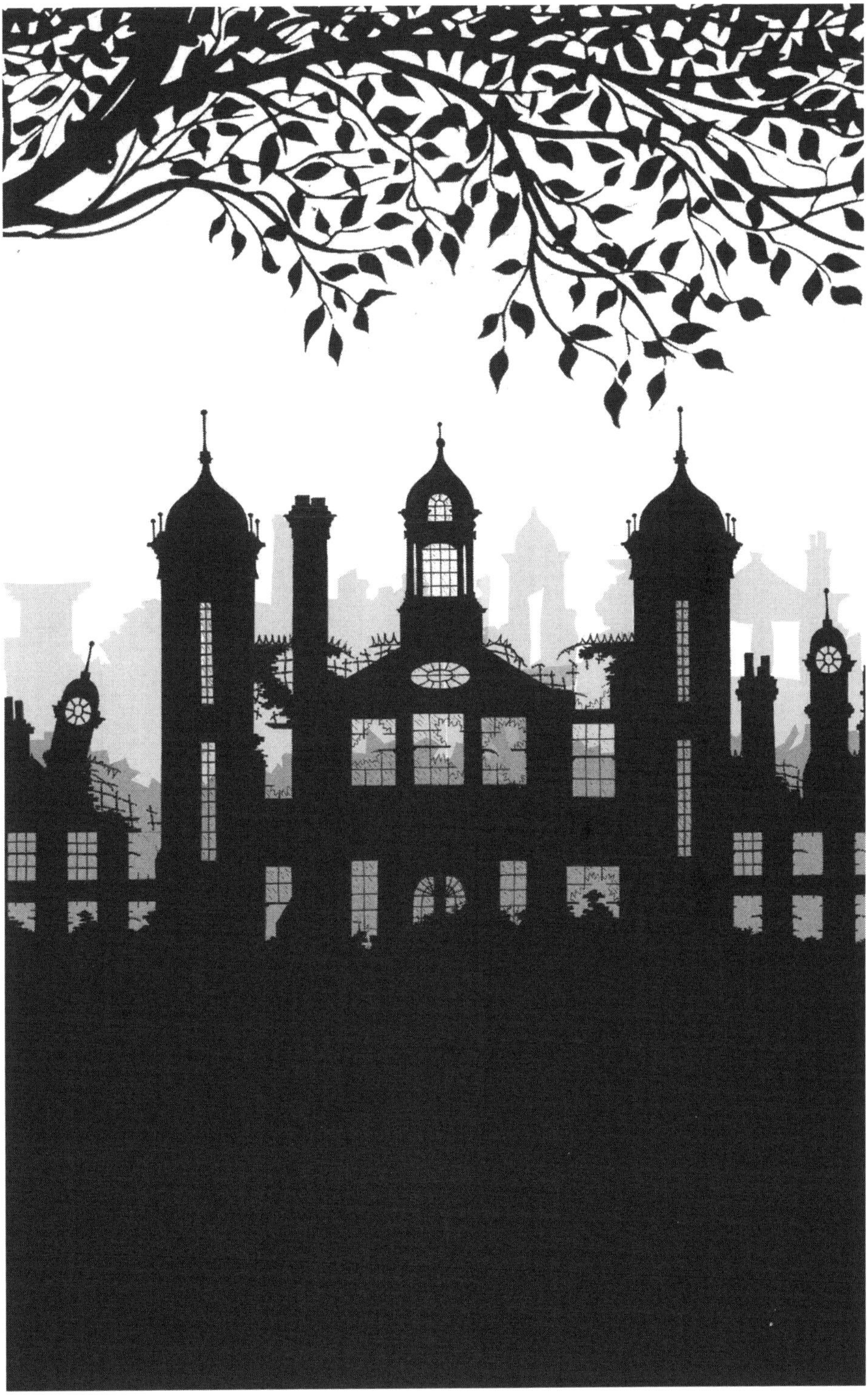

Printed in Great Britain
by Amazon